D0301648

ALL THE DARK VOICES

PHILIP MYLES DANE

Copyright © 2023 by Philip Myles Dane

ISBN 97989891533-1-2

Book design and formatting by Damonza

For my three sons

We live in a very unusual world where we desire—in fact, one could say need—science and culture to reconcile peacefully with the human spirit; where our hopes and our senses, passions and desires might be fulfilled completely in the rapidly changing world around us. Where the notion of heaven and the threat of hell are reconciled.

CHAPTER ONE

THE SATURDAY EVENING rush was underway at the small cafe on Prospect Street. Sunlight streamed through the front windows of the red brick building. The evening shift manager yelled an order at the young woman behind the register. Without hesitation, she darted out from behind the counter and looked up just in time to avoid colliding with Thomas Shelton. The watchful shift manager shook his head at the employee's carelessness. Shelton smiled at the cashier's enthusiasm, grateful at having avoided the collision. He walked past the SEAT YOUR- SELF sign and headed toward an open table in the back of the restaurant.

He sat at the table in the far corner of the dining room next to the front window. The cashier greeted him as she pulled the cord, lowering the sunshade next to his table. The smell of his cologne wafted up and into her nose. The sweet smell brought a smile to her face.

Shelton studied the attractive cashier walking away. The curves of her body in her tight jeans, her warm smile, and the pace at which she did her job all made his heart beat faster. He loved women. He loved everything about them. The blend of intelligence, grit, softness, compassion, and drive was a combination that the male gender could rarely understand, let alone appreciate.

Shelton sighed, trying to clear the image of the cashier's beautiful face and the vision of her naked body inside her jeans from his mind. He opened his small gray notebook and double-checked his notes. Jeanie's Cafe was not on the list. He started to make a new entry, then stopped. He closed the notebook and placed it back in his pack.

Thomas Shelton had made the trip to the DC area at least nine times over the past two years. Each time keeping meticulous notes of where he stayed, where he ate, who he talked to, and what stores he visited. He was careful to never visit the same place more than once. He had the entire neighborhood committed to memory. Every street, alley, business, and camera location was embedded in his photographic memory.

The drive from Evanston had taken all day. The fatigue of finals week combined with the long hours behind the wheel of his six-year-old Volkswagen showed in his bloodshot eyes. Making the trip by car meant no airline tickets or credit card charges to track. His mobile phone was in his apartment. This would be his last trip. He would do what he came to do, then drive back to the university nestled on the north shore of Lake Michigan.

Tomorrow was graduation day for twenty-two-year-old Shelton. The four years studying physics and psychology had buzzed by for him. When he wasn't doing academic work, he was in the studio studying martial arts with a local master. His natural ability in the art and with weapons had quickly caught the teacher's attention. It didn't take long before Shelton was earning money as an instructor. In between his busy schedule, he had made one close friendship in four years. Mitchell Donovan.

Donovan was from the same area in Northern Virginia where Shelton grew up. He was from a wealthy, multi-generational family with a long legacy at the top-tier university. Shelton's admission to the prestigious school was far different. It had nothing to do with his interest in higher education or his family roots. Shelton's high-school counselor had used his perfect grades and low-income status and somehow turned it into a full academic scholarship.

Shelton and Donovan were two introverts from very different backgrounds. Regardless, they had connected during orientation of their first semester on campus. While they spent little time together, the two friends made it a point to drink a beer together twice a month.

Now both had achieved their goal. Twenty-four hours from now, they would graduate with top academic honors. Donovan with his degree in bio med and heading off to medical school. Shelton with his two degrees and no idea what was next. He had his whole life ahead of him to figure it out. After tonight, the past would be settled, and he would focus on the future.

⚜

An hour later, Shelton paid the cashier and departed from Jeanie's Cafe. The girl behind the register smiled as he walked out. She had captured a picture of the handsome, wonderful-smelling young man as he made his way toward the exit.

The light in the western sky had disappeared over the tops of the buildings as Shelton began his walk through the streets of Georgetown. He checked the time on his watch, then picked up his pace as he turned north toward the middle of town. The parochial school's campus was two blocks ahead. He casually strolled down the sidewalk, crossed the street, then dropped the to-go coffee cup in the recycle receptacle without missing a stride.

The last shreds of sunlight faded as Shelton sat down on a cast-iron park bench in the courtyard of the church grounds. He took a deep breath and exhaled slowly. He removed the burner phone from his pocket. The light from the screen completed the disguise. He was just another person resting on a park bench, focused on the world at the other end of the cellular signal. Seemingly oblivious to the natural world around him.

Across the courtyard in front of him was a preparatory school. Behind him was the monastery. To his left was the back entrance of the church sanctuary. From his position, he had a clear line of sight to the door of the church that clergy and staff used to come and go.

After a few minutes, Shelton closed the phone and placed it back in his pocket. He sat there quietly as his vision adjusted to the growing darkness. The branches and leaves from the large old oak trees around him looked black against the night sky. The tree trunks provided perfect cover. No person or camera could see the stranger sitting on the bench.

The dimly lit bulb above the back entrance to the church gave off just enough yellowish light to see the door and steps. Shelton sat there in the dark, watching and waiting.

Across the courtyard, the back door of the church burst open. A young boy emerged, jumped down the steps, and trotted down the walkway. Shelton could hear him whistling as he passed on his way to the waiting car parked at the curb. The passenger side car door opened and closed. The car pulled away and disappeared from sight.

A brief sense of relief washed across Shelton's face. The boy had somehow escaped the hands of the pedophile lurking inside the back hallways of the house of God.

Shelton stood and walked toward the sanctuary, then stopped. Every ounce of him wanted to run into the church and rescue what he knew was happening to a less fortunate boy. The one who did not escape, like his two best friends when they were ten years old. The one who, like many others, was having his life destroyed by the family clergyman.

Twenty minutes later, the door opened again. A young boy with disheveled hair stepped out and stood at the top of the steps as the door closed behind him. His head hung low as he wiped tears from his face. Shelton watched the boy slowly walk across the courtyard, dragging his backpack on the ground behind him.

The sound of an approaching car caught Shelton's attention. He reached into his jacket and pulled out a night vision monocular. As the car pulled to the curb, he trained the device on it. He recognized the driver immediately. It was the reverend's assistant. He watched the demoralized victim climb into the back seat of the car and pull away. Shelton placed the monocular back in his jacket, then patted his other pockets. His other tools were in place.

The heavy evening air was growing cooler, and moisture was collecting on the seat of the metal bench beside him. He reached down with his finger and wiped the dew off the cold metal. He looked up just as the door opened. Reverend Brooks stepped out into the night air, closed the door behind him, and then pulled on it to make sure it was locked. Brooks turned and started slowly making his way toward the street.

Shelton sat quietly, watching as the monster walked down the sidewalk across the courtyard from his position. He slipped on his gloves as he watched, never taking his eyes off the clergyman. When Brooks reached the street, he rounded the corner of the prep school and was soon out of view.

Shelton was moving now. He exited the courtyard and made his way to the other side of the street. Brooks was back in his sights. Shelton increased his pace to the next corner. He turned onto the dark side street and sprinted half a block, then ducked behind a set of concrete steps. His breathing was quickly back to normal. He stood there listening intently, a sense of tranquility softening his face.

The sound of approaching footsteps was distinct. He recognized the cadence of Brook's gait as his shoes made contact on the pavement. The click of heels against the asphalt grew louder. Soon the dark shape walked past Shelton's position, oblivious to the stranger waiting in the darkness. Shelton stepped out and approached Brooks from behind.

"Good evening," Shelton said, surprising Brooks.

The priest immediately stopped and turned.

"May I help you?" Brooks said, a pleasant smile on his face.

Shelton stepped closer. "I was wondering if you remembered me."

The sixty-two-year-old Brooks squinted, trying to get a better look in the low light.

"You look familiar. What is your name, son?"

"Thomas Shelton."

Brooks's eyebrows lifted in surprise.

A sudden gust of wind swept down the dark side street. Shelton could feel the air swirling around them. He looked up, then side to side. The buildings and sidewalks were no longer visible. It was just him and Brooks in a strange veil of concealment. Shelton drew his knife and placed it under the clergyman's chin.

"I need you to pass along a message for me," Shelton said.

The unplanned words came flowing out of his mouth in perfect ancient Hebrew. Surprised, Shelton's focus shifted slightly back and forth, confused by the words he had spoken. Before Shelton could say another word, Brooks lifted his arms and began praying. The words were Latin. Again, to his surprise, Shelton had a perfect understanding of what Brooks was saying.

"Keep praying to your gods," Shelton said calmly in Hebrew. "You can tell all of them I'm here. I have arrived."

Shelton did not know why these strange words were coming out of his mouth, but the terror on Brooks's face was better than he could have imagined. This low-life person he was driven to take revenge on was in total fear for his life.

In one swift move, Shelton pulled the knife from Brooks's chin, slicing the flesh to the bone as it moved, and plunged it between the clergyman's ribs and into his heart. Shelton looked deep into his victim's soul, his facial expression unchanged. He flexed the blade of the knife back and forth to maximize the agony. He watched as Brooks's contorted face reflected the pain ripping through his body. Shelton could feel the pedophile's heart struggling to find a rhythm at the tip of his blade.

With his left hand, Shelton pulled the twin-bladed dagger from the leg pocket of his tactical pants. He held it up so that Brooks could get a good look. Then, with remarkable speed, Shelton rotated his wrist and drove the daggers into Brooks's eye sockets, smashing the handles against the bridge of his victim's nose. The clergyman opened his mouth to scream, but no sound came out.

With the blades buried in Brooks's skull, Shelton held the pedophile's body upright, using the knife as a handle. He continued to examine the monster's face with complete scorn. He reached down and drew his last weapon from his pants. With one flowing motion, he brought the short saber around to his right side, released the knife handle, took a firm grip on the saber with both hands, and swung with all his strength. The razor-sharp blade separated Brooks's head from his shoulders. Shelton watched the head and the body fall to the ground.

Shelton looked around. Then he methodically collected his weapons and wiped the blood from the blades using the clergyman's clothes. As he walked away, he lit the gray notebook on fire and tossed it into a nearby trash can, then made the walk back to his car for the drive home.

CHAPTER TWO

Twenty-years later...

THE MIDDAY TRAFFIC up from Coronado into downtown Los Angeles was slow but steady. The quiet air-conditioned car and slow pace of traffic combined with Tom Shelton's jet lag made it difficult for him to keep his eyes open. More than once, he nodded off, dreams of the desert scrolling through his mind. The stress of the past few days spent half a world away was taking its toll.

He lowered the driver and passenger side windows slightly and turned up the music. The sound of the air streaming through helped keep him alert. He exited the 405 and made his way into Century City, slowly weaving through traffic to the entrance of the parking garage. He scanned his digital pass at the kiosk and waited for the steel safety barrier to lower and the gate to rise. In his peripheral vision, shadowy forms emerged. He paused. Something, or someone, was watching him.

The encounters were becoming more frequent. Now there were two watchers where normally there was one. Shelton had learned to ignore the observers over the years. They had never approached him. Never attempted to harm him. They went about their business, and he went about his. Today felt different. The two dressed in black were larger than the usual one dressed in gray.

The observers made their first appearance following the death of Reverend Brooks. Now, at forty-two years old, Shelton had come to accept the observers as part of his world. He assumed they were real and invisible to others. No one else had ever reacted to their presence. Real or unreal, it didn't matter to Shelton. He had never felt one once of remorse for eliminating Brooks. Only an overwhelming sense of justice.

Shelton continued to look straight ahead. He took a deep breath, then quickly turned his head to the left. For a brief second, he made eye contact with the faces peering out from under the hoods. Then they disappeared.

Now there were only businesspeople and vacationers moving about. The short beep of a car horn waiting behind jolted Shelton into the present. He released the brake and gently stepped on the accelerator. He wound the car through the parking garage and up to the second level. The private parking garage door opened and closed behind him. He got out, made his way to the executive elevators, and scanned his badge.

❧

Los Angeles was the home of Lambert Capital's new western regional offices. Thomas Shelton was the firm's vice chairman and second in command. His team had developed the firm's global growth plan, and LA was the final expansion office. Under his leadership, the company now had offices in every primary North American and international money center in the world.

Opening a west coast operation had been more difficult than expected. Made more difficult by Herb Lambert, the company's founder. Herb felt strongly about having a competition between several west coast cities. A traditional tactic for companies. This requirement made something as simple as selecting the location more time consuming than necessary for everyone.

Herb got his way. The competition was fierce between San Francisco and Los Angeles politicians. Even Seattle emerged unexpectedly and made a substantial run at Shelton, offering enticing incentives for expanding in their respective cities. The chief executives of the large tech and industrial companies all made at least one phone call to Shelton, while the local politicians used Herb to put pressure on him. However, there was never any question about location in Shelton's mind. It was Southern California or nothing. The new office had to be close to his west coast home. And he much preferred June gloom over the fog of the central coast or the rains of the northwest.

The bigger challenge was attracting the right talent. Southern California traffic jams and taxes weren't exactly attractive features for thirtysomethings with families. But Shelton's reputation made it easier. His network allowed him to attract the attention of the best from around the globe. He had no qualms about using top brass to make the sales pitch for him, and that included presidents and prime ministers. After all, what person could say no to the British Prime Minister when he called and suggested you take the job?

With his many tools, Lambert's Tom Shelton had stolen some of the best strategic business and financial minds in the world. The new team had homes with reasonable commutes, beautifully refurbished offices with a view, and compensation plans that could make them wealthy.

The strategy worked. The west coast team was consistently outperforming New York, London, and Hong Kong offices in securing new mandates and clients. Cash was pouring in, in even larger volumes than anticipated.

His previous two weeks of naval reserve duty left Shelton with a sizable stack of paperwork and phone messages waiting for him. The unshaven, casually dressed executive spent the rest of the afternoon in the office returning phone calls and catching up on business from around the world. Occasionally, he would wistfully glance out his window at the LA country club golf course below.

᥎

By 7:30 p.m. Shelton was on his way home. He pulled into the driveway of his Pacific Palisades mansion just before eight o'clock. The black SUV parked in the circle drive told him his dinner guests had already arrived. His LA home was one of many around the world, which included multiple penthouse apartments in New York City.

Shelton was looking forward to a nice relaxing evening with his close friend and chief of security, Ben Davis. He could think of no better capstone to his military duty. Good whiskey, a good friend, and watching the sunset across the ocean would be a perfect wrap to his long day.

Ben greeted Tom with a firm handshake and hug the moment he walked in.

"Welcome home, Tom," Ben said. "It's good to see you."

"Likewise, my friend. It's good to be seen." Shelton raised his eyebrows slightly, knowing Ben would understand the expression. Returning from any military deployment alive was considered a success. Especially one led by Shelton.

"Hello, Carson," Shelton said, greeting his girlfriend with a kiss. "Did you miss me?"

"Of course," she said, grimacing slightly as the hair on his upper lip got in her mouth.

"Hi, Mattie," Shelton said, greeting Ben's wife.

"Hi there, Thomas," Mattie replied, burying her lips in his bearded cheek with enough passion to make him notice. "It's nice to see you."

"It's nice to see you too Mattie. Did you bring the kid?"

"Not this time," Mattie said as she glanced at Ben. "We decided tonight was for adults only. He's with my parents."

"I was looking forward to seeing the young man." Shelton smiled and stretched out his hand at waist level, indicating the boy's height.

"He was looking forward to see you too," Mattie replied. "We'll have to get together in New York when you can find time."

One of the house staff handed Shelton a glass of his favorite whiskey and refreshed the other drinks.

"Mr. Shelton, what time would you like to have dinner, sir?"

"Does nine o'clock work for you?" Shelton asked.

"Yes, sir."

"Very well. Thank you, Victor." Shelton dismissed him with a nod.

Victor turned and headed for the kitchen.

The four friends walked out onto the deck overlooking the Pacific. Shelton caught Ben staring at two girls in bikinis walking by on the sand. He nudged him slightly to break the more than obvious gaze.

Ben Davis had served under Shelton's command in a Navy special forces unit for almost a decade. When they first met, Shelton was a newly minted officer fresh out of college. Ben was his older Petty Officer 1st Class.

It didn't take long for Shelton to earn the team's respect. His physical ability, planning, and combat skills were undeniable and unmatched. He was faster and stronger than anyone else in the most elite unit. As a result, everyone in the operating groups wanted to be a part of Shelton's squad.

Shelton had taken an immediate liking to Ben. The no-nonsense approach to his job and his dry sense of humor were things Shelton appreciated and enjoyed. After Shelton made his first tens of millions at Lambert, he hired Ben to watch his back.

The wine and conversation flowed freely for the next hour and a half. By the end of dinner, Shelton had achieved his preferred state of bliss from the alcohol. Finding a break in the conversation, Ben suggested the two of them move to a more private place to discuss business.

Shelton didn't mind. In his current state of half soberness, talking business with his friend would be a great way to wrap up an enjoyable, relaxing evening. It would also be a good way to put the watchers out of his mind for the day.

The two friends walked to the study in the private wing of the house, where Shelton opened a fresh bottle of single malt and poured nightcaps.

"This is a great space," Ben said, looking around the boss's den while sipping his drink.

"This is one of my favorite rooms," Shelton said, his voice low and smooth. "I feel refreshed when I walk in here. It makes me want to retire and just hang out. Maybe spend my days working out, diving, and fishing. Maybe play a round of golf or two a week."

"Somehow, I don't think that would last very long," Ben replied. "It's hard to envision you enjoying a normal retirement."

"At some point I am going to need to figure it out." Shelton led the way out onto the smaller, private veranda. The two sat down by the fire pit, its flames dancing in the ocean breeze.

"Do you ever feel like all of this is too good to be true?" Shelton asked in a half-intoxicated tone.

"What do you mean?" Ben leaned forward.

"All of this," Shelton said as he motioned around him. "The home, the money, beautiful women. We have what most people in the world only dream about. Look at me. I'm just a kid from the suburbs, yet somehow I've made more money than I could ever spend. When I think about it, it still seems bizarre to me."

Ben narrowed his stare while looking at his friend through the firelight.

"I don't know, Tom. I think you've worked pretty hard to get to where you are. The successful businesses Lambert creates provide jobs and security for thousands of people and their families. You should feel good about that. Not question it."

"Good?" Shelton raised his head slightly. "That's an interesting word. I find it hard to tell the difference between who's good and who's bad most days. Including myself."

Ben stared at Shelton. "Do you ever talk to Angie?"

Shelton's eyebrows raised slightly, then he turned away, shifting his gaze toward the dark water and crashing ocean waves.

"No, I don't," Shelton said, sipping his drink.

"Why not, Tom?" Ben pressed with a sincere, deliberate tone.

"She doesn't need me complicating her life."

"I see." Ben leaned back in his chair. "I think the summer you two were together was the happiest I have ever seen you. It seemed like you were made for each other. You had a certain settled vibe that I haven't seen in you since."

Shelton smiled as he thought about his friend's observation.

"That was a long time ago, Ben." Shelton took a fortifying drink. "But I still think about her. I think about where we might be if I had done things differently. But it doesn't matter now. Angie would have no interest in all this material stuff, anyway. She's better off on her own, and I'm better off alone. What did you want to talk about?"

"Frank Heitschmidt called me. He said he has a project and wants my help," Ben said.

"Isn't Frank the chief of staff for the CIA director? What's his name?" asked Shelton.

"Exactly. He's the chief of staff for Interim Director Walker," Ben replied.

"What's the project?" asked Shelton.

"Do you remember the places, the locations the intel people thought were some sort of safe havens? Places where no army or people were allowed to go?" asked Ben.

"Vaguely," Shelton answered, sipping his drink. "I never thought it was real. Figured it for folklore."

"Me too," said Ben. "Apparently, Walker's heard about these places. And now he wants a contractor to do surveillance on one of these villages. Collect some baseline information. He's not interested in one of the large defense contractors doing it. He wants a solo act. Someone who has the skills but can't be connected to his shop."

"You said places," Shelton said. "How many are there?"

"I don't know." Ben shrugged. "They can't be real, right? Seems impossible in this day and age."

"I assume you're interested?"

"I am. Seems ridiculous, I know, but it's intriguing. I miss the field work. This is a chance for a minor change of pace."

"How does Mattie feel about it?" asked Shelton.

"She doesn't know. My guess is she won't like it. But she won't tell me no. She will think it's a little irresponsible given I have a child to look after. But she knows I'm a bit jealous of you and your reserve operations. It's a low-risk gig compared to hanging out with you."

Shelton nodded, acknowledging his security chief's words.

"How much time off do you need?"

"Frank said two weeks. But you know that really means six to eight. Then if I discover something, maybe longer."

"It sounds interesting. And to your point, it would be a change of pace. When would you start?"

"If you are okay with it, I'll get back to Frank and plan out the details," said Ben. "It will take at least a couple of weeks to pull things together."

"It's up to you. Take all the time you need. But tell Frank I expect to be a part of the debrief at the end," Shelton said with a serious look on his face. "Nothing is free."

❦

An hour later, the silence of the room filled Shelton's head as he stared into the darkness above his bed. The increased presence of his observers was troubling. The lack of genuine purpose in his life was stressing him out. And Angie. If he had only met her earlier, his life could have been different.

Shelton's eyelids were getting heavy, but he couldn't fall asleep. Thoughts of his childhood never fully left his mind. Many nights as a young boy, he would fall asleep and find himself in a desert or mountainous landscape exacting justice on the ones deserving. In the dreams, there was a sense of purpose. A sense of belonging. He remembered the soft touch of his mother's hand gently stroking his hair when he woke. And then nothing. The dream traveling ended the day his mother died. A reality that made it difficult for him to sleep.

CHAPTER THREE

SHELTON STEPPED OFF the private elevator and walked straight ahead to the single frosted-glass door. He scanned his personal security card and entered. The neatly dressed corporate security agent greeted him from behind the counter. Shelton returned the greeting as the guard opened the back door that led into the main executive office complex.

Lambert Capital's newly renovated offices on New York City's West 57th Street were some of the most well-appointed and expensive real estate holdings in Manhattan. Full-length windows in the main lobby and in Shelton's office framed the city's Central Park from the forty-second floor.

It was a view that never grew old. A view that screamed success, power, and wealth. The halls, offices, and conference rooms were lined with original pieces of art worth millions. Shelton had selected the pieces personally.

"Good morning, Mr. Shelton. Welcome back," greeted his assistant.

"Good morning, Brian," Shelton said in a pleasant, relaxed voice. The two coworkers took the next several minutes to catch up on current events.

Lambert Capital was about to celebrate its fiftieth anniversary. Herb

Lambert had made a living for himself for the first forty years. He had cobbled together a few accounts from several of his father's wealthy friends to get started. The firm benefited from industry growth, but he never came close to achieving his dream of being a serious player on Wall Street.

The day Thomas J. Shelton walked in, that all changed. The once small boutique firm was now one of the top money managers and investment banks in the world.

Over the past ten years, the firm had grown from managing a few hundred million dollars to over five hundred billion dollars. Shelton had done all the heavy lifting.

Shelton and Herb's first meeting was purely a coincidence. It was a Saturday morning at Herb's granddaughter's flag football game. Shelton was there watching his nephew play. It turned out Herb's granddaughter and Shelton's nephew were on the same team.

After the game, the team celebrated at the local creamery near Charlottesville. Shelton had noticed an older gentleman staring at the tattoo on his left bicep and the graphic on his tee shirt. The combination of the trident tattoo and the university logo had caught Herb's attention. Having a Ph.D. in Behavioral Science from Cal Tech and being in naval special ops was unique, if not one of a kind. Herb liked enigmas.

It surprised Shelton how fast Herb moved. Within a week, he had made him an offer. The salary and bonus plan was more than Shelton had dreamed about making in ten years at his new corporate job. He jumped at the chance to join the Lambert team.

Six months later, prior to the banking disaster and Great Recession, Shelton had convinced his boss to adjust client investments to full defense. Meaning, get out of the stock market before the decline. It worked. Clients saved hundreds of millions in losses. Then billions of additional money started flowing into the firm.

The success and insight propelled Shelton to the firm's vice chairman and chief investment officer position. He guided investment strategies, oversaw the investment bank, and led the private equity side of the business. Lambert's returns were the best in the industry. Happy customers drove even more new business their way.

Now the once niche player on Wall Street had become arguably the most respected firm in the business. All based on essentially one principle. When Tom Shelton gave his advice, you were wise to listen.

Shelton's reputation for having superior insights into world economies and business combinations was unmatched. He soon showed up on every top ten list one could think of, including most eligible bachelor.

Shelton was fully aware of the reputation he had created for himself and the firm. As a result, he offered his advice and views sparingly. His critics were abundant, but his results undeniable. Even in the wake of such success, he had maintained his ability to ignore the prevailing views, think critically, analyze the details, and take the risks that made others ill. He believed a few good brains that worked hard, remained humble, and managed the details would beat a mass of smarter brains ten times out of ten. Too much IQ and arrogance created lots of useless by-products that had nothing to do with achieving and making money. At least in his playbook.

This morning, Shelton placed his folio on the side of his desk and sat down. One click of the mouse and his computer came to life. His assistant appeared a minute later with a freshly brewed cup of coffee and placed it on the coaster to the right side of the computer screen without saying a word. Shelton sipped the fresh brew, then opened the morning briefing sheet. He spent the next twenty minutes digesting the world's political, economic, and financial news from the specially prepared document. When finished, he pressed a button on his phone and gazed out over Central Park.

Stephanie Cunningham was waiting in the outer office for the summons she knew was coming.

"Morning, Steph. Come in," Shelton said.

"Welcome back, Tom." She entered his office and took her usual seat.

"Thanks," Shelton said. "Why don't you bring me up to date on things?"

"Nothing has changed materially since we spoke on Saturday. The Project Zephyr team is heading to Paris today. The industrial team is working second round bids on Project Titan, and the health-care team is pitching to the potential buyer tomorrow on Project Meadowlark."

Project names were the convention used to preserve the confidentiality of companies buying companies. The need for secrecy was critical and required to minimize the risk of inside information leaking.

"Did Jeff Meyer give us feedback on our options for his company?" Shelton inquired before taking a sip of his coffee.

"He did. Meyer didn't like our ideas. I called him personally to make sure I understood his concerns. He never called me back. Between you and me, I don't think he knows how to run a company. Frankly, I think he is a dumb ass," Steph concluded.

"I see. But we do a lot of business with his chairman. We can't let this Meyer guy eff it up. It's bad for business."

"Understood," Steph said.

"Call Meyer's chairman and arrange a dinner meeting. Just us two. I'll walk her through our strategy and concerns. If it turns out she's okay with things, then I am."

"Moving on, I kept your calendar open this morning. Your only scheduled meeting today is at two o'clock with the investment committee. They want to give you a preview of bitcoin. You're back in your office at five thirty to meet with the mayor for thirty minutes. Then we'll do a quick read through of your comments for the internal recognition dinner for closing Project Bell. The reception is tonight at six thirty. You're doing the opening welcome and thank-you remarks up front. I'll take it from there. Oh, and you have dinner tonight with Herb. He's expecting you at his home around seven thirty."

"Any idea if Herb has an agenda?"

"When I spoke to him, he didn't specify a subject. But you know this is the time of year when he thinks about succession and promotions."

"He's not currently up to date on the latest performance of individuals. He only spends one day a week in the office," Shelton said, his annoyance clear.

"That doesn't stop him from wanting to ponder and provide input."

Shelton shook his head slightly, dismissing the topic.

"Tomorrow morning," Steph continued, "you and I go to Paris to meet with the French Minister of Finance. He has a few strategic ideas that he wants your opinion on. Apparently they're becoming more and more concerned with the state of the automotive supply chain in the country. My team did some research on the issue. It seems many of the smaller suppliers are struggling financially. The government wants to discuss the feasibility of consolidation. I'll give you the details on the way over.

"Wednesday evening, I have arranged a meeting in London with the PM's chief of staff. He requested a private meeting with you before the World Economic Forum in Davos. His office wouldn't give me any more details."

Shelton took a deep breath and another sip of coffee. "Good to be back, Steph."

"Oh, and the final numbers are in on Project Bell," she said, working to wrap up the briefing. "Our advisory fees and commission earned us a tidy $1.2 billion. By my records, that's the single largest fee ever realized by one firm."

Shelton smiled with satisfaction. Lambert had been the sole adviser to the buyer in a multi-billion-dollar acquisition. A difficult mandate to capture in today's world. Especially on such an enormous deal. Strangely enough, Lambert's customers didn't flinch at paying a higher fee and awarding the deal exclusively to the firm. After all, it was Shelton's idea, and the deal advanced the customer's market share from third to first. The stock shot up 30 percent on the announcement of the deal. Everyone involved was getting richer.

"Anything on your list this morning?" Steph asked.

"No," Shelton responded.

"One more thing, boss. On a personal note, Bob's wife was admitted to the hospital on Friday. She was having difficulty breathing. I didn't hear from him over the weekend, but I'll call this morning to check up. I'll let you know what I find out. See you at six o'clock."

As soon as Steph walked out, Shelton picked up the phone and dialed his old colleague's mobile number. Bob answered on the second ring. Shelton learned they had admitted his wife to the ICU with what the doctors thought was pneumonia. She was also dealing with some sort of kidney infection that had her in terrible shape. The doctors were working to stabilize her but had not yet succeeded.

Shelton knew that Bob and his wife were not big believers in some of the more modern medicines. He offered to help however he could and wished Bob the best.

At 6:25 p.m., Shelton headed down to the recognition event right on schedule.

CHAPTER FOUR

THE CROWDED CONFERENCE center was buzzing as Shelton walked through the main doors. The firm's employees were socializing and enjoying cocktails. Virtually everyone in the room knew the moment Mr. Shelton entered. The junior staff members struggled to glimpse their very own celebrity. The more senior staff did the same but were much less obvious.

Ben stepped up to his boss's side as Shelton worked his way through the crowd shaking hands. Gradually, he made his way to the deal team's table.

The Project Bell team members were beaming with smiles and laughter. Basking in the moment's glory. Their bonus checks would soon have them buying new cars and making down payments on vacation homes. It would make all those long days, weekends, and late nights on the road seem worth it.

Shelton took his time talking shop with the team and congratulated each one personally. Ben lingered in the wings while Steph showed up and took her place by Shelton's side.

Steph and the deal team's leader would be at the top of the banking industry rankings for the year. It was like winning the Academy Award in finance. It would be the first time a female had ever accomplished such a feat on Wall Street, let alone two women. An outcome Shelton was honored to be associated with.

Out of the corner of his eye, Shelton noticed two dark figures standing on the far side of the stage. Their glares sent chills down his spine. He looked around the room. No one was reacting. Ben and the other security staff were acting normally. He took a deep breath and continued his conversation, stretching out the discussion to collect himself. The two figures were dressed in black flowing robes. Hoods mostly concealed their faces. They stood motionless, staring directly at him.

They're taller than usual, Shelton thought. *Dressed in black like the ones in LA. They have what look like sabers hanging from their belts. Perhaps a different rank than the usual gray-robed observers.*

He took another deep breath, then looked up and made eye contact with Ben. Shelton touched the back of his left hand with two fingers from his right. The sign meant there was a problem. Ben reacted immediately, moving to Shelton's side.

"Thanks so much for your hard work on the project, everyone. And again, congratulations." Shelton and Ben stepped away from the group.

"Stay close," Shelton said, keeping a pleasant expression on his face for the crowd.

"What is it?" Ben asked, scanning the room.

"I don't have time to explain right now," Shelton replied. "Just follow me up on stage and stand on my left side toward the back of the stage. Two meters, Ben." Two meters was the standard spacing Shelton used during close proximity combat in his naval special ops unit.

"It's going to look a little strange," advised Ben. "Fighting formation on the big stage."

"Just stay close and alert."

Ben nodded in compliance.

"Let's go," Shelton whispered.

Shelton straightened his jacket, then his tie, and started toward the stage, shaking more hands as he went, Ben by his side politely moving people out of the way for the vice-chairman. The crowd watched as their impeccably dressed and fit boss walked up the steps and across the stage toward the podium. Shelton's gaze locked on the two figures, and their focus was on him.

Shelton stopped at the podium and managed the most glaring look he could produce toward the figures. The one on the right broke eye contact with him and quickly glanced toward its partner. Shelton's training kicked in.

You lose, Shelton thought.

The other one did not flinch.

Ben was still moving in their direction but did not see them. Shelton turned toward the audience with a pleasant smile, then glanced back. The observers were gone.

Shelton turned back toward the microphone and began speaking in his normal confident yet soothing voice. Before he finished his first sentence, the figures reappeared in the back of the room.

Fine, he thought. *Whatever they are, they're avoiding contact. That's good for now. No big scene.*

Shelton finished his remarks to a round of applause and casually exited the stage down the left-side stairs, with Ben following.

Now Shelton and Ben were moving toward the back of the room as Steph began speaking from the podium. Once again, he stared directly at the leader and assessed the opposition as he approached. Fifteen yards, ten yards, and then *poof,* they vanished again. No walking, no turning. Just disappeared.

Shelton continued walking directly over the space where the watchers had been standing. A cold sensation brushed across his face. He stopped.

"Do you feel that?" Shelton whispered to Ben.

"Cold?"

"Yes," Shelton replied.

He casually pulled a pen out of his jacket pocket and dropped it, then bent over to pick it up. As he did, he placed his hand on the floor. The carpet felt like ice where the two figures had been standing. He stood back up and exited through the doors at the back of the conference center.

"What was all of that about?" Ben asked as they made their way toward the elevators.

Shelton kept walking without speaking. As they reached the elevators, Shelton surveyed the hallway. There was no one in sight. Ben pushed the down button, and the two men descended to the parking garage, still without words. Shelton's adrenaline was still pumping. He could see Ben watching him in his peripheral vision.

They walked out of the elevator in the executive parking garage and headed toward the car. Shelton stopped in his tracks. The two figures were now standing at the other end of the garage, watching them.

"Ben, I want you to look straight ahead, down by the trunk of the silver Audi. Fifty yards. Look closely," Shelton said. "Do you see anything? Anything at all?"

Ben turned his head and focused on the white solid-colored wall on the other side of the garage.

"Who are those people?" Ben said in a curious whisper as he continued to focus. A look of confusion emerged on his face. "What the hell are those things, Tom?"

"Keep looking. What do you see?"

"Two figures in black robes. They're staring at us. They're tall with sabers on their belts." The tension was clear in his voice.

Shelton felt a sudden sense of relief. For twenty years, he had wondered if he was hallucinating. Wondered if he was the only anomaly in the world. Now he had a witness. The watchers were real.

"How clearly do you see their faces?" Shelton asked.

"It's hard to see their faces for the hoods. What the fuck are those things? Is it some kind of joke?" Ben said.

"I don't know. I don't think so. I saw them on the stage just before I called you to me, but they disappeared as we approached. Then, while I was speaking, they reappeared at the back of the room. Their eyes were focused directly on me, but when we got closer to them they disappeared, leaving that sense of cold we both felt. No one else seemed to notice them."

"What should we do?" Ben asked.

"They seem to watch me. They've been doing it for a while now. I sure as hell don't know what they are. But they don't look like good guys."

The two men removed their jackets, hung them on the back of the seats of the Carrera, and climbed into the car. Ben's sidearm that had been neatly tucked into his shoulder holster was in his hand. Shelton reached under his seat and pulled out his weapon, then he started the car and slowly backed out of his parking space. He shifted the car into drive.

"Still visible. No movement," Ben said.

"Hold on," Shelton said with determination on his face.

He pushed the accelerator to the floor and turned on the high-beam headlights at exactly the same time. The engine screamed to life, echoing off the concrete walls of the parking garage while the tires broke loose of their grip and squealed. The ear-piercing roar of the engine caused the watchers to flinch as the bright lights illuminated them. They quickly turned and vanished.

Shelton slammed on the brakes as hard as he could, turned the steering wheel, and slid sideways to avoid hitting the wall. Both men jumped out of the car with their weapons raised. They walked toward the place where the things had been standing. At the same moment, they felt it. A sudden wave of cold. Exchanging looks in silence, they surveyed the area. They stood there for a few more minutes, quietly looking, waiting for something else to happen.

"Ben," Shelton said, breaking the silence, "I'm sure you have a lot of questions. I do too. The problem is, I don't have any answers."

"They weren't human," Ben said, staring straight ahead, confusion etched on his face.

"I think I agree. Unless it's some sort of elaborate hoax," Shelton said.

"How long have you been seeing these things, Tom?"

"Just the last few days," Shelton replied.

Ben turned and made eye contact with his friend. "What are you going to do?"

"What can I do?" Shelton shrugged. "I have to get up Herb's place."

"Why don't I take the ride up with you, just in case? I'll hang outside in the car."

"Take the night off," Shelton said. "I'll be okay. If they planned on attacking, they would have done so, don't you think?"

"I guess," Ben said, though he certainly didn't look convinced. "Shit! This is bizarre."

"And Ben," Shelton added, "please keep this confidential. Don't even tell Mattie. The last thing I need anyone to know is that I have spooks following me around."

Ben abruptly turned and started walking toward his own car at the other end of the garage.

"Hey, don't worry about this," Shelton called, causing Ben to stop and face him. "Go do your work with the agency. We can figure this out when you get back." The cold, penetrating look on Ben's face caught Shelton by surprise. It was an expression he had never seen on his friend. The look one of defiance.

Ben stared back, his eyes narrowed, his brows raised and jaw clenched. Then, like a good soldier, he said, "Sure, boss. Let me know if you change your mind."

Ben Davis turned and walked away.

CHAPTER FIVE

Six hundred years earlier...
1423 CE

THE SUN WAS setting over the Sea of Galilee near the Jordan River just north of Ramot in the Golan Heights. It was a magnificent sight from the northeastern shore of the ancient body of water. Waves rolled onto the shore as silhouettes of fishing boats slowly moved across the water, returning to port after the day's work. From the days before the Fertile Crescent into these days of Ottoman rule, the waters of Galilee had provided sustenance and wealth to the cradle of civilization since the beginning of human time. Sitting on its shores was the ancient city of Abdel Kinneret. The oldest inhabited village on earth.

Elias sat on the small wool rug, legs crossed, facing directly into the setting sun, his eyes closed. As he began his daily meditation, the desert breeze warmed his face. The radiation from the sun on his skin eased his body's tension while the dry air cleansed his senses. The daily process balanced the mind and soul. A routine he had practiced for as long as he could remember.

Elias was the village elder. Abdel Kinneret was his responsibility. He was the ruler of the city by the sea. He looked the part with his neat dress, smooth skin, and fit body. Elias appeared to be that of a man in his thirties, but no one in the village really knew how old he was. Stories about him were passed down from generation to generation. Residents referred to him as Chayei Olam. The eternal one. Somehow, everyone else grew old and died while Elias never aged.

He was a gentle leader with a calm demeanor. As a result, Kinneret was a peaceful and serene place. People went about their daily lives farming, fishing, educating their children, and keeping the city impeccably neat and orderly.

Visitors to the city were rare. The village had never made its way onto a chart or map. It had no official name to the outside world, and its obscurity was no accident. No army had ever conquered or occupied the city.

There were many well-known stories and writings about an untouchable, unconquerable city by the sea. Stories of soldiers who had entered the region and never been seen nor heard from again. The tales were persistent and passed down through history.

Still, from time to time, an overzealous military leader would test his luck. The most recent test had occurred just ten years earlier.

A small group of soldiers challenged the village's defenses by breaching the perimeter established by the Syrians. The militia didn't make it within ninety kilometers of Kinneret before they met their fate.

A fate that left mutilated, dismembered skeletons of men and horses strewn about after a hail and lightning storm descended on them from out of the blue sky, ripping them all to pieces.

On that day, all but two men had died. Before the sun had set, the vultures, desert wind, and sand had wiped all evidence of the event from the face of the earth. The two survivors were spared. They were the latest witnesses to attest that the legend of the village was no legend at all.

Before the latest incident, the Chaldeans, Syrians, Arabs, Paddan Aram, and Phoenicians had all tried to commandeer the village on different occasions. Each time, the invaders met a brutal and violent death. The world had learned to avoid the place altogether. The nearest road was at least 100 kilometers away from the city.

Every boat captain knew to steer clear of the sea's northeastern shoreline. The bottom of the lake just offshore was littered with the wreckage and bones of captains and sailors who had come too close.

Kings, pharaohs, and caesars feared the City of Dust. Yet today, a stranger unexpectedly walked into Abdel Kinneret unannounced. As Elias sat on his wool mat before the setting sun, his meditations focused on the visitor.

Just after sunset, Elias folded his meditation rug and walked to the small one-room building just off the village square. The dark tan walls, windows, and clay roof of the new structure were near perfect. The work of a highly skilled craftsman and his crew.

He entered the space but didn't speak, sitting down at the table across from the stranger. In between the two was a small fire in the center of the table giving off the required heat and light to warm and illuminate the space. The evening desert air wafted in through the windows, making the flames dance, and the smoke drifted up through the peak of the roof. In the evening's silence by the light of the fire, Elias observed his guest methodically.

The young man sat there, unable to look his host in the eye. Finally, he found the courage to break the silence.

"Sir, I am sorry to bother you. But thank you for receiving me," the young man of only twenty years said in a shaky voice. "I have traveled here from France. My father sent me."

The young man found the courage to lift his gaze from the ground. Elias looked at his visitor as if he were reading the young man's mind.

"Who is your father?" asked Elias in a gentle voice.

"His name is Jean Pierre Lyon. He is an overseer in Paris. I am Amir Pierre Lyon."

"What is it your father oversees?"

The young man glanced around the room.

"He is the chief magistrate of Paris. He is spiritually independent. There are thousands of us in France and the broader continent who do not subscribe to Roman religions or the thoughts of others. My father is one of the free-thinking leaders. Not openly, of course, or his head would have been removed long ago."

Elias continued staring at Amir. "You are not French."

"You are correct, sir. My father is French back to the beginning of time. My mother is a Persian. I get my complexion and stature from her lineage. My mother's parents are merchants from Basra. They still travel to and from France several times a year with goods. They pass by three days' distance from here. I used to travel with them when I was a boy. The area is familiar to me," said Amir with more confidence.

"Why did your father send you to our village?"

Amir took a deep breath and sighed.

"As my father would say, in the ignorance of my youth, I have been associating with the wrong people." A look of confusion came across Amir's face.

Elias watched. His guest had not intended to be so transparent with his words. The young man was no longer in control of his tongue.

Amir told Elias about a friend he had met several months back. How they started spending time together. Mostly hunting and fishing on some land surrounding a chateau just outside of Paris. The beautiful estate comprised hundreds of kilometers of land with rivers and forest.

As a boy growing up in the city, Amir rarely had access to such wide-open spaces and wonderments. On this day, he rode out to the chateau to meet his new friend. When he arrived, there were other people present. He and his friend spent the morning fishing and swimming. Everything seemed normal. When they returned to the chateau, the owner was there with two very unusual-looking men covered in black robes. They did not speak, they just stared and watched.

Amir went on, describing how the lord of the estate seemed nice enough. How the owner offered Amir and his friend lunch. A normal lunch except for these two strange men lingering about. They ate and drank wine, then went outside to the carriage house, where the owner announced it was time to receive commissions. Amir and his friend did not know what he was talking about. Amir's friend assured him it was nothing, really. At first Amir wasn't concerned. After all, an initiation, a commission would probably be some sort of game. Something that would be meaningless.

Elias listened intently.

"I was wrong," said Amir. "The lord had my friend stand beside him. The owner of the estate said some words in what I think was Latin. I could not understand. Suddenly, he drew his saber and ran my friend through. Right into his chest," Amir said, catching his breath and a sip of wine.

Elias continued his stare without emotion. The shock from the memory was on young Amir's face.

Amir continued describing to Elias how when he realized it wasn't a game, he started looking for an escape. The lord was between him and the door. He knew if he could make it past the man, his horse was ready to ride just outside. When the lord started saying some other words, Amir darted for the door. It took everyone by surprise. As he was moving past the lord, a large hand grabbed his arm and the other hand slammed against his chest. Amir was caught. Everything seemed to stop as this man looked at him intensely. Amir said he could feel something penetrating his skin through the garment where the lord held his hand.

"And his eyes," said Amir. "His eyes were not normal. They were penetrating my mind. His grasp was not enough to stop me. I spun away and bolted through the door and onto my horse. I rode as fast as I could back to Paris and told my father what happened. He immediately packed my bag and sent me on my way."

The exhaustion from the journey and the trauma were showing on Amir's face.

"Did your father ever speak of our village to you before this?" asked Elias.

"No, sir. My father is a very private and reliable man."

"Indeed," said Elias as he glared into the boy's soul. "Before you departed, what did your father tell you about our city?"

"Not much really," said Amir. "Only that my life was in grave danger and, well, and if I made it here alive, I might be safe."

"Your father is a wise man," replied Elias. "You are the fortunate one. You followed your father's direction."

"Thank you, sir. Do you know my father?"

"I know many people," replied Elias. "Tell me about the lord of this estate."

Amir sat back in his chair and took a sip of wine. According to Amir's father, the owner of the chateau was a man named Hauser. Wolfgang Hauser. He was from Germania. The French government gave him the estate. Lord Hauser was tall. Smooth skin. Very handsome. Neatly dressed in the latest fashion, like a wealthy aristocrat. One of the best-dressed men Amir had ever seen. Amir's friend said Hauser was the finest horseman in France. At lunch, Hauser told the boys stories about sailing. He bragged he was the finest captain this world has ever known. Lord Hauser didn't eat, he just sipped on his wine and told stories. Amir had seen a woman in the chateau. Hauser watched her continuously with pursed lips, a slight smile and narrowed eyes.

Elias could see his guest becoming more comfortable.

"But Hauser's eyes mesmerized me. They seemed to change color. They were black as coal one second and then pale the next. It made me dizzy," continued Amir. "I had a difficult time breaking eye contact with him. Then there were his hands. They seemed unusually large and powerful with long fingers." Amir demonstrated the length with his own two fingers. "They didn't look human."

"Did anyone chase after you?" asked Elias.

"No. I looked back several times. As I rounded the first bend in the road, I saw two strange-looking men standing in red robes outside the carriage house, watching me ride away. But no one followed. I am an excellent horseman myself."

Elias stood up from his chair and walked to the window, sipping his wine. He stood there for a moment, thinking as the cool breeze drifted through.

Elias turned back to face his guest.

"Your chest where he touched you. You said you felt something strange. May I see?"

Amir stood, unbuttoned his garment, and slipped it off his shoulders. Elias walked over to him and began studying the mark in the fire's light.

Elias traced around the outside of the symbol with his gaze. Then he examined every inch of the darkened flesh without touching.

"What is it?" Amir asked, staring down at his chest. "Do you know what it is?"

"It appears to be a bruise," Elias said while he continued the examination.

Once finished, he stepped back from Amir, then politely excused himself and exited the room.

✍

Amir rested his head on the table while he waited. Several minutes passed as he drifted in and out of sleep. A sudden touch on his shoulder stirred him. He turned and saw Elias.

Before Amir could say a word, Elias grabbed his clothing and lifted him from the chair with one hand. Amir's face contorted from the sharp pain in his chest and the loud, piercing noise inside his head.

"What are you doing?" Amir screamed with terror in his voice.

Elias clenched the knife in his hand. The only visible part was the handle with his hand wrapped around it. The blade was buried deep in Amir's chest. With his other hand, Elias tightly gripped Amir's arm, holding him steady. A few seconds later, he gently lowered Amir to the ground, supporting the dying man's head as it laid back on the stone floor.

Amir labored for breath. He tried to speak but could not find enough air to get the words past his lips.

Two other people entered the room and held Amir on the ground. Elias wiped the blood from the knife using Amir's shirt.

Then he cut off Amir's shirt and began slowly working his way around what he had told Amir was a bruise. It was not. It was a symbol. A globe and serpent symbol. Elias cut the skin as he went. When the incision was complete, Elias placed the knife on the ground. He rubbed his hands together and began working his fingers into the incision and underneath the skin.

Slowly he peeled the flesh away from Amir's chest. Inch by inch, he carefully removed it in one piece. When the last piece of skin separated from the muscle, Elias turned and tossed the bloody mark into the fire, then sat back on the ground to rest.

Amir's eyelids opened slowly. A look of calm replaced the pain on his face.

"Peace be with you," Elias whispered as Amir closed his eyelids for the last time.

CHAPTER SIX

THE SWELLS OF the Mediterranean were gently rocking the deck of the *Blu Signora*. The sun descended toward the horizon, occasionally peeking through the partly cloudy skies. Aboard, the passengers were enjoying an ice-cold Scottish pint around the fantail table.

Commander Shelton had parachuted in with his team the night before. His drop pack was a case of beer heavier than the regulations allowed. This evening, the team was taking in the magnificent view and relaxing after a grueling week of preparation in the South Pacific.

The boat's captain had the 134-footer anchored in international waters a hundred miles northeast of Tripoli. The team had everything prepared for the next twelve hours of work. They had checked and double-checked all the gear and equipment. They had left nothing to chance. The only thing to do now was to wait.

Echo-Golf-Lima One missions, otherwise known as Eagle One, were a low-priority activity for the White House and the Joint Chiefs. That made it a good fit for the commander's naval reserve special operations unit. There was always more work that needed to be done in a world filled with terrible actors. More work than active-duty personnel and budgets allowed for.

Several of the sailors aboard the CIA-equipped boat were original members of Shelton's active-duty team, a group that had completed multiple tours in the Middle East and survived other covert unnamed missions in unidentified places.

As the members of Shelton's team approached retirement age, he had convinced several of them to continue their service in the reserves with him. The others figured they had pressed their luck enough and checked out.

Commander Shelton's part-time job was to find meaningful yet relatively safe work for his people once or twice per year. Initially, the navy brass had pushed back against having a special operations reserve squad. After several attempts, Shelton found a receptive ear inside the Pentagon. A flag officer named Admiral Nathan Wood had taken the time to listen and review the idea. The unit was perfect for low-priority missions.

Wood had quickly bought into Shelton's idea and funded the squad out of his own budget for the first couple years. The investment had paid off. Twelve successful intelligence and capture missions in ten years. Five of the missions had provided significant positive press for the previous US administration. They were happy to take credit for Shelton's success. The beauty was, there was no downside risk letting Eagle One operate. If a mission failed, no one would have ever known. Not even the president. But they hadn't failed.

Eagle One was not a sanctioned operating unit inside the US Navy. There was no record of the team anywhere. However, every special ops team member, leader, and support personnel knew about Eagle One through its success. So when the commander of Eagle One or his executive officer called for resources or support, they received it. No questions asked. The special operations community enjoyed bending the rules for one of their own.

Woods was smart enough to keep his distance from the team, even though his career and pension were bolstered by at least two additional stars due solely to Eagle One's accomplishments over the past decade.

Now, Wood was the current acting chairman of the Joint Chiefs of Staff for President Staley. The position made Wood the highest-ranking military officer in the country. Wood knew his career would be over if something went wrong and the news media traced it back to him. The longer Eagle One operated, the more likely it was to end badly for him. Staley would not think twice about throwing him under the bus to save his own skin.

The good news was, Wood's house on Chesapeake Bay was paid for, and his ex-wife was off the payroll. The cash the commander had collected from the bad people and shared with the admiral over the years made his government pension look like gas money. Somehow, Wood and Shelton had both justified that killing and taking the enemy's money was not theft. It was more like the price of justice.

Currently, two Americans were being held against their will in Libya, and the mission was to rescue them. The journalists' Libyan captors didn't like what these two reporters were up to and sequestered them. The State Department didn't define them as hostages because no ransom had been demanded. For all the government recognized, the Americans were simply missing and presumed to be living in a terrorist state of their own free will.

The families had reported them missing and engaged the government for help. As of now, no one had heard from the reporters in over two years. The sitting US president despised reporters. He probably even liked the fact that there were two less running around the world.

One of the Americans was a freelance reporter named Bret Baldwin. He was from a wealthy family, and his mother was a major contributor to the president's election campaign fund.

The story was, Baldwin had been looking to make a name for himself. He hired a young photojournalist named James Lower from Oregon to help. The two had set off to Libya, looking for an international story to launch Baldwin's career. Lower's family had told the US State Department that Baldwin had misled their son, who now found himself in a hostile country against his will.

Woods brought the mission to the Eagle One commander for consideration. Baldwin's family had privately offered the admiral $10 million to rescue their son. Shelton agreed to do it for $20 million. They placed the money in escrow in two Swiss accounts. Ten for Woods and ten for the Eagle One team.

Shelton's motivation was to rescue Jim Lower and make it painful for the Baldwins. He couldn't care less about an arrogant manipulator trying to create a name for himself. The Lower kid was obviously duped and didn't know that the rich kid was being reckless.

Eagle One's intelligence showed that a civilian group of Libyan criminals was holding the two US citizens. The group would be no match for Eagle One. The only way the Lower kid was going to get home alive was if his captors let him go or Shelton and his team went in and got him. The US military simply could not spare the active-duty personnel to rescue every less-than-smart citizen who found themselves in a hard spot.

At exactly 11:15 p.m. local time, the *Blu Signora* hoisted anchor. The boat went dark, and the captain pushed the throttles forward and headed for the Libyan coast. Three hours later, at two miles out, the captain pulled the power back and locked in the global positioning system. The lights of Tripoli were just over the horizon. Shelton checked the radar scope. No other traffic was visible.

The rescue team launched the RHIBs and headed for the coast. The group, including Shelton, was dressed in upscale casual wear. The disguise would allow them to blend in with the locals. Anyone who might see them arriving at the dock would simply think they were a group of friends out for an evening ride and drinking.

The command boat was staffed with the captain, three CIA field officers, and a signals officer who was monitoring all Libyan police and military communications with the help of an E-3 aircraft circling above.

The Americans blended perfectly with the local street crowds in the city's nightclub district. Alex and Kurt took the lead, casually strolling in and out of crowds until they reached the front of Club Diamond. The four found a table across the street from the club, ordered a round of drinks, and began assessing the area and the people.

Thirty minutes later, the group entered Club Diamond through the main entrance. Shelton and Jamie immediately split off and took the elevator to the fourth floor while Alex and Kurt took the stairs. The main hallway on the top floor of the building was empty. Shelton and Jamie walked to the end of the hall and turned right, where they met what appeared to be a security guard. Jamie spoke to him in perfect native language.

"We have an appointment with Salem," Jamie said.

The security guard looked confused but assumed the request was legitimate. He headed down the hallway. Shelton watched as the guard walked to a large double door and turned to go in. Before the guard could react, Jamie was behind him. The unsuspecting guard's lifeless body slowly crumpled to the floor.

Commander Shelton opened the door and walked in with Jamie following. Behind a large desk was a heavyset man looking up at the strangers in his office. Before he could speak, Shelton had his 9mm handgun pressed against the man's forehead.

"Keep your hands on top of the desk and make no sound," Shelton ordered quietly.

The man complied.

"We are here to take the Americans home," Shelton said. "Just tell me which room they are in, and we will be on our way."

The fat man paused for a moment, then said, "Other side of the hallway, two doors down."

"If you are lying to me, I will kill you," Shelton said in a matter-of-fact tone. "If you waste my time, I will kill you. Just like I killed your security guard." He pointed to the body lying on the floor just inside the doorway of the room.

"Do you understand?" he asked.

The man nodded. "Just as I told you, across the hall. Take them. They are a hassle for me, anyway. They waste my time."

Jamie stepped out of the room and gave Alex and Kurt directions. The two maneuvered down the hall and quietly picked the lock on the door. Inside, the two young men were sound asleep in separate beds. Alex woke them one at a time. Within two minutes, Alex and Kurt were back in the doorway with the two men ready to go.

"You are a wise man," Shelton observed.

He told Alex and Kurt to take the journalists and return to the command boat and put team two on notice. With no questions asked, they departed.

All Eagle One members knew to prepare for the primary mission, as well as a secondary mission, when deploying with Commander Shelton. He was notorious for adding on objectives in the field real-time based on his assessment of the situation. The assessment of Libyan criminals was that they were amateurs. Amateurs driven because police and government enforcement of rules and law in the country was almost nonexistent. Therefore, criminals really did not need to be overly paranoid or sophisticated.

Shelton sat down in front of the fat man's desk and relaxed.

"Tell me, sir, who is your biggest adversary in your line of work?" he asked.

The man immediately said, "Riccardo. Riccardo Flores. He operates a despicable human trade network between Tripoli and Barcelona. Kids, adults, men, women, girls, and boys. It does not matter to him. If we eliminated him, life in our city would improve," the man offered, assuming the American was looking to return a favor.

Over the next ten minutes, the man told Shelton all about Riccardo's operation and where to find him. Shelton and Jamie departed through the back entrance with the keys to man's Mercedes.

Two blocks from the harbor, the Americans found the location. They parked the car on a side street and took up surveillance across the street from the Hotel Med. A few minutes later, they were on Riccardo's doorstep.

Shelton and Jamie walked toward the two men in the hallway as if they were residents. One of the security guards glanced up as the strangers approached the suite. The two sailors walked slightly past the two men, then turned around suddenly. The other security guard awoke just in time to see the flashes from the suppressors that ended their lives.

Shelton listened for movement inside the suite. Nothing. Jamie removed a room key from one of the dead men's pockets and opened the door. They walked into the bedroom where Riccardo was sound asleep with a woman in the bed beside him. Shelton strapped a piece of tape on Riccardo's mouth and ripped back the sheets with lightning speed. Jamie did the same to the woman.

Riccardo woke from his deep sleep, confused by what was happening. Within a minute, the woman was bound and placed in the bathroom. Two minutes later, the three men were making their way down the seventeen flights of stairs. Jamie led their guest, and Shelton carried a bag of money. They exited into the alley. Jamie sprinted ahead and backed the car up. Shelton pushed Riccardo into the trunk and slammed the lid.

"Two minutes, standing by," came the voice from the radio into Shelton's earpiece.

The recovery team watched as the car approached on the beachfront road. There were no other cars in sight. Shelton estimated from the road to the water was about fifty yards.

"Ready?" asked Shelton.

"Affirmative."

"Now," ordered Shelton.

Jamie stopped the car. They pulled on their headgear and climbed from the car and opened the trunk.

Shelton keyed his mic. "Recon status?"

"All clear," came the immediate reply.

"Inbound… Ready, now," ordered Shelton.

The specially equipped recovery boat lifted out of the water and was at full speed, headed for the shore, within seconds.

"Two minutes."

Jamie and Shelton lifted Riccardo out of the trunk and onto their shoulders almost without effort. They turned and began sprinting toward the water, each carrying their part of Riccardo.

"Keep working," Shelton told himself as his feet struggled to find traction in the sand. "Work through the pain. Keep going." The distance between Shelton and the beach didn't seem to get any shorter. The sand was getting deeper. "I am running out of breath. I will not make it. Shit!"

Suddenly, Shelton woke up, confused and huffing. He slowly calmed himself as he stared at the ceiling of the hotel. His heart rate slowed as he relaxed and the nerves in his back recognized the soft bed of the London Ritz Hotel.

Less than a week had passed since he led the Eagle One mission in Libya. They had quietly reunited the Americans with their families; Woods and Shelton's team had added another layer to their personal wealth; and the information he extracted from the Riccardo interrogation regarding a human trafficking operation in Spain had been useful.

Post-mission dreams were common for Shelton. He had learned to use the playback to analyze details of operations, looking for flaws. He rolled onto his side and went back to sleep.

CHAPTER SEVEN

THE WORLD ECONOMIC Forum was in full swing, and the small Swiss town of Davos was buzzing with activity. Once a year, leaders from governments, businesses, and civil society from around the world descended on the resort town nestled in the eastern Alps. It was an opportunity for the rich and powerful to collaborate on solutions to the world's most pressing problems.

The reality was it was a chance for presidents and prime ministers, billionaires and celebrities to get together and show they cared about the rest of the world. Any A-list person with a cause could and would show up to capture the spotlight for their ten minutes of exposure, all hoping to advance their own agenda. The hordes of reporters from the business and political media took every opportunity to beam the interesting, irrelevant, or outright lies around the globe with equal vigor within seconds.

Lambert Capital had been attending the forum since Shelton joined the firm. At first, both Herb and Shelton attended. During the first few years, it was hard work to get a single private meeting with anyone useful. Several years later, that had all changed. Now Shelton was one of the hottest tickets in town. The secretaries and assistants of the most powerful people on the planet would interrupt their principal just to point Shelton out as he walked across the hotel lobby, sat in a restaurant, or got into or out of a car. Davos was Shelton's Hollywood. There was no bigger star. Not because of his position or rank but because of his enormous financial success.

Shelton had quickly learned to use his position effectively. He always kept a low profile, which added to the mystique and intrigue. That made a Tom Shelton sighting even bigger news. The fact was, Shelton's reputation was much better known than his face. Only those who knew him or had a well-trained eye could pick him out of a crowd. To most people, he looked like just another handsome, well-groomed, and well-dressed businessman.

The informal aspect of the conference was much more productive for Shelton and the company. So many decision makers and influencers in one place at one time presented tremendous opportunities. One-stop shopping for a deal maker.

Despite the objectives of the meeting, the world's biggest challenge at the moment was not on the agenda. But it was on everyone's mind. The problem was the recently inaugurated president of the United States. Somehow, the American electorate had put a media personality with no sense of ethics or integrity in the White House. A person who inherited his family's money and had no comprehension of a working person's reality. Ironically, the hard-working people of America had elected a person who had never done an honest day's work in his life. The very people that President Staley despised the most had voted him into office.

For government and business leaders, it was a serious situation. The determination of the best behavioral professionals in the world judged the US president to be mentally unstable. That meant a mentally challenged person was the leader of the most powerful economy and military on the planet.

Every major political leader was searching for ideas and suggestions on how to deal with the new US administration. They were looking for someone who might influence the administration into a more constructive approach to world trade and foreign relations. Someone who could at least give useful advice on how to navigate with the new president. The European leaders quickly recognized Shelton as one who might be useful in either case. A logical choice, especially given Shelton's PhD in Neurological Psych and Behavioral Science from Cal Tech.

The president's first chief of staff had paid Shelton to interface with the new president socially. The chief arranged a business roundtable meeting with Shelton in attendance. Shelton's professional opinion was extreme narcissism. Pathological narcissism was the medical term. His advice to the cabinet was to get the best psychiatrists in the world together and develop a playbook. One that would allow them to manage the information and, therefore, the reaction from the patient. In a normal situation, Shelton and the others would view the recommendation as treasonous. The brutal reality was it was going to be necessary for survival.

Steph had spent the months before Davos building Shelton's itinerary for the week. The plan would allow Shelton to spend time with key government leaders. The aim was to listen and help sort out a strategy that would help others manage the United States of America effectively. Steph wanted the world's leaders to know Shelton was trying to help. Being visible in the inner circles would be good for business.

The knock on the door was thirty minutes early this morning. Shelton looked through the peephole of his hotel suite door and saw Steph standing outside. The intense expression on her face explained the early arrival.

He opened the door, and Steph walked past with a quick and barely audible greeting.

Shelton closed the door and stood there watching as she placed her briefcase on the dining room table, then turned toward her boss with a serious look.

"Good morning, Steph," Shelton said with a pleasant smile on his face.

"Good morning," Steph replied, frowning while looking at the floor. Shelton stood there in his T-shirt and dry-fit exercise pants, waiting for her to continue. He noticed the expression on her face improved slightly as she looked up before she turned away.

"Coffee?" he asked, pointing toward the freshly brewed carafe. It wasn't time to jump into the first problem of the day.

"Yes, I'll get," Steph replied, shaking the sexual image of her boss out of her mind. She turned and walked to the bar and poured two cups. "You will not believe the call I received this morning. Staley wants to have dinner with you tonight. It's going to blow the entire schedule."

Shelton stood in silence as he processed Steph's words. Then, picking up his cup of coffee on the way, he walked over to the window and looked out into the valley as the sun was about to rise over the mountains.

"Interesting. What should we do?" he said, sipping the steaming liquid.

"How about we say no?" she said in a calm, cool voice. "But how can you turn down the president of the United States? If it were any other person, I wouldn't be agitated, but it's Staley."

"What does he want to talk about?" Shelton asked. "Did his new chief give you a subject?"

"I asked, but he said the president didn't specify. I even pushed him to make an educated guess but got nothing. The White House must be in complete chaos all the time. His chief isn't even smart enough to make up a reason for the meeting. How the hell are they going to run the country?"

"Well, why do you think he wants to meet?" Shelton asked.

She let out a deep sigh.

"Who knows? He may have learned that you're meeting with other heads of state. He wants to know what you are up to." She shrugged as she sipped her coffee.

Shelton turned away from the window and sat down at the table next to Steph.

"Now that makes sense to me," Shelton said, pleased by the thoughtfulness of the answer. "He likely thinks he's entitled to know what I'm discussing with the others. After all, I'm a citizen of his kingdom. A king is entitled to know everything. It helps prevent an overthrow." Shelton smiled at the lunacy of his words.

"Now for the tough question. How should we handle the situation?"

"What are you willing to share with him?" Steph asked.

"Nothing," Shelton said, raising his arms and making an X with his forearms. "I will never violate the trust I've built with the others. However, I could have some fun with him." His raised a brow and offered a slight smile, mischief crossing his face.

"How about this? I sit down with him at dinner. I start off being respectful of his highness. Then I insult him and berate him just as he does to others. A test to see if I could get him to blow his top at the dinner table with others watching. Maybe even with the cameras rolling. That would be exciting." Shelton grinned, returning to his feet to stretch his calf muscles.

Steph smirked at the idea and discretely stole a look at her boss's body. The tights accentuated his muscular shape. "I think we have our answer. I will respectfully decline on your behalf."

"You know they won't let you off that easy. They're going to have you running back and forth with me to make a meeting happen. Not knowing what is being discussed in the back rooms is unbearable for Staley. That characteristic is part of his impairment." Shelton watched her carefully. "I'm completely serious, Steph."

"Well, what do you suggest?"

"Get the chief on the phone." He pointed to her mobile device.

"Are you sure?"

The expression on Shelton's face answered the question.

Steph didn't dally. She pushed the call back button on her phone. The president's chief of staff answered on the third ring.

"Hi, Stephanie. Thanks so much for calling me back. Are we all set for tonight?" General Mack's voice boomed through the phone.

"Good morning, General. This is Tom Shelton."

After a brief pause, the general greeted Shelton with a warm, "Well, good morning, Commander Shelton. This is a surprise. Thanks so much for calling me back personally."

"Yes, you're welcome, General. About tonight. Please understand that my words mean no disrespect to you personally, sir. However, the answer is no. As you would imagine, I already have other plans and, frankly, I have no interest in having dinner with the president."

"Commander," the general implored, "the president has specifically requested a dinner meeting with you tonight. Your president has no other plans. Your president expects a United States Naval Reserve officer to follow orders. I suggest you accept."

Shelton was sure they had briefed General Mack on the successful Libyan mission. It would have been normal protocol to put a summary of such a mission in the president's daily briefing. General Mack was known across services for his extreme attention to detail. His unofficial nickname was "Grinder."

Even knowing this, the next words out of the general's mouth took Shelton by surprise.

"If the president gets wind of your moonlighting job, Commander, he will not hesitate to pull the plug on you and the ranking officer."

The threat was legitimate. Staley had indeed fired scores of people within days of planned retirements, leaving thirty-year government employees without the pensions they had earned. Adding insult to injury, Staley would make sure he splashed his actions all over the press and social media.

"General, I appreciate that you have a hard job," Shelton said. "Perhaps more than most. Frankly, I cannot understand why you would subject yourself to such incompetence. You, sir, are a general in the United States Marine Corps. That said, I know someone must do it. My advice is to let some ass-kissing halfwit do the halfwit's bidding. And, general, you need to take my next words seriously."

Shelton allowed an uncomfortable silence to settle in.

"I do not appreciate your threatening tone toward me or the admiral. Is that clear, sir?" Shelton said. "If I get wind of any repercussions, I will find you, General. I will find your loved ones, General. Eagle One will find you. Do you understand what I am saying to you, sir? If you decide to do the wrong thing here, there is only one slow protracted outcome for you."

Mack's breathing was audible on the phone speaker.

"Now, General, we both know the president has problems. You can tell him that if he wants to talk to me, the best thing he can do is resign. And, General, I am happy to call him personally and give him my answer. Do you have his number?" Shelton asked.

Mack drew one more deep breath and replied, "I understand. Goodbye, Commander."

Steph's eyes were wide and her mouth was hanging open as she pushed the end button.

"What the hell, boss!" came the uncontrolled words out of her mouth. "Oh my God! What was that all about?"

"Don't worry about it. Ignore what you just heard. It was just a couple of old military guys busting each other's balls to get their own way."

The shock on Steph's face faded a little. Shelton's words seemed to make sense to her.

"Don't answer if he calls back. That's an order, Steph," Shelton said with as much seriousness in his voice as he could muster. "What's happening in the presidency is unprecedented. It's easy to poke fun at it. But it is a serious, serious situation."

"I understand, Tom," Steph replied as she shook off the shock and refocused on the day's schedule. "I will see you at the elevators at eleven o'clock."

"One more thing, Steph," Shelton said, causing her to stop and turn around. "Andy Wilkinson phoned this morning. He wants to have dinner tonight."

The skeptical look on her face said it all. First the president and now the prime minister of England.

"I know, I know," Shelton said. "But I am absolutely serious. Wilkinson called me himself. Dinner is at eight thirty. His squad is picking me up at eight o'clock."

"I'll get the schedule adjusted," Steph said. "I'll see you in a few hours."

༄

The small villa on the British government's estate just north of the city was well guarded. On the drive in, Shelton's trained eye observed the layers of security that surrounded the property.

The initial layer was armed observers and roadside checkpoints. Armored security vehicles and fully equipped army personnel protected the entrance to the estate. The open fields between the perimeter wall and the main house contained two layers of heavily armed infantry personnel.

Shelton recognized the silhouettes of the infrared devices and broad night vision machines strategically placed throughout the open spaces and fields. The closer he came to the prime minister's location, the security detail density increased.

The specially equipped Range Rover came to a stop in front of the prime minister's living quarters. From the front porch of the small villa, Shelton turned and looked out into the fields of darkness he had just come through. Only a few security people dressed in black were visible standing post. The small army protecting the PM was not visible.

The small, cozy four-bedroom villa was Wilkinson's preference. He had no need for grandiose accommodations when traveling.

Andrew Wilkinson III was raised in a middle-income household in London. His father and mother were both teachers at the local preparatory school in his neighborhood. He was raised to value education, learning, and hard work.

At twelve, he was employed at the local hardware store on weekends and some weeknights. He found a love of selling and using his interpersonal skills to interact with others.

The young Wilkinson's academic performance and his relentless pestering of the local members of Parliament got him a full grant to Oxford University. There, Wilkinson refined his political skills and positions. By the time he was a senior, he was the newest Member of Parliament, defeating the very one who got him into university.

After a life in politics, Wilkinson had come to accept that he wouldn't get the top job. The British people liked his predecessor for the support of the Church of England. The sudden and untimely death of the beloved PM opened the job for the top member of the cabinet.

Initially, the people and the crown viewed Wilkinson as a gap filler. An acceptable one. But as he settled into the job, his popularity grew. He was now in the fifth year of his second term and only sixty-eight years old. If he made it two more years, he would be the longest-running British prime minister in the modern era.

Tom Shelton and Andrew Wilkinson first met by sheer coincidence in Davos ten years ago. Shelton had stepped out the back door of the hotel to smoke a cigarette. There he stood in the hotel's alleyway enjoying the afternoon air and a smoke when the British prime minister and two of his security people stepped outside to do the same. Shelton and Wilkinson hit it off immediately.

To Shelton's surprise, that same day Wilkinson canceled his original dinner plans and invited his new acquaintance to share a meal with him. They got to know each other a bit more, and by the end of the evening they were both sloshed. Wilkinson retired to his stateroom while Shelton found a sofa to sleep on. The tradition was born. Every year since, the two friends would sneak off one evening during the conference to have dinner and tie one on.

Tonight, Wilkinson's mood seemed more serious. Shelton wasn't interested in prying. His old friend would come around to sharing what was truly on his mind. Most likely after a few fingers of single malt.

They spent dinner conversation catching up on the events of the week. The hand-wringing that Staley was causing among world leaders had precedent and Wilkinson had done his homework. He had gone back into the notes of Churchill, the Cabinet, and Parliament. As much as he hated to say it, the situation was akin to German leadership prior to World War Two. He didn't see it playing out the same way, but the behaviors, rhetoric, and intentions seemed equally dangerous.

Regardless of believability, Wilkinson seemed resolved to do what was necessary to protect England from a potentially hostile United States of America.

After dinner, the two friends made their way to the back porch of the villa. The evening air was crisp. The staff had a warm fire stoked in the pit, wing-backed leather chairs in position, and a fresh bottle of whiskey opened with drinks poured and waiting.

Wilkinson couldn't delay any further, it was time to share what was really on his mind.

"I had tea with the archbishop of Canterbury this afternoon," Wilkinson said, "at this little castle up the road. About ten kilometers north." He pointed with his glass of whiskey. "I had no idea the crown owned a Swiss castle." The gruff tone of Wilkinson's voice and the snarl on the prime minister's face made Shelton laugh.

"So I'm curious. How does the conversation between the Church of England and the prime minister go?" inquired Shelton, lifting his glass of whiskey from the wooden table between their chairs.

"Oh, well, I'm sure you can imagine," said Wilkinson. "They want me to attend their ridiculous sermons more regularly, like my predecessor had done. With the cameras rolling, of course. They want me to mention the Church more in my speeches. I suppose it's all on the up and up, you know. Their membership continues to decline. That means less income from the congregation and more government funding to sustain their business model. The archbishop's argument is a few good words here and there from me require less cash from Parliament. Of course, he reminds me that the new king suggests the same occasionally. I think it's a gigantic leap of faith to think the younger generations of British citizens are going to be influenced by my words or actions regarding religion," concluded Wilkinson.

Shelton sat attentively, enjoying the moment with his friend. He watched the age lines on Wilkinson's face shift downward as a concerned look appeared.

"What is bothering you, Andrew?" Shelton asked. "You look like a person who needs to have a talk."

Wilkinson looked toward him without speaking. He picked a cigarette out of the pack lying on the table and lit it. The first puff of smoke drifted away and out into the night.

"There were two other people accompanying the archbishop this afternoon. One was a cardinal from Rome. Name was Father Bianco," Wilkinson said, gesturing with his cigarette. "The other was a strange-looking fellow. A German named Hauser. We were not expecting either of them. It was supposed to be a one-on-one meeting. It's terribly poor form by the archbishop. Instead of embarrassing him, I let his guests stay. I shall take it up with the Crown at our next meeting, I assure you."

"I suspect that happens frequently to you?" Shelton said, trying to keep the conversation light. "After all, people are less about procedure and more opportunistic. Don't you think?"

The grimace on his friend's face oozed with unhappiness. Wilkinson stood and began pacing around the fire.

"Strange chap, that Hauser. Dr. Wolfgang Hauser. He wore gloves. His suit coat sleeves were over length. I think he was trying to conceal the size of his hands. He didn't say a word. He just sat observing me. I felt like on was on display." Wilkinson resumed his pacing. "Apparently, he works with the Church of England and the Roman Catholics. The cardinal introduced him as a significant financial sponsor to the Catholics and Protestants. He was tall, with remarkably perfect skin and a penetrating look. His face had some resemblance to yours. Here in the eyes." Wilkinson gestured with his fingers toward his own face. "Have you ever heard of this der mensch?" The words were German for "man."

"I'm not familiar with the name," Shelton replied, seeing the tension in his friend's clenched jaw muscles. "But me not knowing a private German contributor to the Church isn't surprising. I'm confident there are tens of thousands of them I don't know."

Wilkinson turned and stared out into the darkness.

"Apparently, someone stormed through Barcelona recently and killed over ten people in one night," said Wilkinson casually. "Four of the victims were clergy. One from the Church of England and two Romans. The fourth was some other flavor. It sounded as if the assailant gave the holy men some extra special treatment." Wilkinson turned back toward the fire. "This Bianco fellow requested my help to find the one responsible. He said he was reaching out to leaders around the world for assistance and that my support would be both expected and appreciated."

Shelton casually reached for the pack of cigarettes sitting on the table.

"Expected?" Shelton narrowed his eyes and clenched his jaw slightly in surprise. "That is strange. I don't recall reading about it in the press." He lit up, then took a sip of whiskey.

"These fellows cover up issues with their personnel frequently," replied Wilkinson. "I got a quick read from my team just before you arrived. The building where they were killed was a Spanish human trafficking operation run out of Libya. The attacker killed all the bad guys and gals in the place, then set the victims free. I say fuck those bastard low-life pedophiles and criminals. I'll give a medal to the son of a bitch doing the good work. What do you say, Sir Thomas?"

One side of Shelton's mouth rose into a half smile. He had forgotten Wilkinson and the late queen had knighted him.

"That's not what is troubling you, is it, Andrew?" Shelton leaned back into the chair. "You deal with such bullshit all the time. Liars, thieves, and crooks. Isn't that what you say?"

Wilkinson walked over to the outdoor bar. The senior house servicer quickly stepped out of the villa to serve the prime minister.

"Sir, may I help you?"

"Cognac, please," Wilkinson said.

The barkeep poured the PM his preferred brand and vintage, then stepped back inside to give him his privacy. Wilkinson returned to the fire and sat down in the chair next to Shelton.

"This Hauser fellow is troubling to me," Wilkinson said, swirling his cognac. "These so-called men of God hanging around such an unusual chap is troubling to me. The archbishop putting me on display for his guests is troubling me. Asking me to help them find a killer of human traffickers in Spain is troubling me. Bloody fucking hell, Tom! It felt like an intimidation mission. The goddamn pope and the archbishop of England threatening me!"

Shelton switched his crossed leg from one side to the other. He took a puff of the cigarette and leaned toward the prime minister.

"Well, sir, I would let your team of professionals sort out this Hauser fellow," Shelton said. "You have the best in the business working for you. But if there is something I can do to help, you have my number."

"I have a question for you," said Wilkinson, working to change the subject. "Why would your people elect such a person as Staley?"

Shelton turned his head, contemplating the question as he looked into the darkness.

"Blind loyalty. It is the fate of those who don't know better, Andrew," he said as he took a drag from his cigarette. "Those of us burdened with the facts, the truth, or in possession of such have a duty to the rest." Shelton turned his head back toward Wilkinson.

"A proper thought to end on," Wilkinson said as he contemplated Shelton's words.

Wilkinson stood and said good night, then excused himself and went into the villa. On the way back into the city, Shelton created two new folders in his secured electronic file: "DWH" for Dr. Wolfgang Hauser and "Bianco."

CHAPTER EIGHT

THE SPECIAL INVESTIGATIONS room on the 22nd floor of the Los Angeles County sheriff's headquarters resembled a corporate boardroom, complete with state-of-the-art audiovisual equipment, personal workstations, and leather chairs. Detective Lexi Rawson offered her guests refreshments and bagels before taking her seat at the head of the table.

Detective Rawson was a sixteen-year veteran of the LA County sheriff's department. She was the most decorated detective in the department's history. She had solved more homicides during her tenure than her colleagues did in an entire career. In her spare time, she worked cold cases for a change of pace. The single greatest challenge of her career was the one on the agenda today.

The meeting had taken almost nine months to coordinate. Rawson had spent much of the time trying to convince lead detectives in New York, Chicago, London, and Washington, DC to meet with her. Coordinating schedules was almost as difficult. At last, she had them all in the same room. Now the real work began.

The faces looking at her from around the table lacked enthusiasm. She was confident that would soon change. The case at hand was one that would likely become a hunt for the most prolific serial killer the world had ever seen. Her goal was to motivate her colleagues to work together to solve the case.

Eight years earlier, she had been called to the scene of a homicide in Long Beach. The victim was a convicted rapist and a known repeat abuser of women. They found his body in an alley with two bullet holes in his chest. Two days later, Rawson got a call from Santa Monica. The victim there had a similar criminal record but was a wealthy businessman who had lived in Westwood. They found him beside his car in the back of a strip club. The fatal strike, a single stab wound in the chest. Both victims had identical puncture marks on their torsos. Marks that would have resembled a snake bite, but the wounds were too far apart. There was no forensic evidence on either victim. No witnesses. Just to two dead people with identical puncture marks left by the killer as a calling card.

Over the years, the body count had climbed to over twenty-two in LA County. All marked with the same snake-bite signature wounds. At least twelve other case in the surrounding counties had the killer's calling card mark. Rich and poor. Different races, genders and ethnicities. Each victim had two similarities. One, they were known as convicted, unreformed offenders of crimes against other humans. Two, the killer left no clues behind to work with other than the signature mark.

The body count and sporadic frequency in LA spurred Rawson to broaden her research to other large cities. She found similar cases throughout the national database. Individual victims with criminal backgrounds who had become victims themselves. She didn't find a single report of an arrest associated with any of the crimes.

Initially Rawson had a hard time getting her colleagues interested in discussing the research. After all, criminals dying wasn't exactly a top priority for any police chief. But after learning the victims all carried the same killer's signature mark, the detectives decided to attend the meeting.

Rawson sat at the head of the table, looking at the stoic faces sitting around her.

"Thank you all for taking the time to be here. I would like to start at the beginning of my research and walk you through the timeline as it relates to cases in southern California."

She spent the next twenty-five minutes summarizing each of the cases using a set of slides on the video screen. The others still showed no signs of interest.

"Based on my research in each of your jurisdictions, the picture looks like this," Rawson said as she pushed the button on the controller. She watched the expressions on the other detectives' faces show interest as they studied the graphic. She sipped her coffee.

"This map shows over a hundred and twenty homicides from the beats sitting in this room. All with the same characteristics. This is the timeline," she continued, advancing to the next chart.

As she continued through the slides, the timeline was filling in. It mostly closed the gaps and frequency in the greater LA area in with the cases in New York, Washington, and Chicago. She tapped the button again, adding the cases from London, Paris, and Frankfurt.

"The data shows that we potentially have a serial killer out there who is killing at an average rate of one per month over the last eight years in these cities," Rawson concluded.

She now had their attention. Rawson stood up from her chair and walked over to the wall and pushed a switch. The curtains on one of the long walls opened.

"This is what the rest of the US looks like," Rawson said as the curtains reached the stops.

On the wall was a large map of the United States. Each red dot on the map represented an unsolved homicide that fit the pattern. Cities across the US from Houston to Detroit, from LA to Boston all had red dots. The total count across all cities was over two hundred and eighty. Three per month over eight years not counting similar cases in Europe.

Rawson walked across the room and pushed another button. The curtains opened, revealing a wall full of the faces and names of the victims.

"Gentlemen, I think we have a problem."

The other detectives sat there quietly exchanging looks between themselves.

New York City's Detective Winslow broke the silence. "Impressive work, detective. Like you, we have no forensic evidence to use. We have habitual criminals being eliminated by someone. I say someone, because it is unlikely that multiple killers could be so consistently clean. But to be blunt about it, the families of the victims have never complained. Not once. We do not have one report of a family member, friend, or loved one showing interest in what happened to their loved one. No follow-up to check progress on a case. Not once. In almost every situation, at least in New York, the families seem relieved. So maybe whoever this person or persons is, is doing us all a favor." Winslow glanced around the room looking for support.

Rawson clenched her teeth, trying not to show her frustration.

"Our jobs are to get the bad guys, detective," she responded, raising her voice.

"We all understand our jobs," Winslow replied, maintaining a calm tone. "But if we tell the public we have a serial killer on the loose when we have not a clue how to solve it, it will create panic. And for what? Good, honorable citizens aren't dying, detective. Bad guys are. This is not the Son of Sam," he said, referring to the 1970s case where a guy went around New York City at night randomly killing couples with a large-caliber handgun.

The words from Winslow were the same conversation she had with her bosses many times over the years. Everything about it seemed wrong to her.

"We're not discussing going public, Mr. Winslow," Rawson said. "I am certainly not proposing we do so. I thought maybe we might work together to solve the mystery. Two brains are better than one, after all."

"This situation is strictly confidential in our department," chipped in Scotland Yard's Peter Gallagher. "The director has only one interest at the moment, which is keeping it quiet. There are only three people in the whole of England who know the facts, such as they are. If, and I say if, we had some tangible evidence to use, I think we would assist. Short of that, there is really nothing to do here."

"I understand. But let's focus on what we know." Rawson advanced the presentation slides.

She proceeded to lay out her profile of the killer. "He uses a seven-inch knife or a 9mm handgun, most likely silenced. He is skilled with a knife and a trained shooter. Maybe military. He travels a lot. Most likely by airplane. He is frequently in major cities and often in financial centers. He uses a tool for the signature. The puncture wound marks are always the same distance apart. We will assume it's a man, though we can't be certain. The killer wants us to know it is him. He needs recognition. He is challenging us to find him."

Rawson paused. "Did I miss anything?"

"Don't you think it could be a retired policeman?" suggested the detective from Chicago. "Somehow, he is remarkably adept at picking his targets. I mean, there are hundreds of murder victims, and we really don't even care. Who has more information about the bad guys than us?"

"The most perplexing thing is, yes, they are convicts, but they, by most all accounts, are still committing crimes," said the detective from DC. "We hear that from family and friends too. Somehow, this person seems to know how to pick his targets. He or they are vigilantes…and damn good ones."

Rawson felt the energy in the room waning. The perspectives being shared only elicited more unanswerable questions.

"I assume we can all agree we are dealing with a professional," said Rawson. "A pro the likes of which the world has never seen. I have one more question for you. Are you willing to assign someone to work on this for the next year? My boss has found the money to fund a three-person team. This guy is going to mess up at some point. Someone needs to hold him accountable."

CHAPTER NINE

THE EARLY MORNING phone call woke Shelton from a deep sleep. The voice on the other end of the line was that of his younger brother, Rob.

Robert Shelton was nineteen months younger than his elder brother. They were close in age, but in many ways, they were opposites.

Physically, Rob took after their father. If he stretched, he stood about five feet seven inches tall and weighed in at one hundred forty-five pounds.

The mostly bald, newly tenured professor at UVA lived in a newer suburban neighborhood of Charlottesville. As his family grew, he carved out his personal space from his wife, two teenage daughters, the cats, and the dogs. The neat third-car garage and small wood-paneled basement office was all he needed to do his work and be happy.

In contrast to Shelton, Rob rarely traveled, knew little about the stock market, and was a devout peace activist in high school and college. He wasn't against defending oneself. But using violence to motivate others with a goal of creating peace and advancing society was a contradiction in values from his point of view. A view he thought he had in common with his brother. That is, until Shelton went off to college, then joined the US Navy after graduation. A decision that seemed rash and out of character for his older sibling.

The news this morning was unwelcome. Rob had the unpleasant task of informing Shelton that their dad had suffered a heart attack. Ed Shelton was in the ICU at the hospital in Leesburg. The doctors were not optimistic.

The cardiologist had the unfortunate task of breaking the news to Rob. Their father's medical records documented a fourteen-year history of heart problems. Ed Shelton had chosen not to have corrective surgery. The years of damage and condition of the vital organ were essentially beyond repair, short of a heart transplant. Days, not weeks, was the prognosis. Everything was in order on the DNR. Ed Shelton had been coherent enough on his arrival to hand the piece of paper to the ER nurse.

Two hours later, Shelton's airplane was climbing and making the turn west toward Virginia after departing London's Gatwick airport.

Shelton's executive protection agent was the first person to step off the aircraft. Slowly and casually, she descended the steps and stopped at the bottom, checking her mobile device. She turned and looked to the far left end of the fence line, slowly worked her way down the line past the FBO office to the right end of the fence. Then checked her device again. A standard practice for his security team.

The executive protection agent keyed the microphone. "Two subjects in a dark-colored sedan, south end of the field."

Inside the airplane, another agent keyed his microphone and acknowledged the situation. The new infrared surveillance device installed on the top of Sandy McCoy's bush hat had easily detected the heat signatures of two people sitting in a car a hundred yards away. She pushed the normal setting on the handheld and rotated the camera directly toward the two people without moving her head, zoomed in, and snapped a dozen high-resolution pictures. She zoomed out and snapped a few more pictures of the car.

McCoy stood at the bottom of the stairs and nodded to the drivers standing by. The two SUVs pulled alongside the airplane.

"Clear," McCoy said into the microphone.

Shelton stepped off the aircraft and climbed into the waiting SUV.

As soon as the bags and security equipment were in the second vehicle, the group pulled away and headed for the hospital.

∾

Ed Shelton was resting peacefully when his oldest son arrived at his bedside. The senior Shelton was looking noticeably older. He was resembling his age. A look he'd avoided throughout his entire adult life. Both sons knew he had worked hard at trying to defy the laws of physics and biology.

Ed Shelton was always busy in retirement. He exercised daily and volunteered at the local high school as well as the local community theater. He was a fixture at high school sporting events, known by most of the kids and their parents.

He was the head statistician for the boys' sports teams. He was also a substitute teacher occasionally. During football and basketball season, he was the small-framed, older gentleman dressed in khaki pants and a UVA jacket.

During football season, he was on the sidelines with a clipboard doing his work. Inside his headphones, a student volunteer reported the numbers from the press box. It was simply not possible for a person to collect the stats from the bench in a football game. You couldn't see enough from field level and the game moved too fast. Ed insisted on being as close to the game as possible.

During basketball and baseball seasons, Ed sat in the stands, focused intently on the game at hand. Watching every move and recording everything on his stat sheet. Never clapping or cheering for his team. He just sat there, undisturbed by the cheers of the surrounding crowd.

Ignoring the world around him was a special skill he had learned to embrace in his young adult life. A skill his late wife had required of him.

Now, at eighty-two and in failing health, Ed Shelton looked aged.

Shelton knew his dad was keenly aware of what was going to happen to him by neglecting his health. While it was sad, it was ultimately his dad's choice. Even if the sons had known about Ed's condition sooner, it was unlikely they would have been able to change their somewhat stubborn-minded father.

Shelton was okay with his dad's choice. He had enjoyed a high quality of life right up to the end. A few days of difficulty at the end of a happy life seemed like a great outcome. After all, there were much worse alternatives available in the human existence.

After discussing his father's status with the medical staff, he found his father sleeping in private hospital room. Shelton decided to take a walk around the small Virginia town while the elder Shelton rested. He had several hours to kill before Rob planned to return.

Agent McCoy tried to insist on going with him, but Shelton quickly dismissed the idea. The hospital was in the neighborhood where he grew up. The tree-lined streets and the city were very familiar. As he passed by homes, the names, faces, and memories came flashing back.

Each home held a unique memory. The white brick, green-trimmed house just ahead had been the home of the Kellys. A widowed insurance agent who was left to raise his three daughters and one son all alone. The outside of the house deteriorated as the years went by. Shelton remembered the rotting window seals and frames on the south side of the house. One window even had a towel jammed into the hole to keep out the wind and rain. The current owners had corrected the problem.

Across the street from the Kellys lived the Mullins. A small well-kept red brick home with a neat and well-maintained lawn. Mrs. Mullins was a mechanical engineer at the local medical device factory. The tidy home reflected her attention to detail. Neighbors wondered how Mr. and Mrs. Mullins put up with seeing such a dump when they looked out the front window.

A few blocks away from the hospital, Shelton spotted their family church. Chills shot down his spine. As he got closer, he moved his gaze around the architecture. He made his way across the street and walked up to the front steps and stopped. The words echoed through his head:

"It's your turn, Tom," Chris said as Stevie looked on.

Shelton, Chris, and Stevie were ten years old. Chris had dared Shelton to ride his skateboard down the church's ramped walkway, make the turn, and jump down the steps to the sidewalk below. Chris had been the first to successfully navigate the course that day. Now Chris was challenging his best friend to do the same.

The church people had told the boys many times to not ride their skateboards on the steps. But when you are ten years old, instructions are just a challenge not to be caught.

Shelton mounted his board and flew down the ramp, made the turn, and into the air he went. It was a perfect takeoff. The board was tight against his shoes. His knees bent. Everything felt good. At the top of the jump, he looked down at his landing spot. A rock big enough to cause problems was waiting for him. He couldn't do anything about it other than try to put down hard and muscle over the obstacle. The moment he touched down, his front wheels stopped. Shelton went flying forward, sliding across the sidewalk on his face. Luckily, his helmet took the brunt of the impact and, therefore, the damage.

His friends had laughed uncontrollably at his misfortune. He recalled the stinging sensation of having his skin ground off by the grit of the concrete. It was a wonderful memory that, at the moment, blocked out the bad.

Shelton stood there motionless. He noticed a newer section of sidewalk with a date stamp etched in the cement. Then he looked up at the bell tower under the steeple of the church. The place from where Chris had jumped to his death when he was fourteen. Chris's blood had stained the cement. The city workers quickly replaced the section where his friend had landed. Chris's continual abuse by the minister was more than his buddy could take.

Shelton was proud of his friend's courage. Chris's actions somehow caused the child-molesting preacher to be transferred out of their community. That meant the children of Leesburg were safer. It also meant that some other city had a problem.

Chris could have just shot himself in his bedroom. It would have been just another teen suicide for unknown reasons. Chris had escaped his destroyed life and caused everyone to take notice.

The loud, clear caw of a single black crow broke the morning silence. Shelton looked up toward the church's roof as the cool morning breeze whisked across his cheek. Again came the clear caw of the crow.

The loud, lonely, eerie sound dampened by the low cloud cover penetrated Shelton. He looked down at the ground, then back up toward the sky. Now a row of blackbirds sat along the peak of the roof. Every creature faced him. Shelton stood motionless, staring up at the birds. He raised his arms from his sides, holding out his open hands with his palms facing upward.

He whispered to the line of ravens, "Come. Come a get me!"

At the utterance of his words, the birds flew off in the opposite direction.

Shelton turned and continued his walk toward Main Street. In his peripheral vision, he noticed the same dark-colored sedan that had been sitting in the hospital parking lot. It was now parked next to the curb a block behind him.

✒

The buildings had changed little in the Leesburg village center. Many of the shops housed different businesses from those that were there during his childhood, although some were the same. Fresh paint, clean brick storefronts, and curbside parking gave the Main Street USA town a down-home feel.

Joe's Coffee Shop was still in business. Shelton remembered the shop from his youth. It was always busy with people coming and going. Doctors, lawyers, businesspeople, construction workers. Everybody liked Joe's. It was a warm, friendly place to be. It was also a favorite place for his dad as he grew older. They had visited there several times over the years.

Shelton went inside Joe's and stood in line. He wondered if anyone would recognize him. Dad had told him that Joe's oldest daughter was the current owner. She was several years older than Shelton, but he remembered her from high school.

She had been very attractive. A cheerleader, a soccer player, and well-liked by the upperclassmen. On his several visits to the shop in recent years, he had noticed no one who looked like her. However, today the woman behind the counter looked like Heather.

Shelton ordered a medium coffee, black, and sat down at one of the small tables facing the window. It was a nice, quiet morning. The clouds were lifting. Patches of blue sky appeared. Sitting there in Joe's Coffee Shop in his hometown was satisfying. He wondered if it would be less satisfying if he were living paycheck to paycheck to earn a living for his family.

"Excuse me?" came a soft voice beside him. Shelton turned toward the words.

"I'm sorry for startling you. But is your name Tom Shelton?" It was the woman from behind the counter.

"It is," he responded.

"I'm Heather Kersting. Joe Frank's daughter," she said as she extended her hand in his direction.

"It's very nice to meet you." Shelton shook her hand.

"It's nice to meet you too. I apologize for disturbing you, but I wanted to introduce myself. My father and your father have known each other for a very long time. I heard your dad is in the hospital. How is he?"

"I'm afraid age is getting the best of him," Shelton replied.

"I am so sorry to hear that. If there is anything we can do for him or you, please let us know. We will pray for him," she said.

"Heather?" Shelton said. "Do you have a few minutes to chat? I'll buy you a cup of coffee."

Her face lit up. "Of course. Give me just one minute," she said, turning to walk back to the counter.

A few minutes later, she returned with her cup and sat down in the chair next to him.

"Mr. Shelton, you want to hear something funny?" Heather smiled. "I don't drink coffee. Just tea." She held up her cup and took a sip of the steaming beverage. The confession brought a smile to Shelton's face.

"Well, that is interesting," Shelton said. "Heather? May I call you Heather?"

"Oh, of course," she replied, accentuated with a hand gesture.

"Please call me Tom. There's no reason for this Mr. Shelton business."

"Well, I didn't know what else to call you. After all, we really don't know each other. And you are a celebrity in Leesburg, you know."

Shelton's eyebrows raised in modesty.

Everyone in the small northern Virginia town was familiar with the name Shelton. One of the world's wealthiest people owned the Shelton Estate, which the community was well aware of. Edwin Shelton's name was on the front of the public library. The upper school of one of the most highly ranked private K–12 institutions in the country was named Shelton Upper School. The local school district received half a million dollars annually from the Shelton Foundation.

"Well, I'm just another person, Heather," Shelton said. "I grew up here just like you. I have very fond memories of Leesburg. Dad was resting this morning, so I took a walk. It's amazing how almost every block brings back vivid memories. I was just strolling down Main when I saw Joe's."

"You just never know who's going to walk down the streets, do you?" Heather smiled.

"I remember you from high school," Shelton said.

"Really?" she replied with a look of surprise on her face.

All the boys at Leesburg High knew who Heather was. She was the most attractive girl in school. And smart.

"It's so interesting," Heather said. "The high school and teenage years. Keeping track of Who's Who? The jocks, the freaks, the nerds, the popular, and the unpopular. It can be such a difficult thing for kids. I suppose I was lucky. I fit in well and had no issues. Weren't you a close friend of the boy who died in the skateboarding accident on the front steps of the church?"

Shelton's gaze narrowed slightly. Chris killed in a skateboard accident? The church and city officials had made up a cover story for Chris's death. A cover story for a monster.

"Chris Howard," Shelton said. "That was his name. Chris Howard. It was no accident Heather. Chris jumped!"

"Oh my God!" she replied. "I'm so sorry. I didn't know. I really didn't mean to bring up such a painful topic."

"It was a tragic day. But I have great memories with Chris," he said, hoping to move on from the subject.

Heather and Shelton spent the next hour visiting while Joe's customers came and went. Eventually, Shelton got around to asking Heather if she was interested in taking over the role of managing the Shelton Estate now that Dad could no longer manage the property. His dad had mentioned on numerous occasions that he thought Heather would be a good choice for running the place after he passed. His dad had gone so far as to discuss it with her several times. Shelton had ideas for the land, and Heather might very well be the perfect person to head it up.

Heather accepted without hesitation. She had already lined up her replacement at the coffee shop and had been expecting Shelton's visit in the wake of his father's hospitalization. Angie would have been a great choice too. But that was too complicated. Heather seemed like the perfect fit. She thanked Shelton for the opportunity and apologized again from bringing up the Chris topic. Shelton opened his arms and gave Heather a gentle hug. Then they shook hands and made plans to talk again soon.

Shelton stepped out of Joe's and noticed the sedan was still parked down the street. He turned and started walking toward it. Within a few steps, Agent McCoy pulled up beside him in one of the SUVs.

"What are you doing here?" Shelton asked, somewhat annoyed.

McCoy acknowledged her boss with a nod and a knowing smile.

"I'm sure you noticed the tail sitting down the street," she said.

"Indeed, I did. I was headed over to introduce myself," he said, speaking to her through the driver's side window.

"Let us figure it out, boss. You have other things to be concerned about today."

"I could use the distraction," he said with a mischievous grin.

"The last thing you need is to be arrested by the feds," McCoy said having run the vehicles license plates through a government database. "Hop in. I'll give you a ride."

꒰

Shelton sat in the chair next to his dad's hospital bed. His face relaxed as he laid his head back in the dimly lit room.

"Tom?" a voice whispered. Shelton opened his eyes without moving. "Tom? Is that you?" a frail voice said. Shelton stood up and looked down at his father, making eye contact.

"Dad, it's Tom," he whispered. "I'm right here."

Ed Shelton blinked slowly, maintaining eye contact with his son.

"Tom, is this it?"

"What do you mean, Dad?" Shelton asked. It seemed awkward answering a question with a question to a dying man. He did not want to answer the wrong question.

"Is this the end for me? Am I dying?"

The question took Shelton by surprise. He assumed the medical staff had informed his father of the situation. Maybe they had, and Dad was just looking for confirmation from someone he trusted. Or maybe he simply forgot. After all, the amount of pain medication being applied was self-regulated and virtually unlimited.

Shelton took a deep breath. "The doctors say they can't fix you this time, Dad. There has been too much damage to your heart. The goal is to keep you comfortable and pain free," he said, doing his best to keep his voice calm and comforting.

"Can you take me home?"

"You're not stable enough, Dad. Let's see how you are doing tomorrow. If the doctors think it is doable, I will take you home."

Ed closed his eyes and took a deep breath, processing the reality of the words from his son.

"Well, I guess I'm not surprised. I was hoping for a different answer. But I can always count on you to be honest, Tom."

Shelton smiled. "I was never very good at lying."

The elder Shelton smiled slightly at the confession.

"Are we alone?" Ed asked.

"Yes. It's just you and me. Rob and his family will be back in a little while."

Ed nodded his head slightly, acknowledging his son's words.

"I love you, son," Ed said. "Your mother loved you, too, Tom. She and I struggled with our differences. But I loved her." A tear spilled over onto Ed's cheek.

"Tom?" Ed continued. "Are you sure we are alone?"

"Yes, Dad. There's no one else in the room."

"There's something you must know," Ed said.

"Dad, please. You don't have to make any last confessions to me. Everything is going to be okay. Rob and I will be fine."

"I've needed to tell you things for a long time." Ed fisted the sheets at his sides. "I could never bring myself to say them."

Edwin Shelton pushed the button for more pain medication, then started talking.

"I'm not your father, Thomas," he said. "A month before your mother and I were married, she became pregnant. As far as I know, Elizabeth remained chaste. Robert is mine, but from another woman. We did everything according to your mother's wishes. When I die, there is a letter from her in my will. The attorney will make sure you get it."

The fact that Shelton's father had conceived his brother with another woman at his mother's direction bounced through his head then vanished. It was just another anomaly in his existence that simply didn't seem to matter in the bigger scheme of things.

CHAPTER TEN

RAWSON AND HER partner had a clear view of the front door of the Upper East Side residential building through the darkness of the night. The lights from the buildings and entryways lit the entire block. Now they just had to wait. Her plan was working out better than she had hoped. The meeting in Los Angeles had convinced the New York and Chicago police chiefs to commit modest resources to the search. That meant Rawson now had access to the jurisdictions where most of the homicides took place.

Her boss in LA had used his relationships inside the FBI to connect her to more in-depth profiling. In less than a week, Rawson had eliminated the possibility that the killer was traveling by car, train, bus, or commercial airline.

Next, she matched up former military and police officers who had jobs or wealth that provided them access to private airplanes.

The next group focused on private security personnel. Usually former cops or military special operations people provided security to corporate executives and the wealthy. These people almost always used private aircraft exclusively.

There were thousands of flights every day of the year with these attributes. Rawson had two problems. One was ownership. The aircraft owners of record were usually limited liability companies or trusts. Finding the actual users of the airplane was going to be challenging. Second was the fact that while some private aircraft flights were tracked publicly, most were not.

The first cut was to figure out exactly what airplane flew from Point A to Point B and how it correlated to the timing of the homicides. If that was useful, then they had to figure out who was on the aircraft. The FBI analyst had her work cut out for her.

Rawson focused on the easiest first. The list of active or former military and police officers who routinely traveled by private aircraft quickly dropped to less than five people. She started with the wealthiest person on the list. The selection had her sitting outside Tom Shelton's Upper East Side residence with a newly minted New York City cop.

The cameras mounted on the lower-level exterior of the residence looked like ordinary security cameras. Rawson walked up and down the block to stretch her legs and counted eight devices. What she couldn't see was the customized cameras higher up, on the outside of the building, which were not visible from the street.

Cables from those cameras ran up to the information center in the building's penthouse directly across the street from Central Park. Every ten seconds, the artificial intelligence program took pictures of everyone on the block, then compared current faces to those in the last four weeks. The program analyzed faces and clothing of the people strolling up and down 89th Street. The algorithm determined whether the person was a local, a visitor, or an unknown. Unknowns were uploaded to the output terminal as exceptions.

The vehicle analytics program matched makes, models, and license plates. It reported exceptions in the output terminal. The program sent every exception to Shelton for review.

The dark blue sedan parked just off Fifth Avenue flashed up on Shelton's monitor sitting on the side of his desk in his library. His mobile device received the same information. The AI program identified the car as an unmarked police vehicle.

Rawson perked up as the night watchman opened the door of the building. The quick glimpse of the profile registered to her as Shelton's. She raised her binoculars to get a closer look. The man matched Tom Shelton's physical description, but she didn't get a clear look at the face, and he was walking away from their location.

Rawson punched her dozing partner in the arm.

"Follow me," she commanded as she jumped out of the car.

The streets and sidewalks of the neighborhood were empty. She had a clear view of her target fifty yards ahead. Shelton turned the corner and disappeared from the detective's view.

Rawson immediately started jogging. Just as she turned the corner, her target closed the door to a taxi and drove away.

Rawson's partner pulled up seconds later. She jumped in and gave orders. A few blocks later they had the taxi in sight.

"Follow it," Rawson said. "But give them some space. We need time to react."

The cab continued south on Madison, cut over to Fifth Avenue, and headed downtown. Ten minutes later, the taxi stopped suddenly in the middle of the street. Rawson watched the passenger get out and begin walking directly toward them. The two cops sat there in the car double parked, trying to look busy and uninterested.

Rawson now knew for certain the person they were following was Thomas J. Shelton. Six foot four inches, two hundred and ten pounds, fit, muscular, and very handsome. He fit the profile perfectly.

Shelton stepped directly in front of their car, almost touching the front bumper as he crossed the street. Rawson could feel her heart pounding as her pulse raced. For a moment, she thought Shelton was going to stop and confront them. Her pulse slowed as she watched him enter the upscale tavern on the other side of the street.

Rawson let out the breath she hadn't realized she was holding and removed the hair tie from her ponytail. Her long straight blond locks fell on her shoulders. She pulled the brush out of her bag and ran it through her hair several times, touched up her makeup, and replaced her neutral-colored lipstick with a deep shade of red.

Then she grabbed her waist-length leather jacket and higher heeled shoes from the back seat and climbed out of the car.

"Park down the street," she ordered, pointing. "I'll see you in a little while. Be ready to move."

Soft jazz music filled the air inside the tavern. Rawson sat down at the end of the bar and ordered a martini. Her pulse was still elevated. She looked around, scanning the room. On the far side of the tavern, she spotted Shelton. He was sitting in the corner booth, visiting with another person. His back was against the wall. The person with him was female, brunette, and well dressed.

Rawson sipped her drink as she watched the television above the bar. Every few minutes, she glanced around the room. Each time lingering on Shelton just long enough to observe his facial expressions. She was checking her mobile phone for messages when her peripheral vision filled with the shape of someone sitting down on the barstool next to her. She glanced up to acknowledge the person creeping into her personal space. Her breath caught, and she quickly returned to her screen.

Rawson tried to remain calm. Shelton was now sitting beside her at the bar. Close enough that she could smell his cologne. Her body responded to the sudden physical attraction to this complete stranger. She adjusted herself ever so slightly on the stool while continuing to stare at her phone.

"Would you like another martini?" a smooth voice asked.

Rawson looked up, making eye contact with Shelton.

She paused for a half second. "Sure, thank you," she replied. "I'm Lexi." She held out her hand to her new acquaintance.

Long fingers wrapped around her hand, giving her a gentle squeeze. Shelton's blue eyes and tan skin were striking. She adjusted herself slightly on the chair again. The physical attraction to her suspect was unexpected. Rawson took a shallow breath and maintained eye contact as she worked to refocus on the task at hand.

"I'm Tom," Shelton said.

The two broke eye contact as the bartender took their orders. Rawson turned back to her phone and pressed the control button. The screen went dark. She placed it in her purse and turned back toward Shelton.

"It's been a long time since a complete stranger sat down beside me in a bar and bought me a drink. I'm not sure what to say without sounding ridiculous," Rawson confessed. "You seem to be rather well practiced." She flashed a warm smile.

"I've been in the corner practicing with my colleague for the past twenty minutes," Shelton responded. "I thought this seat would never become available. The last guy sitting here looked like he was there for the night."

"What has you out this late on a work night?" Rawson asked, keeping her tone casual and pleasant.

"I agreed to have a drink with a coworker who wanted some career advice," Shelton replied as he looked at his watch. "What line of work are you in?"

"I'm a cop," Rawson said, raising her eyebrows and waiting for a reaction. "Actually, a detective in Los Angeles. What do you do?"

Shelton's facial expression didn't change. He just nodded slightly with interest. "I'm a finance person," he replied. "A banker." He reached out and picked up his glass. "Cheers, detective. Welcome to New York."

Twenty minutes later, Shelton and Rawson wrapped up their polite conversation. Rawson watched Shelton place her business card in his jacket and walk out of the tavern. A minute later, she stepped out onto the sidewalk. Shelton was almost to the corner of the block when he held up his hand to hail a cab. Her car was out of position.

"Shit!" Rawson mumbled to herself.

She crossed the street to keep out of Shelton's line of sight. Once on the other side of the street, she removed her high heels and sprinted toward the corner. She needed to get the cab number. It was no use. The yellow taxi sped out of sight before she could get close enough to get the number.

Fifteen minutes later, the unmarked car pulled up and parked across the street from Shelton's building. Rawson had a clear view down the block and of the entrance to the residence.

She checked the time. Midnight. It had been almost an hour since they left the tavern. She assumed he was inside his luxurious apartment, getting ready for bed in a room with expensive art lining the walls.

The tall figure at the far end of the block shocked her back to reality. The man was walking toward them. Rawson caught a look at the person through the binoculars as he passed in front of a lighted building entrance. It was Shelton! She lowered the binoculars and slumped down in the passenger's seat. Shelton stopped in front of his building. He paused, looking directly at the unmarked police car, then turned and went inside.

At the exact moment Rawson lost sight of Shelton, the police dispatcher's voice came through the speakers.

"Potential homicide. Victim DOA. 30th and Park."

Rawson's heart started racing.

"Let's go," she ordered.

The young officer methodically picked up the microphone, acknowledged the call, flipped on the lights, dropped the cruiser into gear, and pressed the accelerator.

"You should relax, detective," said the rookie cop as he navigated the car toward the scene. "Things are harder to get the more you want them. You should lower your expectations. Enjoy life more."

Words the young officer had heard preached throughout his life by his mother, the current New York State Attorney General.

CHAPTER ELEVEN

THE GULFSTREAM TOUCHED down just before 8:00 a.m. local time at Jorge Newbery airport in Buenos Aires. Forty-five minutes later the black SUV pulled into the circle drive of the Four Seasons hotel. George Klein, Shelton's personal attorney, was waiting outside. The bellman opened the driver's side rear door. Klein climbed in and took his seat beside Shelton.

The reading of the last will and testament of Edwin Shelton had been unremarkable. All of his money and possessions were to be split evenly between his two sons. The elder Shelton had just over one hundred and fifty thousand dollars cash in his bank account. A wax-sealed envelope inside their father's legal documents was the surprise. The envelope contained the last Will and Testament of Elizabeth Shelton. Her words to her sons were brief:

"Now that your father has passed, it is my last wish to donate five million dollars to the parish of Father Francis Macari in Buenos Aires, Argentina. The money is available in the bank account listed below. Please honor my wishes. Signed Elizabeth A. Shelton."

Rob had almost been uncontrollable after hearing his mother's wishes. His half of five million dollars was a lot of money. It could change his life forever. He would no longer have money worries. His kids would have college funds. His retirement account would be fully funded.

Shelton settled his brother down. The plan was Shelton would go to Argentina and sort out what their mother was trying to accomplish with the donation. Once the brothers understood her intention, they would decide the best course of action.

"Good morning, George. What have you learned about Father Macari?" Shelton asked, getting right to work.

George cleared his throat.

"Good morning, Tom," George said, returning the greeting. "There really isn't much to share. He is Argentinian by birth. Dual citizenship of the US. He was educated at Georgetown. PhD in theology. Returned to Argentina about twenty years ago and started his own parish."

"St. Elizabeth's?" Shelton said with a slight scowl on his face.

"Right." George looked out the window. "Seems he might have named it after your mother."

Shelton glanced at the floor and then back up at George. "What else?"

"That's the only thing your government contact would share. He took the opportunity to inform me that Argentina has privacy laws. Anyway, there is not much on Macari in the public domain to speak of."

Shelton stared at his lawyer with a blank look.

"I found this," George said with a slight smile as he handed Shelton a printed photograph. It was a picture of the priest. Macari appeared to be at a charity event. "What do you think? Early sixties maybe?" referring to Macari's age.

A few seconds later, the black SUV pulled up in front of St. Elizabeth's Parish. The gardens surrounding the parish were perfectly kept. Lawns were manicured, the fences and buildings coated with fresh paint, and the stone walls appeared recently washed.

The two slid out of the SUV and walked up the sidewalk toward the entrance to St. Elizabeth's Parish. Just inside the doors of the main lobby, a waiting attendant promptly greeted them. The young woman escorted Shelton and George through the sanctuary, then down a long hallway to the administrative offices.

Just outside the main door to the parish offices, Macari's assistant waited for the guests. The middle-aged man introduced himself and showed them inside.

Shelton and George followed the assistant through another set of large double doors, across an expansive lobby to the double doors of Macari's office. The assistant knocked on the door lightly and both doors opened automatically. There, standing in front of a large antique desk facing them, was Father Francis Macari.

The trim, well-groomed Macari didn't resemble the picture. He appeared to be ten years younger without the graying beard. The priest was five feet ten inches tall and weighed not an ounce over 160 pounds. He looked like a model. The perfectly tailored, slim-cut Italian suit and handmade shoes complemented his trim physique.

"Mr. Shelton, Mr. Klein, please come in," Macari said, lowering his head slightly with a warm, welcoming smile on his face.

Shelton walked forward and extended his hand.

"Father Macari. Thomas Shelton. Thank you for making time for me today."

"It is my honor," replied Macari as he reached out with both hands to shake Shelton's.

"Father, I would like to introduce you to Senor George Klein," Shelton said. "Senor Klein is my counsel."

"It is very nice to meet you," Macari replied, extending his hand.

"Likewise," Klein said, offering a quick handshake.

"Please be seated." Macari directed his guests to the sitting area in the center of the large office. "Would you like something? Coffee? Tea?"

"Coffee please, Father," said Shelton.

"For me as well," replied Klein.

Macari took his time and poured three cups of steaming coffee from the ornate carafe sitting on the table in front of them.

"If you wouldn't mind, Mr. Shelton, you may call me Senor Macari," he said, looking up as he finished serving. "It is less formal, you see. It makes non-Catholics more comfortable," he said with a slight smile.

Shelton took a moment to look around the office as he took the first sips of coffee. The space was more densely appointed with art than he had expected. Real original expensive art. Missing was any hint of the priest's religion. No crosses, no picture of the pope, no replica paintings of the last supper or the Virgin Mary.

"You have a lovely office," Shelton said. "Your artwork is very impressive."

"Thank you." Macari looked around the room. "It is a hobby of mine. Although, it isn't very well received when the boss visits. He would prefer more traditional surroundings."

"It's refreshing to see something different for us non-Catholic types," Shelton replied with a wry smile.

"Ah, very good," Macari said, appreciating the humor. "We are going to get along well. Now, what may I do for you this morning, Mr. Shelton?"

"Thank you again for making time for me. I will get right to the point. Recently my father passed."

The pleasant look on Macari's face disappeared.

"My deepest condolences, senor." Macari lowered his head as a sign of respect.

"Thank you." Shelton took another sip. "He had a long and happy life. But now, well, I am the executor of his will. Contained in the will was a letter from my mother, who passed many years ago. In her letter, she asked that you and your parish receive a portion of her remaining wealth upon my father's death."

Shelton continued to watch Macari's body language closely from across the coffee table.

"That is generous of her. I am sure you know it is quite common for people to pass along a donation upon death," Macari said. "It by no means requires you to do it. We do well here, as you can see."

"That is very generous of you to feel that way," Shelton acknowledged as he continued to enjoy the hot beverage. "Senor, I am here to learn more about why my mother, who died thirty years ago, would leave you five million dollars in a letter in my father's last will and testament."

Shelton watched Macari's lighthearted disposition vanish.

Macari took a slow sip from his cup, then reconnected with Shelton's eyes.

"That is an interesting question," Macari said. "I am not sure I have an answer for you, Mr. Shelton."

Shelton gazed deeply into Macari's face and paused.

"Senor, I understand this must be quite a surprise for you. I can assure you, the donation of such an amount of money to your parish, and more specifically to you, was also a surprise to me. Regardless, I am prepared to honor my mother's wishes. I think it is fair to understand the reason for such generosity, though."

The intensity of Shelton's glare caused Macari to break eye contact. The contemplative expression on Macari's face suggested there was much more to discuss. Macari found the courage and politely suggested that he and Shelton speak privately. Shelton agreed, and George collected his satchel and departed the office.

"More coffee?" asked Macari.

"Please," Shelton replied as the doors closed behind George Klein.

Shelton watched Father Francis Macari's every move. The priest had a certain way about him. Fluid, precise movements. Detail focused. Perhaps rehearsed.

Shelton watched Father Macari remove, then replace the lid to the small sugar container. He placed it back in exactly the same spot it had been removed from. Macari stirred his coffee exactly four rotations. The few seconds of silence seemed to last minutes.

"Mr. Shelton," Macari said, standing up, seemingly at a loss for words. "I will, I will tell you what I know." He turned back toward Shelton. "However, I am sure it will not satisfactorily answer all of your questions."

"Senor." Shelton jumped in before Macari could say another word. "I want to put your mind at ease. To be clear, I'm not here to cause trouble for you. What may have been between you and my mother privately is none of my business. I'm not here for a confession," Shelton said in a serious, direct tone. "Please understand, my mother passed when I was just a boy. I barely remember her. I didn't have the opportunity to appreciate her as an adult. This is an opportunity that might help me get to know her a little better. A chance to learn something about her. Knowledge every child should have about their parents. But to put a fine point on it, I am not interested in hearing about love affairs or any other personal experiences. I am here to understand the money. It is a large sum. It requires some explanation, don't you agree?"

Macari's brow raised slightly. Shelton watched as his shoulders lowered and he sat back in the chair, taking a sip, appearing to be deep in thought.

"I appreciate your candor and respectfulness, senor," started Macari. "You have come a long way to see me. And it is a great deal of money. The least I can do is share with you what I know. That is all I can do. You deserve to know what I know. Somehow, I think your mother expected this moment. I can assure you I did not. Do you mind?" Macari asked, pulling a tin of cigarettes from his jacket.

"Not at all," Shelton replied, watching the actor turn into something more.

Macari placed the cigarette in his mouth and lit it using the gold-plated lighter attached to the small container. He drew down and then released the smoke-filled air from his lungs.

"Your mother and I were close friends," Macari said in a calm voice. "Elizabeth was a wonderful person. The most loving human I have ever known."

Macari walked to the window and looked out into the clear blue morning sky.

He went on to tell Shelton that he had met Elizabeth in Tel Aviv. They were both twenty-two years old. She was working for the Israeli government on an engineering project, and Macari was studying abroad working on a PhD. When Macari finished his work, he had to return to the university. He had a job waiting for him as an assistant professor at Georgetown. Elizabeth demanded to return to the States with him. The two lived together in Macari's apartment. Elizabeth secured a job at a DC area think tank, and he began teaching. Macari loved her. He loved who she was and how her brain worked. She was the smartest person he had ever met. But they were only friends. Nothing more. Macari wondered sometimes why he wasn't attracted to her in that way—she was an exquisite woman—but he wasn't. Their magic was they understood each other. They trusted each other. They enjoyed each other's company, and they needed each other. Neither of them had many friends, really. That made them even closer. Macari actually introduced Elizabeth to Edwin not long after they arrived back in the States. Elizabeth and Edwin got married quickly, and Macari became a priest.

Shelton sat there for a few moments, processing what he had just heard.

"Interesting, senor. I appreciate you sharing with me. It makes me feel good that my mother had such a close, caring friend," Shelton said. "What about the money? What do you suppose that is about?"

Macari turned and walked back to the sitting area. He stared at his guest for another moment, then sat down.

"I don't know why Elizabeth would leave me so much money or where she would get it. She was a generous person, Thomas. She was self-sacrificing, that is sure," Macari said, lighting another cigarette.

"Senor, do we know each other?" Shelton asked from out of nowhere.

Macari looked at Shelton with pursed lips and a narrowed stare.

"Yes. We have met before. You were ten years old," Macari replied. "It was the day of the incident at the church. I was at your home that morning."

Shelton's body tightened. The veins in his neck became more visible as his jaw muscle contracted.

"What exactly are your referring to?" Shelton asked, his face unreadable.

Macari leaned in.

"The evening when the minister first abused your friends, and you had to watch. The evening you almost killed his accomplice with a candelabra."

The words paralyzed Shelton.

"I suppose you saved yourself from the same fate as your friends.

Quite a feat for a ten-year-old," Macari said. "Try not to be so shocked, Thomas. Mothers know everything. Especially Elizabeth."

"Why didn't she just go to the police? After all, it was self-defense," Shelton said, standing up and raising his voice.

"We didn't want you in the middle of a scandal," Macari said. "Who knew what the police would do? It was a small community. Lots of politics in those types of situations."

Shelton could see and hear a confident calm in Macari's expression and voice.

"The good news was things calmed down quickly. Then Elizabeth passed. You grew into a young man, then took justice into your own hands. That was a surprise."

Shelton turned toward Macari with a look of disbelief.

"Edwin informed me of the situation. He needed advice on what to do. I was the one who pushed your father to get you to join the service after you killed Brooks and then his assistant in Philadelphia. I thought you would be safe in the military. Your strong desire for justice would be more measured and blend into your job. It worked out well, don't you think?"

"What are you talking about?" Shelton demanded, his head spinning inside.

"You know your father strongly suspected you of killing Brooks?" Macari said. "Your college friend, Donovan, he was worried about you. He spoke to Edwin about it. Then your father learned from his police friend what kind of weapon was used. And Edwin discovered his knife was missing. Your father connected the dots."

Shelton continued looking around the room without saying a word.

"You talk about these things casually, senor. As if it were normal," Shelton said. "All the dots you are connecting are completely random."

"Your mother was a unique person, Thomas. She had a special purpose. Somehow, I knew in my heart she was special. Her purpose, all of that purpose, revolved around raising and protecting you."

"Protecting me from what?" he asked.

"That is what I do not know," Macari answered. "Let's just say it is hard to make someone understand the concept of unwavering faith and loyalty. Why one has faith in a person but not all people? My faith in your mother's words and beliefs was strong. She guided my life. I can't explain it. I quickly came to accept it. When I met her, I knew she was my job. My life's work."

"What about the money?" Shelton asked, looking for a factual answer to the reason for having made the trip.

Macari smiled and looked at his guest. "I suppose Elizabeth knew at the right point in time you would follow the money to me. And look, here you are," Macari said softly, attempting to ease the intensity of the conversation. "She trusted me, and you can trust me. Keep your money. I'm sure Rob can use it. Now, what can I do for you, Thomas?"

CHAPTER TWELVE

THE ALARM FROM the mobile phone on the bedside table roused Shelton from a deep sleep. He rolled onto his side, reached out, and tapped the screen until the sound stopped. Slowly, he woke up.

Outside the hotel window, the yellowish incandescent lights stretched out across the night sky to the dark shoreline. From his bed on the 55th floor, he could see the nighttime running lights of a dozen ships slowly moving up and down the coast.

Shelton lay in bed looking at the ceiling. The secret revenge he had kept to himself his entire life wasn't a secret. The dad he had known relied on directions from another man. The mother he'd loved with all his heart kept her own secrets, and took them to her grave, leaving him searching. The only thing that gave Shelton hope at the moment was the thought of Angie Brady. The potential to have a life with her somewhere in the future. The hope wasn't lost. He had done the right thing not to involve her in his strange world. His life was upside-down and getting more complicated by the day.

Shelton and Macari's discussion had lasted late into the afternoon. The simple task of understanding his mother's last wishes had taken an unexpected turn. Then there was Macari.

A man who was technically a Catholic priest, but only on paper. It was his disguise. A disguise Elizabeth Shelton had told him to use. Whatever was going on in his mother's world had caused her to fear for Macari's life. And she'd needed him. So he did it. He became a priest and was hiding in plain sight. Macari didn't know what he was hiding from. But Shelton sensed the man knew more than he was telling. Maybe he didn't have answers, but he didn't share everything. At least not yet. Shelton laughed to himself as he stepped into the shower, recalling Macari's story.

Frances Macari had learned to embrace the role of a priest and make the most of it. He trusted Elizabeth to know what was best. On the side, he had a large home in the best neighborhood that overlooked the city, a beautiful wife, and four healthy children. His assistant did all the priest work and Catholic stuff, and Macari ran the business end, doing fundraisers and collecting and trading art on the side. The monsignor and cardinal knew all about the arrangements. They had no problem looking the other way. Macari's capable fundraising skills placed the parish at the top of the Vatican's source of funds list every year. The senior church officials, up to and including the pope, found it easy to make accommodations for Father Macari of St. Elizabeth's Parish.

Shelton finished dressing for the evening, then poured a small bottle of whiskey from the honor bar into a glass. He punched in the password on his device and pulled up the notepad while sipping the alcohol. The most recent note contained the address of a glassmaker that Macari had given him. Shelton had shared the information about his paranormal watchers, and although Macari didn't know how to help, he suggested the glassmaker might.

Inside the hotel compound, the staff went about the business of greeting guests and opening doors while hotel security kept a watchful eye. The security of its customers could not be assured outside the walls. Buenos Aires was a dangerous city. Crime and gangs didn't know any boundaries. Shelton walked out the front sliding doors and ambled down the sidewalk, then slipped out of the hotel compound and onto the city streets.

The evening onshore breeze was refreshing. It made the first four blocks of the walk enjoyable. The farther away from the hotel Shelton got, the more suspect the neighborhoods became. Tension replaced the soothing feeling of cool air on his face.

The last city block was filled with busy shops and businesses during the day. At night, prostitutes, gangs, and what appeared to be drug dealers took over. Shelton's defense senses were at full alert by the time he arrived at the glassmaker's shop.

The shades of the corner shop were drawn. Shelton slowly opened the door and stepped inside as the muted door chimes clanked against each other. A well-groomed, trim man stepped out of the back room.

"Good evening," the man said. "May I help you?"

Shelton looked around the shop and then back at the man.

"I believe I have an appointment. Francis Macari referred me," Shelton said.

"Certainly," the man said in a pleasant tone. "I've been expecting you. I am Amir." He held out his hand. "And you are?"

"Thomas Shelton," he replied.

"Welcome, Mr. Shelton. It is my pleasure to meet you. Excuse me," Amir said as he stepped past Shelton and flipped the Open sign to Closed and turned off the outside lights.

"Standard practice." Amir smiled. "You are my last appointment of the evening, and, well, the locals roaming the streets at this time of night can be unpredictable. Please step this way." Amir gestured behind him and led the way to a room off the small lobby.

Shelton followed into the dimly lit room and sat down on the sofa across from the ornate walnut desk. Amir closed the security door to his office.

"Would you like something to drink?" Amir offered.

"A bottle of water would be nice," Shelton replied. He watched as Amir retrieved the customary, recyclable paper bottle from the small refrigerator in the corner.

The office was decorated in French country. Every item seemed perfectly placed. Not overdone or underdone. The paintings appeared to be originals. The antique furniture looked unused. The custom glass-work impeccable.

"How do you know Francis?" Amir asked, breaking the ice.

"We have been doing some business," Shelton said. "I shared with him a problem I was having, and he suggested I meet with you. He spoke quite highly of you."

"Francis is a fine human," said Amir, smiling. "I wished I had his eye for fashion."

Shelton nodded.

"So Francis tells me you are being watched by demons," Amir said, getting right to the point. The pleasant expression disappeared from Amir's face. "He said you have been seeing them for twenty years? Is that true?"

Shelton sat quietly for a minute. Hearing those words out loud was unsettling. Then he acknowledged the comment as true.

"Tell me about them, Mr. Shelton. When did you start seeing them? What is it you see? And tell me about every time you have seen one." Amir leaned forward with an inquisitive look.

Forty minutes later, Amir stood and stretched. He walked to the small window, pulled back the shade, and looked outside through the steel security bars, then poured himself a glass of water and sat back down. Shelton had hit the unremarkable highlights of when the watching began and how it progressed. He knew someday he would have to tell the whole story. But it wasn't going to be with a stranger in Argentina.

"Mr. Shelton, do you dream?" Amir asked.

Shelton paused.

"Senor Amir, what does it matter if I dream or not?" Shelton said.

"Dreams sometimes have meaning. Especially in my line of work." Amir continued, "What do you dream about, Mr. Shelton?"

Shelton stood and began pacing behind the sofa. He stopped and turned and looked at Amir.

"I dream occasionally, senor. It is always the same dream. It has been the same dream since my mother died," Shelton said. "I am in a crowd of people in the desert. It is too crowded for me, so I push my way through, trying to get out. I spot a rocky, treeless hill in the distance, so I make my way to it. On the hill, I can see the entire valley below where all the people are. There are thousands and thousands of people moving about. There is sand and rock as far as the eye can see. On another hill across the valley, there is a person sitting on a horse. It is hard to see. The sun is shining on me. In my face. I think the person is dressed for battle. And the person is observing the people below."

Shelton saw the inquisitive expression drop from Amir's face. A look of concern replaced it.

"In the blink of an eye, I am on the same hill as this soldier mounted on a horse. It's still hard to see. The sun is too bright. I have a saber. I look closely at the person. There is something familiar about him," Shelton said, looking into the air, glancing around the room. "The posture? The stature? Something about the face?" He reconnects with Amir's gaze. "I'm not sure if the soldier is an adversary or friend. My instinct tells me to attack. I never delay, never! I attack, but my weapon never touches him. I try over and over. He just sits there, looking at me." Shelton stares down at the table in front of him. "The soldier turns and rides down into the crowd and is gone. I go looking for him to do my duty, which is to kill him. But I cannot find him."

Shelton looked up and saw Amir staring at a letter lying on the desk in front of him. Written at the top were the words "The Dream of One Standing in the Sun." Amir, his face pale, casually placed the letter back in the top desk drawer and collected himself "Mr. Shelton, sir. You are in grave danger. You must leave the city immediately."

Shelton looked at the glassmaker across from him. Amir had a troubled look on his face.

"It is just a dream, senor. Aren't you overreacting?"

"There is no time to explain," Amir urged. "Buenos Aires is the center of the universe for nonhuman spirits. Evil spirits. The unseen. You might see guardians in New York or other places. Only because they were dispatched to find and observe you. Perhaps intimidate you. Here, there is no such guaranty. My advice to you is to leave the city immediately. Do not go back to your hotel. Walk out this door and get in the first cab you see and drive north to a town called Los Alamos. You will be safe there overnight."

Shelton began to ask a question, but Amir held up his hand, stopping him.

"One more thing," said Amir. "There are also immortals around. A few. Sometimes they will look like normal humans. You will only know them by their actions. Now you must go! Every moment you are here, the danger increases."

❦

Shelton stepped out of the shop and onto the sidewalk, closing the door behind him. The street and pedestrian traffic to the north of the shop was sparse. In the opposite direction, the nightlife consumed the streets and sidewalks. Shelton traded looks with the taxi driver parked on the other side of the street. He paused, contemplating Amir's words. The glassmaker had strongly encouraged him to get out of town. Shelton began walking. He crossed the street just in front of the cab and began the walk back to the hotel.

Three blocks east, one block north, and Shelton would be back inside the safety of the hotel compound. He estimated six minutes at a brisk pace. The bright streetlights from the major thoroughfare made it difficult to see on the poorly lit side street. Every few seconds, his night vision was improving as he moved deeper into the darkness. There was no one in sight on the block ahead. He could feel his weapons still neatly tucked into their harnesses. A feeling that increased his sense of security.

Shelton's mind was turning, processing all that Amir had said. The look on the man's face when he mentioned the dream was stuck in his mind. It meant something. He was certain of it. Amir's entire demeanor had changed. Demons, guardians, and immortals. Nothing made sense.

The sudden impact on the left side of his body knocked Shelton off his feet and into a dark alley. Everything went black as he lost consciousness. Seconds later, he woke face down on the pavement. He could feel his brain rebooting, trying to comprehend what had just happened.

He opened his eyes slowly, staring into the pavement. In his peripheral vision, he could see four figures in gray robes. One standing to his right, one to the left, and two in front of him. The figures were not moving. Shelton stayed motionless for a few more seconds as he regained awareness.

Then, with remarkable speed, Shelton was on his feet with his gun drawn. The first shot hit the gray-robbed guardian to his right in the chest, sending it flying backward while its saber fell to the ground.

The next shot hit one of the guardians in front of him. Working to his left, the next two shots dropped the third guardian. With the fourth one in his sights, he stopped firing and slowly stepped backward. He had all his attackers in view and in front of him.

Shelton watched as the three guardians he had just shot returned to their feet. The assailants moved to block his exit from the alley. He placed his gun back into the shoulder harness while continuing to observe his attackers.

In unison, three of the guardians drew their halfling sabers and held them at their sides. The fourth blade was lying on the ground between Shelton and the creatures.

In one fluid move, Shelton dove forward and rolled across the pavement while grabbing the blade from the ground, then returned to his feet. Without hesitating, he sliced through the defenseless figure closest to him, causing it to explode into a cloud of dust.

Spinning, he sliced through a second guardian. Just before his weapon met the next one, he felt the sharp edge of a blade pierce his skin. The impact of his saber against the attacker's weapon knocked it out of the guardian's hands and to the ground. Shelton reversed direction and sent a third explosion of dust skyward.

The last attacker knocked Shelton to the ground and pounced on top of him, wrapping its hands around his throat. Shelton was face to face with the nonhuman life form. Its white skin stretched tightly to its facial structure. Its lifeless, dark stare delved deep into Shelton's soul. The hatred emanating from the guardian's face was forcefully draining his energy.

Shelton's neck muscles were losing the battle. He drew a final deep breath. The blast of air exited Shelton's mouth, hitting the guardian in the chest and sending it flying into the air. Shelton jumped to his feet and with one strike sliced the last attacker in half. The dust from its body drifted back to the ground as silence returned.

The throbbing from Shelton's side intensified, drawing his attention. He opened his jacket slightly and saw the blood slowly seeping through his shirt. He tucked the demon's saber inside his jacket and carefully made his way back to the hotel.

CHAPTER THIRTEEN

THE LIVE MUSIC from the other side of the ranch drifted to the stables a half mile away. Angela Brady could hear the drums and electric guitar clearly in the cool night air. The cheers and whooping began as one song ended and another began. The sound of music and happiness rolling through the valley brought a smile to her face.

Brady was the new head of operations at Lookout Point Ranch. A five-hundred-acre spread nestled in the hills of northern Virginia. The landscape was picturesque. Rolling green hills, valleys, fresh-water ponds, and running creeks were natural works of art. The experienced forty-year-old ranch boss was living her dream—a dream she had kept alive since she was a little girl.

Brady's father had taught her to ride horses when she was four years old. Training horses and raising cattle was the family business. The elder Brady was pure Wiyot. A descendant of a small group of indigenous people. The Brady ranch in Northern California had been in her family since the early 1800s. As far back as Angie could remember, she was cleaning stables and exercising horses after school and every weekend. She learned quickly that ranching was an around-the-clock job seven days a week, every week. Sometimes she got paid and sometimes not.

After two hundred years in the ranching business, the current Brady generation couldn't compete with the large corporate operations moving into the area. When Angie was a little girl, her dad decided to close the business and lease the homestead. Leasing the land and renting the home would keep the property in the family. Maybe someday Angie would restart the business. Hopes, dreams, and ancestry were part of being a Native American.

Angie's mother, Samantha Kearns, was a career diplomat and a field intelligence officer. The British-born dual-citizenship agent was one of the highest decorated spies in American and British history. After a lifetime of service and being away from home, Kearns was ready to stay in one place.

Her appointment to the National Security Administration was perfect. The family moved to Northern Virginia. Sam Kearns could keep doing the job she loved. She could also be at home with her daughter and her husband. A daily routine the field officer had to get used to.

The change worked out well for Angie. She made a few good friends as she went through high school. She replaced working on the ranch with track & field and lacrosse. Occasionally, she would talk her mom into paying for a half day's rental of a horse at a local farm. It wasn't enough time in the saddle for the teenager, but it was better than nothing.

Following high school graduation, Angie attended the University of Virginia. She wasn't sure her parents had the money to pay for a private or out-of-state college, and her mom never introduced another alternative. To Angie, there was something strange about it. Her mother was a graduate of Cambridge and Berkeley. Kearns could have paved the way for her only child to one of her alma maters. Her mother never offered.

UVA worked out well for the young Angie Brady. She graduated with a degree in physics, moved back home, and went to work on a small ranch outside of Bethesda, Maryland. The night Angie's mom brought home the handsome naval officer from the NSA changed her life.

At first she was annoyed that her mother was trying to play matchmaker. After all, Angie didn't require a man in her life. She was quite content and happy in her self-sufficiency. But young Lieutenant

Commander Thomas Shelton was gorgeous, polite, and soft-spoken. Attributes she simply could not ignore.

After an awkward introduction by her mother, Angie and Tom became inseparable. While Shelton was stationed at the NSA, hardly a night went by where Angie and her new boyfriend were not together. Then one weekend the summer love affair ended. They sent Lt. Commander Shelton back to his unit in Virginia Beach for deployment.

Angie watched Shelton struggle with his revised orders from the Navy. She knew he loved her with all his being and that leaving meant risking losing her forever. She had no doubt he would have walked out of the Navy if she had asked him to. Shelton would not have given it a second thought. But Angie didn't ask, and Shelton didn't offer. She knew he needed his crew, but she wasn't sure why.

His parting words still echoed through her mind: "I will love you until the end of time."

Angie contemplated those words over and over through the years. It wasn't the words as much as it was Shelton's voice. His sincerity. To Angie, it didn't feel like the end but the beginning. It was as if there was more promised for them out there somewhere in the future. She could feel it.

Dreams were one thing but Angie needed to move on with her life. What would be would be. The reality was she needed to move on with her life without him. Thomas deployed and the young, expecting Angie Brady left home to make her own way into the world. She packed her bags and headed west one night, leaving her parents behind with a simple note about her departure, with no explanation as to why.

Over the past seventeen years, Angie had worked her way up the chain of command at cattle ranches in northwestern Wyoming and southern Montana. She had worked hard, navigated the politics of business in a male world, all while raising her son.

Over those years, she built an excellent reputation in the ranching industry. Her expertise with horses and cattle operations was well known among ranchers and operators. When the recruiter for Lookout Point Ranch showed up, Angie was surprised. The Northern Virginia ranch was east of the Mississippi River, a landmark that bifurcated the industry. The wild open west versus the tree-lined east. A brown landscape versus green. Real cowboys versus daddy's money.

She had never expected the opportunity to practice her profession in her home state and was hesitant to consider the opportunity. The open skies and spaces in the west was an environment she embraced. She was proud of the reputation she had established. Moving east would degrade her value as a ranching professional.

A bigger title, a much bigger paycheck, a new home on property, a new truck, and a smaller, less complex ranch was intriguing, though. Angie was quite aware she was getting older, and so was Daniel, her son.

The opportunity to live closer to her mother was a positive. Daniel would have family around him and her mother would dot on him. The regrets Angie had about her dad missing time with his grandson weighed on her. But his passing happened too soon, and the opportunity was lost.

On the third recruiting trip to Wyoming's Henderson Ranch, Heather Kersting made the offer to Angela Brady personally. She got her new VP signed up, and soon Angie Brady and her son, Daniel, were on their way to Virginia. Another item Heather could check off the boss's list.

Angie was aware that she was taking a job on Tom Shelton's ranch. Heather had disclosed the name of the owner during the final recruiting trip. Heather wasn't aware of the relationship between Tom and Angie or that Daniel was their son. Heather was simply following orders from Shelton to get the best ranch boss in the mountain west region of the country. That was hands down Angela Brady.

❦

Lookout Point Ranch's long paved drive from the main road snaked up the Potomac River valley. Angie watched as a car turned right from the county road at the top of the hill and descended to the valley floor.

She sipped her coffee, looking out as the vehicle made its way toward her house. She could see the long blond ponytail of her old friend being blown by the wind through the open car window. She turned and walked to the door and stepped out onto the front porch, stopping at the top of the steps. All five feet eleven inches of Angie Brady's slim, lean body wrapped in jeans and boots stood there waiting. She hadn't seen her best friend and roommate from college since graduation.

Following their graduation eighteen years ago, Taylor went on vacation with her family, and Angie spent the summer with her boyfriend, then disappeared, never to be heard from again.

Several months ago, the text message from Taylor Reed popped up on Angie's phone. At first, she didn't know what to do. She wanted to answer but didn't know what to say. So she waited. Every day that went by without responding to her old friend's message, her anxiety grew. Every day she imagined Taylor looking at messages, wondering why Angie hadn't answered. Angie eventually called her old friend, and they planned the reunion at Lookout Point.

Angie met Taylor as she climbed out of the car.

"Look at you," Taylor said with amazement in her voice. "You look like a model." The two friends held a long embrace.

Angie stepped back, looking at Taylor and taking hold of Taylor's hand. "It's so nice to see you," she said softly. "I can't believe you're here. I missed you so much. So much." Her voice quivered.

"I've missed you too." Taylor gave her arm a squeeze.

Angela Brady and Taylor Reed had been the stars of their sorority class at the University of Virginia. Both were straight-A students. Each enjoyed their alone time more than they enjoyed partying. Both were very attractive and constantly pursued by fraternity boys. The friends found the pursuit of males interesting but a distant priority. Their other sorority sisters were curious that Angie and Taylor were so much alike.

The two friends shared everything for four years of their lives. But when Taylor returned from her summer abroad with her family, Angie Brady was gone, with no forwarding address.

The two friends spent the day exploring Lookout Point, riding horses, and catching up on life. After dinner at Angie's favorite restaurant, the two arrived back at the ranch.

Angie tossed several logs into the fire ring on the back patio and lit them while Taylor was inside selecting the wine. A few minutes later, the two friends were sharing another toast. They sat there quietly, enjoying the stillness of the night and the fire.

Somehow Angie had made it through the day and dinner without having to explain her eighteen-year silence to Taylor. She knew she wouldn't be so lucky now. There was only the darkness, the fire, and the conversation left unsaid.

"So where did you say your son was?" Taylor asked in a slightly higher-pitched voice. The effects of several glasses of wine were beginning to show.

"Daniel is with his grandmother in Arlington," Angie replied. "He likes it there. He enjoys hanging out in the city. Mostly at the DC memorials. He loves to watch people and is a kind of history buff like you."

"I bet he's a great kid. He has a splendid mother," Taylor said warmly. "Cheers!"

The two friends raised their wineglasses.

Angie was quiet, still in disbelief at the dinner conversation. Taylor shared the story of her ex-husband, a religious zealot from a radical southern family. Somewhere along the way, Taylor wasn't living up to her in-laws' expectations. She was criticized for not raising her son correctly, and having had enough, the in-laws, her husband, and their preacher conducted an intervention. Somehow, they had her committed to a hospital for psychiatric evaluation.

Taylor hired a talented lawyer, and they constructed their own plan. She passed their psychological evaluations with flying colors, then counter-sued the family and the church. She walked away with full custody and one and a half million dollars. Just for fun, she filed kidnapping charges against her ex-husband. The judge sentenced him to prison for two years to teach him and the others like him a hard lesson. To make the lesson even more memorable, the judge made him serve the time in a maximum-security facility. They released him after six months. The lessons had been learned, and Taylor was set for life.

Angie was heartbroken that she hadn't been there to support her best friend in a time of need. She sipped her wine as she stared into the fire.

"You know, Angie," Taylor said as she finished a drink of wine, "you don't have to tell me why you disappeared after that summer. After all, I'm the one who left town the day after graduation. We were so close at school, then I just went off to Europe like an arrogant, thoughtless person. It was totally self-centered of me. I guess I took for granted you would always be there. It makes me sad. But I'm not angry with you. You don't owe me any explanation. I'm just thrilled we are here now. There is no place I would rather be." She reached for Angie's hand.

Angie smiled slightly, then broke eye contact. She raised her glass and gazed into the darkness beyond the fire.

"There really isn't much to tell about that summer," Angie said. "I met a boy. I fell head over heels in love with him. When we weren't working, we were together. Every minute. He received new orders from the Navy and left. I learned I was pregnant just after he departed."

Angie paused, stood up, stretched, and refilled their wineglasses. Then she placed more wood on the fire.

"Law school as a single parent seemed impossible to me," Angie continued as she sat back down. "I decided it was time to make my way in life. I had always wanted to work on a ranch out west. So I packed up and left."

"What did your parents say?" Taylor said. "Mine would have blown their tops."

"I didn't ask them," Angie replied. "I wrote them a note and departed. They didn't know I was pregnant. I didn't feel like explaining anything to anyone. It seemed like the simplest thing to do."

"When did you tell them?" Taylor asked with a shocked look on her face. "Your parents?"

Angie raised her eyebrows at the question as she looked at Taylor. "Two years later, I think."

Taylor gasped. "Your mother must have been pissed. Oh my god!"

"My mother is pretty unique," Angie responded. "There isn't much that can rattle that woman. She has spent a lifetime focused on herself and her career, which she loves. I felt the most sorry for my father. He raised me. He was closest to me. Anyway, by the time I told them and they came to see me, I was established. I had a job I liked, a house, a new truck, and a beautiful two-year-old baby boy. I expected the worst from my mom. But she actually seemed quite proud of me, and my dad was beaming. You know…his baby girl was kicking ass and taking names in a man's world. It made me feel good."

Angie reached down, picked up another piece of wood, and tossed it on the fire.

"So tell me about this summer love and the father of your son?" Taylor said.

Angie stared at the ground before she looked back at the fire and continued her story.

"He was a sailor. Naval officer, actually." Angie's voice grew warm and wistful. "He was a simple happy boy. He used to say less is better and simple is happiness. He seemed to take life in stride. Nothing rattled him. He loved life. Very handsome. Gentle. Wouldn't hurt a fly. He joined the service because he didn't know what else to do after college. He was smart. Like really smart. Shit, I introduced him to horses that summer," Angie said, feeling the effects of the wine. "The moment he took the saddle, he was the best rider I'd ever seen. Still is to this day. It's like he could communicate with the animal," Angie said with passion in her voice.

"Did you ever tell him he had a son?" Taylor asked bluntly. "By the way, what's this mystery man's name?"

The straightforward question poured cold water on Angie's passionate thoughts.

"He knows he has a son." Angie sighed. "I'm not a complete bitch."

"Do you ever talk to him? Does he visit or at least talk to his son?" Taylor asked, her voice growing louder.

Angie took a drink of wine and paused.

"Taylor," Angie said, "relax. I'm thrilled with my life. I have made my own way. I'm doing what I love to do. My son is being raised right. He will be a good person, just like me and his father. My life is a dream. I had three months with a man that was full of love and passion. I have a child with the man I loved and still love. Even though he isn't here physically, that doesn't mean he isn't present."

Taylor raised her eyebrows and looked confused.

"I think you are drunk, woman," Taylor said, smiling. "Are you living on another planet?"

Angie shook her head slightly and laughed. "It feels like it sometimes. But I like it."

CHAPTER FOURTEEN

SHELTON STARED OUT his office window toward Central Park while he sipped his second cup of morning coffee. He studied the rain-soaked city park and low-hanging clouds. The last words of his father, combined with Macari's story about his mother and the attack, were churning in his mind. He sat down at his desk and scribbled the key events on a legal pad of paper. He stared at it, hoping to connect the dots.

The tap on the door broke his concentration.

"There is a Professor Baker on the phone," announced his assistant.

Shelton paused, put his pen down, and then looked up slowly. "Thanks, Brian. I'll pick up."

On his way back to New York from Buenos Aires, Shelton stopped at his brother's home in Charlottesville. Rob was pleased with the outcome of the meeting at St. Elizabeth's Parish. It thrilled him to hear that the priest would not accept the money. Even better yet, did not need it. The college professor was now five million dollars richer.

Shelton figured Rob's conscience was clear. He would never know that his big brother insisted Macari take the money according to their mother's wishes. Then he paid Rob out of his own pocket.

Shelton's second order of business was to enlist some help from Rob.

He needed someone to help him figure out what was happening to him. A research professional was needed. Someone who was respected in their field and was a practitioner, not just purely academic.

Shelton concocted a cover story for Rob. He told his brother he had made an investment in an antique company and needed a consultant to help him sort out a strategy. Without hesitation, Rob offered the name of Professor Ann Baker as the best in the business.

Baker was the Co-Head of International Studies at the University of Virginia. She had written three books on the ancient civilization and human empires. Baker was the youngest full professor in the college's history. Ivy League schools constantly recruited her. According to Rob, she was happy where she was and didn't desire the politics of other institutions. Rob made the introduction, and Shelton had been waiting for a response from Baker.

He took a deep breath, then pushed the speaker button on the phone.

"Good morning, Professor."

"Good morning," came a warm voice through the speaker. "Do you have a few minutes to talk, Mr. Shelton?"

"Certainly," Shelton said, trying to calm his nerves. "It's a quiet, rainy New York morning. I'm having a bit of trouble getting motivated. How are you?"

"I see. Well, it's a gorgeous day here. Clear and cool," Ann said. "Just the way I like it."

"Thank you for calling, Professor," Shelton said. "I assume Rob has passed along some details about my project?"

"He has. It sounds very interesting. I would like to hear more about it, though. Coincidentally, Mr. Shelton, I have plans to be in the city this weekend. I have meetings on Saturday until four or five, but I am free after that. Would you like to get together and discuss things in person?"

A slight look of optimism washed across Shelton's face. "I think I can make it work. How does dinner Saturday evening sound?"

Ann agreed.

"Professor," Shelton added, "I was planning on being out on Long Island this weekend. I have a home there. It has an excellent guest room.

I would love to have you as my guest. It might make logistics easier. The house staff enjoys having guests. How does that sound?"

The slight pause in the conversation brought a smile to Shelton's face.

"I am not sure what to say?" Ann replied. "I suppose that would be fine as long as it's no inconvenience."

"Not at all," he responded. "Just let me know when and where to pick you up on Saturday, and I will handle the rest."

⁂

The black Mercedes sedan pulled up to the main entrance of Shelton's Long Island estate right on schedule. Slowly, the large iron gates swung open. Two minutes later, the driver stopped under the cover next to the side doors of the mansion. Patricia, the estate manager, opened the car door for Ann, then introduced herself. The driver placed Ann's bag beside her, then Patricia showed her inside and to her room.

"Please take your time settling in," Patricia said. "I will be back shortly to show you to the library."

Shelton had watched Ann's arrival from the library windows as he sipped a cold generous pour of whiskey. A few minutes later, there was a light tap on the door. He turned as the door opened and Professor Ann Baker walked in.

"Welcome," Shelton said, making his way toward the guest. "It's very nice to meet you." He reached out his hand.

"Thank you," Ann replied. "It's nice to meet you as well. Robert didn't prepare me for this. I'm speechless. This is an impressive home."

Shelton smiled. "Thank you. Can I get you something to drink?"

Shelton poured the whiskey and handed it to Ann as she took a seat on the sofa. He sat down in the armchair next to her.

"Frankly, your compliment is embarrassing, Professor," Shelton said sheepishly. "I suppose it reminds me of my excesses. Cheers! Thank you for that," he said with a slight laugh.

Ann raised her glass and smiled. "Sorry about that. It's just somewhat overwhelming. I don't hang around with this crowd in Charlottesville. I don't think this crowd exists there."

"I never dreamed or even desired any of this. I know it sounds contrite and ridiculous. Poor me. When you think about how people work, the sacrifices they make striving to achieve a small part of this, it is troubling. For me, it just seemed to happen. One thing led to another," Shelton said with a straight face. "To this very day, I am not sure what happened. What I mean is, I know *how* it happened, it is the *why* that is not clear. A person works and makes money. You make more money. You buy things that make life more efficient, comfortable, and secure. Then you buy things that fulfill your personal needs and wants. The unanswered question is, why me? I'm just a middle-class person. I didn't have dreams of being rich and powerful. I did not seek any of this out."

"Well, that's interesting," Ann said. "Rob said you were in the navy?"

"I was a naval officer for ten years," Shelton said. "I joined up right out of college. I'm still in the reserves."

Ann's stomach rumbled loud enough that her host noticed. "Of course you are hungry, Professor. So am I. Let's go to dinner." Shelton stood and motioned her to the door.

✌

At the restaurant, they were seated in a semiprivate booth with a view of the other patrons and the beach. A table just far enough away from others where nobody could overhear their conversation. It was the only table like it in the restaurant. Shelton had paid for the construction of the area.

Over dinner, Shelton learned Professor Ann Baker's personal story. The motivated student had worked nonstop through breaks and summers. At twenty-three years old, she had completed her PhD. She was awarded tenure and full professor status at twenty-six and promoted to department head a year after that. The professor had written and published three books on Western Asia history and cultures. She was married for five years and divorced for three. Her only son was six years old. Her father was a retired professor of engineering.

The calm and energetic seventy-year-old was Baker's primary child-care provider. Her mother was the headmaster of a private preparatory school in the area. While the professor pursued her career with vigor, her young son was in excellent hands with his grandpa.

Shelton relaxed as they got to know each other. He liked Baker. She seemed passionate about life and her work. And she hadn't sacrificed her son for her career. She was doing it all successfully.

"Are you ready to get to work?" Shelton asked as they walked back into the house from the SUV.

Ann looked surprised.

"I hadn't expected to work after three glasses of wine," she replied.

"I understand. But there is something I want to show you."

In the library, Shelton walked over to a case lying on the side table. He picked it up and moved it to the larger table. He opened the case, laid the object on the table, then folded the cloth back, revealing the saber.

"What do you make of this?" he asked.

Ann's eyes narrowed as she gazed at the shiny silver sword lying on the table. She lifted her eyeglasses to her face and stepped in for a closer look. Shelton watched as Ann stared at the blade tip and worked up to the guard, grip, and the pommel. Her gaze rested on the spherical-shaped pommel, a globe wrapped by a snake with seven red eyes.

Ann's head suddenly snapped up, and she looked Shelton in the eye. She slowly returned her focus to the pommel and studied the image again. She looked at the door, then the windows, and then back at Shelton.

"Tom," she said a bit hesitantly. "I am not an expert on these things. However, I know this symbol. I remember seeing it during my under-graduate work. My professor used this symbol as the grand finale for his class."

"What does it mean?"

"Professor Schwartz described it as one of the oldest spiritual symbols known to humans," she said. "A round sphere wrapped in a serpent represents the good earth surrounded by evil. The serpent represents evil, and the multiple eyes are always watching to ensure survival. The underlying implication, according to the professor, is evil does not possess the power of the good. Therefore, evil can only exist at the will of the good."

Shelton cocked his head. "And?"

"Well, it's a very obscure symbol," she replied. "If I recall, there have only been two or three artifacts ever discovered with this symbol. Those artifacts were fossils that dated back to 3000–4000 BCE. I had never seen the symbol before that semester in Israel. And I have not seen it since." Ann looked at it again, studying the shapes and pondering its meaning. "I am not sure western historians and archaeologists even acknowledge it as significant because it's so rare. That just means the symbol is likely considered a local artifact. One that was, for whatever reason, never shared with the broader world community."

Shelton nodded his head with a contemplative expression on his face.

"When you first saw the pommel, you looked frightened. What was that about?"

"Surprised…yes. Frightened, no," Ann replied. "Where did you find this?"

Shelton paused for a moment, thinking.

"The answer is a little complicated. What I can do is assure you I did not steal it," he said, knowing his words were not exactly true. "I'm told the weapon is rare and, therefore, valuable. Your professor, he sounds like the expert?" Shelton said, trying to move the conversation along.

"I think he could give us a more informed view of its value, or point us in the right direction," she replied. "I suppose he may determine the authenticity. But he would want to know the origin of the piece and be able to verify it."

Shelton looked at Ann with an expectant stare.

"I could contact Schwartz and ask him to look at it," she offered.

"Look at it, as in send him a picture?" Shelton asked.

"Initially, yes. That's the easiest and fastest way. But of course, I'm sure he will want to see it in person. That is the only way to make a definitive determination."

"The problem is, Professor, in business, sharing electronic pictures of priceless pieces without the proper security is a bad idea," Shelton said.

Ann wrinkled her nose, contemplating Shelton's words.

"I understand. Perhaps you can meet with him in person."

Shelton covered the saber with the cloth and closed the case.

"It's late, professor. I'm going to turn in," Shelton said. "I like the idea of you and me going to see your guy. But before we go, I'm not sure I believe this symbol doesn't scare you."

"And I want to know where you found it, Mr. Shelton. The piece didn't just show up at the local antique store."

Shelton's eyebrows raised, impressed and surprised by Baker's words. "I'll show you to your room, Professor."

CHAPTER FIFTEEN

ANN SETTLED INTO a seat with her hot tea and a book. Several pages later, the gentle movement of the airplane made her eyelids heavy. Shelton sat across the aisle, checking his messages and nodding off.

In a few hours they would touch down in Tel Aviv. The Gulfstream was the newest addition to Shelton's fleet of personal airplanes. The custom configurations of each aircraft were like five-star hotel rooms, complete with a dining room, bedroom, shower, and office.

Shelton's flight operations department housed the small fleet of airplanes at Smith Field in Texas. Aircraft maintenance businesses surrounded the midsized commercial airport that included almost a hundred other private jet owners. Shelton's four large, unmarked hangers blended in nicely.

The flight operations team was required to have at least two other airplanes operating besides the one Shelton was on. Each aircraft's passenger manifest listed Thomas J. Shelton, US Citizen, Height 6'4", Weight 210 lbs. While he was on his way to Israel, a second and third aircraft were headed for Paris and Istanbul without passengers. Anyone trying to track his movements would find it impossible, if they could even get the information.

The previous morning, Shelton and Ann took turns exchanging their respective stories. Shelton poured Ann a cup of coffee, and she launched into her story.

Ann had first seen the symbol on the saber's pommel while studying in Israel. Her professor's lecture had been followed by a strange occurrence. The night of the lecture, she and three classmates had the same dream. All awoke from the dream with the sense that someone was in the room watching them sleep. The next morning, they each discovered an image of the symbol on the door of their dorm room. Burnt into the wooden doors.

Ann and her roommates approached the professor with the issue. He dismissed it, telling them that every year someone pulled a prank following the topic. The university replaced the doors, and the professor encouraged them to forget about it. Ann and her roommates followed instructions. Another one of their classmates took pictures of the symbol and began showing them around. A few days later, she vanished while on a weekend field trip. She was never heard from again.

The local authorities investigated the disappearance for only a few days before concluding that it was a case of deliberate and willful withdrawal by the girl. Case closed. The family, as well as friends, appealed to the authorities, but the government had no interest in pursuing the case. She was never found.

Then it was Shelton's turn. He methodically walked Ann through the attack in Buenos Aires. As the story advanced, Ann's face transformed from curious to concern.

"You were attacked by evil paranormal beings? Personally?" she exclaimed with a look of disbelief and skepticism in her voice. "And you took one of their weapons?"

It took a few more iterations from Shelton as he tried to convince his new partner his story was real. He showed Ann the wound on his side from the attacker. Eventually, she believed him.

"So you made up the advisory role story in order to get me here? It was a cover?"

Shelton looked at the floor and then back up at Ann, then made his confession. For the first time, he had someone to rely on. Someone to openly discuss things with. A person who was on his side trying to help. Someone he could trust.

It was only the second time in Shelton's adult life that he hadn't felt alone. The other time was with Angie. But that was twenty years ago. In the end, Ann and Shelton both agreed that the best place to start was with Professor Schwartz at the Hebrew University in Jerusalem.

❦

The jet touched down in Tel Aviv on Monday morning. The driver chauffeured Shelton and Ann to Jerusalem. A message from Schwartz to Ann confirmed an evening meeting at his office.

The new partners had both managed to sleep on the flight, so they spent the day in the old city being tourists. Ann took the lead, showing the boss around. She knew every inch of the city. They wandered in and out of alleyways and narrow passages. Shelton was amused to see Ann had the passion of a college student again, reminiscing as they explored the sights.

Shelton was less enamored with the place. Most of the city only dated back to the sixteenth century, although you wouldn't know it from the emotional reaction of visitors. It was as if they were walking in the actual hallowed halls of religion. Historians and archaeologists alike agreed, the current 300-year-old version of the city looked nothing like the original. In most cases, the location of the original historical sites was unknown, making the current shrines technically manufactured. It didn't matter to visitors to the region. The cultural stories and the emotional association to the general location overwhelmed logic and facts. People simply didn't care that it wasn't authentic. It was close enough.

As the two browsed in the shops, Ann made it a point to ensure her boss understood the vendors and their goods. She complained that very few of the arts and crafts were domestic. Like every other market in the world that catered to tourists, most of the product was Chinese or South East Asian. Somehow, the deception seemed more violating in the "Holy Land."

Shelton was on watch the entire day as they strolled through the different sections of the city. The attack in Argentina still had him on edge. The story of Ann's colleague was also a concern.

Their last stop before going to meet with Schwartz was the Western Wall, a stone wall where people write their prayers on tiny pieces of paper, then stuff them in the cracks. The idea is God would read their prayers and grant them.

As Shelton and Ann turned a corner, Shelton stopped suddenly. Guardians in black robes stood fifty yards away next to a side wall.

Shelton casually and gently touched Ann's arm while reaching for his mobile phone. He held the phone up and leaned over toward her as if to show her something on the screen.

"What is it?" she said, surprised by the physical contact.

Shelton pointed to the screen and said, "Do not react to what I am going to say. Just look at the phone and act interested. Okay?"

"Okay," Ann replied, wrinkling her brow with suspicion.

"Now, when I tell you to, look up casually at the bottom stairs on the other side of the square in front of us. Left side of the staircase against the wall."

She nodded, smiling, still looking at the phone.

"What is it?" she asked again, maintaining a calm voice.

"It is the same type of thing that attacked me in Buenos Aires," Shelton said. "Two guardians. They are watching us now. When you look up, stare intensely right at that point. Again, six feet above the ground, at the wall, left side of the stairs. If you understand, keep looking at the screen, smile and nod, and say okay," he said.

Ann complied as her pulse increased. Shelton looked at her, smiling and pointing to the screen.

"Relax your breathing just a little," Shelton coached.

Ann tried but failed. Shelton wasn't sure she'd be able to see what he was trying to show her.

"Are you ready?" he asked.

Ann took a deep breath, smiled, and said, "Yes. Do I have a choice?"

"Welcome to the field," Shelton said, smiling slightly. "Okay. On three."

On the count, Professor Baker slowly raised and turned her head, looking up at the exact spot Shelton had directed her to. She stared intently, looking for anything. Anything at all.

She blinked two times to clear her vision and then, "There!" she said. "Never mind. I think it's just a heat mirage."

The mirage Ann saw consumed the space from the ground up to about eight feet high onto the wall. She blinked and refocused at the same time Shelton touched her face with his fingertip. At that moment, the guardians came into focus.

It was as if someone had changed her vision. Two tall, black-robed figures. Both faces looking directly at her and Shelton from underneath draped hoods. One figure moved its head slightly and looked directly at her. A sudden expression of concern came across the guardian's smooth, pale face. The figure raised its hand and placed it on the other's shoulder. They disappeared.

"Shit! That was awesome," Ann said in a whisper.

Shelton smiled at her enthusiasm. Silently, they continued to survey the area, looking for any trace of the creatures.

"They're gone," Ann said.

"Let's go see." Shelton grabbed her hand and hurried down the stairs and across the square to the spot where the guardians had been standing. He bent down and touched the spot. Ann followed Shelton's lead. She knelt down and placed her palm next to his on the ice-cold stones. She turned her head toward Shelton and made eye contact. Their faces were only inches away from each other.

Shelton had touched Ann's face and that had somehow enabled her to see the goons. *Ben Davis didn't require enabling in the parking garage,* thought Shelton thought.

❦

Professor Schwartz was waiting for them in the café outside his office when Shelton and Ann arrived. Shelton watched as Professor Baker and Professor Yaakov Schwartz embraced. They seemed happy to see each other again after so many years.

They consumed the first cup of tea while the two academics caught up on their accomplishments and journeys over the past years. Shelton kept a pleasant, engaged look on his face but was wondering if they were going to spend the entire evening catching up. Then he noticed Schwartz glance his way.

As the server poured them all a cup of fresh tea, Schwartz used the moment to change subjects.

"Ann, what brings you and your colleague to Israel?"

Ann glanced at Shelton expectantly.

Shelton furrowed his brow slightly, then made eye contact with Schwartz.

"Professor, excuse me for getting right to the point," Shelton said. "Ann shared with me the story of her friend's disappearance while she was studying with you. I found it intriguing. The symbol. The dreams. The disappearance. So I offered to do some follow-up on the matter. I thought the best place to start was with you. What can you tell me about the situation?"

Shelton watched as Schwartz glanced down at the table, then back up, then from one side to the other.

Professor Schwartz stuck to his story. How every year someone played a prank with students following the Ancient Artifacts section of study. In Ann's year, the disappearance was unusual and devastating but simply coincidental.

"Professor, I understand you are one of the foremost experts in this field. How can you, on one hand, acknowledge the true nature of evil yet dismiss a corroborated encounter? An encounter that you downplay but do not deny. In fact, these pranks happen every year by your own admission. How do you conclude that the experience is a prank? What are you hiding, Professor?" Shelton stared deep into Schwartz's soul.

"Mr. Shelton, you certainly know how to get to the point. However, your accusation that I might have knowledge about the young woman's disappearance is off base," Schwartz said.

"I did not accuse you of anything," Shelton said, quickly following up. "I simply think you know this symbol has real consequences. I think it's deliberate on your part. You have been collecting data on this subject for a long time. Somehow, that particular year, something got out of hand. You know it, and now I know it. Why don't you share with me what happened?"

"What is it you are after, Mr. Shelton?"

"I am not a cop. I'm not here to arrest you. What happened took place many years ago and is not my affair. I need to know what you know about the spirit world. I need to know what you know about nonhumans running around amongst us," Shelton said. "I want to hear about your decades of unpublished research."

⤴

The professor walked ahead of Shelton and Ann, leading the way across the dimly lit campus through a maze of buildings.

"He knows something," Ann whispered to Shelton in disbelief. "That bastard! The intensity of the situation when his student disappeared was severe. He never once cracked. You apply some pressure over a cup of tea and he capitulates."

Shelton glanced sideways at his partner.

"Human nature is strange, Ann. Time is the enemy of good people that have done regretful things. It never leaves you. Maybe this is the old man's opportunity to come clean. Unburden himself of his own demons from the past," Shelton said.

Yaakov Schwartz escorted them into his personal library. Books were spread across a table in front of the fireplace. Schwartz pulled a green-covered book from a shelf and set it down.

"Mr. Shelton, Professor Baker, thank you for your patience. I realize you have come a long distance to speak with me. Your efforts show conviction in your research. I must admit this conversation is a great surprise to me," said Schwartz. "It is a conversation that I have thought about having many times over the years. However, I am sure you appreciate the fact that there are very few people with which to discuss such a subject."

"Indeed," Shelton responded with a sympathetic tone.

"Ann," Schwartz continued, "I am not sure what happened to your colleague that year. I truly do not know. However, I am confident that something sinister took place. Something associated with that symbol. The previous twenty-five years of giving the same lecture on the subject elicited almost the exact same situation every year. At first, it was harmless and interesting. It offered a young professor some excitement at least once a year. It always reminded me that history is the past and the current world is real and alive. Good and evil have never been more real and alive," Schwartz added. "It was my brief blast of reality in a world of make believe and deception."

Schwartz told Shelton and Ann about the year his student disappeared. It was the last time he ever delivered the lesson. His theory was that the young woman must have somehow threatened or challenged the entity, and they simply eliminated her. He apologized again for his cover-up. He explained that telling the police investigators what happened would have been problematic. It would have ended his career and livelihood. It would have changed nothing.

Shelton could see the logic and look of relief on Ann's face. Knowing the truth was important to her.

"Professor, I understand you departed from religion at some point?" Shelton asked.

"That is correct," answered Schwartz.

"Why? Why did you leave?" Shelton pressed.

"Let us just say as time went by, I found it increasingly difficult to subscribe to institutional beliefs. It motivated me to do my research. Make my own determinations without relying on biased, politically motivated organizational interpretations. I decided based on the facts and data at my disposal. Frankly, I have everything at my disposal."

"I see," Shelton replied hearing the arrogance of Schwartz's comment. "So, what can you share with us about the nonhuman world, Professor?" Shelton prodded.

Schwartz took a deep breath and placed his hand on the green leather-bound book sitting on the table in front of him.

"This book is the missing link. The story that no one ever told,"

Schwartz said. "The ancient writings are factual. This book shares additional information not known to most. It is unclear how many copies exist. I was once told that a copy lives in the Pagan Roman archives inside the Vatican, but I'm not sure that is true."

Schwartz continued explaining that the original record tells of disobedient spirits that would materialize in human form. The spirits fathered a hybrid generation known as Nephilim. These spirits and offspring were destroyed when the great cleansing came. Some spirits escaped to the spiritual world but did not regain their original positions. Instead, they discovered their misdeeds had caused them to lose their stature in the spiritual world. Not only did they lose their positions, they were deemed antagonists. They found themselves in dense emotional darkness. The dark places in the universe were their only refuge.

Schwartz explained that Heylel, who is the devil, and his demons still had the ability to influence the minds and lives of humans. However, it was difficult for them. It required great effort, coordination, and planning. It required human organizations and decision makers to advance and ultimately achieve the aim. The objective being the elimination of the species. If Heylel could wipe away the humans with the wave of a hand, he would have done it long ago.

Schwartz looked at Shelton.

"In this book, it refers to a soul that possesses such power. He's referred to as one standing in the sun. One who commands all elements of the earth and all living creatures. One who killed thousands of people and destroyed cities in the Hebrew and Aramaic scriptures. This One is not God or even a god. In the Greek writings, a solider did the work. It's logical that a solider did the work in the Hebrew writings as well. No one knows his name. But Heylel does."

"Why would they be following me, Professor?"

"I suppose you have threatened them," Schwartz said.

Shelton and Schwartz stared at each other. The pause in the conversation hung in the air.

"Look, Mr. Shelton, I am an old man. I will turn eighty-seven in several weeks—"

"Who controls these demons, Professor?" Shelton interrupted.

"I do not know his human name," confessed Schwartz. "But Heylel is here. On earth somewhere. Moving about. Influencing. If he is successful, all the stories and worries about Armageddon will come true. That is the natural end of this system of things, unless someone or something changes it."

Shelton stood and walked over to pour himself a cup of tea. He could feel the warmth from the fireplace.

"Professor Schwartz," Shelton said. "I would like to show you something."

Shelton opened his backpack and placed the saber on the table. He folded back the protective cloth. The professor raised his brow with interest.

"It's a guardian's saber," Schwartz said, peering closer.

"How do you know that?" Shelton asked.

"It's just like the drawing in the book." Schwartz pointed to the green leather-bound book lying on the table. "Where did you get this? The craftsmanship is excellent."

"I took it from its owner. A guardian. Dressed in a gray robe," Shelton said, his voice dry.

Schwartz turned and looked Shelton in the eye. "I understand. Let me get to the point. There is no heaven or hell, Mr. Shelton. It was all contrived. Made up. A tool for humans to dominate one another. Fear of hell is a powerful motivator. It herds humans into the arms of those with power. The ones who can save them from eternal torment."

The office door exploded inward. The shock wave knocked Shelton and Ann backward, slamming them against the wall. Shelton quickly jumped back to his feet. As he did, he saw the tall black-robed figure standing in the doorway.

Shelton glanced over and saw the lifeless body of Schwartz impaled and stuck to the wooden fireplace mantel. The guardian's saber had penetrated the professor through the heart with such force the only visible part of the saber was the handle. A handle with a globe and a serpent on it.

Shelton darted toward the table for his saber. The rapid movement caught the guardian by surprise. It responded. The adversaries were on a collision course. At the last second, Shelton shifted direction toward Schwartz's body, and in a flowing motion, he pulled the sword from the mantel and turned toward the demon.

The last remaining air to leave the professor's lungs made a hissing sound as the body collapsed to the floor. Shelton stood facing the guardian, holding the bloody weapon at the ready.

"What do you want with me?" Shelton asked in a calm, steady voice. Ann had caught her breath and was sitting against the wall, watching.

Without hesitation, the guardian attacked. The enormous sword-wielding creature moved rapidly toward Shelton, who dove to his left, rolled on to the floor, and was back to his feet in one swift motion, causing the demon to miss. As the guardian turned back toward its target, Shelton swung the saber with all his strength, striking the attacker just above the shoulders. The ear-piercing scream penetrated deep into Shelton's head. And the guardian exploded into a cloud of dust.

CHAPTER SIXTEEN

As the winter storm moved across northern Germany, ice and snow pinged against the upper chamber windows of the castle. The strong cold wind moved the leafless tree branches against the leaded window glass making a scratching sound inside the centuries old architecture.

The flickering fire in the centuries-old fireplace created dancing shadows on the stone walls. A lone figure stood at the window, peering out into the darkness of the bitter snowy night.

Dr. Wolfgang Hauser turned from the window and strolled toward the fireplace. As he did, he studied the large painting above the mantel. The art was the centerpiece of his private library. He never grew tired of looking upon it.

The painter had done a remarkable job perfectly capturing the moment in time with texture, color, and movement. He'd portrayed Hauser at the helm of *Le Majestic* on a beautiful day sailing the blue waters of the Mediterranean Sea off the coast of Spain.

Hauser sat down in the armchair next to the fireplace and began playing the glorious day back in his mind, moment by moment.

ॐ

Wolfgang Hauser was not human. He was an unseen spirit trapped in a human body. His true existence transcended time. His work spanned across all the universes that contained life. As the supreme governor of worlds, he determined how best to govern and create productive societies across thousands of galaxies. Freedom of choice was not an option or even a thought in the societies he oversaw. Only the earth, with its human class, was different.

The Sovereign Principals of the Universe had given the human species enough intelligence to harness the resources of the earth for sustainment, advancement, and enjoyment. The type was provided self-choice with no limits. A sort of life that could operate in a free, self-generating society on a living planet wouldn't need Hauser. And that was a problem. The human kind, if the experiment succeeded, would put Hauser out of a job.

Hauser marveled at the beauty of earth more than anyone. He had carefully watched as it developed through millions of years of evolution, trial and error. The earth was one of a kind. The other thousands of inhabited planets looked nothing like it. It was to be the model for all future development. But if the biology experiment was successful, what would he do?

Fortunately, time was on Hauser's side. The slow degradation of the species governing themselves was clear to all. There was no perfect model or controllable way to let life self-govern. A little pressure here, a little enticement there, and suddenly you had a creature that would eat their young and each other for self-satisfaction, power, and glory. Humans worked endlessly to dominate one another. Hardly a template for future life anywhere. Hauser needed the species marked as a failed experiment. End of story.

So, for the many centuries before World War I, Hauser didn't overly burden himself with the human condition. The natural progression of the species, with a push and prod here and there toward self-destruction, was enough to make his point to the principals.

Instead he spent his days on the high seas transiting the oceans of the world. Moving across the vast oceans of water with the wind in his face, delighting in the power and beauty of earth. He found the raw exposure of his human body to the natural world intoxicating. On this day, the artist in tow had captured it on canvas.

Hauser and his two confidants had sailed from a Spanish port. Just out of the harbor, they hoisted the mainsail and watched it fill with a brisk east wind. The perfect day passed by as they zigzagged across the water with expert skill. It was also the day he met his obsession.

Sitting in the chair next to the fire, Hauser lifted his nose slightly and inhaled. He could remember the smell. The sweet scent of his companion's captivating fragrance. He could feel her hands touching his flesh. He could hear her breathing as she lay beside him. The lust for human interaction Hauser had resisted throughout time changed that day.

In the years ahead, the lovers spent all their time together. They traveled the world side by side. The presence of her beauty, his infatuation with power, greed, and now lust consumed his consciousness, feeding his arrogance and ego. His human companion died eventually and he spent the centuries on earth influencing governments, religions, and humans while transiting between his posts across galaxies.

As the twentieth century arrived on earth, an unexpected visitor to Hauser's Parisian home one spring day changed everything. The visitor had traveled from Abdel Kinneret, where the Sovereign Principals of the Universe reside, to deliver a message.

The message was clear. Hauser had overstepped his role by negatively influencing the human species instead of supporting them. Hauser was being confined to the earth, no longer free to transit between his posts across the galaxies. He was relieved of duty. Never again to serve.

In his rage, Hauser attempted to end the human experiment once and for all by pushing humans into the world of war. To his dismay, somehow the species had stopped short of complete annihilation in the Great War. He had underestimated the human ability to learn, problem solve, and exercise self-preservation instincts.

The next time, Hauser made certain he had the people in place armed with the right tools to do the job. Again, those not under the direct influence of his demons had beaten him at his own game. The

European Allies and the Americans had overcome and defeated the Germans and developed the nuclear bomb before Hauser's madman could get the job done.

The expert sailor and lover had lost his way. Power, greed, and lust, the very things Hauser had inflicted on the humans for thousands of years, had snared him. His anger grew. But the earth would not survive his next attempt. This time he had incompetent humans lining up perfectly so that no one would escape when the bombs started flying.

⌁

The black sedans pulled into the courtyard of the castle just after two o'clock in the morning. Three men quickly exited the second car and made their way toward the main doors. But not before a blast of icy wind came rushing down the valley, almost knocking them to the ground.

The sound of strangers' voices echoing up the staircase stirred Hauser back from his thoughts. A few minutes later, Steven Walker III strode in through the open French doors of the upper chamber and into the presence of Dr. Wolfgang Hauser.

Walker was the acting director of the US Central Intelligence Agency. New England born and raised, he was the great grandson of a Boston-area real estate tycoon. His family wealth had bought him the best education money could provide. The Ivy League law degree had provided him the opportunity to practice at one of the most prestigious law firms in the country.

The cronyism only lasted long enough to preserve the firm's relationship with the university. Before Walker's first year with the firm was complete, the new, less than adequate lawyer found himself tossed onto the street and looking for a job.

After two years of jumping from shop to shop, the failed lawyer relented and went to work in the family business. A business that systemically took advantage of honest, hard-working people. Walker fit into the mold just like his father and grandfather before him.

Now Walker found himself as the acting director of the US Central Intelligence Agency. He had left the family business and gone to work for the CIA director, who was a friend of his from college. When President Staley suddenly fired Walker's mentor and friend, he found himself in the position of the top intelligence officer of the most powerful nation on the planet.

Unqualified by any measure, Walker knew how to follow orders and suck up to a boss. Ethics never got in his way. Attributes the current US administration valued.

The figure standing in front of the fireplace did not move when the acting director entered the room. Walker's swearing under his breath about the weather and the lack of heat in the "dingy stone shithole" did not go unheard.

"Dr. Hauser, Steven Walker," Walker announced, throwing his damp coat on the antique leather sofa and extending his hand toward Hauser.

Without acknowledging his guest, Hauser turned and slowly walked past Walker and sat down at the desk.

Wolfgang Hauser was a picture of elegance. Tall, thin, and impeccably dressed in a perfectly tailored suit. He sat upright, shoulders back in a commanding posture behind the walnut desk in the leather high-backed chair. Walker helped himself to a seat in front of the desk. When Walker looked up, the two men's eyes met for the first time.

Walker had a smitten look on his face. Hauser was a stunningly attractive man. The host did not react to his guest's expression. He just stared into Walker's dimly lit soul as the agent worked to regain his composure.

"Doctor, I am going to get right to the point. It is imperative that you knock off the bullshit. The President of the United States has the world situation under control. He sent me to tell you to stop creating these regional skirmishes all over the fucking place. Stop funding warring governments in the Middle East and Africa. Stop encouraging the Russians to interfere with politics and make land grabs. There is enough chaos in the world. The president needs a little more cooperation out of you."

Hauser continued to stare at Walker without saying a word.

"And, by the way, what the hell are you doing letting one of your people attack an American citizen? I'm told your men almost killed that guy in Argentina. We need a quieter, more peaceful existence, doctor. I am sure you know the president is trying to get reelected. If you allow him to help calm the waters, his reelection should be a given. Well, doctor? Do we have an agreement?"

"You are an imbecile," Hauser said in a calm voice that matched his appearance. "You think you can stroll into my drawing room and make such demands? Have you no idea whom you are speaking to?"

"Look, I don't know you. I assume you are some rich German businessperson who has more money than God. So whatever you are, or who you think you are, is irrelevant to me. My instruction is to get your commitment to stop the nonsense. The president demands it."

"You are failing me," Hauser said. "Has your president forgotten who gave him his job?"

Hauser stood up, walked around the desk, and stopped beside Walker, peering down at him. Walker looked up at the man towering above him.

"How did it feel to have daddy do everything for you? How does it feel to be such a miserable failure, Mr. Walker? How does it feel to be the worst of the worst? When animals have offspring like you, they kill and eat them. They leave no trace of weakness behind."

Hauser continued looking down at his guest with the blank, emotionless facial expression.

"When you fail me," said Hauser, "there is a price to be paid."

"What are you talking about?" Walker asked, concern suddenly appearing on his face. "The president is doing everything right. The problem is that for him to be successful, we need more time to focus. Too much unrest causes problems for everyone."

Hauser turned and walked to the fireplace.

"Were you aware the American who was attacked by my people actually killed all of my associates?" asked Hauser.

"Impossible!" Walker exclaimed.

Hauser turned to face his guest.

"Are you stupid, incompetent, and deaf, Mr. Walker?"

"Our sources gave me no such report. We are the absolute best in the intelligence business," Walker said, trying to ignore the insults.

"We have been watching this American for years," Hauser continued as he paced about the room. "He is a danger to us all. He is even more of a threat now that he knows his life is in danger. He will not stop! You and your people need to manage him. You must track him down and convince him to move on with his miserable human life. He has everything he could want. Give him more."

"If he is the problem, we will just eliminate the threat," Walker responded in a cavalier tone.

Hauser burst out laughing. The loud sound reverberated off the stone walls inside the library.

"Oh, you small-minded animal. You are indeed stupid. You do not know what you are dealing with." Hauser glared intensely at his guest.

Before Walker could manage another word, Hauser had moved across the room in one swift motion. Walker's eyes involuntarily flickered at the rapid movement. Hauser stood in front of Walker, removed his gloves, and slowly raised his hand, revealing his pale skin and long thin fingers.

"This is the hand that feeds you. This is the hand that will destroy you if you fail me. Just let things go. We are close now."

In one swift motion, Hauser gripped Walker by the neck and lifted him out of the chair.

"Now, what should I do with you?" Hauser asked rhetorically, staring at his guest's face. "Should I kill you like I did your pathetic friends downstairs? Yes, they have been eliminated. Should I let you go? You come into my home and insult and make demands of me?"

Walker could feel the hand tightening around his neck as Hauser's anger grew.

"Give me a chance," Walker begged, getting the words out between gasps. "I will manage the president."

"You tell your president that I am the commander in chief. I am the ruler of your little world. I helped create all of this. Everything your president has is because I caused it to be so. His money. His power.

Everything! Now go do your duty." Hauser threw the man across the room.

Walker's body smashed into a far wall before falling to the floor.

"Get out of my sight," yelled Hauser. "Rest assured, if you ever see me again, I will tear your limbs from your body one by one."

Walker scrambled to his feet, ran down the stairs, and jumped into the waiting car, then punched the connect button on his secure phone.

Hauser sat back down by the fire in deep thought. The strategy to pit nation against nation had failed twice. He wasn't about to fail again. It was about divide and conquer. Europeans against Europeans, Americans against Americans. Deconstruct the unity that held the nationalistic cultures and societies together. The US president was doing a masterful job of alienating allies and dividing his country internally. The Russians were underway as well. If Bianco and the Archbishop of Canterbury did their job, a new British prime minister would do his part shortly. After the bombs fell and the internal civil wars were complete, it would render the experiment of the human species on earth useless.

"Diakonos," Hauser yelled, his voice echoing off the stone walls.

"Yes, my lord?" the servant responded as it entered the room.

"We are going on a holiday. Make the arrangements. One more thing. Get in touch with Mr. Ben Davis. Tell him I need to see him in France immediately."

᭥

Five hours later and four hundred miles to the west, the aid placed a classified packet in the center of the prime minister's desk. Wilkinson removed the seal and methodically opened the folder. He read the briefing papers while he sipped his morning tea.

The phone call from Walker to the US president had been intercepted by British intelligence. The military satellite link had captured the conversation but not Walker's location. The prime minister was a target. A few minutes later, Wilkinson placed the papers in the shredder next to his desk and picked up the phone.

CHAPTER SEVENTEEN

ANN BAKER GLANCED up from the stack of essays to check the small battery-powered clock on the faded tan wall. Office hours were almost over. She stood up from behind the desk, walked over and closed the door, turned off the lights, and laid down on the sofa. She closed her eyes just before her head touched the cushion.

Ann was back at the university teaching, advising, and preparing for spring graduations. She had been working nonstop since she and Shelton returned from Israel. The lack of sleep was catching up with her.

During the week she was the department head and professor. On Friday afternoon she was on an airplane crossing the country, working on the plan she and Shelton had dreamed up. Sunday afternoon she would return in time for dinner with her parents and son.

The research plan had been more her idea than Shelton's. She needed to make sense of what happened to Professor Schwartz. Sitting around lamenting about it wasn't her style. Idle time to think about her changed reality was the enemy. Activity to fill the space was good. Even if it would likely provide no value.

Her former professor impaled and staked to the fireplace mantel was an image she couldn't get out of her mind. The expression on his face kept popping into her brain during lectures, meetings, and in dreams. Shelton had changed her life forever. He was the only person she could talk to about it. He had made his problem her problem. A fact that angered her when she thought about it.

She had witnessed a paranormal life form kill a human. Then she watched Shelton strike the creature, and it vaporized in front of her. Life could never be the same. Now helping Shelton was the same as helping herself.

The sheer exhilaration of what she'd seen was phenomenal by any account. Ann found the existence of other life forms cleansing in some strange way. It meant there were much more than humans in the universe. Much more to the story. Perhaps hope!

The information that there was more to the world than meets the eye meant the possibilities of life forms were truly endless. Ann's broadened perspective and love of learning had arrested all the angry feelings toward Shelton. Now she was working on solutions and answers.

But feelings of guilt emerged occasionally. She was spending very little time with her young son. She was thankful her parents were willing and able to take care of him while she focused 100 percent on her research project. Baker had convinced herself that the work she was doing could very well save her son and her family. If not mankind.

Ann and Shelton agreed they needed to find the one directing the guardians. Schwartz called him Heylel. But that was just the generic word for light bearer, morning star, or Lucifer.

Ann proposed interviewing religious leaders. After all, who studied Satan more than theologians? Past and current generations of popes acknowledged evil spirits roamed the world. The profession knew something others did not. It was a long shot, but doing something was better than doing nothing.

Ann selected a list of clergy from North America to get started. Her cover story was she was doing research on the Holy Trinity, a Christian concept that was in most respects benign and easy for a theologian or preacher to talk openly about. The opportunity to be quoted in a research report as an authority on the subject could only be good for a career.

Once Professor Baker had established a repartee with the interviewee, she would transition to her actual subject, hoping to learn something or picking up a clue.

The work took her to New York, Boston, Toronto, Chicago, San Francisco, and Salt Lake City. The southern route took her to Atlanta, Birmingham, New Orleans, Little Rock, and Tulsa.

After weeks of traveling and interviews, she had found a reasonably good commitment by the professionals to their respective doctrines. Although the depth of analytical thinking regarding the dogma that they espoused was almost nonexistent.

Baker found it remarkable that a person could stand up in front of a group of people day after day, week after week, and preach words they didn't truly understand. In some cases they didn't even believe it themselves.

All the emotions, theatrics, and dogma were nothing more than a job and a business for most of these church leaders. Congregations and followers believed their priest or preacher was a person of God with the ability to understand and comprehend things the nonprofessionals could not. But the profession was not about the truth. It was about perpetuating the culture. The business. It was an industry. There was very little sacred or holy about any of it.

The question Baker kept asking herself was, how had she missed this reality her entire life? After all, she was one of the top ancient history professors in the country. She knew all about cultures, governmental systems, and their religions.

Ann's conclusion made her nauseous. She had been so focused on being a successful professor and respected researcher that she simply missed what was right in front of her. She missed the fact that religions were man-made. In most cases, they stemmed from combined belief systems with a few facts and a lot of fiction in the mix. All designed for humans to govern over humans. A hierarchy for society and cultures.

Ann had completed interviews with eleven of the twelve names on her list over the past several weekends. She was exhausted. One more meeting with a local North Texas-based evangelical, and she'd be done. After that, she and Shelton would have to figure out the next step.

Friday at midday, Ann climbed aboard the private jet and headed west. The Reverend Steve Chapman met her in the lobby of the Three Forks Church just after two thirty in the afternoon.

Ann had chosen Chapman after reading his biography and using one of Shelton's colleagues in the intelligence community to dig deeper. The preacher's associations with a variety of churches and religions made him an interesting prospect. She was eager to learn about why he had disassociated himself with other groups and formed his own church.

Chapman had been a senior clergyman with one of the world's most popular religions at a very young age. It was a long shot, but he was a statistical anomaly. Outliers always had interesting stories. Something had motivated him to change course. Just like Professor Schwartz.

Chapman's church had been up and running for eleven years. Over three hundred people from throughout the Dallas and Fort Worth area were members. The medium-size tan metal building sat back in a grove of trees just off Pipeline Road. A slight color difference in the metal panels suggested they had expanded the original building as the membership increased. The parking lot was freshly paved. The inside of the building was modern, clean, and orderly, just like the exterior. The flowers in the garden were newly planted. If you didn't know you were fifteen minutes from one of the largest airports in the world, you would think you were at a rural church in a quiet, small Texas town.

Chapman invited Ann into the sanctuary. They sat down on the soft blue fabric of cushioned chairs in the front row. Ann took a moment to refresh the preacher on the reason for the meeting, her background, and research. Chapman's aging skin and expressionless face said he was less than excited by the topic.

Ann started off wading through the standard opening questions as she had with the other interviewees. Can you walk me through the history of the trinity? How it came about? Why is it significant to Christianity and your church?

Unlike the others that chose not to spend time explaining concepts to a professor, Chapman methodically made his way through the detailed history of the topic. He explained the Council of Nicaea and how the notion of the Father, Son, and Holy Spirit, all equal, became a solidified notion in the decades following the Council. From his point of view, the Trinitarian concept exists today much as it did after Nicaea. They did not fully reconcile it with the religious leaders of the time. They simply needed a unified view to help govern the pagan Roman state after their attempts at killing religion failed.

"That's why the question confounds most preachers," concluded Chapman. "They simply cannot explain it rationally to a layperson."

Ann was impressed by the preacher's candor and objective reasoning. His thoughtfulness and carefully chosen words reminded her of an academic.

"Why couldn't they collectively confirm the doctrine?" pried Ann.

Chapman simply replied, "The principle has no basis in fact. There is no support for the concept in the accurate translations of the Hebrew or Greek writings. Triune gods are pagan."

Chapman had impressively and successfully recited what anyone could read in any encyclopedia or reference source.

"So, what you are describing is the convergence of political expediency and religion?" Ann asked.

"Essentially," Chapman replied.

"Keep in mind, Professor, it was the Roman Empire that brought Jerusalem to ruin in 70 CE. Rome! Pagan Rome!" Chapman said. "Roman leaders tolerated almost any sort of social practice, moral or immoral, as long as the people would pay taxes and share in worship of the emperor. Emperor worship was an important factor in uniting the empire," he continued. "One person decides all. Political expediency, as you call it. But when a culture and its belief system, such as the Christian religion, became too big, the politicians brought them into the tent. A larger tax base to fund their country is important. To a politician, accepting the unseemly is cheaper than funding a war."

Ann glanced at her watch.

"What do you think about the interaction between political governments and religious governments in today's world?" she asked, diverging from her script.

Chapman paused and continued to look her with tight lips and a narrowed stare.

"Perhaps we are getting to the reason for your visit, Professor Baker? You surely did not come all the way from Virginia just to speak to a minor-league Texas preacher about a well-known concept?"

"You would be surprised what a college professor would do to earn a few bucks," Ann replied with a smile.

Chapman's expression loosened. He almost smiled at the comment.

"Professor, I would offer you this thought. The behaviors and actions that Roman emperors took to govern, the compromises that religious leaders made to advance their organizations, those dynamics are still alive and well in the world today. More so now than ever before."

"Say more," Ann encouraged.

"These things we are talking about are happening today. As we speak. Just as Jerusalem was destroyed because of their misdeeds, there may well be an end to the cultural and societal organizations of today. The only question might be, is when and how the end will come."

"Let's slow down for a moment, Mr. Chapman," Ann said preferring not to address him using a clerical title.

The pastor stood to stretch his legs.

"I'm not completely following you," Ann said.

"You seem sincere, Professor," Chapman said, turning to face Ann. "Today, the religious organizations are mainly academic. They debate, what is the nature of good? How does the Holy Spirit work? What is the responsibility of Christian religions in the modern world? Marry you, bury you, and farewell," he quipped. "All these questions evolve around philosophy, different perspectives, and ideas. They make no decisions. No dogma is revised materially. The status quo always remains. Maintaining the cultural status quo in a rapidly advancing scientific world, that is the most important outcome."

Ann could see the passion flowing through Chapman now. A person with this passion and knowledge could never tolerate the establishment.

"It is not about serving and obeying a God," Chapman continued. "It's about compliance to man-made concepts. By the way, you don't maintain the status quo by osmosis. You need organizations that are aligned. Resources. Action. Reinforcement. People doing things. It is all happening now in front of us. It is not some heavenly activity that we cannot see. The leader has a goal and a strategy. A leader with a plan and an organization to execute the plan. Religious organizations doing things to accomplish the pieces of the plan. Plans are going well and working. Plans implemented poorly fail. They recruit people, people are fired, and they kill people. Internal conflicts among governments and religious leaders. No one really cares. It doesn't bleed, so it is not front-page news. It's in the background. It's in the hallways and the alleys of governments and religions. They carry it out in the side rooms out of sight. It is politically incorrect to challenge someone's culture, beliefs, or doctrine. The loosening of norms and values gives the establishment great autonomy. Greater autonomy in the hands of the wrong people is very dangerous."

Ann's expression was one of relief when Chapman stopped talking. She checked the time on her watch.

"How is your church different?" she asked, moving on.

Chapman described his approach as simple and fundamental. "Humans are physical and spiritual. People have an innate need to connect with their origins and other like-minded humans. No matter the experiences in life, people desire these connections. Humans can comprehend the vastness of the universe we live in and its creation. They seek to know how it all works. They wonder how it was created. Some people lose themselves in trying to answer these questions. Some simply accept the world as it is, knowing that nothing as complex as the human body or the vastness of the universe happens by accident or coincidence. Intelligence is in the mix somewhere."

Chapman built his church focused on living with integrity and treating each other with respect as human beings, regardless of where you come from, your circumstances, or what you look like. His church has no borders or alliances. In the end, Chapman believed that good prevails and evil fails. It was a message others gravitated to.

"What are you running from, Mr. Chapman?" Ann said, staring intently into the man's soul.

The faint sound of a distant train horn penetrated the metal walls and broke the silence of the sanctuary.

"You were a high-ranking administrator. You were personal friends with popes and others. You tried other religions. The inner circle of some of the most prestigious organizations in the world welcomed you. But those didn't work for you. So, here you are. Just hiding out in Texas. What are you hiding from?" Ann repeated.

The conciliatory look on Chapman's face said she was right. He sighed and took a deep breath.

"I'm not running from anyone or anything, Professor. I'm simply trying to find my way through life, just like everyone else in the world. Yes, I walked out of my post at the Vatican. I resigned from other organizations as well."

"Why?" she repeated. "What was so bad that Steven Chapman couldn't stand it?"

"The organizations I have been associated with previously don't resemble spiritual organizations internally. They are political organizations. Period," he concluded.

This time, Ann took the deep breath.

"Have you ever seen an evil spirit or had a paranormal experience?"

Chapman raised his eyebrows, appearing perplexed by the question.

"Well look," Ann said. "You talk about here and now. I was just wondering if you had ever seen any visible signs of the conflict at hand between good and evil."

Chapman's stare narrowed. Ann noticed the look of concern on his face.

"I mean no disrespect, Mr. Chapman, but you have, as you say, a "rational view" of the current situation. Your conclusions mean that governments and religions are misleading people. That would make them antagonistic. You are looking for the truth about matters. That would make you an enemy of the state, would it not? I imagine many of your former organizations might like to see you eliminated. Especially with your knowledge."

"Professor, I am afraid we need to wrap things up. I really need to get on with my day."

"But you didn't answer my question," Ann said. "I did not come here to be put off."

"Professor," Chapman interrupted, "we are a small church. We do not pose a threat to anyone or anything."

"I disagree," Ann replied adamantly. "Three hundred people turn to three thousand becomes three hundred thousand becomes...? Well, you see what I am saying. Especially if you are the good guy and the good wins."

Chapman sat down without saying a word.

"I need your help, Mr. Chapman," Ann whispered. "I have a client who is in deep trouble. He sees spirits. Evil spirits. Real-life nonhuman creatures. I have seen them as well. We are involved in the here and now conflict. We need answers. I need answers."

Ann took a breath.

"Demons attacked my client in Buenos Aires and again in Jerusalem. I was there in Israel. I saw it happen. He killed the attacking creatures with their own weapons."

Chapman slowly looked around the room and back at Ann, then sighed.

"I am sorry about Professor Schwartz. I knew him well," Chapman said.

"You knew him?" Ann asked with a stunned look on her face. *How would a small-town preacher in Texas know Schwartz?*

"He was a colleague of mine when I was younger. What happened to him?"

Ann's open mouth and a look of disbelief came across her face.

"A seven-fucking-foot-tall demon nailed him to a fireplace mantel with a saber," Ann replied, glaring at Chapman. "Get the picture? And how did the news of his death reach your ears?"

"Did Schwartz give you a green book?" Chapman asked calmly, ignoring Baker's inquiry.

"He didn't give it to us. I grabbed it as I was running for my life out the door," Ann said as she pulled the book out of her satchel.

"I see," Chapman said. "Professor Baker, I do not need my name showing up in any research or news article on this topic. Do you understand?"

"Of course I understand," Ann replied. "I'm not a goddamn reporter. I have no desire to disclose any of this conversation. I need your help, not your head on a platter."

Chapman hesitated for a more few seconds. Ann watched as her interviewee processed his thoughts. There were only a few people on the planet aware of the green book. And here Ann Baker was sitting in Chapman's church waving it around.

"There is an organization run by a person named Charles Edwards. Charles is also a former colleague of mine. He also knew Schwartz. He may be able to help." Chapman took out a pen and wrote a phone number on the back of his business card.

"What does this organization do?"

"Edwards will have to provide that information. Call him. Let him know I sent you. He will have to take it from there. I am just a small-town preacher," Chapman said with a contrived southern accent and a slight smile.

Ann walked out into the sunlight and climbed into the back of the black Mercedes. She opened her notebook and put a star beside number twelve on the list, then picked up her phone and pushed the dial button.

CHAPTER EIGHTEEN

SHELTON WAS UP early and on his way out of the city. By eight o'clock he was across the George Washington Bridge headed west across the New Jersey countryside. He reached down and reclined the seat back slightly and sipped the steaming cup of hot coffee.

Shelton was in the best shape of his life. For the past weeks, he had been training relentlessly. Mostly to relieve stress while Ann was doing her work. A few weeks in the icy Atlantic waters off Virginia Beach beside a group of new naval recruits did the trick. The squadron officers welcomed the alumnus with open arms. They were always happy to provide remedial training to a senior officer.

Shelton's nine-month relationship with Carson was now officially over. He had planned on having the difficult discussion with her before going to Virginia. Somehow, he had missed the signs of her dissatisfaction. She ended it before he could. The long list of grievances she had collected helped her conclude there was no future with Thomas Shelton.

As Shelton checked his rear-view mirror, a smile washed across his face. He was not being followed. His disciplined routine of surveilling his residence had discovered Detective Rawson watching him. His investment in high-tech gear had paid off. A satisfying feeling. Now he needed to figure out what this detective was up to. Why did she suddenly show up and start watching him out of the blue?

Shelton's plan to find his true purpose was taking shape. Steph Cunningham was settled in and in full control of Shelton's duties at Lambert. It turned out that Herb was not happy with Shelton's decision to take a leave of absence. Shelton bluntly reminded his boss that without him, Lambert would still be another small boutique Wall Street firm scrounging for quarterly retainers to help keep the lights on. Shelton had made Herb and his family very wealthy and didn't mind giving Herb a reminder from time to time.

Ben Davis was on sabbatical from his head of security role at Lambert and working with the CIA boss. Shelton had put a call into Admiral Woods asking him to see what he could learn about Walker's assignment. Woods wasn't aware of any such operation but was going to keep his ears open.

Heather Kersting was president and part owner of Lookout Point Ranch, formerly known as the Shelton Estate, just outside of Leesburg. Angie and Daniel were settling into their new jobs there and doing well.

The handheld GPS beeped again and announced, "turn right in one mile." Shelton made the turn onto the freshly paved one-lane road. As he rounded the first tree-lined curve, the road widened into two lanes. Several more curves through the woods and he arrived at a security checkpoint.

The size of the security building was impressive. The new two-story, modern-looking structure was enormous enough to house a small police department. Four unarmed guards stepped out of the door in formation. Two took up position on opposite sides of the car while one stood directly in front, staring at Shelton. The fourth guard approached the car and greeted him.

The officer methodically checked Shelton's identification, glancing back and forth from the credentials to Shelton's face. A green light lit up on the officer's handheld device. The facial recognition program had confirmed the person driving the car was Thomas Shelton.

Shelton followed the road another half mile, then parked in one of the visitor parking spaces in front of a new modern office building. Ann Baker was waiting for him on the front steps. The brushed brass engraved sign on one of the building's white columns read The Providence Institute.

Ann had done her due diligence on Providence. The research turned up nothing remarkable. It was a nonprofit focused on helping private foundations target and allocate resources to areas of need around the globe. The institute had contracts with the varying branches of the US federal government, including the intelligence agencies. There was also information that suggested connections to international agencies. But nothing specific.

The dossier Ann assembled on Providence's leader was much more interesting. The head of the institute was a man named Charles Edwards. Edwards was in his early seventies. He was a graduate of Cornell Law and had a Master's in Religious Studies. He had begun his practice as a criminal defense attorney in Washington, DC, then switched his focus to constitutional law and went back to school to get his doctorate.

According to the dossier, Edwards found his niche in the space between constitutional law and religion. He worked his way up to being one of the top attorneys in the United States on the subject. He had argued several cases before the Supreme Court and prevailed.

Turns out Edwards, while steeped in religious knowledge, was not a personal subscriber. Somewhere in reconciling the fact and fiction embedded in the various dogmas, he had met a younger theologian named Chapman who seemed to have sorted it out. Interested in expanding a more fundamental kind of spiritual existence, he and several partners, including Reverend Steve Chapman, formed the Providence Institute. At one point, Professor Schwartz was involved. Several years later, the institute had attracted more interest than the founders had envisioned. Chapman resigned and moved on.

Edwards was in his mid-fifties when the organization was large enough to require his full-time attention. Now he was one of seven members of the PI leadership. Each member had equal authority, and each was assigned a unique area of leadership responsibility. Edwards handled legal affairs and public relations. He was also the figurehead for the organization and the president of the record.

The call to Edwards from Professor Ann Baker several weeks ago piqued his interest. The follow-up call from Chapman cinched the meeting.

Over the past several weeks, Ann and Charles Edwards had been discussing and sharing information with each other about the attacks and Tom Shelton's situation. Edwards and his team had been working full-time on the topic. Now it was time for a face-to-face meeting.

Shelton climbed out of the car. Ann gave him a wide smile from the top of the steps.

"Good morning, Professor Baker," Shelton said as he reached the top of the stairs. He opened his arms and gave her a warm hug. "How are you?" he whispered in her ear.

Ann's dash of perfume drifted up from her neck, catching Shelton's senses.

"You're in a good mood this morning," Ann said, looking at him sideways.

"Some days are better than others," he replied, appearing relaxed. "The morning drive and the fresh air were nice."

Ann smiled slightly, catching a hint of his smell.

"How am I? I don't really know," she answered. "Anxious. Excited. Numb. Although it really is just another meeting. You know, one where we discuss why demons from hell killed my professor and are trying to kill my boss? But that's a pretty normal day hanging out with you."

Shelton's smile was big enough to show his perfect white teeth. "A sense of humor is good. So what is Edwards going to tell us?"

Ann raised her eyebrows slightly, glancing at her watch. "I wish I knew. I really…wish I knew."

She turned toward the door as Shelton opened it.

"After you, Professor." He motioned her inside.

❧

The attractive young woman in the outer office caught Shelton's attention. He observed her face as she offered him a fresh cup of coffee.

Shelton loved looking at a beautiful woman. A few minutes later, Shelton and Professor Baker were standing across the desk from Edwards.

"Mr. Shelton, it is nice to meet you," Edwards said, reaching out to shake his hand. "Thank you for making the trip. Please have a seat." He gestured to the chairs in front of his desk.

Shelton returned the greeting as he studied the slender gentleman behind the desk.

Edwards's warm pursed-lip smile and gentle demeanor projected a sense of ease. The lines in his face were only slightly carved, making him look younger than he was. His strong, distinct chin gave him a look of confidence and command.

"Mr. Shelton, first let me assure you that all, all of your information is secure in our hands," Edwards said. "I suspect as you learn more about our mission here at Providence, the more comfortable and convinced you will be about our commitment to our clients' privacy."

Shelton maintained eye contact with Edwards but showed no emotion. He could see Ann in his peripheral vision, looking pleasant and inquisitive.

Edwards cleared his throat and continued.

"Your associate, Professor Baker, has been very generous with her time and information. My colleagues and I have been researching and discussing your situation. Obviously, it is unique. But we think we can offer you some perspective."

"Thank you for your efforts. I look forward to hearing what you have to say," Shelton said, taking a sip of coffee.

"First, if you do not mind," continued Edwards, "I would like to provide you with some background of our organization."

Shelton nodded in agreement, having already read the information in the dossier.

Edwards described Providence as a research institute. A global research nonprofit organization focused on sociology. They studied human social and cultural organizations and interrelationships. The group's specific concentration was at the societal and global levels. They examined and sought to explain crime and law, poverty and wealth, prejudice and discrimination, schools and education, business firms, urban communities, and social movements. At the global level, they studied phenomena such as population growth and migration, war and peace, economic development, and religions.

According to Edwards, Providence had some of the most skilled and reputable sociologist, psychologist, psychiatrist, theologian, economist, and net assessment brains on earth. He estimated the organization had six million people in over two hundred countries around the world. Inside that group, Providence had key experts among the associates. All of those experts' personal needs were taken care of so they could focus on the work. Their task was collecting information, analyzing and providing insights about the current situation in their respective countries. It was essentially a network of non-governmental, peaceful intelligence professionals, in Edwards's words. He suggested that Providence's effectiveness was many times more effective than governmental agencies.

"That seems a little presumptuous," Shelton said respectfully, challenging Edwards.

"I realize that may sound arrogant given your background and education, Mr. Shelton," replied Edwards. "However, we frequently know about governmental strategies, decisions, and actions before others. For example, when the President of the United States was evaluating whether to launch the mission to kill Saad Ashour, we already had the intelligence of the mission and pictures of the target," Edwards said. "In fact, nine years earlier we watched the US-funded Pakistani contractors build the compound that imprisoned Ashour until he was captured and killed. You get the picture, Mr. Shelton?" Edwards asked.

Shelton knew all about the compound and the prisoner Edwards was referring to. Shelton's active-duty special ops unit made the initial capture of Ashour in the Afghan mountains twelve days after the terrorist attacks on US soil. Several years later, his team delivered the target from a US military prison to the Pakistani compound on a dark, cloudy winter night. Edwards had no idea Shelton was involved.

"We also educate and support people doing research for their own accord. It is an expanded role we've taken on. Above all else, we seek good and invest in what is right. We are peaceful and spiritual people, Mr. Shelton."

"Mr. Edwards," Shelton said.

"Charles, please," Edwards requested.

Shelton lowered his head slightly in acknowledgment.

"How do you fund such a large endeavor?" Shelton asked.

"A private benefactor backstops the entire operation," Edwards said without blinking.

Shelton raised his eyebrows and didn't seem interested in pursuing the topic.

"Well, Charles, there lies the problem. I am not a spiritual man," Shelton said bluntly. "I have seen what so-called good, upstanding "spiritual" people do to each other. I have no use for any of it."

Edwards tactfully navigated his way out of a philosophical discussion about the difference between being spiritual and practicing a religion, so as to get on with the heart of the matter. He opened his top desk drawer and removed what looked like a diploma cover made from sheep hide.

Edwards told Shelton a story about a colleague who disappeared twenty years ago while traveling in the Golan Heights. They thought he had died or been killed.

"You can imagine my surprise when my colleague showed up at the office one evening," Edwards said. "Turns out, while hiking in the desert, a small group of people had captured him. The price for his freedom was to bring this manuscript to me." Edwards pointed to the sheep hide. "My instructions were to stay awake and on watch. I would know the right time and how to use this writing."

Edwards pushed the sheepskin across the table to Shelton.

Ann leaned toward Shelton to get a better look. Shelton stared at the document cover for a moment, examining the front cover and the binding. Inside was a piece of paper carefully stitched to the silk lining of the hide. The handwritten words were in some form of Hebrew. Shelton raised his head slightly, looking to meet Ann's gaze.

"Can you read it?" Edwards asked.

Shelton looked toward Edwards without turning his head. Then he shifted his eyes to the words on the parchment.

"It looks to be in Hebrew. I cannot read the language," Shelton answered.

Shelton watched in silence as Edwards gave him a questioning look. Edwards obviously expected a different answer.

"Very well, Mr. Shelton," Edwards said. "I think that is enough for today. We'll keep working on things here. Let's touch base next week." Edwards stood and extended his hand to Shelton.

❧

Ann and Shelton made their way down the steps and climbed into Shelton's car without talking. Shelton slowly navigated the vehicle around the curves of Providence with a contemplative expression on his face. He turned out of Providence and onto the county road and sped up.

A few miles ahead, Shelton pulled off the road into a road-side park. He walked to the observation point and looked out over the green hills of Pennsylvania.

Ann walked up beside him and gently touched his arm.

"Are you okay?"

Shelton turned.

"'The great adversary has been thrown down into the world, misleading the entire inhabited earth; and his angels were hurled down with him. To the ones in the heavens and you who live in them, be happy. Woe for the earth and for the sea because the dragon has come down to you, having great anger, knowing he has a short period.'"

Ann's mouth opened in surprise as she heard the words.

"You could read it!" she replied in a quiet but surprised tone.

Shelton raised his eyebrows slightly, confirming her statement.

"It's just a scripture from Revelations in the Christian writings," Shelton said in a matter-of-fact tone. "The second paragraph was more interesting."

Ann stared at him, waiting as the late-morning sunlight broke through between the clouds and glistened off the trees in the green valley below.

"'To the one standing in the sun who can read these words and can see these evil angels, be on guard. Their lord of the earth knows you and you know him.'"

CHAPTER NINETEEN

AMIR SAT QUIETLY just outside the gate area at Los Angeles International Airport. The thin, small-stature man sat waiting to board the flight to Tokyo. He had made the trip from Argentina to Colorado and hand delivered the meeting invitation to Shelton's Colorado estate, as instructed by the Principal in Abdel Kinneret. Then he made the flight from Colorado to Los Angeles.

Amir looked straight ahead as people moved about in front of him. Most were staring down at their mobile phones, oblivious to the surrounding environment. Others seemed more like him. Observers.

Each time a person looked up from their device long enough to glimpse Amir, they would do a double take. Even the most preoccupied person noticed something striking about him, then looked again.

Amir's skin was a perfectly even olive color. There were no imperfections or blemishes. No signs of aging. The combination of the uniform tone of his flesh, dark even-colored hair, and light blue eyes was striking.

Amir could see at night as well as he could see during daylight. His distance vision was at least three times that of a human. Amir was not human. He was an immortal in human form. A connection between humans and the spiritual realm. One of the last two roaming the earth freely.

The night Shelton killed the guardians had sent panic through the ranks of the spirit world. Amir assumed that Buenos Aires was no longer safe for Shelton. He was concerned that the guardians might have watched Shelton exit his glass shop. His calm, peaceful existence in South America had vanished with the swing of Shelton's saber. Although the spirits had no knowledge of Amir or who he was, he knew he was now at risk of being seen and attacked by the guardians. Amir was not a warrior. He was simply a liaison with a job to do.

Now Malaysia was Amir's destination. The country was a relatively eclectic mix of people. A mix that would represent safety for him and Shelton. A country where Indigenous, Chinese, and Indian nationalities created a melting pot. There was no information from Kinneret about guardians being present in the Southeast Asian region. So that is where he headed.

⌘

The customized Airbus A320 jet lifted off just before eight o'clock in the morning from Colorado's Pitkin County Airport. Detective Rawson took her last pictures as the passengers walked up the stairs and into the airplane. She watched helplessly as the airplane sped down the runway, then ascended into the clear blue morning sky.

Yesterday, she had tailed Shelton and Ann from his New York residence to a regional airport north of New York City. Her connection at the Federal Aviation Administration had supplied her with the destination of the flight. She boarded the first flight to Colorado, hoping to get there to resume her surveillance.

Remington was a small town in the mountains. Despite her best efforts, she had been unsuccessful at finding Shelton. As a last resort, she staked out his airplane.

Sipping her morning coffee while sitting in the rental car, Rawson saw the aircraft's lights come on. She dialed her connection at the FAA. No one answered. The frustration showed on her face. The world's most prolific suspected serial killer was about to board the airplane right in front of her, and there was nothing she could do.

Shelton watched the tarmac of the Pitkin County Airport disappear below. The person with a camera standing beside the car in the parking lot looked familiar. He turned his head back as the aircraft sped past to get another look. For a second, they made eye contact.

"What are you smiling about?" Ann asked in a warm voice.

"The mountains are beautiful. I love being here," Shelton answered, turning his head to look at her. It had been his idea to get out of New York for a while. He needed space after the experience at Providence.

A day earlier, a letter arrived at Shelton's Colorado ranch. Amir had been made aware by the Kinneret Principal of Shelton's destination. The letter requested a meeting. A meeting in Malaysia, half a world away. Shelton and Ann had debated whether to go. The fact was, they had no better option, and Amir seemed to be the closest connection to the other realm.

The flight to Kuala Lumpur would take just over fourteen hours. A distance the large jet could do nonstop.

Ann was getting used to private air travel. Her usual seat was on the left side of the cabin across from Shelton. She moved about the airplane with confidence. She was now on a first-name basis with the flight crews and stewards. They made a special effort to have on board all the items Professor Ann Baker preferred. Her favorite snacks, wine, and menu items were in the pantry. Her preferred shampoo, conditioner, and body lotions were all available in her private bath toward the back of the aircraft.

As they headed out over the Pacific Ocean, Shelton retired to his bedroom to rest. A long nap would have him ready for the early afternoon arrival and meeting. He changed into his flannel bottoms, laid back on the bed, and rested. The cool air from the conditioner drifted down, settling on his shirtless torso. He stared at the ceiling, knowing he had yet to provide full disclosure to Ann and Charles Edwards.

They knew nothing about the preacher he had killed that started all of this. He'd killed the preacher's assistant out of anger. They didn't know that killing the preacher and his assistant were the firsts, but far from the last. They didn't know that he could see the evil inside of people. More accurately, he could see people with no soul. He could easily identify them. They had no faces. He looked at these people but saw emptiness. They were living bodies with no chance of finding their way back to humanity. People that were so corrupted, there was no hope of recovery. When he would see one, he felt compelled to eliminate them. It was an instinct. If Ann knew the complete story, she would only see a murderer. An indiscriminate killer. Edwards might be more circumspect. Bigger picture. Assuming there was a big picture.

An hour before landing, the lead steward tapped on Ann's bedroom door and then Shelton's. Shelton was waiting for Ann at the dining room table sipping a cup of coffee when she arrived.

"Good morning, Ann," Shelton said in a warm friendly voice.

"Good morning, your highness," Ann quipped as she sat down at the table.

Shelton picked up on the humor and smiled slightly.

"Well, I am just saying, I don't think king's travel this well. I'm getting spoiled, you know."

Shelton lifted and lowered his eyebrows slightly at the comment. Then a contemplative look appeared on his face. He was very aware of the excesses that filled his life. Multiple expensive homes, cars, and a small fleet of private jets. Conveniences that were enjoyable and efficient at the moment but not required for happiness in life. He would rather know what his purpose in life was and be with Angie in a small town somewhere in the mountains.

"Did you rest well?" Shelton asked.

"Surprisingly well," Ann replied. "The combination of the morning workout and the wine at lunch helped. Normally, I can't sleep at all on airplanes. How about you? Did you get some rest?"

"My little pills helped. I'm still groggy. But I feel good enough."

"You know you really shouldn't take those things too often. Those little pills can be addictive," Ann said.

"That's what the doc says too. I'm not sure I care, really." He looked up at the television monitor.

The live camera feed from the tail of the airplane showed a bird's-eye view of the aircraft as it descended through the moisture layer of clouds on their final approach to Kuala Lumpur International.

The aircraft slowed as the flaps extended and the landing gear lowered. A few minutes later, the plane touched down on the runway. The engines revved slightly as they taxied toward the private terminal where a black Mercedes was waiting for the passengers of tail number NEGL1. The air traffic controllers pronounced it Eagle One.

The size of the private aircraft, along with the Eagle One call sign, usually attracted the attention of local airport personnel and aviators. Today was no different. Observers and officials at the airport were wondering who was on board such an extravagant airplane with such a call sign.

The customs officials didn't waste any time boarding the aircraft. They worked their way through the passenger manifest, checking passports, starting with the crew. Shelton was the last person the senior customs agent greeted. As Ann moved aside, Shelton peered down at the agent.

"Passport please," the agent requested in a demanding tone.

Shelton handed the man his document. The agent studied the US passport and then glanced back and forth from the document picture to Shelton's face.

"Do you have anything to declare?"

"No," Shelton replied.

"Mr. Shelton, what is your reason for coming to Malaysia?"

"I am visiting a friend."

"What is your friend's name?" the agent asked as he scribbled notes in his pocket notebook.

"The Honorable Mohammed Alanzawour," Shelton replied. "The Malaysian Minister of Finance."

The agent's demeanor changed immediately.

"Very well, sir," replied the agent. "Thank you, sir."

It had been three years since Shelton had visited the country. He knew Alan Mohammed well. One text message and Alan had arranged the visit. No questions asked. It was clear the message hadn't flowed down to the customs office.

Regardless, Shelton could tell Alan was thrilled to have such a distinguished guest back in his country. Even if it was for personal business. The minister could report the visit to the prime minister. Shelton also assumed it meant government agents would follow him. If not physically, then by the network of cameras deployed throughout the city. The Malaysian government had the most thorough and sophisticated civilian surveillance program in the world after the Israelis.

The short drive from the airport to the hotel was quiet. Shelton watched as Ann looked out her window. The dense trees and vegetation alongside the freeway represented the entire landscape of the equatorial country. Cities and villages had been carved out of the jungles many centuries before. Occasionally, a human-made opening in the trees provided a deeper look into the rolling landscape and dense forests that stretched for miles on end. Where humans had stopped maintaining the deforesting, nature quickly retook control of the space and land.

As they entered the city, the view outside the car window changed. The dense jungle was replaced by dense dwellings and shops. Small residences, stores, and shops jammed against one another. Many stacked on top of each other. The stores were on the ground level and a residence on the higher levels. Aging, faded, multicolored exteriors and crumbling poverty-stricken housing projects were no match for the year-round 100 percent humidity. Every day, the earth worked to undo what humans had built in the region. The colorful chaos extended for miles and miles on the outskirts of Kuala Lumpur.

The main metropolitan area of the city, however, was stunning. A modern, clean, high-tech city by any standard. High-rise buildings set the skyline anchored by the twin Petronas Towers and Sky Bridge.

The car pulled into the circle drive of the Palmdale Resort's more exclusive wing, then stopped. Before exiting, Shelton surveyed the area and the people. Nothing looked out of place. No guardians. He counted at least seven cameras with microphones.

Shelton and Ann casually made their way to the front desk located just inside the front door. They checked in and set their bags in the two-bedroom suite, then headed back down to the lobby for tea and a light snack.

Alan's text arrived just as Shelton sat down at the small table.

"Welcome to Malaysia! Please sir, let me know if you need anything, Mr. Shelton. We will be happy to accommodate you."

Ann and Shelton were at a table on the terrace just outside the hotel's main lobby. The large-leafed plants and gentle sound of running water from the garden stream created a relaxed environment. Shelton sat back in his chair and sipped the hot tea. He blinked slowly, taking in the relaxing sensation of the hot liquid, soothing sounds, and the damp heavy air.

A voice from behind broke the silence. "Excuse me. May I join you?"

Shelton had spotted Amir approaching from the garden walkway.

"Hello, Amir," Shelton said, standing to greet him and bowing slightly to show respect.

"Good morning, Mr. Shelton," said Amir. "It is nice to see you again, sir."

"Thank you." Shelton offered him a slight smile.

Amir nodded slightly.

"You did well," Amir said, referring to the attack in Buenos Aires.

Amir then turned and introduced himself to Ann before taking a seat next to Shelton.

"How was your flight?" Amir asked.

"Uneventful, and long," Shelton said. "And yours?"

"Well, I don't fly much," replied Amir. "So, I must say it was rather exhausting. I think I will fly first class from now on."

"When did you arrive?"

"Last evening," said Amir. "I was able to get a good night's rest. I feel quite fine today, all things considered."

Shelton listened as Amir and Ann exchanged pleasantries. Amir described himself as a glassmaker and psychologist. His passion was helping people work through life's challenges. Ann glanced over at Shelton as the conversation waned.

"What is so important that it required us to meet half a world away?" Shelton finally asked, his tone friendly. "You could have just knocked on the door in Colorado and saved us both a lot of time."

Amir hesitated. "Perhaps you and I could take a walk, Mr. Shelton, to discuss business."

"We can discuss anything we need to among us. Professor Baker is fully aware of our previous discussions," Shelton said.

"I see. Very well," replied Amir. "Shall we all take a walk?"

Amir understood that the Malaysian government was notorious for eavesdropping on private citizens. Especially in pleasant hotels where businesspersons, government officials, and diplomats frequented.

The three casually strolled down the garden pathway, away from the main building. Each looked about the garden, seeming to enjoy the flowers and greenery. The slight sound of the cars passing by on a distant roadway made its way through the ficus trees and ferns. Amir stopped beside a small waterfall. He methodically looked around the garden, checking to see if anyone was watching or listening from the shadows. Shelton stood there, continuing to be impressed while Amir performed his reconnaissance.

"Mr. Shelton, I have instructions for you," Amir said.

Shelton looked up with interest.

"You are to go to Jerusalem. Specifically, to Gethsemane. There is a garden there. You are to stay there until given additional instructions. You are not to step foot out of the garden until instructed. You will be safe there."

Shelton looked at Amir. Shelton's slightly narrowed stare and serious face persisted as he contemplated what he had just heard.

"What is the purpose of this?" Shelton asked, lowering the sound of his voice to almost a whisper.

"Mr. Shelton," said Amir, "it is perfectly understandable that you would desire additional information. Unfortunately, I have little else to offer you. I am no more than the messenger."

"Whose messenger are you?" Shelton asked. He glanced toward Ann to see if she was following the conversation.

"I'm sorry, Mr. Shelton. I cannot answer that question."

"Well, none of this makes any sense, Amir. The riddles. The lack of transparency from you and Macari. You both know more than you are telling me."

Amir gently held up his hand. Shelton took the signal and stopped speaking mid-sentence. Ann looked on.

"I understand your frustration," said Amir as he glanced toward Ann and then back at Shelton. "But your words surprise me, sir. You of all people know you are not a normal human being."

"Not a normal human?" Shelton turned and took a few steps away from Amir and Ann. He scratched his face as he contemplated the words. Then he slowly made his way back to Amir and faced him.

"How come you didn't tell me the guardians were going to kill me in Buenos Aires?" he demanded with a quiet but tense tone.

"With all due respect, sir, I strongly suggested you leave the city immediately following our discussion. I told you what to do and how to do it. You chose not to listen," rebutted Amir. "You made a poor decision."

Shelton glared at Amir.

Ann turned and took a few steps down the path away from the men to give them privacy.

"Who are you?" Shelton asked, returning to a normal tone while looking down at the shorter man.

"I'm your friend," said Amir. "I am here to help you."

Amir double checked to see where Ann was standing, then took one step closer to Shelton and whispered, "The events in Buenos Aires have sped up everything. You must go to the garden. Stay there until I come to you. There is no time to waste."

Shelton stood there, his face emotionless, looking at Amir.

"If you ignore my instructions, Mr. Shelton, you'll regret it."

CHAPTER TWENTY

CARDINAL FERNANDO BIANCO entered the meeting hall from the side door of the secret conference room. The conversation among the others in the room fell silent. The sixty-two-year-old priest took his place at the head of the table. Bianco's graying, still noticeably auburn head of hair fit neatly under the scarlet zucchetto.

The church's seven most senior cardinals lined both sides of the table, each having governance responsibility for one of the world's continents. A role that made them some of the most powerful men on earth. Not because of their wealth but because of their ability to influence powerful and wealthy people.

The cardinals sat quietly, looking down at the table, waiting for Bianco to speak. At exactly two o'clock in the morning, Bianco opened his notebook, took a deep breath, then looked up, moving his stare down one side of the table, then the other.

"My brothers, I have just come from a meeting with his Holy Father and the adviser. The news is encouraging. We will soon see the vision of the popes and emperors. We will assume the role of the universal church. Soon we will play an even larger role within governments. Soon we will create a more dignified world."

Bianco paused with an emotionless mask on his face while he observed the faces of his colleagues.

"Imagine," he resumed, raising the volume of his voice, "non-Catholics will look up to us instead of down upon us as celibate pariah. We will rise! We will be respected!" His voice boomed even louder. "We will stand taller to lead the world into the future. We will muster the nonbelievers and the unfaithful. If they don't comply, they will pay the ultimate price. They will listen, respond to our teachings, and become a part of our faith. Else, their fate will be their own. The blood from their bodies on their hands, not ours."

Bianco lowered his volume yet grew more intense.

"This is the moment we have worked for." The ranking priest held up his open hand. "The glory of God will give us the power to rule over men and women for eternity. We will help them see the error of their ways. Then we will help them comply with the divine rules."

Bianco stretched his arms above his head with his hands made into fists.

"Can you feel the power rising? Can you? Can you feel it? This is our time," he exclaimed.

Applause filled the darkly lit chamber.

Bianco went around the room, one by one, asking for each cardinal's commitment to the church. Each time he looked deep into the face of his subject. Each time he looked for weakness.

Convinced his words had taken hold, Bianco took his leave.

"Fernando?" came a loud whisper that echoed off the stone walls as Bianco made his way toward his private quarters. The portly Bianco turned to see who it was. The tall, gray-haired European cardinal exited from the same room as Bianco and approached him.

"What the hell are you doing making statements like that from your official post? Are you trying to get us all killed?" Bianco was well known for making extravagant statements in an effort to appear in command. The cardinal's agreement with Bianco in camera, behind the scenes, was often polite not authentic.

"Relax, my friend," Bianco said calmly, placing his hand on the cardinal's shoulder. "His highness was just briefed by Dr. Hauser. Everything is happening. The apocalypse for the unrighteous will soon unfold. I will reward our dedication and faith. We must be prepared to lead our nations. We must be prepared to perfect our faith."

"Are you mad?" said the cardinal. This time in a quiet whisper. "The politicians will not allow that to happen. No one in that room knows how to make anything happen. You and I both know that. Before dawn, the leaders of every nation will know what you said. That is the only certainty."

Bianco looked down at the ground, then he looked back up, meeting the cardinal's gaze.

"There is a plan for the political system. I'm not sure we can really do anything about it," Bianco said. "All Hauser needs is for them to fire nuclear weapons at each other. We will take it from there."

"The Russians, the Chinese, Brits, and Americans are not that stupid," said the cardinal.

"Get your head on straight, father," Bianco ordered, looking sternly at his subordinate. "We can't change anything. You, of all people, need to be ready. Europe is where wars start and end. If anybody is alive afterward, we will pick up the pieces."

Less than thirty meters away on the other side of the thick stone wall, the black Mercedes sat idling in the darkness just outside the private entrance to the Apostolic Palace. The hot exhaust from the twin tailpipes slowly rose into the dense night air and disappeared. The doorman swung open the exterior door of the building and Dr. Wolfgang Hauser stepped out of the residence. A tall, thin shape made its way beneath the covered walkway to the waiting car. The chauffeur opened the rear door of the vehicle. Hauser folded his lanky frame into the seat on the right side of the car. From the second floor of the residence, a face watched from the pope's bedroom window as Hauser's car pulled away, turned a corner, and disappeared from sight.

❧

The morning sun rose above the hilltop, beaming warm rays onto Shelton's face. He slowly turned his head to shield his eyes from the bright light and surveyed the surroundings as he blinked slowly, attempting to fully wake. He listened. The sound of his own slow-paced rhythmic breathing and that of a car horn in the distance was all he could hear. He lifted his head to complete his assessment. He was alone. There was no one in sight.

Shelton and Ann departed Kuala Lumpur immediately after the meeting with Amir. The partners agreed Shelton had no choice. He must follow Amir's instructions. There was no better idea on the table. No other path to follow.

Although, Edwards *had* presented the sheepskin to Shelton. That could have been an alternative path. If Shelton had been honest with Edwards and read the letter, what would have been Edwards's next step?

Shelton and Ann debated the issue. Ann's point of view prevailed. Regardless of what might have been Edwards's next best advice, all roads led to Amir.

It was crystal clear to her that Amir was not a complete product of the human species. His physical appearance hinted he was not a normal human. His dropping off the meeting request for Malaysia at Shelton's ranch mailbox, then disappearing in front of the security camera clinched it. Amir was guiding Shelton to his destiny.

Less than eight hours ago, Shelton and Ann had arrived in Tel Aviv. The car dropped Ann off at the hotel and the two said their goodbyes. Then Shelton headed for Jerusalem. Ann would be back on the private jet the next morning headed home after the pilots and crew got their required rest.

The car had dropped Shelton off in At-tur, a half mile from his destination. He made the short walk up a steep hill to the top of the Mount of Olives. In the darkness below him, on the other side of the walkway wall, was the oldest grove of olive trees on the planet. From the top of the hill, looking across the Kidron Valley, Shelton could see the lights of the old city of Jerusalem.

He did his reconnaissance in the surrounding area as he walked.

Convinced there were no cameras or people watching, he sat down on the top of the short rock wall and made the fifteen-foot drop into the garden.

Crouched, he had waited while his eyes adjusted to the darkness of the night. A few minutes later, the rocks, stones, and shapes of the trees were clearly visible. He worked his way to the Garden of Gethsemane, well away from the path of tourists, and found a tree with a broad canopy and sat down at the base. He laid down, resting his head on the small supply pack he carried. Within minutes, he had fallen asleep.

❧

Seven hours later the gentle breeze brushed against Shelton's face. The warm morning sunlight was fading in and out as clouds moved across the sky. The sound of distant thunder caught his attention. Without hesitating, he retrieved the rain tarp from his backpack and stretched it between the two trees. Just as he tied on the last knot, the clouds let loose.

The rain poured from the sky onto the eastern slope of Kidron Valley. Shelton sat on a rock beneath the cover. He watched as water drops hit the stones on the floor of the garden. Within minutes, the liquid was dancing across the tops of the rocks as it landed and began making its way down the hillside. The gray light from the now cloudy sky reflected off the water flowing toward the valley below. The garden floor looked as if it was in motion and moving down the hill.

Shelton spent the day and the next exploring the mountain and the garden. He moved about warm and dry underneath a rain poncho. The garden and olive trees stretched down the valley for over two miles. Hundreds of smaller groves bunched together, each creating its own secluded island in the middle of the rocky and arid landscape that overlooked the old city of Jerusalem.

Tourists came and went from public spaces of the mountain and the garden, most arriving and departing on large buses next to the Church of All Nations, a church that the Roman Catholics had built in the 1920s.

Mosaic images covered the front of the building. The exterior gables displayed an elaborate work of art depicting Yeshua as the mediator between God and humans. To his left, a throng of people in tears looked up to Yeshua for confidence. On his right, a group of powerful and wise people acknowledged the shortcomings of their might and learning. At the peak of the gable, two stags stood on either side of Yeshua. The stag on the right represented evil. The stag on the left represented good.

The interior of the church was dark and somber. The dark blue color of a star-filled night sky covered the ceilings and dome. In front of the large wooden Roman altar, was a flat outcrop of rock. A rock which tradition suggested was the "Rock of Agony," where Yeshua prayed two thousand years ago.

Hundreds of people streamed in and out of the shrine every day, taking pictures in front of the main doors and the gable. Some with tears flowing down their faces. Tears of happiness at walking upon such a holy place.

The reality was, prior to construction of the church in the 1920s, the site had been abandoned for hundreds of years. There was no fact-based record that anything ever happened at the location. Historians thought the location was the site of a Byzantine church in the eighth century before an unexpected earthquake destroyed it.

Shelton sat under a tree in the garden, watching the people come and go. He also witnessed hundreds of guardians move in and out of the church. Gray, black, and red robes. The spirits outnumbered the tourists. Each was oblivious to the other's presence. Each life form in its own world yet occupying the same space.

Amir had told Shelton that the guardians could not see inside the garden. They wouldn't be able to see or sense Shelton sitting just a few feet away.

As the days went by, Shelton's thinning, unshaven, and increasingly disheveled appearance was visible to tourists. He appeared to be a local garden regular. Just part of the landscape and experience. Occasionally, a tourist would take a picture of him sitting under the olive tree.

Unbeknownst to the guardians, Shelton filled his days sitting under the trees observing and making notes of the comings, goings, and behaviors of the robed beings. They moved freely and casually around the church property, coming and going with the energy and intellect of young people on a college campus.

One day bled into another. Shelton hadn't eaten in more than seven days. He was moving slower now, his focus and mental process less precise. Just before sunset, he returned to the lower garden. The tourists and the guardian numbers at the church were much less as the end of the day approached. The bright lights of an automobile caught his eye.

A black SUV stopped in front of the church. Cardinal Bianco emerged from the back seat. Shelton recognized the priest from his research following his meeting with Wilkinson at Davos.

Bianco stood on the sidewalk and adjusted his black robe and red sash. He glanced up at the stallions at the top of the mosaic, then made his way up the stairs and into the church.

Shelton stood from underneath the tree, grabbed his pack, and began making his way up the slope to the back of the church. He focused directly in front of himself, trying not to step across the boundary of the garden. He stopped beside an olive tree. From of the darkness of the garden, he watched the glass-lined corridor connecting the church with the office building behind it. A minute later, the cardinal appeared in the passage.

Shelton mustered all his energy and began sprinting up the hill to the side entrance of the building. Across the sidewalk, through the glass door, he saw Bianco standing in front of the elevators at the far end of the corridor. The elevator opened and Bianco stepped in, reached down to push a button, then the door closed.

Shelton watched as the lift indicator went past two and stopped at three. Going against the instructions Amir had given him, Shelton bolted across the sidewalk, out of the garden and into the building. He had to figure out what this priest was up to. Just inside the exterior door was the fire staircase. He made his way, slowly at first, listening, then at a full run up to the third floor.

Breathing heavily, Shelton opened the door slowly and peered down the dark corridor. He made his way toward the elevator. The sudden sound of voices surprised him. He stopped dead in his tracks. As the footsteps grew louder, Shelton slipped into a conference room and closed the door quietly behind him. On the other side of the room, through the windows, he could see Bianco standing in an office in the adjacent wing of the building. He removed the binoculars from his pack and turned the zoom dial until the cardinal was in perfect focus.

Two large guardians dressed in red flanked Bianco. He watched as the priest picked up the telephone and began speaking. The guardians stood watching. Bianco held the phone out as one guardian turned its head to listen, then Bianco placed the phone down. Shelton adjusted the focus. Now Bianco was staring directly at Shelton and pointing.

"Shit," Shelton said under his breath as he tossed the device in his pack and darted toward the door.

He descended the stairs as fast as his weakened legs could carry him and burst through the first-floor door into the corridor. He turned his head just in time to see the large red shapes racing toward him. Shelton sprinted for the exit.

His arms and legs were pumping and striding as fast as he could move now. He glanced back. His clenched jaw and stressed face said it all. He couldn't get to the exit before the guardians would catch him.

As he approached the exit, a blast of cold air rolled across the back of his neck. Chills rocketed down his spine. As his next foot touched the floor, he pushed off with all his strength and dove toward the floor, sliding off to the side of the corridor. As his back hit the wall, the momentum of the demons rocketed them forward. Both demons were glaring at him as they shot past and slammed into the outside doors.

The sound of breaking glass and splitting metal was deafening. Shelton buried his face into the floor and covered his head with his hands. The backflow shrapnel from the disintegrating doors pelted him as he heard the same decompression sounds he'd heard when killing his attackers in Buenos Aires. He looked up as the dusty remains of the high-ranking demons filled the air. In the dust and darkness, Shelton crawled out of the building, sprinted across the sidewalk, and disappeared into the garden.

The sleep-deprived Bianco sat in the main floor parlor of the French Chateau waiting for Dr. Wolfgang Hauser to arrive.

After hearing the breaking glass and chaos at the Church of All Nations offices, Bianco had wasted no time. He made the dash east to the Jordanian border. There, they smuggled him out of Israel. The same camel-mounted sheepherders that smuggled him into the country extracted him. The Israeli authorities had no official record of Bianco ever being there.

From Amman, Bianco flew to Cairo, where he switched aircraft. From Cairo, he stopped in Istanbul before landing in Copenhagen. Dressed as a civilian, he boarded public transportation to France. The journey had taken almost sixteen hours.

The French press was covering the breaking of the doors at the famous church in what was reported as a robbery. Bianco watched the report that showed Israeli authorities swarming the area. The tourist site was closed until further notice.

Bianco had failed. The one he was supposed to stop from entering the garden was already there.

❧

The sun was setting as Shelton sat on a stone fence overlooking a massive Jewish cemetery. Following the encounter at the church, he had made his way back to base camp in the dark. He spent the entire day sleeping under the shade of an olive tree, with a vague memory of a young Israeli policewoman trying to wake him up. She'd failed. Shelton had watched through his slightly cracked eyelids as the officer took pictures of him. Now he was awake and energized after a long rest.

As nightfall arrived, Shelton watched a line of guardians dressed in gold robes marching from a tomb down in the valley of the Silwan necropolis. The tomb was the most important resting place in ancient Judea. Silwan housed the highest-ranking officials in early-century Jerusalem and was outside the boundaries of the garden and off limits to Shelton.

Shelton repositioned and stood observing just inside the lower boundary of Gethsemane. The group of gold-dressed guardian marched across the valley in a single line to old Jerusalem. They took up watch from the top of the old city walls, looking out across the Kidron Valley toward the garden.

A second group surrounded the garden. Hundreds of them, about twenty feet apart, facing inward, looking into the garden. The guardian centuries walked back and forth, staring into the garden, looking for something or someone.

Shelton stood less than six feet away, observing one of the paranormal life forms. The gold-robed demons were at least eight feet tall. Their facial features and skin tones were similar to humans of varying races and ethnicities. They looked relativity normal, all except for the eyes.

"Good evening," said Amir.

The familiar voice from behind Shelton surprised him. He turned to face his visitor.

"Good evening," Shelton said in a quiet voice.

"You look better than I would have expected," Amir said, smiling slightly.

Shelton stared back.

"Their faces." Shelton pointed to one of the guardian centuries. "They are like yours."

"Maybe they are immortals," Amir said.

"Immortal? I have no doubt these giants are immortal," said Shelton.

"Don't concern yourself with them. We have other things to do"

"Other things?" Shelton said, lifting his hand to show the century guards. The enemy surrounded him.

"It seems you escaped with your life again last night," said Amir. "Now they know for certain you are here. Regardless, it is time to go. You are to leave the garden and make your way to the village of Abdel Kinneret."

Amir went on and detailed the location of the village for Shelton on a map.

"Exactly how am I going to get out of here?" Shelton asked.

Amir handed him a small bag of food and water.

"Wait until midnight. Then go down to the lower garden next to the church. When you are ready, step out of the garden and keep walking. Do not stop. Keep your head covered and look down. Do not make eye contact with anything or anyone. If you do, they will attack."

Amir gave Shelton instructions to keep walking until he was out of the city and into the desert. He assured him he would be safe there. A guardian's form of paranormal life didn't function well with the heat.

Shelton opened the bag and began taking small bits of the flatbread and sips of water.

"Just walk out of here? Just like that?" he said, chewing. "These things have been following me for two decades. They know how to find me. I hope you—"

Amir held up his hand.

"Your arrogance may have killed you," said Amir. "You were told to not leave the garden. You did. Now the centuries are on alert. Going past them is the only way out. If you stay here, you will die," Amir added in a definitive tone.

Shelton sat down on a rock, contemplating Amir's words.

"Thanks for the food, Amir." Shelton looked down at the ground in thought. "Thank you for helping me. If I don't make it, it's not your fault. It's mine."

"Open your mind, Thomas," Amir said warmly. "What you see in front of you, all of this"—Amir raised both arms into the air— "is but a fraction of existence and life. Finish the journey. Do what you do. You'll never be sorry. Just follow my instructions this time."

Shelton lifted his head. Then he glanced at his watch, checking the time. He then placed the food in his pack, swung it onto his shoulders, and pulled the hood from his coat tightly over his head. He stepped toward Amir and placed both hands on his friend's shoulders. Without saying a word, Shelton nodded slightly as if to acknowledge Amir's ultimate words to follow the instructions. Then he turned and began making his way toward the church.

CHAPTER TWENTY-ONE

IT HAD BEEN four days since Shelton had departed Gethsemane. The food rations Amir had given him lasted two. The pain from hunger had come and gone. His body was now consuming energy from his muscles in order to function. His strength slowly declining as he made the trek through the desert from Jerusalem to Kinneret.

The afternoon of the fourth day the sun broke past the southern wall of the rock overhang and directly onto the sleeping Shelton's face. His eyelids opened without moving another muscle of his lean 195-pound body. He looked around to survey his surroundings. The wind had shifted from a southerly breeze to a northerly one while he slept. He tried to relax as the cooler air brushed across his skin.

After a few minutes, Shelton looked at his watch, then sat up. Ten minutes later, he was heading down the sloping landscape toward Abdel Kinneret. It was his final push. The windswept rock on the desert floor provided a hard trail that made going easier.

As the sunlight faded, the western sky became a deep purple and transitioned to a thin orange glow on the horizon. Shelton slowed his pace. The cool desert evening air striking the perspiration under his clothing sent a chill through his body. Just ahead, a small fire burned at the entrance to the village. He sat down on a bench next to the flames, rubbed his hands together to warm himself, and surveyed the area for any other living soul. He opened his soft-sided flask and slowly drank his last pint of water.

A voice startled him. A man was sitting on the bench next to him. Shelton finished his drink, then set the flask down. He returned a slight head bob in greeting but didn't say a word.

"I am Elias. Allow me to offer you some food and water."

Shelton sighed, his stomach rumbling from hunger.

Elias stood up and began walking. Shelton mustered his energy, stood, and followed. Elias glanced back, then slowed his pace.

The narrow dirt streets of the village were neat and clean. Small shops and modest homes lined both sides of the block. The buildings were freshly painted. Each had fresh flowers planted in the pots just outside the doors.

Shelton followed Elias through the empty streets, doing his best to keep up. Ahead, Elias stopped in front of a small one-room home. Inside was a table with food and drink prepared. Shelton sat down across from his host and began eating without saying a word.

≪

A knock at the door woke Shelton. He opened the door to see Elias standing there.

"It is time to go."

Elias was the elder and overseer of the Abel Kinneret. The past several days, the two men had gotten to know each other. Elias had led them on long walks along the shore of the Sea of Galilee and around the village. They took meals together and discussed current affairs and the history of the desert town. Shelton had resisted asking the obvious question: why am I here?

The previous evening, each had overindulged in wine as they sat beside a fire on the seashore. Elias told stories about the different attempts by various armies to invade the village. Each time meeting a fate almost worse than death. He shared how there were usually one or two survivors allowed to return to their homelands to tell the story. How the "One Standing in the Sun" was the village's protector. What Elias didn't share was that Shelton was the life form known as the "One Standing in the Sun." A name that was ascribed to him in the ancient writings and revelations. Shelton would soon find out his true nature and purpose.

Shelton had slept through the entire day and into the evening, his body working to catch up from the fasting and fatigue from the previous week's stress. A few minutes later, he was dressed and at the door, ready to go.

Elias stepped aside as Shelton exited out of the home and into the street. He didn't look Shelton in the eyes. Instead, he held his head slightly down in a subservient posture. A change from the past several days.

Shelton followed Elias down the narrow streets until they were standing in front of the entrance to the village center. The center's gates were at least four meters in height. Each over a meter wide. Shelton watched as Elias unlocked them and swung the large wooden timbers open with ease.

Stepping aside, Elias extended his hand, inviting Shelton to enter. Shelton crossed the gate's threshold without saying a word. Elias bid Shelton a good evening, then closed the entrance, locked the gates behind him, and walked away.

Shelton stood alone before a set of inner gates. He studied the design and construction. The steel, wood, and gold design was magnificently crafted. Everything in Kinneret was perfectly crafted. Handmade to perfection. He was admiring the work when the inner gates slowly opened.

A woman greeted Shelton by name, then escorted him down a pathway through pristine gardens and small ponds that led to a domed round building with a pillar-lined portico. The bronze dome accented the clean white stone of the outside walls. They made their way up the steps under the portico. The double doors of the building opened, and she escorted him inside.

Standing in the center of a large empty room was a woman dressed in a shimmering red caftan with gold accents. The leather weave of her sandals was trimmed with gold tassels and disappeared under the length of her garment. Her olive-colored, ageless skin was striking. Similar to Amir's complexion, but even more perfect. Her wavy, flowing, and silky brunette hair reached down to her waist.

White Carrara marble glistened on the floor inside. Natural light from the windows surrounding the top of the dome spilled into the room. The evening sun reflected off the walls and the floor, creating a soothing, peaceful ambiance. Next to the woman was a table, two chairs, and a carafe of wine.

"Please come in," said the woman in a smooth, low voice. Shelton made his way toward her.

"Mr. Shelton, I am Adira. Welcome to Abel Kinneret," she said, extending a hand to her guest.

Adira's slight smile and light blue eyes were warm and kind. Her perfect posture projected confidence and strength. Shelton reached out and took her hand. He narrowed his stare at the new acquaintance.

"Please, sit if you wish?" said Adira politely. "Wine?"

Shelton accepted the offer. He looked around the room, observing the architecture. The walls of the main chamber were framed with tall square panels. Each panel stretched from floor to ceiling and formed a section of wall. There were no paintings, statues, or symbols of any kind. Just pristine white walls and marble floors.

The dome ceiling was coated in gold. Each golden section of the dome was trimmed with silver. Around the base of the dome, where it attached to the walls, was a golden ring inlaid with silver and bronze. The simple elegance was stunning.

As the evening sun moved toward the horizon the room grew dimmer. Shelton watched as two people worked their way around the room, lighting the large candle stands and torches. He looked across the table at Adira. The welcoming look on her face seemed to ease his angst.

"Relax," Adira said. "There is nothing to fear here."

Shelton leaned forward and picked up the glass from the table, then sat back in the soft cushioned chair and took a sip of wine. He lowered his brow in concentration as he studied the taste of the vintage. His face relaxed and a slight smile of satisfaction appeared. It was without question the best wine he had ever tasted. He took a second, larger sip to keep the feeling of nirvana alive for another second or two as Adira watched.

"You have done well on your journey," Adira said. "The world outside is treacherous. It's filled with many things that can consume, degrade, and kill a person's soul."

"Very true," Shelton said. "Your village is impressive…" He paused, unsure how to address his host.

"Adira will do, Mr. Shelton. You can call me by my name."

"If you wish," Shelton replied. "It seems impolite given the company, mademoiselle."

"Yes, well, in good time, Mr. Shelton. We have to start somewhere."

Shelton took a deep breath and sighed, looking unsure of what to say.

"We have much to discuss," Adira continued. "I've given a great deal of thought about how to approach this conversation with you. In the end, you will have the reason and purpose you have been searching for your entire life. How you proceed afterward will be up to you."

Adira pointed her finger up and moved it across her body. Midair in front of them, six universes of galaxies and stars appeared. The large three-dimensional images floated in the air in front of them. Adira commanded the graphics and images with the movement of her finger.

"This is Apex One," she said, pointing to the first universe on the right.

Methodically, she worked her way across the systems, universe by universe, galaxy by galaxy. Apex One through Apex Six. Each universe contained at least one planet with life forms similar to humans, with each progressive system having a more advanced intelligent species. Each species building on the previous one.

"To be clear, Mr. Shelton," Adira said, "Apex One through Six is the limit of all life and science in existence. It is known and understood. Capabilities and intellectual capacity of all life forms are contained in one through six. There is nothing left to know or to be discovered. Birds can fly. Fish can breathe air from water. Chameleons can change color in an instant. Life forms have rational thought and can communicate. Life on Six is a thousand times more intelligent than any human that has ever lived on Apex Seven."

Adira paused and moved her finger again. This time shifting the images to the left. From the far right appeared an alternative universe. Apex Seven, Earth.

"Seven changes everything," said Adira. "It is a development effort. Can living, breathing, self-sustaining life govern itself? There is nothing else like it in any universe. We reduced the intelligence of the species to test self-governance. If we get seven right, human life on earth will be the basis from which all future species evolve. The possibilities are truly endless, Mr. Shelton. We did not design humans on earth to die. They were designed to live, thrive, explore, and regenerate in perpetuity."

Shelton raised his eyebrows in skepticism, then took a sip of wine.

"Exactly," Adira replied. "Not a pleasant thought at the moment. The species is on a path to self-destruction."

"Fix it," Shelton said. "It seems you have the ability to do so."

Adira proceeded to provide Shelton a discourse on science. How science cannot be undone in the way cultures and organizations can. With science, there is only learning and moving forward. Finding a better solution that is understood, repeatable, rational, and useful.

"What went wrong?" Shelton asked.

Adira paused. With another flick of her finger, the images vanished.

"The question is, *who* went wrong?" Adira said. "His name is Simeon. We appointed him governor of all life forms across the systems. Species on One through Six required his leadership. The life forms do not have a full complement of emotions available. They cannot choose one path over another. Simeon was an excellent leader of the worlds before seven. But we purposefully evolved the human species on earth to self-govern. Simeon's sole purpose became proving to us all that the species is incapable of doing so. He will stop at nothing to prove his point. It is that simple."

Shelton looked toward the floor as Adira completed her sentence. The magnitude of her words settled into his mind.

He thought about Angie and Daniel. He thought about his deep love for them. The thought of reconciling and a future together. With Adira's words, their reconciliation was at risk.

"Why are you telling me this?" he asked. "I'm one of them. One of the species, as you call us. In fact, I am the worst of the species."

Adira's gaze locked on Shelton. "You are only half human," Adira said. "Your real name is Magnus Elian. The Prime Chief Justice of Seven. You are the judge, the jury, and"—she paused—"the executioner."

Shelton's face remained stoic but his mouth dropped opened slightly.

"When things on Seven didn't go according to the original plan," continued Adira, "it was your job to deal with it and you did. But it didn't end. Now you are back to deal with Simeon once and for all."

Shelton couldn't sit quietly any longer. He stood and began pacing around the sitting area. His head moved side to side as if he were calculating and analyzing the news. He turned back toward Adira. "How can that be? Who are you?"

"Sit down, Mr. Shelton," Adira said in a commanding voice.

The wine and the intensity of Adira's revelations were overwhelming his senses. He took a deep breath and returned to his seat.

"I am the new Chancellor of Apex Seven," Adira said. "I am the Supreme Chair of all systems. This situation is now my personal responsibility. If you cannot turn this human experiment in the right direction, then I will end the species."

Adira looked deep into Shelton's soul. "Listen to me, Magnus," she said, returning to a calm and comforting but intense voice. "There is still time. I will reconnect you with the powers you once possessed. I will educate you. I will provide you with everything you need to know. Yes, you were born with one foot in humanity and the other in the full spectrum. You were born as a human precisely for this purpose. Nothing more. So when you are ready, you will leave Kinneret and immerse yourself in humanity again. You will keep wading through all the dark places, the lies, and the greed. You must find Simeon and stop him."

Shelton reached up and refilled their wineglasses. He paused a moment to collect his thoughts, then took a deep breath.

"I have many questions," he said, speaking slowly and thoughtfully. "But the first is, how would I find this Simeon?"

Adira didn't blink or twitch. "He goes by the name Wolfgang Hauser. He and his henchmen perpetuate lies and mislead this world. You must stop him."

CHAPTER TWENTY-TWO

THE UVA CAMPUS was quiet except for the birds singing in the morning air. The occasional sound of a squirrel chattering echoed off the brick buildings while a few summer students moved along the sidewalks to and from classes.

Ann was back on campus finishing up her post-spring semester office cleaning ritual. She stood back and observed her work. The desk and credenza were clean. Everything was in its place. The paper shredder bin in the outer office was full. The fresh smell of dusting spray hung in the air.

Almost two weeks had gone by since she dropped Shelton off in Tel Aviv. She caught herself glancing at the door to her office frequently. Some part of her expected to see him standing there. There had been no communication from Shelton. Only silence.

Ann was filling her days, catching up on day-to-day life of being a mother and a daughter. Every day that went by made the drama of the past several months seem more and more like a dream. Almost like it never happened. The thought and image of Professor Schwartz nailed to his mantel with his eyes stuck wide open always brought her back to reality. It was all very real.

Every couple of days now, Edwards called Ann to check in. Each time the phone rang, she hoped it was Shelton. She had not told Edwards about Shelton reading the Hebrew manuscript in perfect dialect. She hadn't mentioned meeting with Amir in Malaysia or the drop-off in Tel Aviv. She'd thought about it. After all, Shelton hadn't told her to not share. But keeping quiet seemed like the right thing for the time being. Maybe Shelton didn't want Edwards to know. Regardless, there was something about watching Shelton slay the huge, black-robed demon in Schwartz's office that said he might not really need Edwards's help.

Unbeknownst to Ann, the Providence intelligence network around the world was pinging hard, trying to locate Tom Shelton. Edwards knew he lied about not being able to read the Hebrew at their first face-to-face meeting. Ann had slipped and accidently referred to Shelton reading the passage. The system had received the passport information the night Shelton and Ann arrived in Tel Aviv. Edwards had his team monitoring camera networks in the capital city and Jerusalem using facial recognition technology. They were also listening to cellular communications across the country. They had people on the street corners all over Jerusalem looking for him. So far, they had turned up nothing. Shelton had disappeared.

When Edwards's phone rang. Within minutes he had his Providence team on a conference call. The next morning he packed his bags and headed to the local airport and waited for Shelton's airplane to arrive.

✍

Shelton stood on the veranda of his Colorado home, gazing out over the valley. He watched the late-afternoon sun slowly lowering toward the western peaks on the other side of the Remington Valley as he contemplated what awaited him. The steam from his afternoon tea rose into the cool summer air.

Elk Creek Holdings was the largest landowner in Pitkin County, which included most of the property of the city of Remington. City and county records showed Elk Creek owned over twenty billion dollars in land and real estate throughout the central Colorado valley. The owner of record for Elk Creek Holdings was Travers Real Estate Investments. Travers was owned by Travers Holdings, which was part of a Dutch company named New Bedford Advisors. New Bedford was wholly owned by a company based in Bermuda named Crystal View Partners. CVP Inc. had one shareholder, TS Enterprises, a privately held trust company owned by one Thomas J. Shelton. The chain of ownership could not be tracked back to Shelton. Once the chain reached Bermuda, the trail stopped.

Pitkin County politicians and police didn't know or care about the intricacies of the city's ownership structure. They were close friends of Shelton. That is all that mattered. They did their jobs and received their above-average salaries from the Remington Foundation, which was funded solely by Shelton.

Shelton had gone the extra step to see that the city manager had enough funds to pay top wages and salaries to all city workers, as well as local and county police and fire. Every two years, a fleet of new vehicles, weapons, and uniforms arrived for departments. All courtesy of donations made by the Remington Foundation.

Thirty minutes later, the sun was touching the western ridge of the mountain peaks. The summer sunshine had warmed the main gathering spaces of Shelton's Elk Creek mansion. The 15,000-square-foot custom estate was nestled on an eastern slope of the valley in the middle of ten thousand acres of trees, valleys, and streams. It was Shelton's dream home. He had designed it for his family. The family he and Angie would have. A family that didn't exist at the moment and most likely never would.

Just down the hall from the large main family room was a more intimate hearth room. The space had a private balcony and was well-equipped with a custom bar, TV, and seating for eight to ten. It was a room where Shelton spent his evenings reading, drinking, and watching the occasional sports game on the big screen.

What wasn't visible was the bulletproof, armored walls and the hidden door to the left of the bar. The hearth room was the ultimate safe room. Complete with hidden steel doors along with the walls, the room could be sealed off and withstand a heavy armor attack. The electronics and coatings made the space impenetrable by listening devices. The door next to the bar was an emergency exit that led down two levels to a fully equipped armory that included survival gear.

The room was designed to withstand an assault while allowing Shelton and up to five other people to escape down to the armory, put on survival gear, climb aboard two gas/electric utility four wheelers, and be into the escape tunnel with a door closed behind them within ninety seconds.

The carefully constructed escape route led deep into the backcountry where the survival bunker was located. The bunker was a large underground custom habitat, which was supplied with provisions that could sustain a group of six adults for at least two years. Shelton and Ben had tested the escape route many times. The two of them could be on their way in just over sixty seconds.

As the sun disappeared behind the mountains, Shelton turned and went inside the house. Charles Edwards sat in the armchair reading a book and sipping tea in front of the fireplace.

The advisors at Providence had cautioned Edwards not to take the meeting at Shelton's place. The new acquaintance was still an unknown. It would not deter Edwards. He was old school. He believed in following his instincts. His instincts said to get on the airplane and see what Thomas Shelton was up to. Unbeknownst to anyone, Shelton had been practicing his powers that Adira had reconstituted in him. He now had resumed control of all elements of the earth including the ability to generate powerful electricity from his fingertips.

The expression on Edwards's face when he stepped off the airplane and saw Shelton waiting for him said he was having second thoughts. Shelton looked almost like a different man. His skin was smooth and darker. He looked thirty pounds lighter. And most alarming, his irises were a lighter shade of blue. He was an attractive man before. Now he was strikingly handsome, thin, and muscular. His jawline and cheekbones were more pronounced. The veins in his muscles showed through his skin.

Shelton poured himself a drink, lit a small, thin cigar, and sat down across from Edwards, crossing his legs.

"Charles, I have given a great deal of thought about our initial meeting. You offered to help. I've been thinking about that," Shelton said in a clinical tone. "To be frank, it still isn't clear to me how this all works. However, if you are going to help me figure it out, I think you need to have a little more perspective. A more comprehensive view of the situation. That's the reason I asked you here. I thought it would be best for you and me to discuss these things face to face outside of your headquarters. So we could both focus."

Shelton had assumed that every room at Providence had microphones and video. He was right. He didn't want any record of this conversation. That became clear to Edwards when Shelton requested he put his mobile phone in the secure box behind the bar.

"What I share with you must be kept in the highest confidence," Shelton said. "You are an attorney, right?"

Edwards nodded.

"Good," Shelton continued. "You are now my attorney. What we discuss is privileged, right?"

"Yes," Edwards replied.

"If after our discussion you don't feel up to the task, I will understand. However, just as I am coming to terms with things as you suggested, I believe you will have some soul-searching to do at some point," Shelton said, smiling slightly to lighten the intensity.

The nervous expression on Edwards's face didn't change. Shelton stood, walked over to the bar, and refreshed his whiskey.

"We need to maintain our sense of humor here, don't you think?" Shelton asked. "This whole situation is extraordinary. The good news is, we are in the driver's seat, Charles. We didn't create this shit show. But we might fix it."

Charles Edwards smiled slightly at the levity.

"We are on the same team, Charles. The more you know, the better we can work together."

"I must admit you have my curiosity aroused," Edwards replied. "Yet I am scared to death about what you are going to tell me. It's easier to be an observer, academic and more circumspect about things, than on the front lines. I suppose reality is hitting us all in the face right now. It just seems unbelievable."

"Indeed, it does," Shelton responded more lightheartedly. "The moment that people have speculated about, dreamed about, lamented over, killed each other over since the beginning of time is arriving. Yet it is not what people expect. It's not what we have been trained to believe through hundreds of years of culture. What will the believers say when the clouds don't part and they aren't swept away to some esoteric place in the heavens? Everyone will feel as though they are being attacked, yet they are being saved. You Charles will feel you are being violent, yet it is what Providence was designed to do. We will have to work through paradox after paradox, Charles."

Shelton sat down in the chair next to Edwards, took a long drag on the cigar, and began telling his story.

⁊

Ann had noticed the black SUV parked several rows over as she climbed into her car in the UVA parking garage. Through the tinted windows, she saw someone in the driver's seat. Shelton's level of paranoia and caution was rubbing off on her.

An hour later, she noticed another black SUV at the grocery store. This one was parked out toward the street, away from the front of the store in the dark. She kept an eye on it as she loaded her groceries into the back seat. She continued watching her rearview mirror carefully as she turned out of the grocery store parking lot onto the city streets.

She glanced behind every few seconds. There was no sign of being followed. Ann took a deep breath to relax. She had just two more stops before heading home.

The locally owned pet store Ann frequented was rarely busy. Especially at eight thirty in the evening. The local proprietors were friends of her mom and dad. Giving them her business instead of the national chain store made Ann feel good, even though the decision ate away a little more of her disposable income. It was worth it to support a local owner and friend.

Ann's financial situation was much improved these days. The money she had earned from the Shelton adventure had made her worries over money virtually disappear. For that, she was very grateful.

She took her time walking up and down every aisle in the small store, picking up products that looked interesting, reading their labels, then placing them back on the shelf. Twenty minutes later, she was pushing the shopping cart filled with large bags of dog and cat food toward her new German-made sedan.

The shopping cart vibrated across the gravel-based asphalt as Ann pushed. The metal frame and hard rubber wheels rattled loudly. She pushed the unlock button on her key ring, then pushed the trunk release button. She grasped the large bags of animal food one at a time and rolled them into the trunk of the car. She looked around her, then pushed the shopping cart over to the corral and made the way back to the car and climbed in.

The figure in the back seat moved swiftly. With one motion, the chloroform-filled cloth was over Ann's mouth and nose. Before she could process what was happening, she lost consciousness.

A second person opened the passenger door and pulled Ann out of the driver's seat and over the center console. The attacker climbed behind the wheel and started Ann's car. Within seconds, Ann's sedan and a black SUV were pulling out of the parking lot.

CHAPTER TWENTY-THREE

Samantha Kearns and her boss had become accustomed to listening to the daily ranting of the sitting US president. Fortunately, President Staley's personal insecurities usually overwhelmed his big blustering talk. It took some getting used to. Kearns and the National Security Administration top brass had it figured out.

The president's emotional volatility and unpredictable, frequently unhinged comments created a daily feeding frenzy for twenty-four-hour opinion news networks. NoYos, as Kearns referred to them. Short for "Not Yoda," meaning no value or insight for the pubic. The erratic behavior of the sixty-eight-year-old president made everyone else on the planet nervous. Especially the European allies.

For the president's cabinet, every day was like a new beginning. Each day Staley's behavior hung on his perceived public perception of himself. Nothing else mattered. Not governing, leading, or advancing "the greatest" country on the planet. Not surprising, considering Staley had never really worked a day in his life. He was the only child of a wealthy German businessman and an amateur fashion model.

Kearns felt somewhat sorry for the president. After all, the international authorities believed Staley's late father was also one of the largest illegal traders of opium in the world. The FBI had Staley's father pegged as a brutal, drug-dealing crime boss. One they could never quite pin down.

Staley had grown up in a violent, largely isolated environment, where he was never good enough for his father and his mother wasn't around much.

The rebellious young Staley had taken the money from his father's estate and invested it in casinos and real estate. By the age of fifty, he had been bankrupt five times. Each time he had clawed his way back through his influential, wealthy friends in the media—and with money, most likely from the still-functioning criminal network.

Blackmail was Staley's tactic of choice. He had pictures and recordings of New York's wealthiest people in compromising situations. Such power and influence funded his presidential campaign, along with a large stream of laundered money that started with Wolfgang Hauser.

The revolving door in the West Wing was a testament to the challenges of working around the president. Most of the cabinet members were "acting" in their respective positions. The original appointed members either had departed on their own or were fired. It took little to get fired by Staley. He had ended three people's careers because he didn't like their choice of clothing.

The National Security staff, led by the assistant director Samantha Kearns, had moved quickly after Staley was elected. Before the inauguration, Kearns had put together a team of psychiatrists. A group of nine of the best mental health professionals from across the globe. The goal was to figure out how to work with the new president given his personality issues. The initial meeting took place in Edinburgh. A planned two-day meeting turned into a six-day working session.

The consensus of the "group of nine" was to share information with the president selectively. Focus Staley on benign matters whenever possible. More consequential issues would be managed on the side by competent professionals. And they'd only involve Staley when required.

Kearns shared this advice with her old friend and now British Prime Minister, Andrew Wilkinson. Wilkinson used the counsel when dealing with the US president. However, he and the other European leaders were an order of magnitude more concerned about Staley than the American establishment. The continent had a history of wars caused by mad men.

The unpredictable state of the world's largest superpower was unnerving. Staley seemed to admire dictators. It was clear to all, including the CIA and the NSA that Staley was working to develop a deeper relationship with several of them around the world.

For the British PM and his European peers, Staley's actions and instability, combined with their geographic proximity to one of the world's remaining autocrats, was troubling. A history of two world wars in their neighborhood was not forgotten. A need to change the current situation was vital. The threat to European security was proliferating. A situation that was unacceptable.

⤜

The staff of the small bed-and-breakfast were completing preparations for the mid-week guests. The employees of the inn had been working long hours with two of Kearns's technicians from NSA. They were making the property ready for the Hancock Company's board of directors meeting. The hotel staff didn't know they were actually working with the US intelligence apparatus.

The Hancock Company was a real but hollow company. Kearns had hired a Delaware law firm to establish the legal entity owned by the deceased Mr. Hancock of Los Angeles, CA. Shell companies were basic field craft used by government intelligence agencies. Even fictitious companies required authentic websites. That was the job of two people sitting in a control room in the NSA's operations center in Northern Virginia.

On site at the B&B, the NSA chef had the kitchen and bar restocked with the preferred food and drink choices of the directors. They had swept the building for listening devices and cameras. The installation of the NSA's own temporary security system was almost complete. Within the hour, Kearns's team would have full control of the small country estate in the foothills of the Appalachian Mountains.

Just after dark, guests began to arrive. The first was Lamar Harris, director of NSA and Sam Kearns's boss. Shortly thereafter, the Republican

Party leader stepped out of the rain and through the front door. Then the ranking democratic senator from Illinois and Speaker of the House. The Speaker was third in line for the presidency after the vice president, a fact in the US system that was important to the allies at the moment.

Before the reception and dinner, each guest had time to get into their rooms and freshen up. The joint chief, Admiral Nathaniel Wood, arrived just as the group was gathering for cocktails in the main lodge of the facility. The same Admiral Wood that handled Commander Shelton's special projects.

Kearns and her boss had exhausted every idea as to how to open such a delicate conversation and be taken seriously. A conversation that was technically not taking place at a meeting that did not exist on any calendar anywhere.

Dinner conversation had gone better than Kearns had expected. After a few pleasantries, the group of ranking US decision makers began lamenting about the president. The stories, concerns, and hand wringing were nonstop. The setup for the next discussion was perfect. Kearns found the right moment and moved the group to the bar lounge.

A flash of lightning lit up the room as the group settled in. Thunder began rolling a few seconds later. The rain was coming down harder now, and the sound of the drops hitting the rooftop grew louder.

"Again, thank you all for making time to be here," Director Harris said. "I would like to toast the United States of America and its dedicated leaders." Harris raised his glass. "To the leaders who strive to make a difference and serve all the people of our great country. Long live and God Bless the United States of America."

Each person raised their glass to the toast and took a drink.

"Following on our dinner conversation, we would like to spend the next hour and shift to a different focus," Harris said. "Assistant Director Kearns will lead this discussion."

Kearns sat comfortably in the armchair next to Wood's chair adjacent to the fireplace. All eyes shifted to her.

"Thank you, Director Harris. We at NSA believe it is time to start a serious discussion about the current state of national security," Kearns began. "I'm speaking of security that affects us both domestically and abroad. Security that affects our allies around the globe."

She looked around the group, making eye contact with each person as she spoke.

"The current administration's approach to government is unacceptable. It is insular, arrogant, and shortsighted relative to both domestic and foreign policy. The tactics of President Staley and actions of the US Congress have the American people deeply concerned about the future," Kearns continued. "Our European allies are even more concerned than the American people. How would I know? I have spent the last several months collaborating with the PMs and presidents across Europe. Conversations at the highest levels, in confidence, with our closest allies."

Kearns continued to adjust her look from person to person while taking a sip of wine. Her audience followed suit and took a drink.

"Isn't that the State Department's job, Ms. Kearns?" asked the ranking GOP member in his deep southern accent.

"Simply put, our European partners do not believe our system of politics can address the issue at hand, Senator," responded Kearns. "Director Harris and I have been working with French, English, and German officials in order to understand their concerns. We have arrived at a point where I think it is appropriate to consider solutions."

Harris spent the next twenty minutes sharing the allies' concerns and answering questions. When the dialog was exhausted, Kearns watched Admiral Wood swallow hard, then ask, "What do they propose we do?"

In silence, Harris looked across the table at Kearns. Everyone in the room had read the dossier of Samantha Kearns. She was mother to one daughter, Angela Brady. Her career of service was well known. Her accomplishments were highly respected. She created fear among enemies, even among her colleagues.

Early in her career in the intelligence business, she had single-handedly tracked down a US state department analyst who was disclosing US undercover agent names to the Soviets. Six of the US agents disappeared because of the leak. They assigned Kearns a solo mission to find the ones responsible. When she found them, she took it upon herself to administer justice to the Soviet agent and the US spy. Her video recorded the process while never revealing her identity. Everyone knew it was the work of Kearns. She signed off on the classified records confirming it as such. The tape showed a tan, fit woman in her panties and bra executing and disassembling the two spies piece by piece. No bodies or body parts were ever found. The Kearns legend was born.

"Our European allies want to know what we are going to do about the administration," Kearns said in a firm, commanding tone. "Our allies have made it very clear that if we will not act, they will. They want to know whether we will support them. If we cannot find the courage to support them, then they will ask us to stand aside and not interfere. If we cannot find our way to do that, they are prepared to act alone."

"What do they want us to do?" Senator Waner of Mississippi asked.

"They," said Kearns, holding up an official jointly signed letter, "have concluded that the president of the United States represents a present and imminent danger to the collective security and sovereignty of the European Union. The declaration requires them to take all necessary action to abate or eliminate the threat."

Kearns passed the letter around the group. Each seemed to carefully read every word, their faces tight and avoiding eye contact. Kearns walked to the bar and refilled her wineglass.

"They are prepared to declare war on the United States of America? Are they joking?" Waner asked, concern clear in his voice.

Kearns watched Admiral Wood's face as she spoke.

"That is exactly what they are prepared to do," Kearns said.

She turned to Waner. "Do you blame them, Senator?"

"It seems to be a huge overreaction, if you ask me." Waner tugged at his collar.

"How so, Senator?" interjected Admiral Wood. "What options do they have? We have backed our allies into a corner. If they support us, they are collaborating with a madman who is befriending dictators. If they do not support us, they are on their own, anyway. We have left them with no options. No options while our president snuggles up to dictators."

"I cannot sit here and discuss a conspiracy to eliminate the president," said Congresswoman Rodriguez of Illinois. "That is what we are talking about, isn't it?"

The observation from the Speaker stopped the conversation in its tracks. Kearns watched as the others traded glances.

"To be clear," Kearns said at a slower cadence, "it has not risen to that level of action yet. There are actions that congress could take to remove the president. However—"

"Oh my God," Waner said. "Don't even go there."

Kearns paused, waiting to see if the senator had anything else to say.

"However, I believe we are perhaps one or two erratic decisions away from that being the situation," Kearns concluded.

Harris's complexion changed to a slightly deeper color as his heart pounded and pulse raced. What they were discussing was tantamount to treason. If they didn't all agree, heads would surely roll.

To be truthful, Kearns and Harris had had difficulty talking about such a thing between the two of them as they prepared for this meeting. Now, hearing the words aloud in front of others was almost unbearable. Harris stood up and walked over to the bar, rubbing the back of his neck.

Kearns sat there calmly sipping wine. She watched her guests continue to trade glances. The discomfort with the subject filled the room.

"Ms. Kearns," Waner said, having brought his emotions under control, "I assume you are making no record of this meeting?"

Kearns smiled. "No, Senator. There are no recordings. No video. No record of this meeting ever taking place. The only way anyone will ever know is if one of you talk."

Waner's wrinkled brow said he mostly believed her.

"Then to be clear, I am not on board," Waner said, his voice soft. He turned to look directly at Wood and Kearns. "At least not yet," he said. "But…but as the republican in the room, I get it. Behind the scenes, we are all frustrated and concerned. When the cameras are rolling, our heads are so far up the president's ass it is embarrassing. We can't believe he was elected. We don't know what to do other than show support and align with the people who elected him. That is a democracy. That's the way it works. We have no solution. The people elected Staley, and the people must take him out. Not the Brits, for God's sake. Our hope is that the people will choose more wisely in the future. This is a civics lesson for the American people. Be careful who you vote for."

"I suppose that is the problem, isn't it?" said Senator Rodriguez. "We all know that Staley is unstable. It is a fact. Ms. Kearns's point is we cannot wait until the people vote him out of office. More proactive measures may be required. We might only be one unthoughtful action away from World War III. It could be nukes flying both ways this time."

"What is the military view, Admiral?" Kearns asked, turning to Wood.

"Staley is unfit for command. There is no debate," Woods said matter-of-factly. "The military establishment will never disobey an order from a president. If we did, it would be the end of a people's democracy. However, we will not commit illegal acts either. There is a process to determine the legality of a president's orders. With Staley, we significantly censure the information we provide, like everyone else in the west wing does. He cannot act or overreact on what he does not know."

"That's an interesting form of democracy," quipped Kearns, smiling slightly.

Wood sat up in his chair. "Ms. Kearns, what do you propose we do?"

Sam Kearns took a sip of wine and drew a deep breath.

"First, I think if any one of you is uncomfortable with the discussion, we need to stop now. We get a good night's rest, have breakfast, and head back to our jobs tomorrow morning. We forget about this entire conversation. If anyone asks, we simply had a joint working session on international relations sponsored by the NSA."

Just as Kearns was finishing her words, Admiral Wood's secured phone vibrated. He removed it from his jacket pocket, looked at the identification, stood, and excused himself from the room.

"If we decide not to stand still, I recommend we simply support the European plan. It would not require your direct involvement. The support would come from other channels. Channels you would never know about. Politically, there would be little to no risk," Kearns continued.

"Then why are you involving us now?" Senator Waner asked, his frustration evident. "You must need something. You have poisoned us all with this information."

"We need your input, Senator," said Kearns. "We are intelligence professionals, not politicians. We operate in the shadows to carry out the policies of the country. Some should never see the light of day. You and Senator Rodriguez are the leaders we rely on to do something. Lead the way. Be who 'we the people' need you to be."

Waner and Rodriguez both sat hanging their heads, staring at the floor.

"Our Congress and now our president seem to have lost their way," Kearns continued as her boss looked on. "I suggest you get your shit together, congressmen. Our allies will only ask our permission for so long. Then they will do what they need to do."

Wood walked back into the room just as Kearns finished.

"You look like you have seen a ghost, Admiral," said Senator Waner.

Wood poured himself a fresh glass of whiskey.

"Acting CIA Director Walker just informed me the president is canceling his meeting with the lead NATO allies. He is going to Moscow instead." Wood shook his head. "I couldn't talk him out of it."

Kearns looked around the room.

"Walker asked me how long it would take to remove US troops from Europe and Asia," the admiral continued. "He told me to expect the order from the president any day now."

"Staley cannot do that without congressional support," said Waner flatly.

"He doesn't need Congress to withdraw troops. Only to go to war," said Rodriguez.

"What do you recommend we do, Admiral?" Waner asked.

All eyes were on Wood.

"We have a rogue president who threatens western civilization, Senator. I think I speak for all of us," Wood replied. "Ms. Kearns, tell our European allies they have our full support. You and I need to go see Andy and his team," Wood concluded, referring to the British prime minister and the head of MI6.

CHAPTER TWENTY-FOUR

FOR THE FIRST time in Thomas Shelton's life, he had told almost all of his story to another human. That person was Charles Edwards, cofounder of the Providence Institute.

For the past hours, Shelton had laid out his story, step by step. Detail by detail. The stunned look on Edwards's face was fading now that the bigger picture was emerging.

Shelton's first thought of being something other than human was waking up from a dream with his mother sitting on his bed next to him. He was lying on his side with his head on the pillow, his mother gently stroking his long, uncut hair, softly singing to him. He opened his eyelids and saw her beautiful smiling face. For a moment, he saw a second face, a man's face, peering over his mother's shoulder. That was how Shelton recognized Macari at their meeting in Argentina.

Elizabeth Shelton was tall and slender with brown hair and blue irises surrounding her soft-spoken and focused.

The next thing Shelton remembered that morning was he was out of bed heading to a salon for a haircut. He recalled the staff commenting on how beautiful his hair was and his mother making the salon staff sweep up every piece of his hair and place it in a bag for her to take with her. That evening, he was off to the church with his friends to help the preacher with the late service. Shelton was ten years old. It was the day he started believing his dreams were real and his persistent need for justice not just a passing thought. He had always known he was different. He had always had more physical ability than his friends. He was a faster runner, could jump higher and was stronger. Until this point in his life his dreams had been just graphic violent dreams that his mother soothed with her gentle touch.

Shelton's two best friends were Steve and Chris. The boys were in the same class at school. They played together, did homework together, and roamed the streets of Leesburg together. They did everything together. It was their own little kingdom. Their own piece of the world where nobody bothered them. It was safe, and they were free.

There was no place that was considered off-limits. They would ride bikes or walk anywhere they wanted: to the local pool, through the woods by the creek, to the river, or to the convenience store. The only requirement was Shelton had to check in with his mom from time to time. It was the perfect way to grow up. Naïve, safe, and carefree.

The best friends each had their families together. No divorces or separations. Each had siblings at home. Dads and moms went off to work every morning and returned in the early evening. Dinner was on the table by six o'clock, and their parents were in front of the television or doing laundry by seven. They were middle-class, comfortable, with all their needs met.

Every Sunday, Shelton would see his friends in church with their families. Occasionally, their parents would let the boys sit together. Usually regretting the decision by the end of the sermon. The giggling and whispering from the boys always garnered a few sharp looks from the preacher toward the parents.

Church was a required act as far as Shelton was concerned. Something that people did on Sunday morning in Virginia. Shelton and his friends didn't really pay attention to the message from the pulpit. What could an old guy possibly know about heaven and hell? What qualified him as a person of God? The passing thoughts of a ten-year-old before he put his head back down and continued drawing pictures in his notebook. The fifty-minute service seemed to last hours.

Shelton and his friends were the age when kids were asked to serve as church helpers. The boys had no interest in helping the preacher with candles, incense, or anything else. Shelton's mom did not require him to do it. However, Steve and Chris didn't have a choice. Their parents made them serve. Shelton joined them. It was another chance to hang out together on Saturday night.

The work was all routine for the first few weeks. Then one Saturday evening, things changed. Shelton and his friends had finished cleaning and putting away candle stands and offering plates in the storage room behind the sanctuary. Reverend Brooks and his adult assistant, James Dilfer, trapped the three boys in the storage room. Shelton thought it was a joke at first. Then Brooks, using his kind voice, showed them pornographic pictures. Shelton and his friends thought they had underestimated their preacher. Instead of being boring and old, he was really cool.

Then things took an unexpected turn. Brooks blackmailed the ten-year-olds. He threatened to tell their parents that he caught them with pornographic pictures. Brooks also told the boys that part of their duty was to submit to his needs. The act would be a show of humility before God. Subservience to the church and God were the words he used.

Dilfer whispered to them that if they didn't do what Brooks asked, or if they talked about any of this to anyone, they would be killed. Then their families would be killed. To make his point, Dilfer showed them gruesome pictures of dead boys dumped in a grave with their eyelids still open. The message was simple: This will be you if you don't comply or if you talk.

Shelton watched as Brooks and Dilfer assaulted his two friends. Tears of fear flowed down their faces. They were not sure what was happening to them. Shelton wanted to stop it. He was frozen and in shock about what was happening. He knew he was next.

When it was Shelton's turn, Dilfer came toward him, smiling as if he were taking great pleasure in dominating the young boys. No one had noticed that Shelton had repositioned himself to where a candle stand was within reach. When Dilfer was in range, Shelton grabbed the stand and smashed it into Dilfer's face as hard as he could. The old man dropped to the floor, screaming in pain. The wound in his face poured blood onto the floor. Shelton hit Dilfer three more times in the head, doing his best to kill the attacker. Then he turned his attention to Brooks.

Shocked, Brooks was zipping up his pants when he saw the candelabra moving toward his head. The preacher raised his hands just in time to block Shelton's strike, sending the weapon flying across the floor.

Shelton grabbed his friends and bolted out of the room. On the way out, Brooks screamed they would be killed if they talked.

Shelton led his friends out of the church and down to the woods as fast as he could. Chris and Steve cried in between throwing up for at least an hour. Shelton had just sat there, trying to comfort them with words. He never cried. He wanted to but couldn't. After a couple of hours, they collected themselves. They agreed to tell their parents. Their parents would take care of it. The preachers would be arrested and sent to prison. The boys would never talk about it again.

Shelton never told his mom or dad. He just never went back to the church. Steve told his dad, and he never went back. His parents did nothing. They just told him to tell no one and it would be okay. Chris told his parents. They didn't believe him. They made him go back the next week.

Shelton tried to help Chris. He had found the courage to tell a city policeman. He pointed to Dilfer's face as proof. The next day after school, the police officer pulled him aside after track practice and told Shelton that if he ever discussed what he saw with anyone, he would disappear. That Shelton would just vanish one day. No one would ever know what happened to him. Not his mom, dad, or friends. No one would ever find him in the Potomac River were the words of the officer.

There was nothing else to do. The adults had won. Shelton remembered having a great sense of satisfaction as he watched Dilfer's blood spilling onto the floor. He wished he had killed him. He tried. Dilfer survived. But not without a deep scar on his forehead and a touch of brain damage.

Elizabeth Shelton passed away shortly after that night. Heart failure, supposedly. From that point on, Shelton's father rarely spoke to him. His younger brother, Rob, was his only friend.

After Chris's suicide two years later, the church promoted Brooks and transferred him to a different location.

As life went on, schoolwork was easy for Shelton. He always got perfect marks without really trying. He was good at sports but didn't play. Shelton did only what he had to do. In his free time, he watched television, rode bikes, and hung out at the local arcade. He never had a friend besides Rob, until he got to university. Steve's parents packed their bags after the assault by Brooks and moved to the high plains of Wyoming.

At Northwestern, Shelton studied physics and psychology. The subjects intrigued him. The blend of science and culture. One Friday morning, as he was reading the Chicago news, his past came flooding back. The reporter's short piece, buried on page ten below the fold in the *Tribune*, told a story about abusive preachers, priests, and church cover-ups.

The story woke Shelton. He followed up on Reverend Brooks. It didn't take long. A few keystrokes on the computer and he learned Brooks was still at the church in Georgetown. It seemed he had been promoted to one of the top-ranking clergy positions in the country. Brooks was a senior member of the United Nations Council of Religions. Later that same day, Shelton was on the way to Washington, DC, to see Brooks for himself.

On that Saturday evening, Shelton watched Brooks deliver a sermon while Dilfer sat on a bench off to the side of the pulpit. Just like in Leesburg nine years earlier. Brooks delivered a talk about loving one another and treating each other with respect.

An hour later, Shelton sat in a dark corner under a tree and watched two young boys come out. Both wiping tears from their faces.

Shelton spent the next three years of college preparing. He became an expert in the martial arts. He made trips back and forth, observing Brooks's every move. The weekend he was to graduate, he executed the plan. A couple of weeks later, he caught up with Dilfer in Philadelphia and finished the job.

Shelton stood up from the chair and refilled their drinks, then stepped out on the veranda for fresh air. Edwards returned from the washroom and joined Shelton outside.

"What happened next?" Edwards asked, intrigued, scared, and fascinated by the story all at the same time.

"After I returned to the university, the next day, before graduation, was the first time I saw Saint Xavier," Shelton said.

"Saint Xavier?" Edwards asked, looking a little confused.

"An observer. A guardian. That's what Amir calls them. They don't seem to guard much," Shelton said.

"Why do you call it Saint Xavier?"

"Well, it was a rather formidable-looking thing. Tall. Weapons. And it has a red X on the front of its black robe." Shelton used his finger to show the location of the X on the chest panel of Xavier's robe. "I could see the spook, but it was obvious no one else could. I decided to name it Saint Xavier. I only see that one occasionally. It's usually the smaller ones wearing gray, unarmed."

Shelton could see on Edwards's face that he was battling his own thoughts.

"All the violence," said Edwards in a disparaging tone. "I am not a violent person. Providence is not a violent organization. Quite the opposite, Tom."

"Charles," Shelton said, drawing in a breath slowly and then releasing it. "You need to listen closely. I feel your frustration, your anxiety, perhaps even disbelief. There is a reality of the situation that we have to embrace. You and the Providence team need to be very clear on this point. The Saturday night that Steve, Chris, and I were running from the church, I knew at that second what had to be done. I knew I would do it. I was sorry I didn't get it done that night." Shelton looked to the distance, remembering. "Imagine my despair. Day after day. Week after week. Knowing that every night I did not act, another young person's life was destroyed. It tormented me. It still torments me, Charles. When it came time to act, I did. They awoke something inside me that night. Like an element of physics that is undefined. So as awful as what I did seems, how violent, a force appeared that night to shroud my actions in secrecy. A veil surrounded me. Protected me. It supported what I was there to do. If it had not arrived, I'm sure I would be in prison right now."

Edwards listened intently to Shelton's words. The two men went back inside the hearth room and sat down next to the fireplace.

"Think about it, Charles," Shelton continued. "A church that is supposed to be a haven for families, a source of spiritual nourishment for its congregation, is instead raping and pillaging young, defenseless humans. There is no lower form of human life than Reverend Brooks, those like him, those that support it. Nothing lower in all the dark places of the universe! Any form of death or torture for such a person is still not enough. Abolishing them from all existence is justice. The damage they inflict cannot be undone."

Shelton sat back in the chair, taking a sip of his drink.

"What does it mean when what we know as good has become corrupted beyond repair? What happens now, Charles? What happens next? And what are you willing to do to help?"

"What happened to your wrists?" Edwards asked, changing the subject. He had noticed medical wraps visible just below Shelton's jacket on both wrists.

Shelton stared at his guest with a blank expression. He stood and methodically rolled up his sleeves. He removed the right wristband and then the left. Then he lifted his arms and turned both wrists inward to examine them himself. The wounds from the branded, burned skin were perfectly healed. The raised flesh marks he received at Abdel Kinneret were clearly visible. Shelton turned the inside of his wrists outward toward his guest.

Edwards stood up for a closer look. He examined the right wrist, then moved to the left wrist. In silence, their eyes met as Edwards looked at Shelton's face between raised arms.

Edwards broke eye contact, turned away, walked toward the bar, and sat down as Shelton watched.

Edwards recognized the Hebrew Tetragrammaton branded on Shelton's right wrist. "YHWH." The symbols were the name of the Hebrew God. A name that was considered too sacred to be spoken. The one whose name was ignored by modern-day scholars. The one who extracted justice from wrongdoers in ancient times. The one whose actions were well documented in the scrolls. On Shelton's left wrist was the Hebrew word for the number seven.

Edwards lifted his head from his hands and looked back at his host.

Shelton's mobile phone began vibrating against the granite bar countertop, breaking the tension in the room. Shelton walked to the bar, looked at the caller identification, and answered.

Shelton stared at Edwards as he listened to his brother's voice on the phone. Ann Baker was missing.

CHAPTER TWENTY-FIVE

Heather Kersting was hard at work getting Lookout Point Ranch in order. All the improvements she and Shelton had agreed to were in process. They had renovated the main house, construction was under-way on a new home for Angie, the new larger horse paddock was in place, and everything had a fresh coat of paint.

The ranch's cattle operation was ramping up to full functionality under Angie's leadership, and the thoroughbred business was attracting attention around the region. Daniel was working every hour outside of school, training and exercising horses.

The teenage son of Tom Shelton looked like his father. The six-foot, four-inch, hundred and eighty pound seventeen-year-old had a thin face, high cheekbones, and strong jawline. Like his dad, he was stronger and faster than every kid in his high school and had earned a reputation for his athletic abilities back in Wyoming. A reputation Angie was happy for her son to leave behind. She wanted him to be normal and fit in.

The late-afternoon sun was coming through the stable doors as Angie wrapped up her end-of-day checklist, a routine she did after the day's work was done and before the crew went home. Clean, maintained equipment in the right place meant the next day's start-up would go smoothly. She was meticulous about ropes being properly wound and stored, the tack being clean, and the floors swept.

From the door of the barn, Angie stepped out of sight and watched from behind her sunglasses as a black SUV parked in front of the main house. A man got out of the car, stood, and surveyed the estate.

Angie recognized Ben Davis even from the distance. It had been almost twenty years since she had seen him, but his tall, medium build, muscular frame, and wavy blond hair were the same. They had met the summer she and Tom were together. They had hung out frequently. She wondered if something had happened to Tom. Was that the reason for his visit to the ranch?

Angie watched from the shadows of the stable as Ben stared out into the primary field with interest. The cowboy riding a horse had caught Ben's eye. Daniel trotted the young horse from side to side, maneuvering without using his hands. Ben watched Daniel intently.

"Hello, Ben," the voice behind him said.

Ben turned and greeted Heather. Angie continued watching from the shadows of the stable, which was close to the house. She could hear their words.

"This is a surprise. What brings you back to Virginia? Your security team wrapped up work two weeks ago."

Heather, at Shelton's direction, had consulted with Ben on a new security system for the ranch. Ben owned a small security company on the side. He had managed most of the project virtually while his team performed the onsite work.

"I was doing some work in DC and thought I would stop by and check in," answered Ben. "The place looks amazing."

Angie recognized the higher pitched voice with a slight southern twang. There was no doubt it was Ben Davis.

"Thank you," Heather replied, beaming. Her white teeth shined from ear to ear. "We have been working day and night. It's all coming together nicely. Do you have time for a quick tour?"

"Sure," Ben replied. "I would love to see it."

Angie watched warily as the two climbed into Heather's truck. She stepped back behind the stable wall as the truck moved slowly past.

She'd never trusted Ben. Not from the moment she'd met him. There was something about him that made her suspicious. She had mentioned it to Shelton several times, but he didn't see it.

Less than an hour later, Heather and Ben arrived back at the main house. Heather gushed with pride at what the team had accomplished so far.

Inside the main house, Angie was starting dinner when Ben and Heather walked in the front door.

"Down by the river, it looked like contractors were putting the final touches on the log cabin and a boat dock. Did I see that right?" Ben asked.

Angie could hear the conversation and the patronizing question from Ben.

"Are you planning on having a boat?" he asked.

"The boss wants two jet boats," Heather answered. "The type that backwoodsmen used to navigate up and down rivers with rapids. Thick-bottom aluminum, shallow draft, and no prop. I think it's the frogman in him. He plans on spending more time here at some point, you know. By the way, how is Tom? I haven't seen or heard from him in a while."

"Interesting enough, I've been on a special assignment. Unrelated to Lambert. Honestly, I'm having trouble reaching him as well. That's why I'm here," Ben said. "He seems to have disappeared."

Just before she turned the corner into the kitchen, Heather stopped in her tracks.

"What? What do you mean disappeared?" Heather said.

"Well, I was with him in New York a few months ago. Then I left to do some fieldwork abroad. Apparently, he's on leave from Lambert Capital. Mr. Lambert doesn't even know where he is. I thought you might."

"How can you not know where he is?" Heather said, narrowing her stare with a concerned tone. "You're his security person."

"Yes, yes, I know." Ben lowered his voice. "But you know Tom. He doesn't really need or want staff following him around everywhere. That's the problem. He's operating solo and not communicating with anyone."

Heather turned away from her guest and walked into the kitchen. Ben followed. Angie closed the oven door after putting the fresh chicken in, then stood tall, turned, and looked at Ben.

Heather introduced the two of them. Angie extended her arm and shook Ben's hand, never breaking eye contact. Angie stood just over six feet tall with her work boots on. The height had her looking slightly down at Ben.

"It's nice to meet you," Ben said, raising his eyebrows slightly. After all it had been decades since they had met each other. Angie paused for a slight moment contemplating her next words. Her clinched jaw and penetrating stare indicated it wasn't nice to see Ben. She never liked him. Heather had no idea about Tom and Angie's past. Angie returned the greeting.

Before another word was spoken, Daniel appeared at the entryway to the kitchen. Angie watched as her son's emotionless and unblinking stare beamed down upon Ben, seeming to penetrate his psyche. Ben turned away abruptly with a concerned look on his face.

"Daniel, this is Ben," Heather said. "Ben is a friend of Mr. Shelton. Daniel is Angie's son."

Ben stepped forward and extended his hand to Daniel. Angie watched as Daniel gripped Ben's hand without breaking eye contact or saying a word. Angie could see the surprise on Ben's face as her son's large hands and long fingers engulfed Ben's smaller extremities.

"I saw you riding in the field. You're an excellent horseman," Ben said. "Where did you learn to ride like that?"

"Daniel has been riding since he could walk," Angie answered. "He loves horses, and they love him."

"I'm going to shower before dinner," Daniel said and departed.

Ben turned to look at Angie as Daniel walked down the hallway toward the staircase. Daniel's voice sounded like his father's, and he noticed. He wasn't aware that Shelton had a son.

"I'm going to get some vegetables steaming for dinner," Heather said. "Why don't you two get to know each other in the hearth room?"

Angie poured herself a glass of wine, then walked from the kitchen to the other end of the large open space and entered the hearth room. She sat down in a chair next to the fireplace, crossing her legs. Ben sat down next to her.

Ben leaned forward and whispered, "I know who you are, Angela Brady. I know who the father of your son is. I know what your son is. He looks just like him and commands his horse every bit as well as his dad."

At the base of the stairs, just off the hearth room, Daniel stood listening.

"I never liked you, Ben Davis," Angie said, glaring into his face. "I don't know what you are up to, but I don't trust you. So why don't you just come out with it? What do you want from us?"

"It's simple. If you see or hear from Tom, I need you to call this number immediately. He's in trouble. There are some powerful and bad people looking for him. I need to get to him before they do. Do you understand?"

"I haven't seen him since before Daniel was born," Angie said. "Yes, I know he owns this ranch. Yes, I know he sent Heather to recruit me. So what? He feels bad. He wants to take care of his son. A son he has never seen. The problem is, you're threatening the wrong people. What happened? He was your best friend. Why do you need us to help you find your boss?"

"It's complicated," Ben said, looking away. "Just do as I ask and everything will be fine."

"What does that mean?"

"It means, if I learn that you have knowledge of his whereabouts or hide him from me, let's just say I could make it very difficult for you." Ben wasn't smart enough to at least act like he was concerned for Tom.

"You are threatening us? Me and my son?"

"I am asking for your help, Angie," Ben repeated. "But I am confident your son would be valuable to certain people."

Angie's pursed lips, clenched jaw, and narrow stare said more than her words.

"The first time I met you, I knew you were trouble. Somehow, I just knew it. Fuck you, Ben!"

"Your son, Angie. Think about Daniel," Ben warned. "No matter what you think of me, think of your son. One phone call and I can destroy your world. One phone call, and you and your son will be eliminated. You will never be heard from again. Or you do what I ask and live out your life in a calm, quiet existence."

"Hey, Ben?" Heather called from the kitchen. "Would you like to stay for dinner?"

"No, thank you, dear. I need to get back to the city. I have work left to do. Let me know if you hear from Tom. Otherwise, we will assume he's okay."

"Sounds good," Heather said.

Angie watched the taillights of the SUV as it turned out of the gates and onto the main road. She walked over to her purse sitting on the bench, unzipped the inside pocket, and removed a small manila packet. She took a key from the packet and stared at it, her heart pounding.

The sound of footsteps approaching from the kitchen brought her back to reality. She quickly reassembled everything and replaced the key in her purse.

"Is he already gone?" Heather asked.

"Yes," Angie replied. "I think we need to close the front security gates. Ben suggested it."

"Your call," Heather said dismissively. "It's a little strange that Ben doesn't know where the boss is. Don't you think?"

CHAPTER TWENTY-SIX

THE BUSTLING NIGHTLIFE of Paris made it easy for the modern-day stranger to move about. Hauser's tall frame and black hooded coat made him one of the hundreds of odd-looking revelers roaming the streets of the seventh arrondissement in the middle of the night.

The cool air and the smell of bakeries preparing the next day's assortment of breads and pastries were soothing to Wolfgang Hauser. The fresh smells contrasted with street garbage, and the unbridled drunkenness, lust, and bestiality were visible on the sidewalks, products of human weakness. A testament and yet another fact in an endless stream of evidence that he was right. Humans were incapable of governing themselves. Every day the species degraded further into the abyss of greed, hate, and delusion. Each day having the ability to change, reverse course, but never doing so.

The tall lighted concrete gateway to Paris through the Arc de Triomphe and brick-paved, torch-lined roadway of the Champs-Élysées at night reminded Hauser of a less chaotic time. Hundreds of years before the First World War, he had roamed freely through the streets, cleverly disguised in the period garb of wigs, skin powders, and heavy, colorful fabrics. He'd blended in nicely.

The French aristocracy of the day knew him as the Duke of Rondeau. His love of music was well known among the elite of Paris, who bowed to his every desire. It was a time when his name demanded more respect than royalty. Kings and courts revered him. Judges didn't dare cross him.

As the centuries wore on, Hauser grew impatient. He was changing. His ability to command the elements of the earth waned but remained powerful. His sensitivity to light increased. Now, moving around the world at night was his only option. The changes were a sign that the end was drawing near. Perhaps his end. No. Denial was something weaker minds engaged in, not superior life forms like Hauser.

He was not in denial. The one standing in the sun was coming to save the species from themselves. That meant eliminating Hauser. He needed to prove that self-governance of any form of life could never work. If humans self-destroyed, his point would be proven right. He could revert back to performing his governor duties on apex one through six. Seven would have to be reconstructed.

The past months had taken Hauser to Istanbul, Rome, London, Singapore, and Beijing on holiday. Paris was his last stop. Europe was home. Civilized, by his definition. The best of humanity such that it could be. The rest of the world had been a feeble attempt at colonization and government. The worst of which was the new English colony called the United States. The name screamed arrogance and stupidity. Hauser didn't think humans could unite anything.

The maturity of the American democratic system was proving useful now. Free choice and wealth in the new world had produced greed, hate, and delusion at a remarkable pace. Now, a wealthy criminal narcissist was the leader of the free world. A president who spent his whole life lying while using and abusing the common person. The very people that the US president despised and trampled were the very ones who had elected him. An elegance that summed up the human existence from Hauser's point of view.

Benjamin Scott Davis had done well in the service of Hauser. The young boy from the streets of Ohio had exceeded his expectations. While the guardians watched and observed the murderous Tom Shelton,

Davis had befriended Hauser's potential adversary. Ben had gotten close enough to know Shelton's own demons. After twenty years, he had concluded that Shelton wasn't a threat to anyone. Especially to Wolfgang Hauser. Regardless, his orders were to find Shelton so Hauser's henchmen could eliminate him. That is what kept the big money coming in and pleased Hauser.

A Paris Summit meeting was the right place to start the next and final war. The chaos it would create in the power structure along with Staley's volatile mental state should light off World War III, a nuclear holocaust that would accomplish Hauser's mission.

Hauser made his way back to the King George Hotel just as the glow of morning light touched the eastern sky. The hotel was one of the finest in all of Europe. A hotel that Hauser had owned since the 17th century.

At the top of the Parisian architecture was Hauser's exclusive residence, a penthouse adorned with silver and gold. The furniture was handmade by French craftsmen. The original artwork throughout the 6,000-square-foot space was priceless.

Hauser walked into the library, closed the drapes, and sat down behind his desk. He picked up the phone and dialed.

"Ben Davis," said the voice over the speaker.

"Is everything in order, Benjamin?" Hauser asked.

"All the preparations are in place, sir," Ben replied.

"Fine," Hauser said. "Now go deal with our other problem." Hauser was referring to Tom Shelton.

"I'm already working it, sir," Ben replied in a confident tone.

"You should remove that smile from your face," Hauser demanded. "If he is who Xavier thinks he is, you have a big problem. You need a big solution."

❦

The next evening, the hotel lobby was bustling with international businesspeople. Oil barons, fashion moguls, and technology entrepreneurs from Europe and Asia crowded the hotel restaurant and club. The line of Rolls Royce's, Bentleys, McLarens, and Lamborghinis in front of the hotel was impressive. Tourists and locals were routinely stopping to gawk and take pictures of the expensive toys of the worlds most wealthy.

Hotel security and personal security people were everywhere. These serious-looking men and women were easily identifiable, dressed in black with jackets and earpieces for communication. Anyone walking through the lobby or club was videoed. Within seconds, the security detail evaluated each individual using facial recognition tools. If they identified a problem person, the hotel's general security quickly communicated the details to all others, and hotel security resolved the issue. A routine that was required at least twice per night. The team was so adept at the process that legitimate guests rarely noticed.

Tonight, the back entrance to the hotel was also crawling with security. French commandos guarded the access gate to the rear lot of the building. After presenting the proper credentials, the custom limousines drove through the back lot and into a covered parking pavilion. Only when the pavilion door closed behind the car did the occupants of the special transports emerge. The private elevator then whisked the VIPs to the top floor of the building. Car after car arrived for the special, invitation-only reception and dinner with Dr. Wolfgang Hauser.

Hauser examined himself in the mirrors as he prepared to join his guests for a reception and dinner. Perfection was what the satisfied expression on his face said. His ageless light-colored skin was perfect. His new hand-tailored dark blue French suit fit his torso neatly. The fabric had the right amount of silk woven in to create the preferred amount of shimmer. His dark brown Italian shoes, belt, white silk shirt, and royal blue silk tie satisfied his dress expectations for the events of the evening. There was no doubt in his mind that he would be the best dressed person in the room.

By nine o'clock, the chief diplomats representing the world's governments had gathered for cocktails in the foyer of the penthouse main dining room. The group was well on their way to a second round when Hauser entered. The politicians had all been well briefed on the decorum for the evening. Speak only when spoken to and try not to look into Hauser's eyes any longer than necessary. As a diplomat, the goal was to get through the evening and back to their embassy without messing up their boss's agenda.

Hauser made his way around the group, shaking hands and exchanging pleasantries. With each touch, he could sense the mind and tension of his guest. An inhuman ability that he used to manipulate others.

What once was a room full of presidents and prime ministers was now a group of high-ranking diplomats. A fact that angered Hauser. The show of disrespect was yet another indicator that they all deserved to die.

At the moment, the most obvious question on everyone's mind was, where were the Americans? Then again, with the unpredictable nature of the current US president their absence was no surprise. The reality was Ben Davis had passed along intelligence to the US administration not to attend.

"Thank you for coming this evening," Hauser said, addressing the group. "It is my great pleasure to host such a distinguished group. We have much to discuss this evening. Shall we move to the dining room?" He gestured toward the arched entrance. As the small crowd moved, Hauser looked at his watch.

✑

At twenty after the hour, Ben sent the catering delivery truck from the warehouse. The driver and the passenger began the trip toward central Paris. Passing around the Arc, they slowly navigated the vehicle down the Champs-Élysées before diverting onto a side street. The older section of the famous road was still cobblestone. The pavers bounced the delivery truck around. A small detail that Ben Davis had missed.

Ben watched on the tracking device as the truck diverted from the planned route. The truck slowly navigated through the narrow streets until it arrived at the back access gates of the hotel. Ben took a deep breath. The guards quickly waved the truck through into the main lot and then into the covered parking pavilion. The dot on the tracker disappeared. Ben stepped onto the electric scooter and headed for his next location.

The dinner conversation flowed freely. Each diplomat had prepared a list of topics for discussion. The coordination between governments was obvious to Hauser. It was as if the exchanges were scripted. Another indicator that it was time to act.

Hauser's viewpoints on political strategies and tactics were once highly sought after but rarely obtained. It was obvious now that the governments of the world were simply placating the once-famous political strategist. They weren't asking hard questions. They didn't seem to need guidance as to how to navigate the corruption. They had become the experts. Dr. Wolfgang Hauser was becoming irrelevant. The level of disrespect angered him.

After dinner, Hauser led the group back to the foyer for drinks, where the conversations continued. He was partially listening to the philosophy of an Eastern European diplomat when his attendant touched him on the arm. Hauser excused himself and stepped away from the gathering. He walked back to the private quarters of the residence.

The public spaces of the hotel were packed with guests as the clock approached midnight. Hauser swiftly slipped on his hooded silk outer garment while he proceeded to his private elevator. The chauffeured car was waiting at the back entrance of the hotel. He noticed the truck positioned exactly where he expected it to be. He looked at the driver of the truck and nodded as he slipped into the car and drove away.

The French security in the parking pavilion was gone. The security captain knew Hauser was in the building. He didn't like or trust the tall strange looking owner. Unmarked trucks made him nervous. The diplomatic details were staged in a room just off the library on the top floor.

The truck driver glanced at his colleague in the passenger seat, then repositioned the vehicle as close to the private entrance as possible. The two men casually got out of the truck, climbed aboard the staged motorcycle, and exited the private entrance of the hotel.

❧

Four blocks away, Ben Davis was sitting on a park bench. The motor-cycle sped past. He removed the device from his jacket, punched in a code, and pushed send.

Five seconds later, the quiet Paris evening erupted into chaos. As the initial explosives penetrated the truck, the entire central city shook. The accelerating force radiated out toward the main pillars of the old hotel. The first set of building supports fragmented, causing the build-ing to lurch upward. Hauser's guests felt the floor lift beneath their feet. Eyebrows raised, they each looked at the other, trying to process the sudden strange sensation as the floor dropped away from below them. Screams and confusion followed. The secondary blast ripped through the main floor lobby walls and into the private club, extinguishing all human sounds and sending body parts through the front windows of the building and out onto the streets of Paris. Dust from the eviscerated cement structure billowed up into the night air as the entire hotel col-lapsed to the ground.

⟨⟩

Sounds of sirens were now blaring across central Paris. The driver of Hauser's black Mercedes navigated around the Arc, obeying traffic laws. The freeway entrance was just ahead. Suddenly, two police vehicles sped past Hauser's car. The driver watched as the police vehicles slammed on their brakes, slid sideways, and blocked the entrance ramp to the freeway.

The driver stepped on the accelerator, quickly adjusting course for the side street just ahead on the right. As the car veered hard right, lights of the approaching van lit up the inside of the Mercedes. The van swerved left to avoid the black sedan.

The sudden sound of the blunt impact on the right rear wheel of Hauser's car sent it spinning toward the freeway entrance and the police barricade. The van tipped hard to the left, then flipped over onto its side, sliding into three other cars. Traffic in the roundabout ground to a halt.

White powder from the air bags filled the inside of the car. Hauser's chauffeur was collecting himself after being pummeled by the safety devices from the front and sides. A strange sound from the back seat caught his attention. The low, animal-like growl turned his disorientation to concern. Through the powdery smoke from the airbags, a set of long fingers attached to a larger than normal hand emerged from the back seat.

Hauser's hand smashed against the driver's face, pressing his head back against the headrest. The bones in the chauffeur's neck popped like snapping twigs. The hand released the driver's face, backed up, extending two of the fingers as it moved. Hauser plunged the fingers into the driver's eye sockets. Then, with one swift jerk, he tore the head from the driver's body and dropped it in the passenger's seat.

ᢞ

A police officer slowly made his way toward the black sedan sitting sideways in the roundabout. A second officer approached the van lying on its side. Bystanders were taking pictures and videos of the accident.

The annoyed look on the officer's face said it all. His city had just been terrorized and he was responsible for securing central Paris. The last thing he wanted to do was deal with some arrogant aristocrat who had just had his luxury car smashed in a traffic incident.

The officer approached the driver's side of the Mercedes, looking for movement inside. He opened the door and a headless body dressed in a black tuxedo tumbled out of the seat onto the brick roadway. The officer jumped back, gasping in surprise. The screeches and gasps from the bystanders quickly abated and turned into picture flashes and videos. Seconds later, three more officers were doing their best to push the crowd back.

Sirens echoed throughout the city as the passenger side back door opened. Dust powder from the airbags billowed out of the back compartment into the night air. The officer moved around the car, removing the holster strap from his sidearm as he walked.

A figure emerged from the back seat. The officer watched as the tall, slim figure made its way to a full standing position. The officer's observation worked its way up to the face of the imposing figure. A chill shot down his spine when the large black pupils looked at him from under the hood. The officer raised his revolver and pointed it at Hauser.

"What are you doing?" Hauser asked.

"Just don't make any sudden moves, sir," said the officer. "Are you okay? Are you injured?"

"I am fine," replied Hauser. "Put your weapon away. Go about your business."

"What happened to the driver?"

"He was fatally injured, you idiot," Hauser replied in a slightly raised voice.

"Take off your hood so that I can see you," ordered the officer.

The bystanders were moving around to Hauser's side of the car now. The camera flashes were more frequent as the onlookers observed the tall stranger covered in a black silk robe dusted in white powder.

"Turn around and put your hands on the car," the officer ordered. The police radio crackled as the second officer requested an ambulance for the passenger of the van.

Facing the officer, Hauser slowly raised both arms into the air. He opened his hands, stretching out his fingers.

"What the fuck?" the officer said under his breath, shocked by the inhuman appearance of Hauser's hands.

Hauser shook his head, causing the hood to fall to his shoulders. Flashes from cameras increased.

"Turn around," ordered the officer. "Right now."

Hatred and anger filled Hauser's face. He flicked his fingers upward. In an instance, fire shot from his fingertips, reaching up to the sky. Staring straight into the officer's face, Hauser let out a scream.

The penetrating sound caused the officer to drop his gun, grab his ears, and fall to the ground. Onlookers followed, screaming in pain as their eardrums burst. Windows in every nearby building shattered simultaneously. Chaos, panic, and horror filled the air.

Hauser stepped farther away from the car, spreading his fingers as he moved. The pillars of fire expanded into a wall of flames reaching higher into the sky. He lowered his hands to direct the intense flames of destruction toward the city and its humans. He turned slowly in a circle, the wall of fire extending from each hand scorched, killed, and destroyed everyone and everything in its path. Inch by inch, foot by foot, the fire consumed it all. Screams of people burning, cars exploding, and buildings falling echoed through the seventh arrondissement.

CHAPTER TWENTY-SEVEN

THE NEWS OF Ann's abduction hit Shelton hard. Finding her was now his top priority. Edwards was confident Providence could help. Within an hour of the call, they were in the air heading east back to the institute.

The private jet touched down just after twelve thirty in the morning at the small county airport near the Providence campus. A waiting car shuttled Shelton and Edwards to the operations center. The secured facility was located a quarter mile from the main offices, just off the back garden and four stories underground.

It impressed Shelton when the roadway in front of the car suddenly became a ramp leading down into a large underground bunker parking garage. Shelton and Edwards climbed out of the car and entered the operations center. The security people at Providence were now openly carrying weapons and on a higher state of alert.

The lead analyst was relaxing and sipping coffee when Edwards and Shelton entered the room. Shelton glanced at Edwards and noticed the look of disappointment on his face.

Without saying a word, the analyst pushed the play icon on the computer monitor. Together, they watched the latest recorded video footage from the hidden camera inside Ann's car. There it was on the monitor. The abduction of Ann Baker.

The woman behind the wheel was not Ann. The analyst played it back. This time, pausing on the perpetrator's picture.

"Anyone know this person by chance?" she asked, skepticism lining her face. "We are working on facial recognition at the moment..."

"I do," Shelton said, interrupting.

Edwards and the analyst both turned and looked at him expectantly.

"She's a detective I met in New York a few months ago," Shelton said. "Her name is Rawson. Los Angeles County Detective Lexi Rawson."

Shelton turned to Edwards.

"Why is there a camera in Ann's car?"

"When you went missing in Israel, we put her under surveillance," Edwards replied without missing a beat. "It's just good practice. Sometimes it's hard to know the good guys from the bad."

Shelton nodded, accepting Edwards's explanation.

"Indeed it is," Shelton said, turning to walk toward the refreshment station.

"Coffee?"

"Thank you, yes," Edwards replied, seeming to realize he should have been the one to serve his guest.

Shelton poured two steaming cups from the freshly brewed pot, then sat down at the table next to the attractive thirtysomething analyst.

"I noticed Rawson following me around New York one evening. First, outside my apartment. Then a little later the same night, at a club. She really isn't very good at surveillance," Shelton added. "I introduced myself. I didn't confront her. I thought I would see how she handled the surprise interface. She did an excellent job of playing it straight. We chatted. Then she gave me her business card." Shelton smiled slightly as he fished it out of his wallet. "It has her cell phone number on it. Can you trace the device?"

The analyst looked at Shelton confidently and took the card from his fingertips.

"I saw her again in Colorado as Ann and I were leaving for Asia. The detective was watching us at the airport. She was taking pictures. That must be where she saw Ann. Boarding the aircraft, that is…"

"Ann is the bait to get to you? But Rawson had you in New York?" Edwards said, looking a little perplexed.

"She had him in a bar in New York," said the analyst. "She had no reason to arrest him. Or jurisdiction. She wants to talk to you, doesn't she? Alone. No record."

"It seems to be very unconventional, frankly extreme, even an amateur approach for a professional," Edwards said.

"She's the most decorated detective in California," the analyst interjected, reading Rawson's background from the screen. "And she's way out of her jurisdiction. They—the locals and federals—must be giving her some latitude and support. She's on a mission, for sure. She must have a wild-ass theory about you, Mr. Shelton. My guess is her bosses have you on the no-touch list for obvious reasons."

"Wealthy, powerful friends," Edwards chimed in.

"Not to mention your personal skill set," the analyst said. "You could probably have them all ended with a phone call."

"She struck me as an aggressive, passionate person," Shelton said.

"Not very smart for a high-achieving detective," Edwards said, shaking his head in disbelief. "What do you think she wants to talk to you about?"

⦌

By that afternoon, the team at Providence was pretty certain their analysis of the situation was spot on. There were two abductors that kidnapped Ann from the parking lot. Perpetrator One, Rawson, was hiding in the back seat of the car. When Ann got in the driver's seat, Rawson reached around and placed a towel over Ann's nose and mouth. Presumably, there was a chemical on the towel that put Ann under.

Perp Two, a dark-haired male, early forties, opened the passenger door and dragged Ann into the passenger seat. Rawson jumped into the driver's seat and drove away. The video captured Rawson's partner getting into the driver's side of a black SUV in the parking lot.

Ten minutes later, they transferred Ann to the SUV on a side road and parked her car in a shopping center. The SUV drove directly to a Maryland location. The tracking device Edwards had given Ann for safety had worked perfectly.

The Maryland home was an "out of use" safe house, according to the FBI's asset list. It had been out of service for over a year. The Washington, DC-based Providence team had mobilized within minutes of Ann arriving at the safe house. A drone equipped with a night optical camera was in the air within an hour. The next day drone video footage had captured Ann taking a walk in the garden behind the home. She appeared unharmed. A young male agent with blond hair accompanied her. Shelton examined the pictures of the three cops as the analyst wrapped up the briefing.

"What does the area around the safe house look like?" Shelton asked.

"Fairly isolated," answered the analyst. "As you would expect. Nearest home is about a half mile away in any direction," she said as she handed Shelton a set of high-resolution pictures. "This utility corridor," said the analyst, pointing to the picture, "is a good covert approach path. If you give us another day or two, we can get more info on the comings and goings."

"Keep working," Shelton replied. "Call me when you have something new."

૭

The early morning drive to Maryland took Shelton just over four hours. Every hour or so he adjusted the FM radio frequency to the next available public station. The early media reports from Paris suggested the attacks were the work of two different assailants. The initial indications from the Parisian authorities pointed toward terrorism.

Shelton turned off the highway onto an unpaved road that led to a hiking trail. The trailhead parking area was almost full. Shelton parked, slipped on his pack, and set off.

The morning sun was rising above the hills. There wasn't a cloud in the sky. Two miles up the trail, Shelton studied his map. He took a drink of water, and looked up and down the trail. No one was in sight. He stepped off the trail into the woods and began sprinting up the hillside. With precision and smoothness, he weaved between trees, ducked under bushes, and leaped over fallen timber. Three minutes later, he reached the top of the hill and disappeared over the crest.

Another half mile and he came to the utility corridor. The enormous towers with high-voltage wires stretched from hilltop to hilltop. He followed the edge of the tree line for another mile to the private road that led to the safe house and Ann Baker.

⨕

Just after sunset, Shelton broke camp. He moved through the trees, slogging his way to the main security gates in front of the safe house. He took up position behind a large tree, pulled out his phone, typed the message, and pressed send.

Almost an hour later, lights from an approaching vehicle beamed through the forest as it rounded a bend in the road. The state forestry official pulled up to the gates and stopped. The woman pressed a button and spoke a few words into the speaker. A few seconds later, the gates opened. Shelton crouched and followed the pickup truck up the driveway. As the truck turned left onto the circle drive toward the front doors, he slipped into the shrubbery for cover.

Before the ranger was fully out of the truck, the front door of the house opened. A perplexed-looking, blond-haired young man stepped out and began speaking to the ranger. After a brief exchange, the ranger climbed back into the truck and headed down the drive and out the gate. The FBI agent stood on the front steps looking out into the darkness.

⨕

The next morning, Rawson and NYC rookie officer Redmond stood trading looks outside the front door of the safe house. Rawson had reached for the doorknob, but there wasn't one. What had been the doorknob and latch had been melted onto the surface of the door. The cops looked at each other and drew their revolvers without speaking. Rawson slowly pushed the door open. There was no one in the main entryway. The house was quiet.

Rawson looked around and saw the young FBI agent sitting on the living room sofa, quietly staring straight ahead. She moved toward him slowly while Redmond kept watch from behind.

Agent Cody's weapon was lying on the cushion beside him. Spent shells were lying on the area rug in front of him.

"Where is the house guest, Agent Cody?" Rawson asked.

Cody turned his head toward Rawson, making eye contact. "She's gone," he said in an emotionless voice.

"Is there anyone else in the house?" Rawson asked quietly.

Cody shook his head. "She left with him," he said without additional prompting.

"Who is 'him'?" Rawson asked.

"I don't know who he was. He walked in the front door. I drew my gun and told him to get down on the floor. He didn't comply. He looked at me as if he was going to kill me. I fired three shots directly at him. He simply held out his hand, and the bullets disintegrated in midair."

Shelton's power and capabilities were increasing since his meeting with Adira. His ability to command nature and the physical universe were now limitless.

"I emptied my clip on him," the young agent continued. "He stood there looking at me. Then he went upstairs to get the guest. I tried to call you, but my phone wouldn't work and the landlines were dead. When he came back downstairs, I attacked him again. But…but he just threw me across the room with a brush of his arm. Then he walked over to me and pulled out his gun. He pointed it at my forehead. I thought I was going to die. He demanded the keys to the car. Then he suggested I find a new line of work. They both walked out the front door together and drove away."

Rawson stood there stunned, her mouth open. "What time did this happen?" she asked once she'd collected herself.

Cody looked up at the clock on the mantel and pointed. The clock read 1:10 a.m.

"The clocked stopped when he walked in the door."

Rawson demanded a description of the man. Agent Cody complied. Rawson froze when she realized who Cody was describing. Panic emerged on her face.

"Clean this place up, Agent Cody," Rawson demanded. "Let's get the hell out here."

Redmond walked into the room just as Rawson gave the order.

"I found these in the guest room upstairs," he said. Redmond handed Rawson the pictures.

Her face went blank with disbelief. There they were. Abducting Ann from the store parking lot. The next picture showed the two of them entering the safe house with Ann.

"The car!" Rawson said. "Did you say he took your car?"

Cody nodded.

"Then whose car is out front?"

Cody looked outside to see what Rawson was talking about. He thought his car was gone.

"That is the agency car I'm driving," Cody said, his voice cracking slightly from nerves and concern. "But he took it."

The voice from behind came as a complete surprise. "That is your car. I borrowed it for a while."

Rawson and Redmond turned and started for their guns, then stopped. Shelton's gun was pointing at them.

"Have a seat," Shelton instructed, using his gun to motion toward the sofa. Shelton sat down in the chair across from the three cops.

"Now why don't you start by telling me what you are up to," Shelton asked politely.

Rawson quickly retorted, "Go to hell."

Shelton snickered. "Maybe I will. If you want to save your careers, I recommend you start talking. Oh, and by the way, if you try to get away, I will kill you. If you tell me who put you up to this nonsense, I will walk away. You can clean up the place and get back to work as if nothing ever happened. Just that simple."

"How much is it worth to you?" Rawson said.

Shelton looked at the detective blankly. "Is there something about your current situation that leads you to believe we are negotiating, detective?"

"You're rich," Rawson said. "I figure if you want information, you might pay for it. After all, you will not kill three cops," Rawson replied confidently.

"You are right, detective. I do not suppose it really matters whom you are working for. However, it makes me furious that you abducted a wonderful friend of mine. A friend who is the mother of a young son; a daughter to a lovely family; and a valued professor for her students. Presumably your efforts were aimed to get to me?

"Well, here I am. What do you want to talk about? Do you want to arrest me? Would you like to deliver me to your employer?"

Without warning, Redmond suddenly dove across the coffee table toward Shelton. With quick precision, Shelton jumped to his feet, caught Redmond by the throat out of midair with his left hand, all while keeping the gun trained on Rawson with his right.

Shelton held Redmond in the air with one hand, squeezing his neck, causing the cop to gasp for air. During the commotion, Rawson managed to get her backup gun drawn and pointed at Shelton.

As she fired her weapon, Shelton moved Redmond into the path of the bullet, using him as a shield. All three rounds from Rawson's gun hit Redmond in the center of the back, killing him.

Shelton tossed Redmond's body at Rawson, knocking her back onto the sofa. He then kicked the gun out of her hand and stood there looking at her with an emotionless stare.

The LA detective had reached for Redmond's backup gun without Shelton seeing it. With all her strength, she shoved the dead body off her lap, leveled the gun at Shelton, and attempted to squeeze the trigger.

Before Rawson's weapon fired, the bullet entered her ear canal, tunneling into her head and blowing the other side of her skull into the fireplace.

Agent Cody slowly lowered his weapon and holstered it.

After a moment of staring at the remains of Rawson's head, Shelton turned and looked at the junior agent with a curious expression.

"You didn't have to do that," Shelton said.

Agent Cody looked Shelton in the eye. "They were bad people, sir."

CHAPTER TWENTY-EIGHT

THE EUROPEAN ARTIFICIAL Intelligence Command had concluded that it was a 99.72 percent certainty that the US had carried out the attacks in Paris. The world's leading experts in the field had analyzed every recorded word, phrase, sentence, and voice inflection available from the US president. Based on Staley's past words and behaviors, the AI analysis showed it was virtually certain he had ordered the attacks. Hauser's plan was working.

The group of experts were now working on forecasting the future. Program logic, running on banks of super computers, could predict with almost certainty what Staley was going to say before he said it. And it could predict what the reaction would be to his words. The AI group had run countless future scenarios of what could or would happen next. The problem was the Monte Carlo analysis was consistently arriving at the same conclusion. It was 99.93 percent likely that Staley would launch a first strike nuclear weapon into Europe while he was president. The seemingly unfathomable act was now highly likely.

The only suggested course of action from the AI model to avoid a nuclear strike was for the leaders of Europe to do whatever Staley told them to do. Which, at the moment, meant Europe was to buy all their oil from the US and Russians as a show of appreciation for the world's true superpowers. A narrative that Staley was pushing harder and harder in recent public appearances.

Andrew Wilkinson wasn't convinced the AI computers had it right. He and Shelton had discussed and debated Staley's condition many times. The president was a juvenile in a man's body. A bully who was virtually all talk but little action. A puppet in the hands of those around him. Those who were more sophisticated, perhaps more devious, could influence Staley's actions. The one pulling Staley's strings was the imminent threat.

The overwhelming human political support for the AI predictions was something Wilkinson hadn't expected. Computers predicting what humans would do. Humans acting on the information. Even the AI experts tried to highlight the need for human judgment in critical decision paths.

However, when the experts flashed the percentages showing certainty and an imminent threat, the call to act against the US was overwhelming. Turning back was not an option.

The conclusions were proving useful for Wilkinson. He now had wide latitude to take any action necessary to preserve the European way of life.

In his own words, "Europe will never capitulate to a madman. Regardless of whence it comes. Never! Not while I am breathing."

❧

The private aircraft touched down just after dark in Cheyenne. The black sedan pulled up to the aircraft stairs. Shelton stepped off the aircraft and into the car.

Waiting for Shelton in the back seat was Admiral Nate Wood. Wood had made the call to Shelton following a secret meeting in South Carolina. The two didn't waste any time. Within hours they were on their way to Edinburgh with Sam Kearns to meet with Wilkinson. Three days later, they had a plan.

Wood had completed his task. He had convinced acting CIA

Director Walker to persuade the president to meet with the Europeans. Wood had also casually mentioned to Walker that Lambert Capital's Vice Chairman Tom Shelton may have information about the events in Paris and would attend the meeting.

Walker's initial hesitance vanished when he heard that Shelton might be in attendance. Wood had made a mental note of it. Within days, Walker had the meeting set. The CIA director selected the location in Boulder, Colorado. It was remote but assessable compared to the east coast. It would be Walker's opportunity to have Shelton killed. Hauser would be pleased.

∽

The southbound traffic out of Cheyenne on I-25 was light down to Boulder. Shelton and Wood had barely said a word to each other as the Flat Iron Mountains came into view under the light of a full moon. Shelton wanted to take in the cool night Rocky Mountain air. It soothed him. The driver made his way through the neighborhoods at Shelton's direction. Then four blocks away from the hotel, the driver stopped. Shelton got out and made the short walk up to Pearl Street and over to the hotel.

The secret service was waiting for Shelton in the front drive of the hotel. A young woman in a dark suit directed him to a waiting government SUV.

Five minutes later, up the hill from the city center, they turned onto the University of Colorado's campus. Two turns later, the road ended at the university's Institute for Behavioral Science. The plain four-story building on the north edge of campus was secluded. The fleet of security vehicles lined the side street in front of former homes converted to university offices.

The heads of state had already arrived, and the meeting was in progress. Shelton stepped into the library quietly. The French president, Wilkinson, and the German prime minister turned to see Shelton standing in the doorway.

Shelton greeted the European leaders. After exchanging pleasantries with the officials, he walked over to President Staley and extended his hand.

"Good evening, Mr. President," Shelton said in a respectful, warm voice.

The president faked a smile, glanced up, grunted slightly, and looked back down at the floor. Shelton lowered his hand while he studied Staley. The president was wringing his hands as he sat there. Shelton turned away and sat down in the remaining wing-backed leather chair.

Wilkinson began by thanking Shelton for taking the time to meet on such short notice. He apologized for the inconvenience, then got right to the point.

"Mr. Shelton, let me be candid. My colleagues believe you are involved in a conspiracy to overthrow our governments," Wilkinson said. "They believe you had a hand in the attacks in Paris. I think it's nonsense."

Shelton stared expressionless at Wilkinson.

"Regardless," Wilkinson continued, holding up his hands to stop Shelton from responding, "if it was you, they are prepared to look the other way. Or if you know who is responsible and disclose to us who the perpetrators are, we have an opportunity for your firm. Legitimate work that will make you wealthy beyond anyone's wildest dreams."

Shelton raised his eyebrows with interest and glanced around the room.

"I'm listening, Mr. Prime Minister," Shelton said.

Wilkinson explained they were looking for a partner to evaluate, recommend, and lead several cross-border business mergers. He spent the next twenty minutes walking Shelton through a variety of ideas.

"We are prepared to grant Lambert or a new firm led by you, if you wish, to take on one hundred percent of the mandate with a minimum fee of one billion dollars payable in advance," Wilkinson concluded. "What do you think, Mr. Shelton?"

Shelton sat there with a contemplative look on his face.

"I am flattered by the offer, ladies and gentlemen. It is certainly intriguing. Such a large undertaking would require several firms. I am afraid I would have difficulty managing such a project unilaterally."

Staley's hands were turning faster now.

"Look, Shelby," Staley began, mispronouncing Shelton's name. "I don't know what the hell you are up to, and I don't really care. These people have convinced me that what they are proposing is the best course of action. Therefore, if I were you, I would jump on the deal. Asking some banker to help manage the balance of power is stupid. After all, what can you do? You are just a dumb fucking banker. You have never really created anything," Staley ranted. "I have created things in my life. Me, many great things." Staley pointed to himself. "You nothing." Staley continued to point his finger toward Shelton. "Do you hear what I am saying?" Staley gave Shelton a pointed scowl. "Now, we have all taken our valuable time to travel to this place in the middle of fucking nowhere. If I had my way, we would simply lock you up in Leavenworth and forget about it. You know why? Do…you…know…why?" asked Staley again.

Shelton remained silent as he continued facing the president.

"Because you are guilty!" Staley said, pounding the table with his fist.

"Are you going to talk? Can you speak, Shelby?" Staley commanded, finally pausing.

"Mr. Shelton, I am confident you can see and hear the president's passion for this matter," Wilkinson interjected. "He has a certain style and viewpoint that the rest of us don't share. But we would welcome your thoughts on the situation."

The plan that Wood and Wilkinson had dreamed up in Edinburgh was working. Shelton had been skeptical. The plan seemed too overly complex to him. At the moment, however, it seemed as if it was working. Resolution began settling in on Shelton's face. Staley was smiling from ear to ear, clearly impressed with his own performance.

"Frankly, everyone, I am afraid all of you are wasting your time," Shelton said in a calm, controlled voice. "The business opportunity you present is obviously very interesting. However, the notion that I somehow influence the world's balance of power is simply not true. Flattering, but ridiculous. President Staley is right," Shelton said, pointing to Staley. "I am just a banker. A dumb banker. I don't really know anything."

A look of satisfaction lit up Staley's face. At the same time, the hand wringing stopped. He rested his arms on the chair. The president's brain was feeding on the compliment from Shelton. The compliment would replay multiple times inside his head to extend the feel-good moment.

Shelton watched as Wilkinson, separately, looked his French and German colleagues in the eye. Each of them nodded their final approval to move forward. Then Wilkinson looked at Shelton and gave him the green light.

Outside the building, a black sedan and small utility van pulled up and parked near the front entrance. In the car's back seat, Walker checked his watch. A bead of perspiration trickled down his face. Field work made him uncomfortable. He was inexperienced. Wood wanted Walker on the scene in case something went wrong. There would be someone to blame.

Walker stepped out of the car and walked back toward the van. He tapped on the cargo door. The panel slid open.

"Why is it so fucking dark around here?" said Walker, asking an agent inside the van. "I can't see shit!"

The senior field agent sat there holding his silenced automatic weapon, watching the acting director.

"Four of the most powerful people in the world are inside that building right there, boss," replied the field officer. "I would imagine secret service had something to do with it."

Walker looked down at the ground, avoiding eye contact with the officer.

"Don't F this up, hero," replied Walker with a shaky voice. "You understand?"

"Get back in your car, sir. It's safer there." The officer's clenched jaw and narrow stare suggested he might consider other, more punitive options for his boss.

Walker looked up as the panel door closed in his face.

"I don't know who you fucking spooks think you are," yelled Walker as he hit the side of the van to emphasize his comment.

The sound from Walker's hand hitting the van was faint but audible inside the library. Shelton's head turned toward Wilkinson. The curious expression on his face confirmed he had heard noise outside as well.

The smug, sideways contemptuous smile on Staley's face beamed as he looked around the room at his colleagues. His condescending expression oozed arrogance and disrespect.

"Mr. President," Shelton said, breaking the silence.

The sudden voice startled Staley.

"Why did you order the attacks in Paris?"

Staley's contemptuous look shifted to anger in the blink of an eye.

"I didn't order any attack. Are you stupid?" Staley exclaimed. "Not that it was a bad idea, you know. But I didn't do it. But you guys know," Staley said, pointing to the European leaders. "You know you have gotten away with making us superpowers pay for everything. You sit around sipping tea and wine while we pay the bills. Do the work. Maybe you need to do a better job with your security."

Shelton glanced at Wilkinson a final time. The prime minister nodded, confirming Shelton's question. Shelton slowly stood up, walked around the coffee table, and positioned himself in front of Staley.

"What are you doing? Get the hell away from me," Staley ordered.

Shelton looked down at the president with a stoic expression.

"If you didn't order the attacks, then who did?"

"Are you trying to interrogate me?" Staley responded as he leaned forward to stand up. "Is that what this is?"

Shelton put his hand in the middle of Staley's chest and firmly planted him back in his seat. Staley grunted as the back of the chair met his body, knocking the wind out of him.

The intensity of Shelton's glare into the president's face made the other leaders twitch.

"You have hurt many people in your lifetime. You will hurt no one else," Shelton said without moving a muscle on his face.

"What the hell is this?" Staley yelled. "Get your hands off me. Security?" Staley flailed his arms as he tried to catch his breath. "Wilkinson, get this son of a bitch away from me. You are all going to pay for this!"

The German prime minister had moved to help Staley, then stopped.

"What are you doing?" Staley yelled again. "Get security! This pussy can't threaten me like this."

The German PM stepped up to Shelton's side, followed by Wilkinson and the French president.

"Your friends here are tired of your idiocy. They want you dead, Mr. President. How do you feel about that?"

Staley leaned forward again, trying to get out of his chair. Shelton's hand planted him back in the chair a second time. This time with more force.

"Don't you idiots realize this guy is a loser? A loser! I am the most powerful man in the world. I am the best president this world has ever seen. You can't stand by and watch this loser treat me like this. Where the fuck is my security?"

Shelton held Staley firmly in the chair. He leaned in toward the president, who tried to move his head back to avoid Shelton but failed.

Shelton leaned in and whispered into Staley's ear.

"Die nakhash."

Electricity started flowing from Shelton's hand into Staley's chest. The sudden jolt of current caused Staley to scream at the top of his voice. Shelton increased the pressure on Staley's body, the voltage racing through the president went higher.

The electricity ripped through the president's arteries and veins, causing his heart to change rhythm. A second later, Staley's heart exploded inside his chest. The grunting and cries for help stopped. Staley's body slumped sideways in the chair, his eyelids open wide. His pupils fixed and dilated.

Shelton stood back and adjusted his suit coat. The sound of the last volume of air exiting the president's lungs was audible.

He turned to the Europeans.

"You are courageous, Andrew. But that was the simple part. See it through to the end. Take care, my friend."

Without another word, Shelton turned and walked out the door of the library.

Wilkinson checked his watch. Then the British PM reaffirmed the agreement with his colleagues. They would stick to the story. The President of the United States simply had a fatal heart attack during a meeting at Camp David.

Admiral Wood and Sam Kearns would handle the body, the falsifying of medical reports, and the announcement.

⮌

Shelton's driver was standing beside the car when he walked out the side door of the building. As he made his way toward the car, he checked the license plates. Same car, but the driver was different.

As Shelton approached the vehicle, the driver opened the back door for him. Shelton noticed the black van parked thirty meters away. He could see the silhouette of two men in the front seats and the rifle barrel sticking up on the passenger side.

"Thank you," Shelton said. "I think those guys are going to be a little while, so I'm going to take a walk to kill some time."

The driver moved quickly, holding out his hand as if to show Shelton into the back seat.

"Sir, my instructions are to take you back to the hotel."

"Fine. But after I stretch my legs," Shelton said in a pleasant tone.

Shelton turned and began walking away from the car. He walked alongside the building toward University Avenue. As he rounded the corner onto the front side of the building, he could see the car and the van moving his way.

As soon as he was out of the driver's line of sight, he began sprinting toward the next corner. He rounded the corner, turning left at a full sprint.

As he approached the backside corner of the institute, he glanced behind him just as a muzzle flash lit up the darkness. The sound of three bullets whizzed past Shelton's left ear and ricocheted off the building in front of him. Another left and he was on the backside of the building out of the line of fire.

Shelton found the path in the trees that he had used at least a hundred times during the summer he studied at the university. Moving as quickly as he could, he followed the steep path down the hill on the north side of the campus to Boulder Creek. He crossed the footbridge, jogged across the park, and climbed into the waiting car with Admiral Wood.

Walker's attempt to eliminate Shelton had failed. Hauser and Ben Davis would not be happy.

CHAPTER TWENTY-NINE

THE EARLY MORNING fog had burned off in the higher elevations of the Virginia hills. In the valleys, tiny water droplets remained suspended in the air, obscuring the visibility. Regardless, every ten minutes Angie exited the main road, turned around, waited, and watched. She noted each car that emerged from the fog, passed, and then disappeared. She doubled back several times to ensure no one was following. An hour and a half later, she arrived in the city of Marshall.

The key to the security deposit box had been in the side pocket of her purse for almost ten years. She'd kept it safe since the day Shelton showed up out of the blue at the Wyoming ranch where she worked. It was the day he'd opened up to the love of his life and shared his childhood memories: the sexual abuse of his friends, the sudden death of his mother, and the suicide of one of his abused friends. That day he professed his love for her, and she learned Shelton could see paranormal life forms. How the guardians used to watch them that summer after her college graduation. That was the day she learned the father of her child was a murderer.

The confession should have shocked her. It didn't. When they first met, she knew there was something different about Tom Shelton. He was strong but gentle, attentive yet distant. He was intrigued by people and life itself. Love was marbled through his body, yet his connection with people seemed uneasy. While he was nothing but gentle, kind, and loving, he seemed dangerous. Angie never dreamed he was a killer. Regardless, she developed an affinity for the dichotomy of the man she loved. While the diversity of his personality made him unpredictable, she liked the potential danger. It made her feel alive. In some strange way, she felt safer around him.

Angie found she loved him even more following his disclosure and confession. He had sought her out and told her the truth, simply because he loved her. Not because she was clamoring to know or dragging it out of him. He bared his soul and took the risk, hoping she would understand and love him anyway. She did.

At that moment, instead of reciprocating, Angie kept her secret to herself. Shelton didn't know they had a ten-year-old son. She wanted to tell him. But she also wanted Shelton to love her for who she was. Not because she was the mother of his child.

A few years later, she showed up at Lambert Capital and made her confession. She handed him a picture of Daniel. She watched his face as he studied the picture. Shelton's stoic expression never changed. Not even a little. He placed the picture in his suit pocket and that was that. She hadn't seen or spoken to him since.

The security deposit box was at the local bank in Marshall, Virginia. Inside was Shelton and Angie's emergency communication plan. Angie had never had a reason to use it. The visit from Ben changed that.

She removed the cash from the box, purchased a burner phone from a local store as instructed, then sent a text to the phone number on the note. Within a few minutes, a reply came back.

"Richmond Airport. Select Aviation. 5 p.m." Angie sighed, took a deep breath, and began the drive south. Before leaving the ranch, she had taken steps to protect their son just in case Ben Davis decided to become more aggressive. Angie was friends with the Leesburg County sheriff. She reported Ben's unexpected visit as trespassing. The sheriff bought the story and committed to having officers in the area watching around the clock until she returned. After all, the owner of Lookout Point was a notable Leesburg figure. Additionally, she had instructed her son to sleep in the bunkhouse away from the main estate home. Angie was confident that with Daniel's physical ability, martial arts skills, and trained competency with weapons, he could defend himself properly with enough warning.

⌁

The Waves Hotel was one of the few luxury hotels in the world that remained privately owned. The resort was nestled between the Atlantic coastline and the Inter Coastal Waterway on a secluded piece of property near Palm Beach. Shelton rarely visited his home at the top of the hotel. No one knew he owned the hotel. Not the employees. Not even those closest to him. It was a true hideaway. Just like his New York City apartment on the upper west side, and several other properties scattered around the globe.

The SUV stopped under the covered drive in front of the private residence entrance. The back door opened, and Angie stepped out. A hotel security guard greeted her.

"Miss Brady?" asked the young woman.

Angie nodded her head slightly, confirming her identity.

"May I show you to your room?"

Angie surveyed the area, looking for anyone suspicious, then agreed.

"This way please," the young woman said, pointing the way.

She led Angie into a private corridor, showed her to the elevator, scanned a badge, and pushed the button for the top floor. Angie was alone in the elevator as it ascended to the penthouse level.

When the elevator doors opened, the hallway in front of Angie led to the front doors of the only room at the top of The Waves. She stepped out of the elevator and walked down the corridor to the double doors of the penthouse. She took a deep breath and pushed the button for the door chime. A few seconds later, the door opened. Shelton and Angie Brady were face to face.

The man and the face standing in front of her had changed. Shelton was thinner, his body leaner, his irises were lighter, and his hair a bit more gray.

"It's nice to see you, Angie," Shelton greeted her warmly. He held out his arms, requesting a hug.

Angie smiled and accepted.

He wrapped his arms around her waist while her arms embraced him around the shoulders.

"It's nice to see you too," Angie replied as she closed her eyelids, seeming to enjoy the moment.

"Please, come in." Shelton stepped out of her embrace. "Let me show you to your room where you can put your things."

Angie followed him down the hallway. Her look worked its way up and down Shelton's body. The view made her smile.

"Here you are." Shelton gestured toward the bedroom. "If you want to put your things away and freshen up or anything, please take your time. I'll open a bottle of wine and meet you on the veranda when you're ready."

Angie set her bags and purse down next to the sofa, then walked over to the window. She stood in front of the floor-to-ceiling glass. The Atlantic Ocean spread out in front of her. Below, she could see people walking on the beach. She freshened up, then made her way out to the veranda.

The sun was below the horizon now as night moved in from the sea. Shelton was sitting in the fading light sipping wine when Angie sat down beside him on the sofa. The slight onshore breeze blew through her long, straight hair.

Shelton handed her a glass of wine.

"Cheers!" he said, holding up his glass.

"Cheers," Angie responded with a warm smile.

"You are a dream to look at, Angela Brady," Shelton said with a smile of his own as he took a drink of wine.

"That's kind of you, Tom." She shifted on the sofa. "It's very nice to see you too."

"How was your trip down? Any concerns?"

"Uneventful, thankfully," Angie said calmly. "I made sure I wasn't followed. I followed the instructions."

Shelton smiled. "I can't even tell you how much I was looking forward to seeing you."

As happy as she was to see her love, Angie was on a mission not a romantic getaway. This was all business. The surprise visit and demeanor of Ben needed to be addressed before any reuniting. "You know, Tom, I'm not here on vacation. This is not a reunion."

She watched as he returned his gaze to the ocean, his warm, loving look fading.

He turned back toward her. "How is Daniel?"

"He's fine," she said. "He's turned into a man. Right in front of me."

Shelton smiled.

"Where is he?"

"He stayed at Lookout Point with Heather," Angie replied. "There's work that has to be done. He's a key member of the team now. He will run the show before he turns twenty-one, if he has his way."

Shelton looked back out at the ocean with a proud expression.

"Ben paid us a visit yesterday," Angie said.

Shelton's gaze quickly narrowed.

"Heather, Daniel, and I. There was, was something about Ben that Daniel didn't like. Watching the two of them stare each other down was like watching two alpha male wolves. Daniel wanted to come with me. He wanted to protect me. But the question is, why is your head of security looking for you? Shouldn't he know where you are?"

"Ben took some time off to work on a special project," Shelton said, taking a sip of wine. "I haven't seen him lately."

"Well, let me tell you what he did." She told Shelton about the conversation and the threat Ben had made toward her and Daniel.

"What I want to know is why he showed up at my doorstep and threatened me and our son?" Angie said in a demanding tone.

Under his breath, Shelton said, "He must be—"

"He must be what?" asked Angie, cutting him off.

Shelton turned and looked at her. "It's complicated."

Just as he finished his words, the doorbell rang.

"Dinner is here," Shelton said as he stood up. "Are you hungry?" He held out his hand to help her up from the sofa.

Angie took his hand and stood. "I want some answers, Tom. That's why I used the key."

Shelton looked down at her, their faces close together. He peered into her eyes.

"I love you, Angie," he said. "I would do anything to protect you and Daniel. If I had known about Ben, I would have already killed him."

⌘

At dinner, Shelton shared with Angie the newfound aggression by the guardians, his father's last words, and Macari's story about his mother. Angie's gaze was locked on his as he described meeting with Amir and the attack in Buenos Aires. By the end of dinner, Shelton had arrived at the story of Abdel Kinneret.

He lifted the phone and called the hotel staff. Ten minutes later, the table was empty and the staff was gone. Shelton and Angie refilled their wineglasses and walked back out onto the veranda. The sound of ocean waves breaking on the beach was louder now. The white foam from the waves rolled up onto the sand and crashed against the rocks, then retreated into the dark waters.

"The tide is coming in," Shelton said, looking out at the water.

Angie sat down on the sofa and sipped her wine. Shelton flipped the switch on the gas fireplace, then sat down beside her. They sat closer together than before, and the subtle smell of her perfume wafted up his nose. A smile washed across his face.

"What are you smiling about?" Angie asked.

He raised his eyebrows and took a breath.

"I've often dreamed about this very moment," he said. "Sitting next to you in front of the fire. The smell of your perfume. The sight of your face and your smile next to me. It's all I want to think about."

Angie leaned against him as he wrapped his arm around her.

"The thought of this moment has sustained me all these years,"

Shelton continued. "The thought of you and I together forever motivates me."

"Tell me about Abdel Kinneret. Tell me about Adira," Angie said.

Shelton took a deep breath and a sip of wine.

"I was trying to have a romantic minute there, in case you didn't notice," he said lightheartedly.

"Another time, my love," Angie said. "We're in two very different places at the moment. You are taking an evening away from your work. I am here to find answers. Your chief of security threatened me and our son. You act like we're on a date. While I am trying to understand what the fuck is going on, not get in your pants. So get me up to speed so we can be on the same page."

Angie watched the strong Tom Shelton look down from the scolding. He took another sip of wine, then a deep breath before walking her through his meeting with Adira. Angie's gaze narrowed as Shelton stared into her soul.

"My name is Magnus Elian," Shelton said. "I was born from a human that was appointed to be my mother. Her name was Elizabeth. In earthly terms, I am half human, half spirit. I am older than dirt. Literally," he said, smiling slightly. "In the spirit realm, age isn't a relevant measure."

Confusion appeared on Angie's face. A look of concern quickly replaced it.

"I know it sounds outrageous. Delusional. But think it through, Angie," he said. "Daniel is my son. You are his mother. I am someone from another realm in a human body. That makes our son unique. Very unique. But you have no doubt discovered that. You know he's different. He has never been like the other kids, has he?"

Angie let out a slight gasp. She looked at the ground and took a deep breath.

"I know." Angie's voice was shallow. "I know. I knew you were different from the moment I met you. Your presence is consuming. Invasive. You were too smart. Too strong. Your body was too perfect. Your skin doesn't even have blemishes like a normal person. Daniel's skin looks just like yours."

She paused and took a big drink of wine. "Only your lover and his mother would know this."

Shelton reached out and touched her hair. Still looking at the ground, she closed her eyelids and drew a breath.

"What does this make me, Tom?" Angie asked, exhaling a breath while pressing up against him harder. "Where do I fit into the world? Your world? Do Daniel and I have to hide the rest of our lives from people like Ben Davis while you are out doing whatever?"

"I didn't know who Ben was until tonight," Shelton said. "I missed it." Ben unexpectedly showing up at Lookout Point and threating Angie and Daniel along with his defiant demeanor in the parking garage after the guardian sighting meant Ben Davis was the enemy. It also meant the enemy had been in Shelton's midst for twenty years, and he hadn't seen it.

Shelton recalled the night at the Lambert Capital party. Ben could see the guardians in the parking garage with no help. Ann saw them in Jerusalem, but only after he had touched her face. Amir had warned him about immortals in Buenos Aires. A chill ran down his spine.

"Angie"—Shelton leaned forward to emphasize his next words—"I will do everything in my power to protect you and Daniel."

She looked up at Shelton. "But how can you protect us?"

Shelton raised his eyebrows. Without saying a word, he removed his wristwatch and bracelet. Then he stretched out his right hand toward the wineglass on the table. Angie sat up straight, watching, noticing the branded marks on his wrist. Without touching the glass, heat began radiating from the palm of Shelton's hand. Slowly, the crystal glass began glowing, then gracefully melted into a puddle of glass on the table.

Shelton turned back toward Angie, then stood up. He held out his hand to help her up from the sofa. He took her hand gently in his and led them toward the rail of the veranda. The breaking waves were now crashing on the beach below. The roar of the water pounding the sand was the only audible sound in the night air.

Shelton raised his left hand, his palm facing the ocean. He stared out into the darkness. Slowly, the pounding surf subsided. Angie watched as crashing breakers turned into gentle waves caressing the sand. The sound of a distant barking dog rolled down the beach.

He then raised both hands and a gentle breeze began to blow. The sunshades on the cabana on the other side of the veranda moved. As the wind intensified, the shades lifted into the air. The fabric on top of the structure flapped violently, almost tearing the top from its supports. Shelton lowered his hands, and the wind stopped on his command.

Angie turned back around toward the ocean. She looked down and watched as the breakers were building back up, the sound of the water drowning out all other sounds once again.

Shelton turned to face Angie. He held out his hands with his palms facing toward the sky. He gazed into her eyes and stepped closer. Angie slowly lifted her hands and placed them in his. He closed his fingers around her hands firmly.

"I have never known love before you. I have never known the love for a son. That is not how I was designed. That is not who I was before. But you humans can love. Can feel the emotion of love. No other life forms anywhere have this ability. Now, I have found human love, and nothing, nothing can change that. Magnus is dead. I know who I am now. I know what I must do. I will carry out Adira's mission. I will succeed, Angie. I will save you and me and Daniel… I will save all of us."

Shelton leaned in and kissed her gently on the lips. Angie raised her hands, placing them on his cheeks.

"I love you, Thomas," she whispered as a tear rolled down her face. "It's hard to understand all of this, but I believe you. I trust you. I will always love you. No matter what happens."

Shelton smiled as her warm hands rested on his face.

"I have to go," Shelton said. "Be careful at the ranch. Don't let your guard down." He took a deep breath, turned, and departed.

CHAPTER THIRTY

THE TAPPING ON the door of the guest house woke Shelton from a restful sleep. He rolled over and looked at the digital clock on the bedside table. It was just after six o'clock in the morning.

He tossed off the bed covers. The cool air hit his skin, making goose bumps form. He quickly slipped on his black exercise tights, hooded sweatshirt, and indoor shoes, then walked to the front door. Charles Edwards was standing on the other side, holding a steaming cup of fresh coffee.

"Good morning, Tom," Edwards said with more enthusiasm than Shelton could muster this early in the morning.

Shelton's narrowed eyelids flickered, and his eyebrows raised at the warm greeting. He sighed, trying to fully wake up.

"Good morning, Charles." Shelton stepped past Edwards onto the brick drive and took a deep breath of fresh morning air.

Shelton had returned to Providence following his meeting with Angie. In front of him the Providence headquarters sat majestically on the hill a half mile away from the guest house. The green field in between the cottage and headquarters was covered in morning dew. A light layer of fog hovered above the treetops.

Shelton turned and smiled at the elder Edwards. "Well, Charles, what brings you calling at the crack of dawn?"

"I would like to talk to you. May I come in?" Edwards replied.

Shelton gestured toward the front door. Edwards walked in and sat down on the sofa next to the cold fireplace.

"Since you didn't bring me a hot cup of coffee, do mind?" Shelton asked, pointing to the empty carafe sitting on the kitchen countertop.

"Of course not." Edwards glanced to the kitchen as Shelton headed to the coffee machine.

The leader of the Providence Institute raised the shades in the hearth room. Gray light poured in through the wall of tall windows. Then he sat down on the sofa and began flipping through his notes.

A few minutes later, Shelton sat down in the chair next to the sofa. He took a few sips of the fresh coffee, then looked at Edwards.

"Well, what is on you mind, Charles?" Shelton held the coffee cup just below his bottom lip.

Edwards looked up from his notes. Shelton watched Edwards survey the marks on his uncovered wrists.

"Tom," Edwards began, shifting his stare from Shelton's wrist to his face, "I think the puzzle pieces are coming together. My team delivered me all the research on the late Reverend Brooks and Dr. Wolfgang Hauser. I've been pouring through it for the last four days."

Shelton raised and lowered his eyebrows as if to say "and?"

"I, I have a quick question first. When was the last time you saw a guardian?"

Shelton's eyelids narrowed slightly. "The evening I walked out of the garden."

"Okay, that's good to know." Edwards made a note on his legal pad. "Now, after Ann contacted us initially and we learned of Professor Schwartz's execution, we were quickly able to take possession of his private library. We purchased it actually," Edwards said. "We've gone through it thoroughly."

Shelton sipped his coffee and stared blankly at his guest.

"Turns out the sole focus of Schwartz's life research was on

Dr. Wolfgang Hauser. The library has documents that date back to 500 BCE," Edwards said. "Five hundred years before the start of the Common Era. Five hundred years before Christianity or any other modern-day religion. Can you believe that?"

"Interesting," Shelton said.

"Yes, interesting," Edwards replied. "We found a diary in the collection that dates back that far. It appears to be the diary of Wolfgang Hauser. We think it is in his own handwriting."

Shelton took another sip of coffee.

"That makes Hauser over two thousand five hundred years old, Tom."

A sympathetic expression arrived on Shelton's face. "What did he write?"

"He mentions his brothers." The enthusiasm faded from his voice. "One he refers to as Michael. The other he refers to as Magnus."

Shelton sat forward, listening intently.

"Hauser laments that he himself is being blamed for the vile transgressions of humans. He refers to humans as 'the species.' While he is blamed for the human condition, his brother Magnus is systematically and indiscriminately killing the species in droves to correct the species experiment gone bad."

Shelton took a deep breath, stood up, and stretched while Edwards watched.

"More coffee, Charles?" he asked.

"Coffee?" Edwards said. "I just told you there's a person walking around today that is thousands of years old, and you stand up and offer me coffee?"

Shelton smiled at Edward's intensity.

"Take it easy, Charles," he said. "We have all day. It's early."

Shelton walked to the kitchen and poured himself another cup.

"I guess that explains why they killed the professor, doesn't it? He knew too much about Houser," Shelton said, standing behind the kitchen bar. "You said you had put the pieces of the puzzle together. Tell me what else you have."

"I'm sorry, Tom," Edwards said, taking a step back. "This is all so unreal! It's fascinating on one hand. On the other, it scares the shit out of me."

Shelton laughed out loud. "I understand, Charles. Trust me. It's a pinch yourself moment, without a doubt."

Edwards paced about the room. "That makes Hauser the chief influence of evil in the world and you are his brother Magnus. Magnus the adjudicator in ancient times. The one in the Hebrew scriptures who carried out Yahweh's commands. The one who slaughtered the irreverent and unseemly for thousands of years."

Edwards was growing increasingly more agitated at the revelation. His voice was becoming louder yet cracking from time to time.

"That makes you the one who rained down waters, killing almost everyone on the planet. But then you stepped back, and the prophets and others tried to set the example for humans. Examples of how to overcome the power and influence of evil. But nothing worked," Edwards concluded, slamming his fist down on the countertop. "Hauser's influence was too strong. His influence remains strong and is growing, Tom. The human condition continues to deteriorate. Armageddon is a foregone conclusion, and humans will destroy themselves. We will all die unless…unless someone stops him." Edwards pulled his handkerchief from his pants pocket and wiped the perspiration from his brow.

"You are the one, Tom. You are the one who can save all of us." Edwards set his notepad down. "You have the mark. But what is the seven for on your other wrist?"

Shelton continued to stare at Edwards as he held up his wrist.

"I have to find seven souls to help me," Shelton replied. "Seven souls to help me find and eliminate my misdirected, narcissistic brother. Willing, helpful souls who are committed to saving the species. Souls who are committed to sacrificing themselves for the greater good, if required."

Edwards's expression looked as if he wanted to ask more questions but couldn't.

"That's not all I have to discuss, Tom." Edwards rubbed his neck and continued to perspire. "Hauser leads a group called the Grand Council of Religion. It's an unofficial United Nations organization. It's the organization he uses to manage the culture. The people. His influence flows down the ranks rapidly. He touches almost everyone on the planet through this channel. Brooks was one of the twelve members of the governing body on the Grand Council. When you killed him, the guardians showed up at your doorstep. Watching. Observing. Then they tried to kill you, but you prevailed. Hauser knows you are here."

Shelton sat looking out the window. The gentle wind moved the leaves and branches of the trees.

"The last time you saw guardians was when you left the garden?" Edwards asked.

"Yes," Shelton replied, continuing to look out the window.

"Strange. What happened while you were in the garden?"

Shelton walked Edwards through his instructions from Amir. He confessed to Edwards that he had stepped out of the garden to follow a priest into the Church of All Nations. He escaped, but they saw him.

"There it is," Edwards said. "The missing piece. If they are not watching any more, then Hauser knows it's you," he concluded. "He is merging his resources. He's trying to speed up an apocalypse."

A knock on the door surprised both Edwards and Shelton. Charles stood and walked to the front door. The senior analyst handed Edwards a piece of paper. Edwards read through the note, talked briefly to the young lady, then thanked her and closed the door.

He turned to face Shelton.

"An emergency meeting of the Grand Council has been called by Hauser. It's scheduled for one week from today in the council's grand hall below the United Nations building." Edwards ran his hands through his hair. "Hauser is expected to be there."

CHAPTER THIRTY-ONE

THE SECURITY AT the United Nations was better than ever, but far from top-notch. Shelton had managed to pass himself off as a British journalist for the past few days. He had become just another reporter covering the day-to-day business of the UN. He hadn't gone unnoticed.

Several of the more seasoned security staff monitoring the entrance checkpoint had noted the well-dressed Englishman. The run-of-the-mill beat reporter assigned to international relations tended to be younger and dressed more casually. After a couple of conversations with Shelton, their curiosity was gone, and they were treating him like a regular.

As the week went on, he moved his reporting location to the south end of the main lobby. There was very little daily traffic past the main elevator bank. It was perfect for self-recording his afternoon and evening reports. More importantly, it positioned him close to the entrance of the corridor leading down to the Grand Council chamber. There he could watch the arrival and departure of the council members and their staffs.

Traffic in and out of the unmarked door increased as the day of the special meeting drew closer. Shelton maintained his cover while discretely capturing videos and taking notes. He made the necessary effort to get interviews and comments from the strangers wandering in and out of the cream-colored door ten meters away from him.

The clergy and their staffs were well disciplined. The sharply dressed, smooth-talking reporter had only gotten three brief interviews the entire week. None of them were on camera. The fake interviews helped validate Shelton's disguise and credentials for the security staff. More importantly, he had gotten photos of the barcodes from council members' identification badges. Now Providence operations had what they needed to create an access badge for Shelton.

❧

The next evening, Shelton stepped out of the taxi onto the sidewalk in front of the United Nations. He entered the building through the main doors, greeted security, and made his way to the south end of the lobby as usual. He stopped next to his group of chairs, turned, and looked back. Everything was normal.

Shelton made his way across the lobby, pretending to look for another camera angle from which to report. With no one else headed his way, he took one more deep breath and scanned his badge. The door clicked as it unlocked, and he stepped through the heavy steel doorway, then paused as the door closed behind him.

A minute later, the quiet voice in his earpiece said, "All clear. No one else is arriving."

The hallway in front of Shelton was empty. The corridor floor sloped gently downward toward the lower levels of the building. A midcentury floor tile, cream-colored cinder block walls, and smell of fresh floor cleaner gave the passageway an old and sterile ambiance.

Providence had done its homework on the entire UN complex. The south end section of the building was the oldest wing on the campus. The research team had pictures of a pre–World War I Catholic church that had once occupied the piece of Manhattan real estate. At the time, it was a known conference location for US religious leaders. Following the war, the League of Nations bought up real estate around the parish with an eye to the future.

The Providence team had found archived photos from a *New York Times* journalist that chronicled the underground construction taking place on the newly acquired land. It turned out the site was on the reporter's path to work. The construction apparently intrigued the journalist enough to document the building of the belowground council chambers in pictures. But seemingly, he never convinced his editor to turn it into a story.

Post World War II, as the new General Assembly building took shape, concrete and serenity pools replaced the grass and trees covering the underground facility. The underground chamber remained but wasn't shown on any building blueprints. The architects had made it vanish.

Shelton assumed the security cameras at each end of the hallway were operational. He slowly walked down the slopping floor with a slight limp, then sat down on the bench just outside a door marked "Conference Chambers."

He slid closer to the door, listening. He could still hear bustling on the other side. A few minutes later, the noise stopped, and he went inside.

The security guard monitoring the hallway watched the black-and-white image of a figure moving down the corridor away from the camera. The guard sat up in her chair, inspecting the screen. She reached out and clicked the mouse button.

"Hey, Stubs, you want some coffee?" her partner asked.

Officer Suzanne Stubs quickly turned away from the monitor to look at her fellow officer.

"Sure, thanks," Stubs said as she stared with interest at Officer LaPlante's body.

"Give me a break," replied LaPlante, shaking her head slightly from side to side. "I'll be back in a few minutes."

Stubs turned back to the monitors. The hallway was clear.

Shelton sat down on a bench and pretended to look through his camera bag while watching the elevator door close across the room. An assistant turned from the elevator and walked over to a door marked "Observation Seating" and went in. Shelton waited a few minutes, then followed.

The balcony was steep. The large wooden beams spanned across the council chamber from wall to wall. Shelton could see the entire floor of the chamber. He took a seat behind the rest of the observers. Several glanced his way. No one reacted to the unfamiliar face in the crowd.

The chamber of the Grand Council was visually stunning. Colorful, intricate paintings lined the domed ceiling. The columned walkway on one side of the chamber floor was adorned with gold lamps, chandeliers, and paintings.

The main gallery was a sea of individual desks. Each member had his or her own workspace. At the front of the room was a long, gently curving table that spanned the width of the council floor. Standing behind each of the eleven chairs at the board table was a flag representing the geographic area of responsibility for each council board member. Behind the eleventh chair stood the United Nations flag.

In front of the board table on the main-floor level was an intricate crystal figure. A world globe with a serpent wrapped around it. The same one that was on the pommel of the guardian's saber Shelton had captured in Argentina. Shelton studied the idol from his seat. The serpent's seven red jeweled eyeballs spanned out toward the council members.

The sound of a gavel striking its base plate brought the quiet chatter in the hall to a stop. Those standing quickly moved to their seats.

From underneath the balcony, a procession of five figures emerged. Four gold-robed guardians emerged into full view. An impeccably dressed, thin figure surrounded by guardians entered the chamber. Shelton watched as they escorted their principal down the main aisle toward the board table and the eleventh chair.

The guardians moved gracefully down the aisle. Dr. Wolfgang Hauser's tall frame was bent over slightly. He moved carefully. Over one hundred years of confinement to the physics of the earth was taking its toll on the immortal. The humans were unaware of the guardians surrounding Hauser, but Shelton could see them clearly.

One by one, Shelton watched the guardians bow before the globe and serpent. Without touching the idol, they moved aside. Hauser made his way around to the backside of the idol, then placed his large hand on top of the globe. Red beams of light shot out of the eye sockets of the serpent, lighting up the council members. Hauser drifted his stare from one side of the chamber to the other, then back again. Then he turned and made his way to his seat in the middle of the leadership table and sat down in the United Nations seat. Cardinal Bianco stepped to the podium positioned to the side of the main table.

Bianco began by paying tribute to the world's religions and the importance of the mission: solidarity, collaboration, and leadership. He stressed the need to work together to continue building their respective enterprises and to work closely with governmental leaders. He advised the council to expect human injustices; expect pain and suffering; expect wars, crime, and despicable things.

Bianco slammed his hand on the podium, exclaiming, "We are not perfect! They made us imperfect. Despite our imperfections, we must endure to perpetuate our organizations. The leaders are us. We must continue to bring along our flocks. We must continue to foster a powerful belief in our truths. Our narrative. Our flocks cannot cope with the realities of this earth. This universe. It is beyond their ability to comprehend without having the knowledge we have. Dr. Wolfgang Hauser has given us this gift."

The council chamber broke out in applause, each member standing to show proper respect.

Although Edwards and Adira had implied such, Bianco's words confirmed the truth. The entire world was being misled. Consciously and deliberately. The system of religions and governments, filled with greed and power, was taking the species not into the heavens but into an apocalypse. Everyone in this room was helping. These were the generals and field officers perpetuating Hauser's lie.

A sudden disturbance in the balcony caught the attention of those on the chamber floor. Several heads turned to see what was happening. A mist filled the air and descended from above. A substance fell on the council, landing as small dark red spots on their skin and clothing.

"It's blood!" someone screamed in a loud, shrill voice.

"Oh my God!" came another voice as panic set in. "It's raining blood!"

Faces looked up to see what was happening, only to feel the sticky moisture land gently on their skin. Members began running toward the columned corridor on the side of the chamber.

A panicked Orthodox priest hurried down the main aisle. His focus was set on a side exit in the hallway. From behind, a young, fast-moving woman wearing a business suit lifted her forearm and knocked the heavy-set elder priest to the floor as she tried to make her escape.

Hauser glared up into the air. He watched as the crimson-colored liquid began dripping from the balcony floor above onto the heads of the council members below.

With one wave of his hand across the balcony, Shelton had executed everyone. Some of the staff had been cut completely in half, others lost their heads. The force and heat of Shelton's strike vaporized skin and human blood at the point of impact, sending it skyward in a fine mist.

Before anyone could escape the chamber, the double-entry doors burst open. The bright light from the anteroom created the outline of a person standing there, looking down the main aisle of the chamber toward Hauser.

The room fell silent as everyone turned toward the figure.

Shelton entered the chamber and began walking down the center aisle toward Hauser. No one moved as they watched the trim, muscular stranger. Shelton had removed his jacket, shirt, and tie on the way to the chamber floor. His black undershirt hugged his torso, revealing his powerful upper body. Halfway down the aisle, a minister jumped in front of him.

"Stop! Who are—" Before the man could finish his words, Shelton, without missing a stride, used the electricity from his right hand like a sword, severing the man's head from his body. A mist of blood puffed into the air as the middle-aged, mustached head fell into another's lap with the eyeglasses still in place.

Gasps and screams again filled the air as Shelton pushed the headless body to the side and continued on his path.

Sitting in his chair with his hood pulled over his head, Hauser watched the stranger coming down the aisle. Shelton and Hauser's eyes met as he stood in front of the globe and serpent.

Shelton squinted slightly as he examined Hauser's face. He closed his eyelids tightly, then reopened them. Nothing had changed. Shelton could see the resemblance between the person staring back at him and himself.

Hauser's lips bent upward slightly.

Shelton assessed the situation. There were only two guardians standing next to Hauser.

As fast as he could, Shelton raised his right hand. The bolt of electricity rocketed toward Hauser, striking the globe and serpent first. The idol disintegrated into millions of pieces of molten glass shrapnel. Before the electricity reached Hauser, both guardians stepped into the path of the shot. The guards exploded into dust. When the dust settled, Hauser was gone.

Shelton turned just in time to see a blade swinging toward his neck by another guardian. He ducked, moving in a circular motion beneath the blade. With his left hand, he grabbed the demon's elbow. With his right, he redirected the swing blade back toward his attacker. The saber stuck the guardian in the face. Shelton reached out with his bare hands, grabbed the demon by the neck, and ripped its head from its body.

Shelton's strength was increasing the more he used his command of the earth's elements.

A burning pain blazed through Shelton's body. He turned quickly, firing electricity across the chamber as he moved. The speed of his rotation tore the saber handle from a guardian's hands, and Shelton blasted the last guardian into dust.

Looking down, Shelton saw the tip of the saber sticking out of his T-shirt. His chest was rising and falling faster as breathing became more difficult.

He stood in the middle of the chamber, looking around at the others in the room staring back at him in shock. The pommel of a saber was buried in his back. The tip of the blade protruded from his chest.

Shelton drew a scant breath, raised his hands to the sky, and screamed. The intensity of the sound cracked the entire structure of the council chamber. The shifting foundation damaged the doors, making leaving the chamber impossible.

Concrete and plaster fell from the ceiling onto the members below. Screams of pain and panic filled the air once again. The balcony broke loose and fell, killing everyone who had moved toward the back of the room.

Shelton slowly strode between the falling debris, passing Bianco hiding behind a pillar as he made his way to the emergency exit. He blasted the door open, turned, and, with all his ability, shot a column of fire down the corridor that incinerated everyone and everything inside the chamber.

✍

Headlights beamed around the corner into the alleyway. The SUV sped toward Shelton as he fell onto his face, motionless. The Providence team lifted Shelton into the car and sped off.

"How much time?" asked Edwards.

"Three minutes to the helicopter," replied the driver.

Shelton looked up to find Edwards staring at him.

"You are in terrible shape, Tom," Edwards said. "There isn't much bleeding. Removing and repairing things might be a little dicey, though."

"I had Hauser in my sights," Shelton said. "He escaped. Charles, I failed you. I failed all of you."

Edwards sighed and looked away.

"Angie is missing, Tom," Edwards said. "There was an enormous explosion and fire at Lookout Point. It's destroyed. Heather is dead. We haven't found Angie or Daniel."

Shelton's eyelids flickered, then closed as he lost consciousness.

✍

Four thousand miles away, at the same moment, the ground beneath the Basilica di San Pietro moved without warning. The quake grew as the seconds passed. The violent shaking knocked hundreds of people standing in St. Peters Square to the bricks. They watched as the Basilica collapsed into a pile of rubble.

CHAPTER THIRTY-TWO

THE EVENING FOG rolled in from Block Island Sound, sweeping across Connecticut, the Hudson River, and down upon Manhattan Island. The lights of the city through the fog cast a calming but ominous look. Ben, Mattie, and her son exited the Upper East Side restaurant. Ben carefully looked up and down the street for anything out of the ordinary. The damp air obscured his view more than he liked. Then they turned and began walking toward their Park Avenue home.

Ben Davis was a stable person, considering his upbringing. He had been raised in a poor neighborhood in Columbus, Ohio, by a substance-dependent uncle. Alcohol and drug use were all around him from a very young age. His uncle's revolving door of men and women partners had been less than a good example for the young boy.

The young Ben found solitude and safety in his bedroom. It was his sanctuary. The slightly oversize room had everything he needed: a desk, TV, refrigerator, and a sitting area. None of the riffraff from his uncle's exploits dared enter the room. Ben once watched his uncle almost kill a guy with his bare hands for opening the door. Ben knew he was safe there. He kept his little home spotless, neat, and orderly.

The safety and solitude of the room and Ben's interest in comic books helped him cope. The comic book characters led to an interest in the military and soldiering. When he was seventeen, he enlisted in the Navy. Five years later, he was assigned to LT JG Thomas Shelton's special operations team.

Shelton reminded Ben of a comic book character he had admired growing up. He was the leader of a super-secret military team. He was faster and smarter than everyone else. The brass looked to him for advice and ideas. It should have been like working for a real-life hero. It wasn't. For Ben, it was like working for someone who had all the advantages in life that he never had. Else the roles might be reversed.

Ben assumed someone had handed Shelton the money to pay for college. He assumed Shelton had a loving father and a mother at home. Maybe Shelton didn't have a silver spoon, but it looked like it from Ben's point of view. The commander had advantages others never had.

Cardinal Bianco changed all of that for Ben. Bianco recruited Ben to stay close to Shelton. To watch. Observe. Then report any out of the ordinary behaviors or actions. For a million dollars in advance, Ben was happy to take on the task. It was a job he had been doing since joining the naval special operations team under Tom's command and before Tom and Angie had met.

It was Ben's big break. His restitution for enduring an upbringing that should have destroyed him. Cardinal Bianco recognized that Ben had value, and that felt good. At that moment in his life, he was the winner and Shelton the loser. The new Range Rover in the team's parking lot was evidence.

Years later, Ben decided that the initial money for his services wasn't enough. He wanted more. He approached Bianco, demanding more money. That's when Bianco introduced Ben to Wolfgang Hauser. Ben was no match for the cunning and persuasive Hauser. Ben received his payday, but Hauser owned his soul.

Ben mentally froze as he, his wife, and her son rounded the last corner before the entryway to their residence. Shelton's satin-gray sports car was parked across the street in plain sight. Ben worked to control his emotions, hoping Mattie wouldn't notice. He increased his pace to get into the building quicker.

The door attendant greeted the family and ushered them into the foyer, where they took the elevator and up to the 36th-floor penthouse. Ben looked straight ahead at the wood-grained panel of the elevator while thoughts whirled through his head.

As the residence door closed behind them, Ben took a deep breath and processed the situation. Shelton was in the area and wanted Ben to know it. A scare tactic.

"Ben?" came Mattie's raised voice, holding up a video game case as she walked back into the main room of the residence. "I thought we agreed Mason was too young for this game." She shook the case. "Zombie Mission! Are you serious, Ben?"

Ben looked at the game with a stoic face and sighed. Without answering Mattie, he turned and walked to the window and looked down. Shelton's car was gone.

"Ben? Really? Why did you buy my thirteen-year-old son this game?"

"I didn't," Ben replied. "Tom sent me a text and said he had dropped off a gift for Mason. The staff must have brought it up." Ben stood a little straighter, pleased with his quick thinking. "I'll return it and get him a more appropriate game."

"That isn't like Tom," Mattie said. "He surely knows me better than that. And why is the staff coming into our home without asking us?"

Ben had been with Mattie Ekelsen for twelve years. The two met at a bar in Virginia Beach one evening while Ben was on a two-week rest from his naval operating team. The first two years together were satisfying and rewarding for both of them. Ben was providing a nice home, life, and companionship for Mattie. She relished the time to be a stay-at-home mom with her young son from a failed marriage. Now, it was question after question. Criticism after criticism. Mattie never stopped. The more she had embraced Ben's money, the nastier she had become. Ben tried encouraging her to get a job, hoping it might bring her back to reality. Just the suggestion of her going to work had spawned a brand-new set of negativity. After she had a few drinks, everything was three times worse for Ben.

"Tom has been going through some difficult stuff," Ben said, controlling his emotion. "Maybe he just got a little off track and forgot."

"That isn't the nice, sweet Tom I know," Mattie said. "Take it!" She pushed the game at his chest. "And go explain to my son why he can't have it."

She turned and stormed down the hallway, slamming the double doors of the owner's suite behind her.

Ben turned and walked over to the bar. He opened the liquor cabinet to retrieve his vodka glass, his concern now turning to anger as he recalled Mattie's words. *That isn't the nice, sweet Tom I know.* His face went pale when he saw the piece of paper leaning against his favorite glass.

Ben looked over his shoulder to make sure Mattie wasn't watching, then he read the note.

"If you harmed Angie and Daniel, you will regret every second of your life."

Below the words was a mark. Two dots. Fang marks. The marks Shelton's twin-bladed dagger would leave on his combat kills. Ben had seen him use the weapon many times. He slowly looked around to make sure Mattie had not reentered the room. He removed his phone from his pocket and dialed.

"He is in the city," Ben said. "Tell Walker to launch Project Patriot ASAP, full scale."

✄

Shelton's rapid recovery from the guardian's saber shocked the medical staff at Providence. What would have taken a normal healthy person months to recover from was now just stiffness and soreness for Shelton. The blade had missed his heart by a fraction of an inch. The difference between life and death for his human body. That fraction of an inch would have ended Adira's mission and been the end of humanity. Hauser would have succeeded in his goal of destroying the species. At the very least, he'd create living hell on earth.

The weight of his mistake made Shelton nauseous. He realized he had jumped the gun. He couldn't make the same mistake again, no matter what opportunity for justice and revenge might present itself. No matter if someone had taken Angie and Daniel from him. It wasn't about justice anymore. It was about love. Love for each other. Love of humankind, the earth, the stars. Arresting the evil influence of Hauser on the species was the greatest act of love. Adira had told him that very thing. But only now was he fully understanding it.

Shelton had to manage his natural instincts for truth and justice, and it would require discipline. A discipline that went against his natural instincts. A discipline that would require managing his anger.

He only now realized he couldn't do this alone. Shelton needed to complete the cadre of seven. The seven humans that Adira required to help him find Hauser and stop him. Shelton was two people short. He had pored over the names thousands of times. He had only five: Ann, Edwards, Wilkinson, Wood, and Macari. They all met the criteria. They believed that the world was more than one dimensional. They believed in him without full knowledge of the situation. They had faith and trust in something greater than themselves and humankind. They were the five who would willingly lay their selfishness aside, hoping to change the trajectory of humanity.

In his zeal for justice at the Council, Shelton had let everyone down. Hauser had escaped.

And through it all, he had been blind to the deception by his best friend. Ben had completely fooled him. He never saw his friend and fellow soldier as a threat. That Ben could see the guardians had been suspicious, but Shelton never followed up. Now Angie and his son were missing. And he was convinced it was Ben's doing.

✧

The evening drive into the city helped settle Shelton's nerves. He was back on his feet, moving around. Edwards called him a modern-day nomad. A label Shelton found fitting.

He checked his phone, then shifted his eyes back to the road. No messages. Each time he looked, he expected to see something from Angie. There was nothing. Only silence.

Shelton was confident Angie had avoided the attack on the estate. She had known to be on full alert. He had warned her. She was too smart to let Ben capture her. The thought of the alternative was unbearable.

Regardless, every ounce of Shelton's being wanted to eliminate his former security chief. His "protector" had deceived him for twenty years. Ben had pretended to be a friend.

After leaving Ben's place, Shelton drove across the park before turning south on to Central Park West. Within minutes, the car was parked in the underground garage, and he was in his suite overlooking Central Park. He slipped on a dinner jacket and made the short walk down to Columbus Circle. He stepped into the main entrance of the restaurant right on time. Dominic, the owner, was waiting for him.

"Good evening, Tom," said Dominic in a low, velvety voice.

"Hello, Dom. It is very nice of you to greet me," Shelton said.

"Of course. Let me show you to your table."

Shelton followed Dominic through the kitchen and out into a private, secluded room in a small alcove off the main dining area. The private room overlooked Columbus Circle from the fifth floor. Shelton had a perfect view down Central Park South.

"Will anyone be joining you this evening, sir?" asked Dominic.

"Not tonight," Shelton said. "I'm just going to sit here by myself and get drunk, if that's okay?"

"Perfect," replied Dominic. "I will send in Susan. She will make sure you are taken care of. Anything you desire, you let her know and she will make it happen. Anything, Thomas."

"Thank you, Dom. You're very kind," replied Shelton.

Dominic turned to exit the room just as Susan appeared with a double whiskey on the rocks and a fresh glass of sparkling water.

Shelton sat alone in the quiet room. He sipped the whiskey as he looked out across the dark park and down the street. He waited for Ben's next move.

Shelton had five properties in the city. Three were safe houses. Even Ben didn't know about them.

Shelton punched the security application on his phone. He watched as the digital cameras captured a tactical team's arrival at his Upper East Side residence. The building manager opened the door for them just as instructed. Fifteen minutes later, the local police unit was streaming out of the building back to their vehicles.

A few minutes later, a much larger convoy of black unmarked squad cars, SUVs, and tactical vehicles streamed through Columbus Circle, making their way east down Central Park South. The convoy spread out at intervals down the street. The large, armored vehicles stopped in front of the old Essex House Hotel.

The penthouse of the historic hotel was Shelton's primary residence of record. Ben started with Shelton's residence on the Upper East Side. The one Ben was familiar with. Shelton wasn't there. Now Ben was moving on to the Essex House residence. What Ben didn't know was that Shelton hadn't used the location in years. Instead, he had bought and refurbished another residence with one of his shell companies on the Upper West Side. No one knew about that location, or the others located around the five boroughs.

Shelton continued watching from his perch at the restaurant. A few more civilian vehicles had now pulled up behind the tactical van. Professionals climbed out of the cars as Shelton watched. Each member of the squad concealed their weapons under long coats.

The flask of whiskey on the table was almost empty. Shelton poured the last shot into his glass and pushed the call button on his phone.

A monotone voice answered.

"Hell Storm, Kilo, any activity?" said Shelton.

The voice from Providence responded.

"Kilo, Hell Storm. A call has gone out citywide activating Project Patriot. We are picking up communications from New York and Washington, DC. Patriot seems to be a terrorist alert. The alert specified an imminent threat of domestic terrorism in large urban cities. The alert just went out across every state on the east coast."

Shelton acknowledged, then pushed the end button. He watched the activity on the street while the desired effects of the alcohol settled in.

Susan came back into the room. Shelton stood up and placed a roll of one hundred dollar bills in her hand. She glanced down. A surprised look washed across her face. She took hold of Shelton's arm, raised up on her tiptoes, and gave him a long kiss on the cheek.

᜶

The streets were much busier than they had looked from the restaurant windows above. Locals, tourists, and everything in between were mulling around the streets. Shelton crossed Columbus Circle, walking east on the park sidewalk. He reached up and checked his blazer pockets. He took the jacket off and tossed it to a panhandler as he walked by. The panhandler, without hesitating, shouted that he would have appreciated cash.

Shelton continued walking east toward Bolivar Plaza and the statue of Jose de San Martin. As he passed in front of the hotel, still enjoying the effects of the alcohol, a sudden movement from behind rattled him back to reality.

At the last moment, Shelton dove to his left toward the grass. Still in the air, he turned his body to his right. A black-robed guardian with saber drawn was almost upon him. Shelton snatched the saber from its hand, rolled into the grass, and was back to his feet with one graceful move.

He stepped back onto the sidewalk and, with the saber by his side, started walking toward the attacker when two others appeared. The dive into the grass had caused some pedestrians to gasp. The commotion, in turn, drew the attention of the police.

The three guardians launched toward Shelton. The first one had no chance. Shelton waved his hand and sent the beast flying across the street. Impaled by the flagpole extending from the awning of the Essex House, the guardian disintegrated into dust.

Shelton caught the second guardian by the neck. He slammed it to the ground, causing the sidewalk to shake. Pedestrians and officers were knocked to the ground. The impact vaporized the spirit into dust.

Shelton looked up just as the last guardian's sword was about to enter his chest. Before the blade touched him, he swept his left arm upward, knocking the saber into the air. The dense physical mass of the spirit hit Shelton squarely, knocking him backward onto the ground. Shelton jumped back to his feet just as the unmistakable sound of a police assault rifle cracked.

Three shots were fired in rapid succession. Without thinking about it, Shelton dropped to the ground. The bullets made a soft puffing sound as they hit the ground just behind him.

He lay on the grass next to the sidewalk, motionless. His head turned facing the park, and he stared at the guardian's saber six inches from his hand.

Across the street, the police snipers stoically gazed through the scopes on their weapons, looking for signs of trauma and movement of Shelton's body.

Shelton lifted his hands above his head and slowly stood up. They trained every weapon on him.

"Get back down on your face," demanded the voice from across the street.

Before the police could fire a single shot, Shelton commanded a blast of wind that ripped down Central Park South. Every person and object not attached to the ground was swept down the street, arms and legs flailing as they flew through the air. Police cars, civilian cars, buses, taxis, carriages, horses, and people. The sudden impact spared no one. With one act, the street was swept clean.

Complete silence and stillness surrounded Shelton. Now, he was the only person on the street. Buildings had been stripped of their awnings and flags. Trees were leafless. Branches broken and twisted. One of the busiest streets in New York had become a ghost town. The faint sound of a police car siren emerged in the distance.

Shelton stood quietly in front of the statue of General Jose de San Martin. He raised both arms again, drew a deep breath, and screamed at the top of his voice. The sound shook the ground of the entire city. Every window in every building on the street in front of him shattered.

Glass rained down on the sidewalks. Fire alarms and security systems wailed throughout the city. Shelton turned and walked into the dark shadows of the park.

CHAPTER THIRTY-THREE

THE DISTANT SIRENS grew louder as Shelton made his way back to his residence. His phone vibrated inside his back pocket. The voice from Providence on the other end gave him the bad news. New York City was fully locked down. The bridges and tunnels connected to Manhattan were all closed. Every flight in and out of the city's airports was stopped. Drones, satellites, and surveillance aircraft were looking and watching from above. Ferries were docked and patrol boats lined the Hudson and East Rivers. There was no way out of the city.

Shelton removed the cover from his car and checked the gear in the trunk of the small, dark-colored sedan. A few minutes later, the Chevrolet slowly exited the private parking garage. Shelton began working his way up toward the George Washington Bridge.

Red lights of emergency vehicles and police cars flashed by in front and behind his car as the responders sped south down the main avenues of the city. Shelton zigzagged from numbered streets to avenues and back to numbered streets as he worked his way north away from Central Park.

The parking lot of a large housing project across from Washington Park was dark. Shelton slipped into one of the few remaining parking spaces and turned off the engine. He sat for a few minutes, listening and watching. There were voices coming from the far end of the lot. He stepped out of the car, opened the trunk, slipped the equipment bag onto his shoulder, and closed the lid. On his way by, he tossed the car keys through the open window onto the dashboard, then walked toward the building.

Traffic on the parkway was light. Shelton strolled across the road from the apartment complex and disappeared into the park. A hundred yards ahead were the banks of the Hudson River.

Searchlights beamed from patrol boats and public authority vessels onto the water. Shelton watched, observing the tactics being used. A few minutes later, he unzipped the bag and put on his wet gear. He placed his street clothes into the bag, cinched the waterproof backpack tight, and waded into the river.

Twenty yards out, he looked back to scan the shoreline. Then he turned his attention to the river and the patrol lights. Shelton swam silently toward the New Jersey shore as the river's current moved him in a southerly direction. His calculations had been good enough. He moved just under the surface of the water in between two search boats. An hour and a half later, he reached the New Jersey shore, changed his clothes, and hailed down a taxi.

꽃

Shelton was waiting in the library sipping coffee when Ann Baker and Charles Edwards walked in. Ann gave Shelton a pleasant hug and a warm hello. Edwards's greeting was cooler. A simple handshake with a contemplative look.

The Providence team had watched and studied the destruction in New York. The intensity and indiscriminate nature of Shelton's actions had shocked them. It was difficult for the nonviolent organization to deal with the situation. And they worried Shelton might lead the authorities to the Institute, putting it at risk. Edwards had kept leadership calm for the time being. But he needed answers that only Shelton could provide.

Shelton watched as Edwards and Ann sat down across the coffee table from him on the opposite sofa. He made eye contact with Edwards, shifted his gaze to look at Ann, and then looked down, staring at the table. He didn't feel like starting the conversation. He knew the questions would come pouring out of his partners soon enough.

"You look very nice," Ann said, her voice warm.

Shelton was tan and shaved with freshly trimmed hair. The white shirt and dark suit on his tall, trim frame completed the look.

"Thank you, Ann," he replied.

"We weren't expecting you today," Edwards said, his tone more serious. "Security wasn't aware you were on the campus. That has never happened before."

Shelton looked up, making eye contact with Edwards.

"Don't take it personal, Charles. Every security system has its issues. I thought it best that we keep this visit as discrete as possible. You never know who is watching and talking."

Edwards smiled sarcastically in agreement. His wrinkled forehead lines and clenched teeth screamed frustration over the breach.

"Where have you been?" asked Ann. "We've been worried about you after… After New York. At first, we thought you might have been caught up in that sudden storm. Then the team here said…"

"Said what, Ann?" Shelton pushed.

"Well, they hijacked the security tape from the city." She nodded her head toward Edwards. "The tape shows you causing all the destruction and killing."

Shelton looked at Edwards with a raised eyebrow.

"We brought her up to speed on the situation. This doesn't seem like the time or the place for secrets. We all need to be on the same page."

Shelton looked back at the ground.

"Charles told me you are cold-blooded killer. Is that true Tom?"

Edwards's raised eyebrows reflected his surprise at Ann's words. Shelton's gaze moved back up to Ann.

"I shouldn't have done that in New York," he said, remorse in his voice. "My frustration, my emotions, got the best of me."

Ann and Charles continued to stare at Shelton.

"I have taken many lives, Ann. So many I stopped counting a long time ago," Shelton said.

Ann glanced down and pursed her lips as Shelton's words settled into her mind.

"Many?" she said, looking him in the eyes. "Many other than the corrupt cops that kidnapped me and a few fucking demons?"

"The detective who kidnapped you has been looking for a serial killer for almost fifteen years," said Shelton. "She was trying to get me off the streets. At least for a while, to see if things calmed down. She used you as bait. But she had no witnesses. No motives. No evidence. All she had was a theory."

"But it *was* you," Ann said, her voice tapering off and disappointment lining her face. "The detective was right!"

"That is who I am," Shelton offered in a conciliatory tone. "Justice transcends every corner of my human body."

"How do you know the people you kill are bad?" she asked.

"I can look at a human and see their soul. If they have no face—no eyes or mouth, no nose, just a smooth void between their ears—they are soulless. Such a person has no purpose other than to create pain and suffering for others. They are like zombies. Staley was soulless. I like to think my work has saved thousands from suffering. Thousands from becoming a victim at the hand of an abusive father, mother, friend, or relative."

"What do you see when you look at me?" Ann asked.

"A normal person, one with a soul." Shelton smiled slightly. "I see your beautiful face. I know you are good. But I can't read your mind."

"That's nice to know," Ann replied. "I might have embarrassed myself when we first met."

She stood up, smiled at Shelton, and stretched. Then she walked toward the carafe of coffee. Just as she picked up the carafe, she stopped and turned.

"When you touched my face in Jerusalem, my vision changed," Ann said, pointing at Shelton. "I could see the guardians that were watching us just as plain as day. I haven't needed my glasses or contacts lenses since that day."

Shelton smiled and nodded, then glanced toward Edwards, then back to Ann. He took a deep breath.

"I need your help. Both of you," he said. "I'm not very good at trusting humans."

The comment made both Edwards and Ann smile slightly.

"Ann, my job is to find Wolfgang Hauser and neutralize him. I am required to rely on seven souls to help me. Seven souls who believe in what I am doing and will lay down their life for the cause. Those seven souls represent the entire human species. The species must save themselves or there is no way to perpetuate the future. If I cannot find seven souls, then there is no future for you."

Ann made her way back to the sitting area.

"Maybe that's for the best," said Ann. "Maybe all the greed, hate, and murder has gone on long enough. Maybe it is time our planet looks like Mars or the moon."

Shelton saw Edwards looking his way.

"We are the hope, Ann," Shelton said. "You are the hope. You, Charles, Prime Minister Wilkinson, Admiral Wood, Father Macari. There must be at least two more. Two more like-minded people who can see through the fog of evil."

"Why do you care, Tom?" Ann asked without emotion. "Why do you care what happens? You will carry on."

Shelton looked down at the floor trying to find the words.

"I… I could have executed thousands more people, Ann. But I resisted," he said.

Shelton looked back up at her as a single teardrop rolled down his face.

"Life is dynamic across the limitless universes," Shelton said, looking squarely into Ann's eyes. "There is no script. No predetermination. I was born with only one foot in humanity. But I discovered love." He reached up and wiped the tear from his chin. "I met a woman who taught me how to love. Like you, I have a son."

Ann stood and wrapped her arms around Shelton. "I did not know," said Ann in a compassionate voice. If she were concerned about her son he was certainly equally worried about his.

Ann sat back down with perfect posture and a determined look. Her mind was working to reconcile the seven names of the seven souls.

"You have five, right? Five of seven souls. Right?"

"That's right," Shelton said, with one eyebrow shifted up slightly higher than the other showing his curiosity with Ann's thinking.

"Who else? Think, Tom, think? Wood? Are you sure Wood counts?" Ann asked, speaking faster now. "He's a military guy and—"

"He counts, Ann," Shelton said, settling the matter.

"Yes, okay, he counts. Fine," she replied. "Fuck, of course. Chapman! Chapman is six," Ann said, jumping up from the chair. "He connected us to you." She turned and pointed at Edwards.

Charles Edwards smiled in agreement.

"If I'm in, then he is in," said Edwards. "Providence was his idea."

"Six we have six," said Ann. "What now?"

Shelton picked up a pen and paper and began writing. Edwards and Ann watched.

The pen floated effortlessly across the paper. Each letter dripped from the tip as if it were a piece of art. His elegant strokes caused the two observers to glance at each other in disbelief.

Shelton pushed the information and instructions across the table to his colleagues.

"Tell them to meet us there tomorrow night," Shelton said.

Ann studied the list.

"Isn't Macari in Argentina?" she asked.

"He's already there. Wood is on his way." Shelton checked his watch. "I will have an airplane ready for Chapman in Dallas. Get him on board. When he is in route, the three of us will head that way. Wilkinson will have our accommodations and meeting space ready when we arrive."

Shelton's list was one person short but included Edwards, Baker, Macari, Chapman, Wood, and Wilkinson. Angie and Daniel seemed like obvious souls that should be on the list. Adira had made it clear to

Shelton that Angie and his son were not independent of him and that would make it eight not seven. Besides, they had no idea of Angie and Daniel's whereabouts. Shelton had received a text from Angie saying they were safe.

ॐ

The assistant showed Ben Davis into the acting director's office. Walker was working on his computer and hadn't bothered looking up as the door opened, then closed. Ben walked to the front of the desk and sat down. Walker glanced his direction without speaking. Ben sat patiently as the CIA leader kept tapping on the keyboard.

Operation Patriot had been running for three weeks now. Every police force, government agency, and bounty hunter around the world was looking for Tom Shelton. Acting CIA director Walker had worked to convince law enforcement and the intelligence community that Shelton was responsible for the attacks and deaths in Pairs and New York.

The narrative of Shelton going rogue and becoming a terrorist fell short. No competent leader in any agency anywhere bought the story. The working people in the intelligence community revered Shelton's body of work. Throughout his naval career and as leader of Eagle One, Shelton was the one taking down the bad guys. A person with such a reputation turning terrorist was the idiocy of the acting director and the late President Staley.

"It's been three weeks," Ben blurted out, no longer interested in being ignored. "Where the fuck is he, Walker?"

"We will find him. He can't hide forever," Walker answered, still typing.

"Did you get the special situation team on it like I told you to?" Ben asked.

"Yes. Yes, of course we did. Everyone, every asset, is looking. Did you know Cardinal Bianco was killed at the UN accident?" Walker said, pointing to his screen.

Ben narrowed his eyes as he glared at Walker.

"I was aware," he replied.

"What is Hauser going to do now?" Walker smiled with satisfaction. Happy to see someone who thinks they are so powerful fail. It helped support his own ego that he was not the only failure in life. "Staley is gone. Bianco is gone. It seems your master's pawns are falling like dominos. Maybe we can get back to a normal world."

Ben clenched his jaw muscle tightly, then spoke. "If I didn't need you, I would shoot you right here, right now, you fucking moron."

"Whoa now, Mr. Davis," said Walker, smirking. "You are the guy that effed everything up. Shelton rattled your cage a little, and you freaked out. You are the one who launched Patriot. You can't put that genie back in the bottle. Now Shelton knows everyone everywhere is looking for him. Big mistake, Benjamin."

Ben pushed a piece of paper across the desk to Walker.

"We're not going back to normal. We need to reestablish the network," Ben said. "Dr. Hauser needs a new Staley and a new Bianco. The most likely successor to Staley is a young British fellow that is in line to be Wilkinson's successor. A greedy young lad. He's already on the payroll. But you need to eliminate Wilkinson in order for the change to happen in a more timely manner."

Walker stared blankly at Ben. "What about Bianco? Who takes his place?"

Ben shook his head slightly.

"I'm pretty sure there is a long line around Vatican City that has already applied for the job. That's not your issue. You deal with Wilkinson. Quickly!" Ben stood and walked out.

CHAPTER THIRTY-FOUR

THE MID-MORNING DRIVE from Le Bourget Airport to the hotel took over an hour. Traffic in central Paris crept along the Champs-Élysées. Armed, stone-faced soldiers peering through their sunglasses regulated traffic flow at each intersection. They examined each car and its occupants before letting them proceed. Others stood watch on sidewalks and street corners, studying pedestrians from head to foot, looking for something, anything that seemed out of place.

No group had taken credit for the Paris attacks that happened almost three months ago. The French government continued to press the narrative of a niche extremist group being responsible. The political establishment was using all its resources to help make the citizens and tourists of Paris feel safe. Behind the scenes, government officials were using every available form of technology and intelligence to determine who was responsible for the destruction.

Ann, Chapman, and Macari dropped their bags at the Hotel Exeter, then set out for the day. The humid morning air greeted them as they made their way across the street to the grounds of the Louvre. A wide, long sidewalk between the museum grounds and the Jardin des Tuileries stretched out in front of them.

Wilkinson's team had been researching and studying Dr. Wolfgang Hauser since the unplanned introduction to Hauser in Davos, Switzerland during the world economic forum months ago. The surprise meeting arranged by the Archbishop of Canterbury and being in the presence of Hauser that January afternoon had rattled the prime minister. Wilkinson had shared his concerns with Shelton that evening following the meeting, then demanded to know every detail about Hauser from his team. British intelligence's search of their newly digitized historical records had found Hauser's name on a fifteenth-century guest list alongside King Henry VI. The well-preserved invitation was a printed birthday celebration for the French ruler Charles VII. This put Hauser squarely in the middle of the European political establishment of the time. Hauser's position in French society made it likely that artists had captured him in a drawing or painting of the day. The world's largest collection of late medieval period art was currently on display at the Musee d'Orsay located on the left bank of the Seine River, just across the river from the gardens.

Ann had used the time on the morning flight from the west coast of England to learn more about Chapman. Macari sat next to Ann and Wilkinson on the private jet, listening intently to the conversation while he flipped through fashion magazines.

Chapman was a mathematics graduate student when he met Professor Schwartz. Schwartz was a visiting professor at Georgetown, where he was teaching an advanced undergraduate course in history. Rumors among the students suggested Schwartz was really studying the occult. Young Chapman was interested in the rumor and the topic. He introduced himself to the professor, and the two hit it off and got to know each other. Turned out Schwartz wasn't in DC to teach. He was there to study the paranormal.

Schwartz was planning to conduct an experiment with the globe and serpent symbol. He had done it many times at his home university, but he had never tried it anywhere else. This was going to be his first summoning of demons outside of Israel. However, before he could launch his experiment, the faculty got wind of the rumors, confronted Schwartz, and ended his assignment prematurely.

Chapman and Schwartz stayed in touch. Over the years, Chapman made several trips to Israel to visit. On the last occasion, Schwartz showed Chapman the green book. According to the professor, a man who lived in the desert gave him the empty book and told him what to write in it.

Schwartz captured hundreds of accounts of a great warrior. Some accounts resembled those battles written about in the ancient Hebrew scrolls. At the end of the manuscript, it distinctly spoke of a day when the warrior would return. A detail suppressed in modern-day theology. According to Schwartz, the man in the desert instructed him to be on the lookout and to help the warrior when he or she arrived.

Chapman bought in to it. He was the one who conceptualized a group of people who were clear-minded and had a genuine interest in truth. Truth instead of tradition. Truth in place of polite fiction. Truth as substitute for blind loyalty. A group that would remain committed to truths, using the same vigor with which patriots defended countries. These attributes would be the way to see and identify such a person. Purity of vision and free from bias.

To Chapman, it made more sense than the clouds parting and everyone being swept away into the heavens or doomed to be tormented in hell forever. Chapman used his inherited wealth to build Providence. He thought an organization could be useful and support Schwartz's mandate. He convinced his colleague Charles Edwards to help him, and they set off.

Halfway across the garden, Ann slowed her pace in order to walk beside Chapman.

"So why did you leave Providence to hide out in Texas? It seems odd for a preacher not to believe in heaven and hell," Ann asked as they walked.

"I was too close to it all. Sometimes you have to know when to step aside," Chapman said. "You don't have to believe in all the religious dogma to believe in a higher power. It's the beauty of free will."

Chapman glanced toward Ann as they continued to walk.

"Charles was agnostic. More analytical about the world. If Schwartz's theory was correct, Charles was perfect for the task at hand. He would have the organization ready."

The three colleagues made their way across the bridge over the Seine River, crossed the street, and continued walking. A few minutes later, they were in front of the Musee d'Orsay.

The museum was a large stone building set neatly on the bank of the river across from Paris's 1st arrondissement. It was once a railway station, then a postal facility. French historians had rescued the building from demolition. They created the Musee d'Orsay, now one of the most notable museums in the world, in one of the most beautiful cities in the world.

The main railway tracks of the former station had become the main gallery hall. A long arched-glass roof spanned the pillars. Natural light poured into the space from above. The museum contained over two thousand original paintings, six hundred sculptures, and countless other items, both on display and stored in warehouses and annexes.

Ann and her colleagues had mapped out the day's plan on the car ride into the city. They would stay together, start on the ground-floor gallery, and work their way clockwise to the upper floors.

By midday, they had made it through the main floor collections. They had discovered nothing of interest. Other than the expected works of Monet, Manet, Degas, Renoir, and others.

By late afternoon, they had covered the upper-floor galleries. Still, nothing had even remotely seemed unusual.

"Strange we haven't come across the medieval gallery that's supposed to be here," Ann said, stopping at the base of the stairs on the main level.

"I'll go speak to the attendant and see if she knows anything about it," offered Macari. "It must be here somewhere."

Before he could walk away, Chapman gently grabbed Macari's arm and stopped him. The two looked at each other.

"Choose your words carefully," whispered Chapman. "Don't be specific. Assume bad guys are everywhere. Someone's sudden interest in medieval art may raise suspicion. We must keep our guard up."

Macari paused, maintaining eye contact, then nodded slightly, acknowledging the guidance. He turned and headed off toward the information desk.

Ann walked over to a bench and sat down. She closed her eyes and took a deep relaxing breath and exhaled slowly. Chapman's arm brushed Ann's as he sat down beside her on the bench.

With her face relaxed she said, "You knew all about this when we met at your church, didn't you?"

"Not exactly, no," replied Chapman. "I thought it was remarkable that you found me."

"You turned the issue over to Edwards. Why?"

"I told you. Charles is good at sorting out fact from fiction. That's his job. That was the idea for Providence."

"But here you are, involved," Ann said.

"Charles has been keeping me updated."

"Well, it seems Charles must have convinced you we are worthy of your time." She raised an eyebrow and a half smile. "What made you a believer?"

Chapman turned his head. His look met Ann's stare.

"Shelton's ability to read an ancient Hebrew letter. It is a skill no modern-day person on earth has," said Chapman. "The writing and symbols are too obscure."

"How would you or Edwards know? Maybe Tom and I are just making it up? Maybe all of this is complete bullshit."

"I was the one who delivered the letter to Charles," Chapman said.

Ann looked intensely into Chapman's face.

"You were the colleague that was in Abdel Kinneret?" she said. "You watched a person write the letter?"

Chapman nodded.

"And the symbols, or letters branded onto his wrists are from the same time period," Chapman continued.

"You have seen them, right?"

"Seen what?" Ann said.

"Demons!"

The smile disappeared from Ann's face.

"Yes. I've seen them," she replied. "Up close and personal."

"Do you see any now?" asked Chapman, staring across the museum.

Ann slowly turned her head and looked out across the large main-floor gallery. Her observation methodically moved from left to right.

"No, I don't" She turned back to Chapman. "Why do you ask?"

"I don't think the destruction of that hotel and the fire near the Arc was terrorism," he said. "Many of the hotel patrons fund extremism. Several of them were killed. The fire…the fire was far too precise for a random act of nature. Somehow, the Arc was untouched while everything within a hundred meters was eviscerated."

"And?" Ann said.

"And we are standing in the middle of Paris, Ann. I assume we are on Hauser's home turf. Let's stay focused. You are our vision. You are the only one who can see the bad guys coming."

Macari returned from the information desk.

"The young man at the desk said there are some medieval pieces on the lower-level annex," said Macari. "Apparently the curator wanted to display as many of the pieces as he could, so he opted for the basement gallery."

The three stood. Ann surveyed the area again and looked at her colleagues. "Let's go," she said, turning for the elevators.

※

The gentle knock on the door of his library told Dr. Wolfgang Hauser that his guest had arrived. He gently gripped the door lever with his long fingers and lifted. Inside the garden room, Ben Davis was waiting.

The late-afternoon sun beamed over the roof of the chateau onto the far edge of the large well-manicured garden. The four-story mansion was already casting a long shadow onto the walkways, shrubs, and flowers.

Hauser walked past his guest and opened the double doors to the veranda. He stood in the doorway and inhaled deeply, seeming to take in the smell of fresh flowers and vegetation. A few more steps and he stood at the sculpted cement rails lining the edge of the outdoor space. He stood there quietly, gazing out into the garden. The winding paths through the green hedges led from one fountain to the next. The peaceful, pleasant look on Hauser's face captured the satisfaction of the moment.

The look fell away as Ben Davis appeared in his peripheral vision.

"Shelton's team is in Paris," said Ben without preface or small talk.

"What team? He has no team?" replied Hauser, scoffing. "He is a hopeless loner. You told me that yourself."

Ben continued to look out into the garden. "Things have changed. He has a group of people at the d'Orsay searching through medieval art."

All expression fell off Hauser's face. He turned toward Ben, his attention captured.

"How do you know this?" asked Hauser.

"I have tour guides and information helpers all over Paris on payroll," said Ben. "One noticed two Americans and another person rushing through the museum this afternoon. They were looking specifically for medieval period artwork. My source sent me a picture. I recognized the woman. Her name is Ann Baker. She has been helping Shelton."

Hauser turned and walked to the far end of the veranda. He gazed silently around the grounds.

"What is it you want me to do?" asked Ben.

"Eliminate them. They are too close. Do not let them leave Paris alive," ordered Hauser. "Make sure you have everyone in Deutschland on alert. Do you understand?"

"They will never track you to Germany, sir," said Davis. "Even though you let Walker and his whole entourage visit you there."

Hauser moved closer to Ben. He stopped, leaned in, and looked down at Davis. Ben's head moved back slightly as Hauser leaned in close.

"You are out of your league again, Mr. Davis," said Hauser.

"Look around," said Ben, unflinching. "There is no one left except me and your goons. You can't rebuild your political and religious power base fast enough. You are going to have to defeat Shelton yourself."

"Take care of the Americans," Hauser said.

He turned to walk away, then stopped.

"Oh, and Mr. Davis," said Hauser, "you will never be as good as your half-human sidekick. So do as I say, and I will let you live."

Hauser turned and walked back into the house. Ben Davis turned back toward the garden.

The sunlight was gone. Shadows consumed the garden. The bright greens were now another shade of dark green. The color of the flowers faded. Hauser watched Davis from behind the drapery in his study.

Hauser turned away and caught a glimpse of himself in the mirror. The slight hunch of his posture bothered him. He continued to examine himself in the reflection. This was the first sign of age he had ever noticed. Ever! After several thousand years of life on earth.

The sound of crashing glass made Ben look up toward the light in the study window. A few minutes later, silence returned. Ben buttoned up his coat and made his way back to Paris.

CHAPTER THIRTY-FIVE

Macari pushed the level 2 button, and the lift began its descent to the lowest level of the d'Orsay. When the doors opened, a musty smell consumed the dimly lit corridor leading to the annex gallery. The motion in the hallway triggered the light sensors.

There were hundreds of densely packed paintings lining the display racks and walls of the cavernous room. Mere inches were left between the frames. Just enough room for the museum staff to place each piece of art on the temporary hangers.

Chapman walked slowly down the rows, studying each painting. Deciding within seconds if the work had something useful to their search. Many of the pieces portrayed religious figures and significant leaders of the day, capturing their piety. There were also pieces of men slaying others, orgies of men with men and women with women, and a variety of dark demonic figures looming in the shadows.

Chapman turned the corner to begin his review of the next section when he heard, "Steven? Over here."

Chapman changed direction and made his way toward the voice. He turned down an aisle and there was Ann standing at the end of a long section, examining a painting in low lighting.

As Chapman approached, she said, "Look," pointing to the piece in front of her. Her face was flushed.

"Take it easy, Ann," said Chapman. "You don't look well." He shifted his attention to the painting.

It was a small portrait of people standing beside a finely dressed, tall gentleman. In the background was a large French chateau. Chapman studied the piece.

"What do you see?" he asked.

"Look at the shield the tall gentleman in the middle is holding," Ann said, finding her breath. "It's a globe with a serpent wrapped around it. It's the same symbol on the saber Shelton took from the guardian."

Next to the gentleman were two men flanking him on either side. The two on the left wore riding clothes. The two on the right were dressed in black robes with their hoods pulled up. One of the black-robed guardians had a red X on his garment. Behind the group were two red-robed figures on horseback.

"This one"—Ann pointed to the guardian with the red X—"was watching us in Jerusalem. Tom calls him Saint Xavier."

Chapman narrowed his gaze as he looked at the piece and processed Ann's words.

"Who is the one in the middle?" Chapman asked. "Do you know him?"

"That would be Wolfgang Hauser," Macari said, walking up from behind. "Look at him. He resembles the sketch Senor Wilkinson gave us. The devil himself posing for a portrait."

Chapman looked closer, then turned to look at Macari, raising his eyebrows.

"Indeed, it is. Very well. We need to find the chateau," Chapman said, glancing around the gallery to see if anyone else was in the area.

"Why don't you two go see what else might be of interest? I'm going to make a few notes here," Chapman said.

Ann and Macari headed off to review more pieces.

Chapman surveyed the room for security devices. He removed his small camera from his jacket pocket, set the shutter speed to low light, and started rapidly snapping pictures. Within thirty seconds, he had over one hundred high-definition digital pictures of the six-hundred-year-old painting. He pulled out his small notebook to make notes.

Chapman finished his work and found Ann and Macari. The three huddled together, pretending to study a random painting. It was a rouse just in case a hidden camera was watching.

"I know our nerves are shattered at the moment," he said, "but it's time to go."

Chapman reminded the group to act natural and move at a leisurely pace. He highlighted the obvious, that there were security cameras everywhere upstairs. The authorities needed no more pictures of them. They took the stairs up to the main floor, exited the museum, and headed back toward the hotel.

The weather in the city had deteriorated throughout the day. As they casually walked down the sidewalk, it started to mist. A light fog had settled over the Seine. They kept a normal pace down the sidewalk, moving away from the museum. They crossed the street. As they rounded the corner onto the bridge sidewalk, Chapman picked up the pace. Ann and Macari matched his stride.

Chapman glanced toward his colleagues as he kept walking.

"Here is the plan," said Chapman. "Ann, call the pilots and tell them we are headed their way. They have to be ready to go within the hour. We're going back to pick up our bags. The driver is standing by at the hotel."

"Where are we going?" Ann asked.

"Out of France," Chapman answered.

The three walked briskly as they began the long trek across the gardens back toward the hotel. Halfway across, Chapman turned off the main path to shorten the distance. The narrow, tree-lined corridor provided them the opportunity to increase pace without drawing attention. Ann suddenly grabbed Chapman's arm, stopping him in his tracks. Macari jumped to the side to avoid a collision.

"What is it?" Chapman asked, looking at Ann with a clenched jaw.

"There," Ann said, nodding down the path. "Guardians!"

Directly in their path stood a group of gray-robed demons. Chapman and Macari looked down the path, squinting.

"Are you sure?" Chapman asked, seeing nothing.

"Let's go," Ann ordered as she reversed course, taking control.

The three broke into a full run. Ann led the way, navigating them through a maze of turns into other tree-lined corridors, all the while still working their way toward the hotel. The three were at a full run when Ann suddenly stopped, causing her two partners to slip on the gravel path and fall.

"There they are again," she said, barely getting the words out while gasping for air.

"Call the driver and have him meet us at the Place de Le Concorde," Ann ordered. "Maybe we can make it into the open where these things might be less inclined to attack."

Before they could turn around, the guardians made their move.

"Run!" Ann yelled.

Although Chapman and Macari could not see the guardians, they could easily see the fear on Ann's face. It was real. As they turned to run in the opposite direction, the bushes between them and the demons exploded. Leaves and branches flew into the air.

A dark figure stood between the guardians and their small group. The guardians didn't slow. The dark figure wielded his sword with lightning speed, slashing through the demons. Bright flashes of light popped loudly as the stranger eliminated each demon from existence, one by one. Angie secretly watched from the shadows as Daniel expertly did the work of his father.

Without hesitating, Ann, Chapman, and Macari sprinted back to the hotel. Fifteen minutes later, they were in the car and on their way to the airport. Chapman was still working to catch his breath as he looked out the car window across the river toward the museum. The flashing blue lights of police cars lit up in front of the d'Orsay.

"What are the police doing at the museum?" asked Ann.

Chapman took a deep breath, glanced Ann's way with a knowing look, and then turned his head back to the front of the car as they dropped onto the freeway headed back to Le Bourget.

"Who was the rescuer from the shadows?" asked Chapman.

"I have no idea," answered Ann. "But it is good to know the boss has someone watching out for us. You two guys weren't up to the task," Ann said, trying to find a thread of humor to break the intensity of the night.

Macari raised his eyebrows in surprise and smiled at Ann's words. "There is one other," quipped the priest. Macari was aware of Daniel. Adira had made sure that he knew about Tom's son.

"Excuse me?" Ann said, leaning in toward Macari.

Macari held up his hand and moved his head slightly from side to side in the dark back seat of the stretched Mercedes. "Not now," he answered. "It will have to wait."

The flight from Paris touched down at Prestwick Airport just before nine that night. Less than ten minutes later, Ann, Chapman, and Macari joined Shelton and the others in the bar of the small Scottish house hotel.

The Lochgrey Hotel sat just off the end of the airport in a small forest in the middle of an enormous field on the outskirts of Monkton. The white-brick, red-roofed hotel was owned by Shelton. It was one of a few five-star hotels in South Ayrshire. For the past several weeks, the hotel had been available for the exclusive use of its owner.

Shelton introduced Amir to the group.

Shelton turned toward Ann. "I didn't expect to see you until morning."

Ann hadn't had a night's sleep since departing Providence. Fatigue was showing on her face.

"We wrapped things up early," she replied with a forced smile. "Paris isn't exactly the most hospitable place at the moment."

Shelton's eyebrows lifted, casting a curious look.

Admiral Wood, Charles Edwards, and Wilkinson's agent, Claire Martin, had spent the past several days in Berlin and Hamburg, combing through local museums, government records, and studying pictures of medieval castles. They looked for anything out of the ordinary. They found nothing.

"A German who has been alive for centuries, using the same name, yet no information on him," said the British agent. "What do you make of that?"

"Hard to say," replied Chapman. "Could be an oversight or just plain arrogance. After all, he seems to be the alpha politician. Nobody eats the king of the jungle."

Chapman reached into his sports coat and removed a small rolled-up canvas. He leaned forward and set it on the table.

Ann's mouth dropped open, as did Macari's.

All eyes were focused on Chapman.

"That is a painting from the Musee d'Orsay," said Chapman. "Five men and two horsemen. One face resembles the composite sketch of Dr. Wolfgang Hauser. There is a French chateau in the background. It might be the place we are looking for. It might be where we will find Hauser."

"You stole a painting from the museum?" asked Edwards with a stunned look on his face.

Chapman reached out and removed the string from the rolled fabric without responding. He slowly unrolled the painting and placed four small rocks he had collected from the parking lot in each corner. The dim lighting in the hotel library made it difficult to see. Wood tapped the light button on his mobile device.

Shelton's face froze. The man in the painting standing next to Hauser in riding clothes was Amir. The man standing on the other side of Hauser was St. Xavier.

Shelton stared straight ahead. He didn't as much as twitch a muscle. His gaze looked over the shoulder of Ann on the other side of the small coffee table, out into the darkness beyond the double French doors.

Chapman leaned forward to speak.

Shelton's voice cut him off. "Quiet! No one move." In his peripheral vision, he watched Amir.

"Mr. Shelton?" Amir said without moving a muscle. "Let me speak. Just let me explain."

Shelton turned toward Amir, lifting both hands up to point his palms toward his adviser.

"Who are you?" Shelton demanded in a calm, direct tone.

"Relax," pleaded Amir as he stood. "Obviously, I am on your side."

Amir slowly unbuttoned his shirt and pulled it back, exposing his left upper chest. Wood shifted his light onto a discolored patch of skin.

"Hauser burned a mark into my chest that day after he killed the boy next to me," said Amir. "Elias, the village elder of Abdel Kinneret, removed it for me. Then took my life."

Shelton's intense stare narrowed.

"When I awoke, I had this mark." Amir lowered his shirt from his right shoulder.

There, seared into Amir's flesh, was a perfectly constructed symbol: YHWH. It matched the one on Shelton's wrist. It was the exact size, color, and inscription.

"Tell me about that?" Shelton demanded, pointing at the canvas.

"That is me in the painting," confessed Amir. "The one next to me is Luke. The one on the other side with the X they called Hans. I didn't know the other one. The riders are obviously guardians."

Amir told the group about the events that led him to Abdel Kinneret so long ago. It was the same story he had told Elias just before the village elder took Amir's life.

"My next conscious moment, I was sitting with several other souls in the village center. Each of us took our turn and received our assignments. Mine was to wait for the arrival. Your arrival," Amir said, looking at Shelton. "The one standing in the sun. The one born from the woman clothed in the sun."

Shelton's head was spinning. He stood and walked to the bar and poured another glass of wine. No one said a word as the tension in the room eased. Ann and Amir joined Shelton at the bar. He glanced at both of them, then stared into his glass of wine.

"Tell me about the chateau," asked Shelton.

Amir's interest was captured by something past Shelton toward the patio doors and windows. Suddenly, his eyelids widened. Shelton's jaws clenched as he saw the grave concern on his colleague's face.

Suddenly, the French doors and windows on the far side of the library exploded inward. The wooden windowpanes were now wooden stakes rocketing through the air mixed with lethal glass shrapnel. The projectiles flew across the room toward where the group was working.

Shelton wrapped his arms around Ann and Amir to shield them from the blast. The wood and glass flew by, missing them. The inset of the bar was just enough where they were not on the main path of the blast.

Shelton turned, swinging his left hand into the air, throwing a blast of air toward the attackers. The pulse of air sent the remaining wall structure and the guardians flying backward. Shelton picked up Ann in his arms and instructed Amir to follow. He set out at a full sprint across the room toward a hallway.

Ann wrapped her arms around Shelton's neck, trying to hang on as the three passed the front desk and sprinted down the hotel's main hallway. They turned at the end of the hall and ran down the connecting corridor. They stopped when they reached the back door of the hotel.

Shelton put Ann down, then turned. Amir was holding an injured Charles Edwards in his arms. Edwards's body was limp, but his eyelids were open. His pupils looked normal.

"The airfield is a half mile through the forest," said Shelton. "Follow the path. Go as fast as you can. Meet me at Exeter."

Shelton opened the door. Ann and Amir, with Edwards in his arms, ran toward the tree line and disappeared into the night.

Shelton quietly made his way around the outside of the hotel. He took a deep breath and peered around the corner. In the distance, he could see the guardians sifting through the rubble. He watched as the demons lifted Chapman's limp body from the debris. Pieces of wood had impaled the preacher and protruded from his back. Shelton watched as the guardian tossed the lifeless body to the side.

A second guardian picked up the dead body of Admiral Wood and tossed it on top of Chapman. Wood's head was barely attached. The glass shrapnel had ended his life instantly.

Shelton continued to observe the guardians as they gathered around Macari. He appeared to be standing. His eyelids open. Shelton stared through the darkness, planning his next move. The blast had blown Macari back against the wall. The flying wood pieces had staked him to the paneling. Shelton took a step forward at the same moment a guardian ended Father Macari's life with its saber.

Shelton stepped back and paused as the demons continued to rifle through the destruction. British intelligence agent Claire Martin was nowhere to be found.

❧

Amir figured he had at least a fifteen-minute head start before the attacking guardians would realize their failure. Unless Shelton had destroyed them. He could hear the familiar sound of an aircraft engine running in the distance. They exited the tree line and ran into the open field leading to the aircraft.

The small private airport lobby was empty. The night attendant's head poked above the counter as the automatic doors opened. Amir entered with Edwards in his arms. He gently laid Edwards on a sofa. As Amir turned toward the attendant, Edwards grabbed Amir's wrist and thanked him.

"You are going to be fine," said Amir.

The airport attendant was soon standing at Amir's side, looking down at Edwards.

"Please get him help. Get him to a local hospital. We were attacked at Lochgrey. He is a close friend of the owner," said Amir.

Without another word, Amir bolted out the door and onto the aircraft with Ann. Neither Ann nor Amir wanted to leave Edwards behind, but it seemed like an easier and safer option than taking Edwards to Paris for treatment and explaining the situation to French border security. Even if that worked, Paris wasn't exactly the most hospitable place to be at the moment.

The distant sound of jet engines washed across the fields to Lochgrey as the aircraft Ann and Amir were on took to the sky. Shelton turned away from the destruction and disappeared into the woods.

CHAPTER THIRTY-SIX

THE SOUND OF helicopter rotors emerged just above the symphony of crickets as Shelton worked his way through the forest. He adjusted course and increased his pace toward the sound of the aircraft. He stopped inside the tree line, using the darkness and brush to remain concealed. A few minutes later, the aircraft made a black hole in the night sky as it appeared over the treetops. Shelton watched as it flared and turned, making its way to the clearing in the trees for landing.

The aircraft was the newest version of a lightweight stealth helicopter. Shelton knew the British had developed it, although he had never seen it in person. He watched as the helicopter skids touched down on the damp grass. The sound of its rotors and engine faded.

Shelton watched as five soldiers jumped from the aircraft and quickly headed toward the tree line thirty yards to his right. A few minutes later, the group was headed back toward the aircraft with a sixth person on a gurney. Shelton stepped out into the open with his hands above his head.

Two of the British special operations team pivoted immediately toward him. With his hands above his head, Shelton closed into a fist and reopened three times quickly.

The gurney was loaded onto the helicopter, and three of the soldiers made their way toward Shelton. As they got closer, their weapons and night vision equipment were visible.

"Mr. Shelton?" came the voice from the darkness.

"Correct. Thomas J. Shelton," he said in a clear, concise burst of words.

"Affirmative, affirmative, affirmative," said the soldier into his headset microphone. "We have three positive identifications."

Shelton could see the outline of the soldier's face as the communication came back.

"This way please, Commander Shelton. Quickly."

Seconds later, the helicopter lifted off into the night sky. Shelton watched out the open side door as the aircraft sped along the treetops. The solider in charge of communications handed Shelton a headset.

"Welcome aboard, Commander," greeted the senior British officer in charge of the rescue mission.

"How is Claire?" asked Shelton, referring to the injured MI6 agent and Wilkinson's proxy at the Lockgrey meeting.

The medical attendant described the injury as a slice wound. The patient had lost some blood but had done a good job self-treating. She would be fine with a few stitches.

Shelton nodded, acknowledging the good prognosis.

"Sir," said Shelton, turning to the officer in charge, "I know your mission was to get Agent Martin. I appreciate you getting me out also. But I need to get to Paris. ASAP. Can you get me there?"

The British intelligence Corps was very familiar with Shelton and his relationship with the Prime Minister. They were also aware of his US naval service and had served with him many times during Shelton's decade of duty around the globe. When Agent Martin was carried aboard the rescue aircraft, she had told the crew to keep a look out for another person. Most likely Shelton. She was right.

⮑

Agent Claire Martin sat across the aisle from Shelton on the plane ride to Paris. She had escaped the Lockgrey attack bleeding but pushed through the forest and radioed for help.

Now, her right hand was busy sending messages and making notes. Her tightly wrapped injured left arm was secured against her body. After hearing Shelton's request aboard the rescue helicopter, Martin had insisted the medics stitch up her wounds immediately. Then she informed her bosses that she would accompany Commander Shelton to France.

Before landing, she handed Shelton an electronic tablet. The secure device had the names and ranks of the British agents on the ground in France who would support him. It also contained maps and satellite pictures of Hauser's chateau. Martin figured out where her passenger was headed after seeing the painting. Shelton studied the maps and geography closely. The slight jolt of the aircraft tires touching the asphalt runway of the small airport informed him of their arrival in France. He made his final mental notes as the airplane taxied to the private hangar.

Minutes later, Shelton sat in darkness in the back seat of the midsize sedan. The driver gracefully navigated the narrow, rolling country roads. The car slowed, turning onto an unpaved road, then stopped.

"We will be right here waiting for you, Commander," said Agent Martin. "Godspeed."

The sudden sound of Martin's voice disturbed the serenity of the night, bringing Shelton back to full consciousness.

"Thank you, Martin," Shelton said, looking her in the eye.

He opened the door, stepped out of the car, and observed his surroundings. Then he sighed, zipped his jacket, and started walking up the unpaved road toward the chateau of Wolfgang Hauser.

A half kilometer up the road, Shelton drifted into the woods and crouched behind a bush. He pulled the tablet from his jacket and pushed the location button. The drones overhead gave him a live view of Hauser's home and his exact location in relation to the home.

Shelton stood and scanned the surrounding forest. There were no signs of guardians. Slowly and methodically, he worked his way between the trees and around ground debris toward the main property. At the edge of the trees, directly in front of him, was the back garden of Hauser's mansion.

The forest was quiet. There were still no guardians. The pathways through the garden were marked with small, low wattage lights. There were two lights on inside the home on the second floor. There were no visible signs of life.

Shelton strode out of the forest toward the chateau. Halfway through the garden he stepped onto the main pathway. Suddenly, he stopped and turned around. A faint crackling of leaves had captured his attention. The sound came from the tree line. He scanned the edge of the forest, turned, and continued toward the main house. A few minutes later he ascended the staircase to the back entrance to the home. Shelton made short work of the locked doorknob and deadbolt sliding lock. One strike with his right hand blasted the wooden door open and off of its hinges. Using military precision he methodically went room by room on the main level searching for any sign of life. Finding none, he worked his way up to the second floor and continued his hunt.

Hauser was gone. The chateau was empty. The office fireplace was still warm. Less than two hours ago, there had been a fire under the stone mantel.

Shelton sat down in the large leather chair behind Hauser's desk and looked around the room. The artwork and paintings hanging all around him were originals. He rocked back in the chair, staring off into space, contemplating how Hauser knew to leave before he arrived. The only practical answer that occurred to him was someone on Hauser's team had tracked Chapman, Ann, and Macari to Scotland. The airplane tail number Ann was using must be compromised. Shelton knew the only one who could put that type of information together was Ben Davis.

Shelton had gone to great lengths to avoid someone tracking his team's travel. His personally owned aircraft were positioned around the world, doing fake missions. The pilots and crews were flying the aircraft from one place to another with no passengers aboard. They would spend a day at a location, then fly to another the next day. One crew was in Southeast Asia, one was in South America, the other was in Europe, making trips from Italy to Southern France, and from Brussels to Dubai and back. Despite Shelton's efforts, Ben Davis had figured it out.

Shelton's phone began buzzing. He unzipped his jacket slightly, pulled out the device, and answered.

His face lost all expression. The voice on the other end was Angie's.

"Are you and Daniel oaky?" asked Shelton.

"We are fine," replied Angie staring at her abductor across the room. "Where are you?"

"The Exeter in Paris. Where you told us to go. Your penthouse floor."

It was the same hotel near the Louvre that Chapman, Baker, and Macari had planned to stay before they were attacked in the Tuileries Garden. Shelton owned the penthouse at the hotel.

"What's a matter Angie?" asked Shelton.

"This thing broke into our room and is demanding to see you. He threatened to kill us if you don't come. Daniel tried to put him out of his misery. But the thing was to strong. Ann and this guy named Amir arrived a little while ago. It won't let them leave either."

"You and Daniel are unharmed?" Shelton asked as he turned the desk chair he was sitting in around to look out onto the garden lights.

"We're fine," Angie replied, staring at her abductor. "This thing wants to see you face to face, Tom. He demands you come to the hotel. When you get here, he says he will let us go."

Angie turned slowly away from the guardian and lowered her voice. In a whisper she said, "This thing has an X on his robe. What does that mean?"

Shelton took a deep breath.

"If he wanted to hurt you, he would have already done so," Shelton said. "I'll be there soon. Then you and Daniel will be safe and can return home."

Shelton pushed the end button and placed the phone back in his jacket. He glared at a gold-framed picture sitting on Hauser's credenza. Underneath the picture, the perfectly handwritten words read:

"The battle against the Devil, which is the principal task of Saint Michael the Archangel, is still being fought today, because the Devil is still alive and active in the world." —Pope John Paul II

The person in the picture with his arm around Wolfgang Hauser was none other than the pope.

Shelton walked to the fireplace with the picture in his hand. The smoldering coals ignited the photo and its frame. He turned and walked to the doors of the veranda and opened them. Shelton looked out into the night as if he were looking into the face of the enemy. He held the flaming picture frame against the curtains. The flames lurched up the drapes immediately. Shelton closed the doors and watched the fire as it reached the planked wooden ceiling. Hauser's office erupted in flames.

⊸⟋

The black windowless van was parked just behind Shelton's sedan. Inside, Martin and four other agents watched the monitors. The video footage from the drones was near perfect. They could see Shelton as he stood at the edge of the veranda, peering into the night.

All four drones inferred heat, and sensor silent alarms began flashing on the agents' screens at the same time.

"We have a fire inside the structure," said an operator.

Martin immediately barked out the order for the operator to focus on the threat while the other three were to keep eyes on Shelton.

They watched as Shelton walked down the stairs of the veranda and into the garden. A few minutes later, he was standing at the edge of the forest looking back at the chateau.

The fire was making its way to the upper floors of the estate. Every worldly possession that Hauser abandoned was going up in flames. Millions and millions of dollars in antique furniture and art were perishing.

Suddenly, Shelton noticed a large puff of white through the office window. The flames were gone. The alarms on the drone screens stopped.

"Fire suppression just kicked in," said the operator. "Better late than never. Might have saved some of the place."

Martin sat there studying Shelton on the monitor. He was still facing the mansion. She moved closer to the screen.

"Zoom in," she ordered.

Suddenly, all the screens went black.

"What the fuck just happened?" barked Martin as she glanced from monitor to monitor.

Just as she got out the last syllable, the van pitched violently to one side. The agents were tossed against the equipment console as the vehicle swayed from side to side.

"Fuck! Fuck! Fuck!" Martin screamed. Her stitched-up, injured shoulder had taken a direct hit.

Grimacing, while regaining her balance, she yelled, "Get the doors open. See what the hell is going on out there? Does anyone have a location on the principal?"

The van's rear doors opened at the same time one of the drone cameras came back online. Martin jumped out to assess the situation. She stopped in her tracks. Then her mouth fell open in disbelief.

A fireball reached into the sky as a mushroom cloud formed. The horizon above the tree line was glowing bright orange. Trees all around Martin's location were bending from the power of the blast.

"We have a feed from drone three, ma'am," said the operator.

Martin stood there looking toward the cloud and the orange sky.

"Well?" she prompted.

"The mansion is gone, ma'am," said the operator.

Agent Claire Martin turned toward the operator inside the van.

"The principal?" she asked.

"Looking now, ma'am. No visual currently," came the reply.

"Find him, damn it!"

"Agent Martin?" came a voice from behind.

She turned around . Shelton's chest was moving up and down as he caught his breath from the sprint through the trees.

"Martin? I need a ride to Paris," Shelton said.

CHAPTER THIRTY-SEVEN

THE PENTHOUSE OF the Hotel Exeter covered the entire top floor of the building. High ceilings and wood-lined walls of the penthouse suite gave the rooms a sense of grandeur. The tapestries and rugs softened the hard textures, providing warmth and color. Each of the six bedrooms had its own unique décor and color based on the original works of different artists. The art gallery and library windows provided a panoramic view of the Louvre and the Tuileries Gardens.

Shelton held his master key against the sensor. The lock on the right main door to his Parisian home unlocked. He opened the door. Standing directly across the room in front of him was St. Xavier.

A black silk robe was neatly draped over Xavier's seven-foot-tall, lean frame. The hood of the garment obscured his face, and a smooth black mask covered his nose and mouth. In his hands were two long sabers. Behind him in the sitting room were Angie, Daniel, Ann, and Amir.

Shelton, imposing in his black tactical gear, stood in the doorway facing Xavier. The saber he had taken from the guardian in Buenos Aires was sitting on the table beside Daniel. The saber he had taken from Schwartz's office protruded from Shelton's backpack. The hilt of the weapon was visible to all over his left shoulder.

Shelton looked past Xavier at the others. His attention was drawn to the unfamiliar face in the group. It was the first time he had ever seen his son in person. His eyes met Daniel's.

Shelton looked away and met Xavier's stare. He reached back with his left hand and drew the saber from his pack. The tip of the blade pointed skyward. He lowered the saber and gently tossed the weapon from his left hand to his right. Xavier stood still like a monument, unflinching. Slowly, Shelton turned the saber sideways and tossed it across the floor. The blade slid to the feet of Xavier and stopped.

Shelton raised his hands as he continued to glare into the dark face of the demon. His black short-sleeve T-shirt stretched across his muscular arms. The veins in his forearms protruded from his skin. The marks on his wrists fully on display.

Xavier's gaze moved from one wrist to the other. Shelton watched as the demon slowly pivoted sideways and nodded toward Amir.

"Let's go," Amir instructed.

The hostages stood and walked across the room toward Shelton. Angie was first. Shelton watched as her tall lean frame moved toward him. Her narrowed stare and clenched jaw showed the tension of the situation. When she got to Shelton, she stopped.

"There's a car downstairs," Shelton whispered. "It will take you to the airport. Ann knows where to go. Stay there until you hear from me."

He shifted his gaze toward Daniel standing beside his mother. Xavier watched from across the room.

Daniel Brady stood the same height as his father. He had the same color eyes and hair. He had his father's strong jawline and lean, muscular body.

"Well done, Daniel," Shelton said, referring to his defense of Chapman, Ann, and Macari in the garden last evening. "I will see you soon."

"He wants to make a deal," came the response in a deep voice.

Shelton raised his brow, hearing the words of his son.

"He could have killed us. But if he had, he would have no chance to get to you," Daniel concluded.

Shelton's eyes narrowed. "Stay on watch, Daniel. Things are going to get more challenging in the days ahead. Continue to be smart."

Daniel stepped away with Angie, then Ann approached Shelton. She faced the door with her back to Xavier.

"Pitkin County?" Ann whispered.

"Oui," replied Shelton.

The reply in French brought a slight smile to Ann Baker's face.

"Good to see you still have a sense of humor."

As Ann walked away, Shelton bent his wrist up and took hold of her hand, stopping her. He looked down at Professor Ann Baker.

"Thank you, Ann," he said. "Thank you for being strong and committed to the light."

Amir stood up from the sofa and walked across the room, passing Shelton without speaking. He waited until the other three had stepped into the elevator and out of sight, then he closed the doors and locked them.

"He wants to talk," said Amir, standing beside Shelton and facing Xavier.

Without waiting for a reply, Amir stepped forward and directed Xavier to the gallery.

Shelton followed. Once in the gallery, he proceeded to the bar and poured himself a drink. He took a large sip and then topped it off. He walked over to the sitting area, removed his pack, and sat down in the chair across from Xavier and crossed his legs. Amir sat down on the end chair, observing.

"Do you mind?" said Xavier, touching his hood.

Shelton remained stone-faced hearing the demon speak for the first time.

Shelton raised and lowered his glass as to say, "No, I don't mind."

He watched the black silk hood slip from Xavier's head and settle on his shoulders. Then Xavier removed the mask from the lower part of his face.

Shelton's eyebrows lifted in surprise. Sitting in front of him was a dark-skinned, somewhat normal looking, middle-aged man with smooth skin, a triangle-shaped face, a high forehead, coal-black eyes, and long dark brown hair.

Shelton took another sip from his glass, gathering himself, then narrowed his stare and looked at Amir before turning his attention back to Xavier.

"Why the X?" said Shelton, breaking the silence.

Xavier drew a deep breath and half smiled while he adjusted his garments and arranged his silky, flowing hair.

"Yes, Mr. Shelton, I can only imagine the questions you must have after decades of coming and going," said Xavier in a slow, deliberate, thoughtful cadence. His voice had a slight British accent.

Xavier again ran his long fingers through his disheveled hair. With several strokes, his hair was in place, hanging down below his shoulders.

He sat up straight and looked at Shelton, then cleared his voice.

"My name is Dr. Hans Leicher," said Xavier. "I am the tenth and last of my kind. An immortal of the human species. We were all marked with our number."

"The others?" asked Shelton.

"All others are gone. Perished by their own hands from their own blades. Their act was their final loyal deed to Master Hauser. They were afraid of being captured by you and forced to betray the Master. So they removed themselves from existence. Cowards!"

"You don't share your colleagues' fear?"

"That is an interesting question," said Xavier. "One answered by the very virtue of me sitting here in front of you at this moment. I do not fear my demise by you or by my saber. My fate was determined long ago. My intent is to help you eliminate all the dark voices from this world by stopping Dr. Wolfgang Hauser."

Shelton stared with disbelief into Leicher's cold black eyes.

"What exactly is it you can do to help?" interjected Amir.

Xavier looked toward the glassmaker.

"Dr. Leicher, why would you want to help me?" Shelton said. "I have no use for you."

Amir looked at Shelton with a confused expression.

Leicher turned his gaze to the floor, then toward Amir and back to Shelton.

"If I may, sir? I have often wondered what it might be like to speak with you, collaborate with you," said Leicher. "A person of your comprehensive intellect. You know your brother, Dr. Hauser, described you as one without emotion or feeling, without subjectivity. Yet with one question, one word, I know that your brother's assessment of you is not factual or true. Such an inquiry would never come from a heartless killer."

"My brother is the master of untruths," said Shelton without blinking an eye.

"Indeed!" said Leicher. "We have already found, discovered, a point at which we are in complete agreement. I'm sitting before you here, in my hybrid immortal existence. I should desire, should embrace the eternity cast upon me. Yet such a gift granted by contemptible hands is not an endowment but an imprecation."

Shelton sipped his drink while continuing to study Leicher's expressions and physical appearance.

"If I may, sir, I will answer your question," said Leicher.

Shelton nodded slightly.

"I'm a scientist. My father and mother were scientists. Greek by birth, raised and educated in England. In our time, we were the founders of real, or shall I say, modern science. Science where theories were developed and nurtured. Ideas were shared and discussed, debated. Most importantly, it was a process of doing and learning. Then doing again, repeating until something new, hopefully useful to humanity, had been learned, discovered."

Leicher had been with his father in Paris the summer he met Hauser. Wolfgang Hauser was incredibly intelligent and an impressive communicator. Leicher spent all the time he could at Hauser's chateau.

"That is the summer I met our mutual friend," said Leicher, looking over at Amir. "In retrospect, I suppose I was the overzealous one that summer. Perhaps I was too curious to explore, to experience science with Wolfgang Hauser." Leicher was referring to his willingness to be turned into an immortal. "As with all science, the experience was irreversible. What I became could not be undone. I've been paying for that mistake my entire existence."

Shelton stood and walked over to the bar.

"You want to repay something now, so that you can feel some sort of vindication? Is that why you sent for me?" Shelton refilled his glass.

"I want no vindication, sir," replied Leicher. "I know what I have done. I do not tell myself polite fictions. When the time comes, I know how to end my existence. My desire is to do something good first. Stopping Hauser's influence on the helpless human species is what I desire. The experiment must go on, continue without his influence. Without such influence, the possibilities of the human species are endless."

Shelton returned to his chair, placed his drink on the side table, sat back, and crossed his legs.

"Tell me about Hauser," Shelton said. "Tell me why he would need a scientist."

"Hauser is an influencer, not a magician or a witch. He has no ability to cast spells on people. He has no interest in torturing people eternally. To him, science is entertainment," said Leicher. "He enjoys watching people discover the power and beauty of informed creation. The chemistry and physics of this planet are unique. There is no other. He never lost his appreciation for the creation. While he despises the characteristics, mainly the latitude granted the species, he found enjoyment in hearing and seeing humans discover the power of the earth beneath them and the sky above."

Leicher paused and collected his thoughts while Shelton remained quiet, pondering the words coming out of the immortal's mouth.

"Keep going," said Shelton, even though Adira had already told him the entire story. He needed to hear it from the demon's own mouth. If Xavier got it wrong or was lying, it would seal his fate to be removed from existence.

"However," Leicher continued, "Hauser knew the clock was ticking because he had to make certain the experiment failed. Then the summer solstice, at the arrival of the twentieth century, changed everything. Hauser was no longer allowed to transit between dimensions. The first in command had confined him to the earth. Humans had no warning. The very world he had great influence over had distracted him. The environment he had created with his misinformation and lies trapped him. His confinement created intense anger and, without hesitation, he set out to destroy the species once and for all by any means available," said Leicher. "Looking back, attempting to learn, I suppose that is when I moved from being his entertainment to a servant. He drove the world to war while I influenced scientific discovery. I had watched the greatest physicists of the day labor and experiment with the very substance of the earth. The substance of subatomic particles. A little nudge, a theory, and a few short decades of experimentation led to the discovery that could indeed change the world."

Shelton sat up straighter in his chair. He hadn't expected to hear the truth from the demon.

"The first war fails. A little while longer, a madman is groomed and rises to power in Germany. The scientific community splits the atom and discovers a chain reaction. Now everything is in place for the species to build a weapon that can destroy the very world they require for life. That, Mr. Shelton, is a very unusual world and very rapid change."

Leicher paused, running his fingers through his hair. Shelton picked up his drink and took two large gulps.

"Science and culture, Mr. Shelton. I worked the science and Hauser worked the culture through our human proxies. A toxic, lethal, perhaps most devastating mix in the end. The scientific process is where discovery, learning, and advancement take place. Learning that hopefully proves useful to humans. Discovering improvements for the betterment of all is the goal. Sometimes these discoveries can result in negative outcomes. Regardless, once discovered, learned, validated through testing and retesting, knowledge is by all respects irreversible. One cannot unlearn or undue scientific discovery. Such was the case with nuclear fission and the chain reaction produced. A process which on the one hand could be quite useful. On the other hand, it could have grave consequences. One can only manage and cope with the new information in such a way that benefits without causing harm. This is not a simple thing to achieve in any profession. Even less so when influenced by one such as Dr. Hauser."

Leicher described culture as something based on perception, emotional attachment, and tradition. How one could argue that the goal of culture, actually, is to stop or prevent change. Leicher suggested it may not be an overstatement to conclude that culture resists change and perpetuates the status quo. Hauser was the master at creating great myths and deception that have permeated completely into the souls of societies and cultures for thousands of years.

"The good news is culture, unlike science, is reversible," noted Leicher. "One can simply change their mind, decide to believe something else, change course, or even regress to past norms, if desired. There are no rules of the natural world that apply. One only has to overcome one's belief or perception. All of which are contained inside the mind."

"Your line of discourse is familiar, Mr. Leicher," said Shelton.

"I suspected it should be, Mr. Shelton," replied Leicher. "I, as with the project team, felt the great regret of pressing the rules of nature to where humans could destroy themselves and the world."

"Ah, you are referring to the Manhattan Project," Shelton said.

Leicher nodded. "The science could not be unlearned. All that Hauser has accomplished with his dark voices, great deception and misleading of cultures and societies, however, can be undone. One simply has to remove the influence, retrain, relearn, change perspectives of what is right and what is not. I suppose that is where you come in, Mr. Shelton," Leicher concluded. "To that end is why I am sitting in front of you now. At this very moment, Hauser is doing everything in his power to influence the world's leaders to use their weapons of mass destruction against one another. Break down the social fabric of society, day by day, week by week, year by year. All so that the species launches the weapons that will wipe them out, ensuring Hauser's belief that the human experiment is doomed to fail. He is not interested in discovery but in being right."

Shelton stood and walked to the windows. He gazed thoughtfully toward the city gardens across the street. The outlines of trees were barely visible through the early morning fog. On the sidewalk, directly below, joggers and walkers appeared, then disappeared. The sidewalk cafe's customers sat enjoying their first cup of coffee and espresso in the moist morning air.

"So, Mr. Leicher," said Amir, "let's talk about how you can help."

"Your colleague, Professor Baker, had a painting on her that the late Reverend Chapman snatched from the d'Orsay," said Leicher. "I watched him take it on the security camera."

Shelton looked toward Amir, then back at Leicher.

"Impressive, that you and Hauser were so paranoid that you were watching the museum and my team," Shelton said, smiling slightly.

Edwards had grabbed the painting from the table at Lochgrey. Edwards gave it to Ann before she and Amir departed Scotland.

Xavier unrolled the painting. "There we are," said Leicher, referring to him and Amir.

"I don't remember Hauser standing there with us," responded Amir. "I recall the artist doing a quick sketch by the stable. It was just you and I."

"Yes indeed. You are correct," replied Leicher. "This is not the original version. It's been altered. Hauser was known for changing paintings to suit his view of reality. He had artists paint over or add and subtract to works of art frequently. This one started as Hauser in front of his castle. At some point he wanted no record of the castle. The artist had captured it perfectly. It was too recognizable. He had the artist add the chateau in the background, then added the group, then you and me. It didn't go quite the way he wanted it to with you. After you departed, Hauser tossed the painting aside," continued Leicher. "Of course, artists destroy nothing, you know. It ended up in the archives. The original version looked like this," said Leicher as he turned over the canvas and picked up the lamp.

The light penetrated through the back side of the thin fabric material. Through the weave on the back of the canvas, the tree-covered mountains of Germany revealed themselves. On top of a lower peak, nestled between the higher elevations, was an enormous castle.

"That is the Castle Janus," Shelton said as he studied the piece.

Days before, Shelton and the team at Providence had poured over every castle picture in France and Germany, looking for anything that might be odd or seem out of place. Edwards's research team had developed the castle theory based on Hauser's estimated age and his assumed need for protection and seclusion during his thousands of years on earth. Janus was unique looking but was most certainly a fortress and secluded. Facing the castle from the lower-level entry road, the light gray stone and dark accents reached into the sky above the mountain top. The narrow width and height of the eighteen-story fortress with twenty-nine spires created an ominous silhouette on the canvas.

"That is very good," said Leicher. "Castle Janus is the only castle on the planet that has been owned by the same family since the fourteenth century. Hauser had it designed and built. He owns the property around it for twenty kilometers in every direction. We registered the property to the wealthiest family in Germany."

Amir stood, excusing himself, and walked to the side of the library with Shelton.

"He's the seventh," Amir whispered to Shelton.

"Impossible," Shelton replied. "He is the adversary. There is only one fate for him."

"There is one more thing you require, Mr. Shelton," Leicher interrupted.

Shelton turned his head back toward Leicher, waiting for his next words.

"A key. You will need the key to the gates of the castle. I know where you can find it."

CHAPTER THIRTY-EIGHT

SHELTON KNEW THE words from Leicher were true. He also knew he needed the key to the gates of Janus—Adira had told him as much. But he couldn't accept that Hans Leicher, St. Xavier, was number seven. The evil he perpetuated was unforgiveable. There could be only one fate for Leicher: death.

Shelton believed Leicher had been fooled, misled by Hauser, like everyone else. He understood Hans was young and naïve when taken advantage of. But was that a good enough excuse? Leicher had influenced scientific advancement and helped develop a weapon that could destroy the entire species with ease. He had helped create Hauser's ultimate weapon. There could be no forgiveness for such an act.

But hadn't Shelton taken thousands of lives? He somehow thought that was different. Because it was his job. His purpose. The reason for his existence. But he hadn't known his purpose when he was doing these things. He had no higher, loftier sense of purpose. Just a drive to eliminate foul humans.

Was Shelton really any different from Leicher? They both followed their basic instincts and sensibilities. They both seemed to accept who and what they were. Neither running from reason or purpose. Both learning from experience and having the ability to apply that learning in the future. Shelton didn't have any regrets. Leicher was reconsidering his fate and his deeds.

In an interesting and strange way, they had both learned lessons from a less intelligent, less capable species. A human species where emotion, compassion, and intelligence combined made for a superior life form. A species Adira was tasked with perpetuating. Life that could progress and build alternative universes. A life form with attributes that Leicher never could fully develop as a young man before Hauser robbed him. Attributes Shelton never had.

However, there was still the question of seven. Shelton didn't have the seven souls required to save the species without Leicher. Adira never disclosed that a reformed demon could count. It didn't make sense to him. Or did it?

Shelton paced the room. He had tasted love. His feelings for Angie were real. Adira hadn't designed him to love, but he did. A short three months of being together with Angie and eighteen years of being apart, and he loved her more today than ever before. Her strong, confident personality didn't need anybody or anything else to survive, to be happy. Living and loving was enough for Angie Brady. Attributes that impressed Shelton. Her happiness lived day in and day out, with love and peace.

How can I forgive and show compassion to Leicher? he wondered.

He knew that Leicher had already shown this ability. Leicher had stepped forward out of his evil existence in an act of compassion and remorse. He stepped forward to help because deep down inside, he was sorry for his actions. He sought forgiveness. Adira spoke of such possibilities, and Shelton could see them in Hans Leicher. For the sake of all humanity, Leicher wanted to stop Hauser—no matter the cost. There he was, sitting across the room from Shelton, ready to help—or ready to die. Leicher wasn't there to barter. He wasn't interested in trading his information for his life. He was simply remorseful, willing to help and suffer the consequences of his past actions.

If I can forgive him, then I have my seven, concluded Shelton.

Shelton had witnessed the power of love. He had felt the love of his mother. He had seen Ann's love for her son. He knew that Edwards and Providence were built around love for others. Helping others. There was no quid pro quo. Generous acts of love and kindness were all around him. When it came down to it, the world was filled with loving, compassionate, good people. The good was billions greater than the bad.

Isn't that worth saving? Shelton stood looking out the glass windows but seeing only the thoughts running through his head. Wasn't it worth giving the human species a chance to blossom without the persistent negative influence of Hauser, his henchmen, and misinformed humans?

Shelton wondered if by embracing love and forgiveness, he would no longer be Magnus. Suddenly that didn't matter. Without another thought, he made his decision. Wisdom, justice with love, was many times more powerful than the pure scales of justice.

He looked at Leicher sitting across from him.

"Mr. Leicher," Shelton said, "I have a plan."

CHAPTER THIRTY-NINE

Spain's Plaza de Zocodover was already bustling with activity when Amir and Shelton arrived. The server at the El Foro Café set two cups of espresso down on the table and departed.

The Spanish Alcazar of Toledo was once home to Wolfgang Hauser. He'd occupied the entire north wing of the large stone fortress. During the Spanish Civil War, the Alcazar was seized, and Hauser was forced to leave in a hurry. All but the north wing of the Alcazar was destroyed. Hauser himself torched the inside of his residence on his way out. He wanted no evidence of himself left behind. But the attempt failed. The stone floors and walls didn't burn, and Hauser's residence remained intact following his departure.

After the war, Hauser sent Leicher to Spain to purchase or steal the main gates from the Alcazar. Either was fine with Hauser. He wanted the large black, silver, and gold iron gates to adorn the front of Janus. They were the most elegant and impressive gates ever constructed. It was only appropriate that such glorious works of art grace the front of the most grandiose castle in the world.

At the same time that the Spanish War was ending, Leicher was busy working with German scientists on nuclear physics. By this time, he realized Hauser intended to use a weapon capable of mass destruction to eliminate the species.

Leicher successfully delivered the Alcazar gates and a set of keys to Hauser at the castle. The moment Leicher handed them over, Hauser destroyed what he thought was the only set of keys to the gates. Keys were only good for locking and unlocking things. Hauser had no interest in either at Janus. No one would dare come after him. Not even his misguided bother Magnus. Leicher had taken the risk that Hauser wouldn't test the keys in the gates. He was right. The arrogant Wolfgang Hauser had lost the ability to think critically. The master's brain was consumed with the need for vindication that he had been right about humans. They were not capable of governing themselves. And his thoughts were becoming increasingly clouded as weapon development progressed. Leicher had successfully slipped Hauser the wrong keys to the gates, placing the actual keys from the north wing safely in the Spanish archives.

Shelton and Amir finished their espresso and began the walk up the hill to the Alcazar. The relaxed morning mood faded. They were now on full alert. After the surprise attack in Scotland, anything was possible.

Shelton was now traveling using British intelligence airplanes. Ben had followed the team from Paris to Prestwick, using a private aircraft tracker. It would be impossible for Ben to track Shelton using British assets. The aircraft information was classified by the British government, and Ben didn't have access to it.

Shelton and Amir observed the people around them as they walked. The crowds thinned the closer they came to the new gates of the Alcazar. By the time the two men made it to the reconstructed fortress, the ticket booth had opened for the day. They purchased tickets, got their map, and planned the day.

The staff members at the Alcazar fortress were plentiful and the tourist traffic was sparse. The slow visitor day provided Shelton and Amir the opportunity to carefully study different informational displays undisturbed by traffic flow.

A young Spanish guide named Emile offered to provide the men with an informal tour. Emile was thorough and enthusiastic in his presentation.

The fortress had been built as a stone fortification on the highest point in Toledo. Originally used as a Roman palace in the third century, then falling into disrepair. The Romans fully restored the structure in the mid 1500s. At that time, the resident of the north wing was an eccentric German businessperson.

"What do you know about this businessman?" Shelton asked.

"Not much really," Emile said. "He was definitely a recluse and was thought to spend his springs and summers in Germany and his falls and winters here in a slightly warmer climate. He also spent a great deal of time on the coast. Supposedly, he was an avid sailor and had a remarkably attractive lady companion."

"Interesting," Shelton said. "I am a businessperson myself. Do you have a picture or painting of him?"

"I am not aware of a painting or picture of him," Emile said.

"During the Spanish Civil War, the fortress was heavily damaged," Emile continued, pointing to several pictures of the aftermath. "Here you can see the sequence of pictures starting with the north, east, south, and the west wings and the damage incurred."

"How very interesting. May I take a photograph?" Shelton asked.

"The policy is no pictures, sir," Emile said. "But one or two should be okay," he said, after looking around to ensure his bosses weren't watching.

"Great!" Shelton punched up the photo app on his phone.

"The north wing is hardly damaged," Amir said as he surveyed and compared the photographs. "The other three wings look like total losses. Although the gates and the gate structure look completely intact."

"Exactly what year was the civil war?" Shelton asked.

"Nineteen thirty-six to nineteen thirty-nine," Emile answered, confidently. "It was a tragic but necessary time in the evolution of our country.

"This case has several artifacts from the post-war days," Emile said, pointing to a large glass display case as he continued to walk. "Of course, shortly after the war, they rebuilt the castle using as much of the original structure as possible. This display shows the different stages of reconstruction."

"What is this?" Shelton asked, pointing to an object inside the glass case.

Emile walked around the case to where Shelton was standing. When he saw the object Shelton was pointing to, he smiled, knowing he had the answer.

"That is the key to the front gates of the fortress," Emile said. "It is the only remaining key to the original gates. There were thought to be five keys produced for the front gates. One key for each of the primary tenants of the wings and one extra for the security and watchmen."

"It looks rather sophisticated," Shelton said, analyzing the handle and the stem. "Isn't that the number one engraved on the stem here?"

"Yes, that is correct," Emile answered. "They numbered the keys. This one belonged to the north-wing tenant. We did not discover it until the final stages of the reconstruction following the war," Emile said proudly, looking thrilled he had actually remembered such a nuanced fact.

"Gentlemen, it has been my pleasure showing you around today," Emile said. "The gift store is just this way." He pointed to the sign at the end of the hall. "You are free to continue to enjoy the grounds. The building closes to visitors at four o'clock."

Shelton and Amir thanked him. Then Shelton handed him 100 euros as a tip, which put a huge smile on Emile's face.

Shelton and Amir hurried through the gift shop without pausing. They stopped just outside the gallery to review their pictures.

"What is it?" Amir asked, noticing the intense look on Shelton's face.

"The key," Shelton said. "The gate key. The handle casting is the globe and snake. It's the same emblem that's on the sword I took from the guardian in Buenos Aires. The same emblem that I smashed into a million pieces at the Grand Council."

Shelton looked out past Amir and examined the front gates of the fortress in the distance.

"These are clearly not the original gates. See here in the picture." He handed his device to Amir so he could look for himself.

Shelton saw Emile making his way through the courtyard, back to the main fountain, ready to answer questions for the next guest.

"Excuse me, Emile," Shelton called out. "Do you mind if I ask you one more question?"

"Please do," Emile said.

"My friend and I noticed the front gates are not the same as those we saw in the pictures. We were wondering if you know what happened to the originals. They were clearly intact post-war," Shelton said.

Emile's face once again lit up, confident he remembered the scripted answer.

"The story of the original gates is interesting," Emile began. "They were removed and placed in storage after the war and during reconstruction. Five years later, when the workers were ready to rehang the gates, they were missing. No one knows what happened. The assumption is someone stole them and salvaged the valuable materials. After all, thievery was simpler back in those days."

"Where were they stored?" Shelton asked.

"From the archive pictures I have seen, they stored most of the salvageable pieces in that general area at the bottom of the hill." Emile pointed down the slope.

"Out in the open, I assume?" Shelton asked.

"Yes. Everything was stored in the open and covered up, if necessary."

"Interesting! Thanks again," Shelton said, making the short walk back to where Amir was sitting.

"He said the original gates were stolen while in storage during reconstruction," Shelton said to Amir, bringing him up to speed. "The story is they were likely stolen and salvaged by the thieves."

"How does someone steal large, heavy gates without someone noticing?" Amir asked rhetorically.

"They don't," Shelton said. "The officials at the time were probably paid to look the other way. In fact, they probably had to help execute the plan, given the size and weight of the gates."

"Leicher's story is hanging together," said Amir.

"Indeed, it is," said Shelton. "We need that key, Amir."

"I'll take care of it," Amir said. "I will meet you back at the hotel."

CHAPTER FORTY

LYCHEN, GERMANY, WAS in the northeastern part of the former German Democratic Republic. The small tourist village had not grown in size since the early 1900s. Surrounded by lakes, the village was a popular weekend destination for high-profile people looking to escape the pressures of life in Berlin.

Limited growth meant limited capacity, which allowed premium pricing for the local proprietors of the small village. Customers did not mind paying up. The quality of service and ability to truly escape life for a while was worth it, if you had the money.

Both Amir and Shelton needed rest. Although Amir did not technically require it, he required recovery time. Without meditation, reflection, and spiritual guidance from Adira, it was easy to become lost in such a chaotic world.

The twenty-room hotel was small but well kept. The service was better than any five-star hotel Shelton had experienced. Excellent service when you need something, insightful staff when necessary, but otherwise invisible and unobtrusive. The small family-owned inn understood how to accomplish such a balance.

Shelton was in the hotel cafe early in the afternoon enjoying his first cup of coffee when Amir sat down across from him at the table.

"Did you get some rest after that late-night flight?" Amir asked.

"As soon as I showered, I fell asleep immediately."

Shelton's voice had a renewed level of energy. "Frankly, I feel more rested this morning than perhaps I ever have been."

Amir smiled. "Excellent!"

"How are you this morning?" Shelton reciprocated.

"I, too, am well healed and energized." Amir looked at the cup on the table in front of Shelton. "The coffee?"

"Remarkable," Shelton said. "I am stunned by this place. I wonder how the logistics team found it."

"I gave them a bit of advice," Amir said, looking down modestly.

"Oh?" Shelton lifted one eyebrow.

"In modern-day terms, we know this as a safe house," Amir said.

"A safe house?"

Amir almost started laughing at Shelton's quick response.

"I realize the term takes on a slightly different meaning from the company we keep. But you and I are safe here." Amir grinned. "The staff here are like me," he whispered.

"Angels?" Shelton asked, his lips curving upward.

"I must give you a great deal of credit, Mr. Shelton. I expected that joke from you a long time ago. You have done well holding it inside for so long," Amir said.

"The city of Lychen is like Abdel Kinneret," continued Amir. "It is a city that the German government simply left alone. The hotel was one of several safe zones that were established around the world. My glass shop and attached home in Buenos Aires was a safe zone. It is the only way to survive in such a saturated enemy environment."

"I don't understand," Shelton said. "Why here?"

"I believe Wilkinson explained it to you at one point," said Amir. "Dots of good in a forest of evil. Wilkinson, Ann, Edwards, Chapman, Wood, Macari, and Leicher. All points of hope. Points of hope must have a place to rest. A great deal of good can come from just a few when connected to a common goal. You have your seven, Mr. Shelton."

"And you," Shelton said, "are the orchestra conductor connecting the notes of hope?"

"Something like that," answered Amir.

"Have you always known that Janus was Hauser's refuge?" Shelton asked directly. "After all, why would one have a safe house in the neighborhood?"

"The answer to your question is no," Amir said. "I learned about Janus when you did. As I shared with you, when the painting was originally commissioned, the backdrop was a French chateau," Amir said sincerely.

Shelton sipped his coffee and poured a fresh cup from the carafe.

"Why here?" Amir continued. "The team briefed me last night. The story is tragic. We are in the heart of Germany. This is the northwestern sector of the state of Brandenburg. We are roughly forty miles northwest of Berlin."

Amir described how Hauser's activity in Germany during the twentieth-century wars was rampant. It was a period when Hauser was aggressively raging against his newly realized fate. He was fostering hate and discord across the planet, the likes of which the world had never seen. This city was a haven for the good people during the first and second world wars. The army tried to invade the city several times. The result was always a very violent death for every soldier and officer of the German militia. No member of the German army had ever escaped alive. A fact that scared military leaders greatly. Even to where they ordered their army to build a wall around the small city. Isolate it and leave it alone. Parts of the wall still existed. Amir offered to show it to Shelton.

"Who defended the city during the war?" Shelton asked.

Amir looked down, hesitating. "You did. You and your team, that is. Before you were born."

"My team?" Shelton sat back in his chair, letting the new information soak in. "In all my dreams, I have never had a team. Never an army. It has always been me against everyone else," Shelton said solemnly.

"You do not require a team. You *desired* a team," clarified Amir. "Your human feelings of being isolated and alone affect your human dreams."

Amir took a deep breath. "In fact, your generals are here at the hotel. They are waiting to meet with you as soon as you are ready."

"Why have they come here? I do not need help in dealing with Hauser. I know what needs to be done," Shelton said.

"You have answered your own question," said Amir. "Your half human side suffers from arrogance. It is exactly why your generals are here. You do not think you need help. You are probably right. To be clear, if you fail, Adira has given Lynxx One, your second in command, instructions to end the experiment on earth. Hauser is a cunning and slippery one. He is a professional, just like you. Once you cross the river and put your foot on the castle grounds, you will either succeed or die. There is no in-between."

~

The generals stood up as Shelton entered the room. They lowered their heads to show respect. All six generals from Apex One to Apex Six were present. They each had assumed the form of a human dressed in a neat-fitting business suit. One by one, Shelton looked into each of their faces to remember his past, then he sat down at the head of the table. Amir stood beside him.

"What do you know about the Castle Janus?"

"Magnus," said Lynxx One, "it is nice to be in your presence, sir. It is good to be with you again. General Axsl has all the information you will need."

Axsl was the commander of Apex Six. He spent the next hour briefing Shelton on Hauser and the castle.

CHAPTER FORTY-ONE

THE TWO-HOUR HIKE from the roadway to the river was uneventful. Axsl and several others had prepared a path through the dense forest and escorted Shelton to the river. The drawbridge on the main road to the castle grounds was raised.

The closer the group came to the river crossing, the more guardians they encountered. Axsl and his team made quick work of the low-density life forms. They could easily identify the exact location of the entity and, without a sound, compress the guardian's matter before the enemy even knew it. The process yielded nothing more than a slight puffing sound before the remains of the creatures fell to the ground as dust.

At the bridge, Axsl and Shelton parted ways. Shelton removed a hook and line from his pack. The first throw across the river to the top edge of the wooden bridge missed. The second one landed perfectly. He gave the rope three powerful tugs to drive the grappling hook into the planks. Then he secured his end of the rope to the bridge pillar. With one swift natural motion, Shelton was pulling himself across the rope line to the other side, just as he had done a hundred times before in the field. Once on the other side, Shelton pulled himself onto the edge, dropped from the bridge to the road below, and collected himself.

Clouds were rolling in now as the evening light grew dimmer. Fog was starting to obscure the distant mountain ridges. Shelton looked around. The veil that protected him was descending around the castle and the surrounding hillsides and forests. The same veil that arrived at his awakening on that dark side street in Georgetown when he was twenty-two years old.

The sudden sound of rushing water caught Shelton's attention. He turned to see a wall of water rounding the bend in the river headed directly for him. The water smashed trees and rolled boulders as it picked up speed, flowing down the valley. Hauser's demons had successfully caused the upstream damn to fail.

Shelton turned to face the wall of water. Patiently, he watched and waited. At just the right moment, he raised his arms as if to embrace the water. Then, with a sweeping motion of his arms, he changed the course of the water, sending it crashing into the forest, ripping through the trees toward the main road below.

The first crack of an automatic weapon firing overhead sent Shelton diving into the trees for cover. Hauser had successful bribed a German military commander to help protect Janus. Thousands of bullets shredded the ground where he had been standing seconds before. Above the treetops, four helicopters surrounded his position, their rotors turning just underneath the low cloud cover in the fading light.

Shelton crawled the next fifty yards on his stomach while the machine guns continued to shred the trees above him. Slowly, he made his way out of the line of fire, jumped to his feet, and began running up the hill through the forest toward the main entrance to Castle Janus. He dove onto the ground and took cover just at the edge of the trees. Shelton looked up.

The castle sat on the mountaintop, rising into the darkening gray sky above. Yet higher mountain peaks protected and surrounded its tall walls and spires in every direction. A long, narrow cobblestone road crossed the bridge that spanned the small valley and led through the castle gates. On either side of the bridge, a line of red-robed guardians sat astride their horses, sabers at the ready.

The unmarked helicopters were now hovering just above the castle spires with weapons aimed toward the tree line just beyond the cobblestone bridge.

Lying in the grass just beyond the tree line, Shelton spotted something on one of the castle spires. It was Axsl standing tall, perfectly balanced on the top of the spire, staring straight at Shelton, waiting for the command. Shelton nodded to give the order.

Axsl raised his arms into the air and pointed four fingers, two from each hand, skyward. One finger for each aircraft. A deafening clash of thunder broke through the evening air. Lightning exploded from the Axsl's fingertips, each bolt striking a helicopter. The aircraft disintegrated in fireballs. Flames, metal, and human parts rained down across Janus.

Shelton's commanders had placed his white horse into position under a tall rock overhang. As the guardians looked skyward to see what was happening, the man on a horse emerged from the tree line, rushing full speed down the cobblestone road toward the gauntlet of demons. The first guardian had just turned his attention to the approaching sound of hooves on stone when Shelton arrived. The blow from Shelton's sword was fatal.

Shelton swung his sword from side to side at a full gallop down the line of guardians, executing each of them as he passed.

At the end of the line, he pulled on his mount's reins, stopping just before the archway and the castle gates. They were the same gates that had once been at the Alcazar castle in Spain. Shelton looked up at the enormity of the structure in front of him. The castle reached endlessly into the sky. It was beautiful and majestic. A grand piece of architecture.

Shelton dismounted and stood beneath the gate arches. He raised his hand to the gates, and they swung open. He walked slowly but purposefully across the cobblestone courtyard toward the castle, stepping over human remains and helicopter parts.

He paused at the main entryway to the castle. The doors opened and St. Xavier stepped out and approached Shelton. Their eyes locked.

"Go away. Leave us, Magnus," came Leicher's voice from beneath the hood. "There is nothing for you to do here. Go back to your money, your women, and your humanity. You will not see us again. You have Wolfgang Hauser's promise."

"A deal? You are offering me a deal?" Shelton said. "There was a time where that may have been of interest, but that time has passed. I have business with Lord Hauser."

"That is not advisable," Xavier warned.

"Not your call," Shelton replied.

"You have no business here. Leave us alone, and we will leave you alone," said Xavier, repeating his offer.

"You are talking to the wrong person if you are looking for a deal." Shelton could see Xavier's hand move slightly toward his saber. "Go ahead and draw your saber," Shelton challenged. "It will be a fitting end to your misled life."

Xavier removed his hand from his weapon, nodded at Shelton, and started walking toward the gates. Just before he stepped through them, he tossed his saber on the ground, removed the hood from his head, and continued walking. Leicher crossed the bridge and disappeared into the forest without looking back.

Shelton cautiously stepped through the front door of the castle. The foyer was enormous and beautiful. He stood for a moment admiring the architecture, the art, and the flowers. To his right, a figure stood in the dimly lit library. The man was dressed impeccably in a perfectly tailored suit.

"Welcome," said the low voice.

Shelton turned and strode into the library. The sheer elegance and character of the large room wasn't lost on Shelton. From the original hand-painted artwork on the ceiling and the handwoven rugs to the fine handmade furniture, richly colored tapestries, and custom unique vases, every item was meticulously placed for spacing and enjoyment.

"Please, sit if you like," said the man as he continued to stare out the window with his back to Shelton.

"Humans?" the man said in a calm voice. "Such an unsophisticated form of life. So easy to distract. So egotistical and driven by the desire for greatness and recognition. They are barely two iterations from being basic animals. Yet they think they are brilliant. It has been unbearable to watch," the figure said, turning toward Shelton. "The smartest among them is the most incompetent. The most simpleminded ones are the most informed. Laughable, isn't it Magnus?"

In the low light of the room, Shelton studied the face of the man speaking to him. It was the same face he had seen at the Grand Council. It was the same face in the painting from the Musee d'Orsay.

"Look at this place," Hauser said, turning back to the window. "Trees that grow out of the ground. Birds that fly. Fish that breathe under the water. Flowers that grow naturally and are so uniquely and beautifully colored. The fragrance, oh it is wonderful. Then there are humans. They try so hard. They can't even imagine the greatness it takes to create such things, yet they think they are so intelligent.

"It is good to see you, brother," Hauser finally said, turning back to Shelton. "It has been a very long time. I have often wondered what this day would be like. Although it is anticlimactic. The earth is not shaking. No clouds are parting. The trumpets do not sound. You just walked up to my front door and walked in. You do not even look like the noble warrior I knew long ago. You look like a weak human."

Shelton remained standing, staring at Hauser intently.

"Tell me," Hauser said, "did Adira provide you with the knowledge of your heritage? Or did she leave that part out? Do you have any recollection of your pre-human existence? Did you even know your real name when I said it?"

Shelton remained silent as his desire to permanently close Hauser's mouth grew. He was expected by Adira to hear Simeon out before acting. He would follow his instructions.

"Ah, of course," Hauser continued. "Your silence. You, too, are the good obedient son, just like our brother, Michael," he said, scoffing. "Adira only gave you part of the story, didn't she? Only the part that would properly motivate your limited human mind. Oh, my dear Magnus, we have much to talk about. Would like something to drink?"

Shelton declined the offer, and Hauser started talking again.

"I look out into the dark sky every night. Every night, Magnus!

From this place I dream of returning to our home and the days when we were together." Hauser took a seat at the table across from Shelton. "We were the doers, the three of us. My brothers and I. Adira and the governing council were the dreamers. The creators. How truly magnificent it was watching them work. Invigorating. Satisfying. The first born, Michael, was the architect, making their dreams come to life. He worked closely with Adira. The worlds they created were magnificent."

Adira had not withheld anything from Shelton during their meeting in Kinneret. His background knowledge was complete.

"I was humbled when they asked me to act as the governor of all the universes," continued Hauser. "Adira set the rules, and I followed them. I handled each domain. I ensured things were properly managed and looked after. It wasn't a difficult job. The superior intellect of life forms across the six universes made everything work. The rules were the rules. Those creations never violated the rules. They were not created with the capability to do so."

"You, my brother, as you have learned, were the scales of justice," said Hauser. "Your legions of soldiers were well trained. Never missed a mark. They were there, always dressed impeccably, with perfectly polished armor and a full complement of weapons. They were my adjudicators and warriors. The commanders of all armies across the all the universe."

"You and your soldiers had nothing to do until Apex Seven," Hauser said, lifting his arms with open hands to show the earth. "When called on, you did a masterful job. Rather barbaric, I must say. None the less, necessary," Hauser said, trying to stroke Shelton's ego.

"We used to enjoy the sunrises, sunsets, the mountains, and the oceans together. It all worked quit well until Seven and the species experiment. How Adira had dreamed it up, I have no idea. She and the council had worked on forming the earth for millions of years. At one point, they were so obsessed with notion and prospects, it was the only project they worked on. It consumed every moment of their time. The science, evolution, and technology they were creating in this planet laboratory was most impressive. I must say, when they were done, it was truly awesome." Hauser raised his arms into the air and stretched out his fingers. "The creation and the evolution of life was remarkable. Life forms quickly learned to adapt to the various environments of the earth. Sea creatures to land. Warm climate life to cold climate life and the weather. How we loved watching the weather, you and I. The atmospheric engine powered all life forms. Wind, rain, snow, heat, cold, storms, lightning, and thunder. All of it a brilliant creation. The cycle of life on earth did not require the services of me or you. It was self-sustaining and regenerative."

Shelton could feel himself being lulled into the dream with Hauser's soft and effective words. Adira had warned him to be on guard.

"Then came humans," said Hauser. "A life form designed and created to thrive, appropriate, and prosper amid this monumental creation. Initially humans flourished like all other life forms. Unlike other inhabited worlds, they could rationalize the experience. All other forms of life were essentially mechanical beings. Eat, sleep, and breed. They didn't have the ability to simply enjoy the beauty of a green meadow, a snow-capped mountain, or waves crashing on the shore."

The muscles in Hauser's face tightened as his anger grew.

"The council should have stopped there," he demanded. "But they did not. They created a soul capable of experiencing the wonders of the earth, just like you and I could. A life form capable of making choices. A species that could problem solve and use the earth and all of its resources to perpetuate life. A species that could discover and transform the resources from the earth into useful things. A living, breathing, autonomous life that could think, rationalize, and self-determine how to manage themselves. Doesn't the thought of that trouble you?" asked Hauser.

"Not in the least," Shelton replied with no emotion in his voice. "Not my call or yours."

"But there were no rules," said Hauser. "No governance required. It was a bad idea from the start. A life form with some intellectual capability and the ability to choose would be a disaster. Adira listened to my thesis, but I lost the debate. With no rules as governor, how would I control the species? So I tested them. The simpleminded human couldn't handle self-governance. When the test failed, Adira and the others continued to believe that humans would self-correct." Hauser sneered. "The whole thing fell apart quickly. Then they dispatched you thousands of times to demonstrate the ramifications of one behaving badly. You, Magnus, snuffed out the awful actors and supported the good ones. But the misbehavior continued to grow and spiral out of control for thousands of years.

"Eventually, you reset the experiment. You killed everyone on earth except for a few," Hauser said, smiling. "But that didn't work either. Then they sent Michael to set the example for the species. The thought was to show humans how to do it and they would do it of their own free will. After all, Michael proved it was possible to have choices and do the right thing."

"The perfect man!" said Hauser. "Laughable, don't you think? He only survived thirty years before the species killed him. Thirty years, Magnus! A drop in the bucket of time. These creatures eat, they breed, they dominate each other, and they killed the perfect human because it threatened their power and egos. And you think I'm arrogant?"

"Your job was to govern and guide the people. Help them succeed. Not to test," said Shelton. "Had you done your job, I would not be here now. We would be sitting on the beach having a delicate glass of wine, admiring your brilliant work."

"You are a liar!" screamed Hauser.

"Am I?" Shelton replied. "No one ever supported your testing. You are the liar. You just couldn't help yourself. You needed to prove that you were right. You were afraid of losing your role, Simeon. Your selfishness and arrogance has destroyed you. I am here to collect."

"Get out of my house!" Hauser demanded. "There has never been a human on this miserable planet that could resist the temptations of greed and power. Providing any life form a choice was the problem. No amount of guidance or governing matters to these morons. These humans believe they can lead themselves. They think they are gods. They are nothing." Hauser pounded the table before him. "They should all die, and you, my brother, should kill them. Do it now, and let's get on with more pleasant matters."

Shelton brought his left hand up to his face and rested his head on his fingertips. Hauser's observations had merits. His demon brother made valid points. Humans in positions of power many times acted like they were a god. Humans had dominated each other throughout their existence. Many times to each other's detriment and ruin. History was filled with examples. Hauser had everything to do with the misdirection of humankind. He had applied undue pressure on a weaker, less developed life form. He was nothing more than a bully trying to prove he was smarter than his superiors. He had been off the rails for thousands of years, trying to prove he was smarter than everyone else. His arrogance and hubris made him dumber than nature ever could.

Adira had cautioned Shelton about this moment. About the strength and persuasiveness of Hauser's words. And she had been clear with her instruction. Shelton must let Hauser's words pass over him and do the work of the day. Reconciliations and debates with a misdirected Hauser were a waste of precious time.

"Why didn't you try to resolve the issue?" Shelton asked.

"Ah," Hauser said, his voice calmer. "For a moment, I had forgotten who I was speaking to. Not just a barbarian, are you, my brother? You are the skilled negotiator, the problem solver, the adjudicator. The answer to your question is intelligence. Humans are simply learning machines with memories. There is no way to purge their brains short of destroying them. They are like runaway machines. Uncontrollable."

Hauser shifted his focus back to Shelton.

"The so-called priest you killed," Hauser said, flicking his fingers to indicate the insignificance of the human, "he deserved it. He was the perfect example of why earthly humans never should have been created. Power hungry, deceitful, immoral, and disgusting!"

"The day I plunged the knife into the heart of your councilman was indeed a good day," Shelton said. "You remind me of him."

Shelton knew the comparison to a human would be an insult. To his surprise, Hauser stood and calmly walked back toward the window.

"Did you really think you were going to walk into my home and destroy me?"

Shelton reached into his pocket and set a letter on the table. "I was instructed to give you this."

"I will not accept it." Hauser looked away.

"The choice is not yours. I suggest you read it."

Hauser walked toward the table. Shelton pushed the piece of paper across to where Hauser had been sitting.

"No. No. No," Hauser said. "She cannot leave me here with these miserable creatures. It is time for my homecoming. I can make all of this right. They have certainly seen the experiment didn't work."

"Take a good look around you, brother," Shelton said, moving his hand around the room. "This is your home. This is your prison cell. No matter how much you rationalize your actions, you were, have been, and will always be the unhinged and disobedient one."

CHAPTER FORTY-TWO

Angie glanced toward the bunkhouse office and saw Ann standing in the window with the phone held to her ear. In the bullpen in front of her, Daniel was exercising his dad's horse as the ranch boss of Elk Creek watched.

The afternoon sun from a clear blue sky warmed the Pitkin valley. The fresh overnight snow on the peaks of the mountains was the first sign that summer was drawing to a close and fall was arriving.

Angie, Ann, and Daniel had spent the morning in Remington buying new clothes. The Bradys' escape from Lookout Point hadn't allowed time to pack. Then the call came from Shelton to Angie requesting they follow Ann, Chapman, and Macari to Paris. Not before stopping in New York for Daniel to pick up the guardian saber for his weapon.

Shelton had warned Angie not to let her guard down at Lookout Point. She had listened. Upon her return from the meeting with Shelton, Angie had a new security system installed that replaced what Ben Davis had set up. She had the system improved, using high-tech pressure and motion sensors that were layered across the grassland areas and open spaces. As an extra precaution, she and Daniel took turns doing night security.

At the first sign of trouble, Angie and Daniel made their escape. They drove the pre-positioned electric utility four-wheeler down to the docks and escaped on the river by boat. Behind them they heard the explosions that destroyed the house and everything in it, including Heather Kersting.

Angie rested her right boot on the bottom rail of the bullpen while the sun warmed her face. She felt the bottom rail move slightly as Ann put both feet on the lower rail and slung her arms over the top rail.

"Edwards is doing fine," Ann said, watching Daniel steer the horse effortlessly without hands. "He seems to be making a quick recovery. No word from Tom or Amir?"

Angie looked past Ann with a blank stare.

"He will be okay," Angie said. "They made him for this moment in time."

"He's a good man," said Ann sincerely. "Not the most cuddly, perhaps, but good."

The words brought a smile to Angie's face. "He has his moments."

Ann's phone buzzed, alerting her to an incoming text message. The levity of the moment vanished. Ann held up the picture received from Edwards. There, on the highest hill of the Providence Institute's vast acreage, near a group of tall trees overlooking a river valley, were seven new gold grave markers. Wood, Macari, and Chapman's names were engraved with the date of death. Baker, Edwards, and Wilkinson's markers were there as well. The seventh marker had no name. Angie and Ann looked up from the picture with deep concern on their faces. Edwards's point in sending the picture was to make sure everyone understood he had made an accounting, and that there was not a number seven. At least not that he knew of. He was trying to reconcile the fact with the others.

❦

Shelton could see the anger on Hauser's distraught face. The rage inside his brother was about to explode.

With one swift move, Hauser's coat flew open. Knives from each hand were suddenly flying straight for Shelton's chest with remarkable speed. Shelton raised his hands just in time to create a blast of wind from each palm. The knives altered course, slicing into the faces of two guardians flanking Hauser.

More guardians appeared, rapidly surrounding the perimeter of the room. Before Shelton could move, they blasted high-voltage electricity from their hands. Each bolt striking Shelton at exactly the same time. Lying on the floor, Shelton turned his head slightly at the sound of Hauser's laughter. Then everything went silent.

The shadows of the clouds painted the desert a beautiful array of colors as far as the eye could see. Magnus looked out across the landscape and marveled at the pristine dunes and canyons in front of him. The reflection of the sunlight off polished steel caught his eye in the distance. His mount moved down the hill toward the valley floor below.

Shelton gradually regained consciousness and opened his eyelids, blinking as he tried to focus. He looked down at the floor, then lifted his head. He turned his head one way, and then the other.

The weight of his body pressed down on the top of the stakes that had been driven into each foot. His arms were stretched out above his head. His wrists impaled with metal rods. Blood from his arms dripped onto his face. His body shook from the pain.

Hauser's laughter brought Shelton back into reality.

"There you have it," said Hauser. "Well done, sir. You have achieved the same fate as our brother. Impaled on a piece of wood to die. And for what?"

Hauser and his assistants had stretched out Shelton's body and nailed him to one of the wooden wall beams in the library. Shelton's bare, limp body was pinned to the wall, helpless.

"Your dreams, my brother, are all coming true. You could not stop me then, and you cannot stop me now. I am the king of this forsaken experiment. My plans will not be derailed. As for you? You will die, just as Michael did. Then I will throw your body to the wolves for dinner. Tomorrow, I will hunt down your son and do the same to him."

Shelton took a deep breath. Then another. He slowly looked at his wrists. The marks were untouched.

"Yes, yes, that is right, you ignorant man," said Hauser. "Look to the heavens to save you. Beg! Cry out! No one came to save our brother, and no one is coming to save you. You are just a poor, helpless bastard. Half human, half pure. I am the only truly pure one. Unadulterated by human loins."

Shelton looked down to survey the rest of the room. With a quick, sudden move, his stare snapped back to Hauser. Their eyes locked. Hauser's proud, smiling face faded as Shelton's anger penetrated his soul.

"You have forgotten one thing, my brother," Shelton whispered. "I am not Michael! And you are not a god."

Shelton opened his hand as wide as he could and commanded the attack. Lightning bolts exploded from his wrists, striking Hauser and the guardians, knocking them backward and on to the floor. Then with one move, the stakes flew from his hands and feet, hitting four of the guardians and exploding on impact, killing them instantly.

Shelton walked over to Hauser lying on the floor. He picked up a saber from the table, turned, and killed three more guardians as they attacked from behind.

He then turned back toward Hauser.

"Stand up," Shelton commanded.

Hauser's tall, thin figure slowly made it to his feet. Shelton moved closer until the two were face to face.

"What now, brother? What else do you have for me?" Shelton asked as more guardians moved in behind their leader. Hauser could feel Shelton's breath on his face.

"Somewhere in there is my brother. I can feel you," whispered Shelton, continuing to stare into Hauser's soulless face.

Hauser grimaced and looked away.

Shelton lifted his arms, turning his marked wrists toward Hauser.

"This cannot fail," Shelton continued. "Yahweh cannot be brought down," he said, "Ever! Whenever or however you attempt it, I will be there. Next time, and there will be a next time, I will remove you from all existence and consciousness forever."

With his right hand, Shelton raised Hauser into the air and slammed him against a wooden pillar at the far end of the room.

"Arm yourselves," Shelton commanded, turning to face the demons. "Let your master observe your death."

Without another word, Shelton jumped to his right, driving his saber into the heart of a guardian with one swift move.

The others descended upon Shelton. They could not match the speed and precision of his blade. Within seconds, all but two of the guardians had perished while Hauser watched helplessly.

The two remaining guardians stood motionless and saw Shelton drop his weapon. He slowly walked toward them. The demons could not move. Shelton stripped the two guardians of their robes, exposing their ghastly forms. Their skin was void of color. Their black, dead eyes sunken into their skulls.

With his hands, Shelton lifted both creatures and pinned them to the wall beside their leader, using stakes he had ripped from the wooden beam.

Shelton drew his dual-bladed knife from his waistband and loosened the nut that held the two blades together. With a dagger in each hand, he approached Hauser.

Hauser summoned all his strength to fight back. It was no use. His power was gone.

"This one is for our brother that you killed," Shelton said, smiling as he plunged the knife into Hauser's wrist above his head.

Hauser let out a deafening screech as the dagger punched through his skin and between his tendons before embedding into the wood.

"This one is for Adira, whom you disobeyed."

Shelton plunged the second knife into the other wrist, pinning Hauser firmly to the wall. Hauser let out a grunt as the weapon sliced through his nerves.

Shelton stepped back and observed the demons and their leader nailed to the library wall of Castle Janus. With a sweep of his hand, he stripped Hauser's garments from his body.

"This is your judgment," Shelton said.

He turned to face the opposite wall and swept his right hand across his body. The entire castle wall in front of him tore away from the building. Stones and mortar flew across the courtyard and the earth shook. The arched entryway and gates to the castle were now visible directly in front of them.

Shelton reached into his garment and turned back to face the gaunt-looking figures nailed to the wall. He raised the object in his hand so that Hauser could see it clearly. Hauser's eyes widened as he realized what Shelton was holding.

"Kill me, you bastard!" screamed Hauser. "Do not leave me to rot behind these forsaken walls. Kill me, Magnus. Kill me!"

Shelton smiled, turned, and began walking toward the gates as Hauser watched. Without pausing, he walked through the courtyard to the main entrance archway and stopped.

He turned to take one last look at Simeon. Without hesitating, he swung the first gate closed, then paused. He took a deep breath and looked toward the sky, then closed the second gate.

Shelton inserted the key into the hole and turned it. The four tumblers fell one by one. The sound echoed off the stone walls and into the castle library, each sound of a tumbler further sealing Hauser's fate. Shelton removed the key, placed it in his pocket, and began his walk across the cobblestone bridge without looking back.

CHAPTER FORTY-THREE

ONE MONTH LATER, Charles Edwards, Andrew Wilkinson, Amir, and Ann Baker took their seats as the governing body in front of the newly created Council of Human Society. Charles Edwards gaveled the meeting to order.

Four thousand miles away in Pitkin County, Shelton tossed another piece of wood into the fireplace and switched on the television to catch up on the news of the day. He poured himself a generous glass of cold Canadian whiskey before taking a seat on the leather sofa. Angie and Daniel had turned in after a long day of skiing and a nice dinner with several of their close friends.

Shelton and Angie were slowly transitioning into what they both hoped would eventually be a more normal family existence.

Shelton's mind drifted as he sipped the spirit. He was pleased Edwards had assumed the top leadership role at the council for now. The Providence Institute's continental and in-country leaders around the world would provide governmental continuity across the globe as the transition to peace and security got underway. Ann Baker was the vice-chairman and would succeed Edwards. They would make a great team. There was a great deal of work to do, and they would need direction in their new positions. Adira was there to support and guide them, and Andrew was there to help transition from the current standalone system to a coordinated, species-focused system of government.

The International News Network was covering the various events as peace was breaking out around the world. Conflicts between countries were now just a part of history. Crime and terrorism had stopped. Former enemies were going to extraordinary lengths to work together now that the veil of Hauser's influence had lifted.

All governments were doing the groundwork to transition. What had once been the offices of the Providence Institute around the world were assuming the roles of governors to usher in a peaceful existence for humanity.

The reflection of movement in a vase beside the television let Shelton know he was not alone.

"Hello, Ben," Shelton said in a quiet voice.

"Tom," Ben replied, standing behind him.

"How did you get into the house?" Shelton asked.

"Really, Tom?" said Ben, surprised by the question. "I helped design this place. Designers always create a back door. You should know this."

Shelton simply nodded his head.

"I never thought about it," Shelton replied. "But that makes sense."

"You've ruined everything. Look at what is happening around the world. It's nonsense. Not sustainable. It looks good for now. It feels good now. Give it time. You will be sorry," Ben said. "We had it all. You had it all. You could have just looked the other way and lived happily ever after. But your insatiable need for purpose ruined everything."

"I figured you were dead," Shelton said, sipping his whiskey. "I assumed Hauser had you eliminated since you failed your mission so completely."

"You never were as smart as you thought you were. Where is the key?" asked Ben.

"Ben," Shelton replied, "you can't change things now. It's too late. Hauser used you. Played you just as he has played the world for thousands of years. The gates are closed and locked. I locked them. Hauser has no power or influence anymore."

"Just give me the damn key," demanded Ben.

Shelton laughed out loud. "No chance. At some point, I will unlock the gates. That day is a long way off. Sit down, Ben. Have a drink. Get your head on straight. There is a lot of good work to do."

"My wife and son are dead," Ben said, anger tinging his words.

A surprised look came across Shelton's face.

"What happened?"

"You killed them. I found them in our home, executed," said Ben.

"I did not kill your family, Ben. Hauser did. He knew all along how this was going to go down. Can't you see? He planned this. He needed to motivate you to do exactly what you have come here to do."

"Can't you see that, Ben?" Shelton asked again. "He misled the entire world for thousands of years. Misleading one person is nothing to him. Your family was nothing to him. You are nothing to him."

Ben's face reddened as the anger inside him intensified. Every word that came out of Shelton's mouth increased his rage. In the glass's reflection, Shelton saw Ben remove his weapon from his waistband and point it at the back of his head.

"Are you going to shoot me in the back?" Shelton asked. "Is that your plan? Why didn't you confront me at the chateau? I know you were there, watching from the trees. You could have saved your master, but you didn't have the courage or the skill to even try."

Shelton continued to slice into Ben's mind, using words as his weapon.

"Hauser and his dark princes, the guardians, all of them are cowards. Sneaking around. Manipulating people. Creating hate and divisiveness. Taking advantage of people when they are most vulnerable. Blaming everyone else for their shortfalls. Is that who you are, Ben? At least your leaders had the courage to look me in the eye. Even Hauser had the courage to look me in the eye while I locked the gates to his prison cell." Shelton stood up from the sofa turned and faced Ben.

Adira quietly stepped out from the decretive room panel and approached Ben from behind without him knowing while Shelton watched. Before Ben could fire his weapon, Adira acted. Her first move was faster than the human eye could see. With her right hand she grasped Ben Davis's wrist in which he was holding the gun handle and twisted. The motion snapped Davis's forearm bones in half pointing the barrel of the gun upward towards the ceiling and unfired. Davis's scream stopped suddenly as Adira sunk her left hand finger nails into his back and unleashed an electrical current that terminated his life instantly. She raised her hands above her head and watched with pleasure as her son's assailant dropped to the floor dead.

ABOUT THE AUTHOR

Dane is a generation Xer, a chief executive officer, and a lifelong student of science and culture. He travels and works with people from around the world. ALL THE DARK VOICES is the first in a three book collection with the next two, and other thrillers in queue for readers in the years ahead. Dane is also musician and a father of three.

PhilipMylesDane.Com